THE DEAD YARD

ADRIAN McKINTY

A complete catalogue record for this book is available from
the British Library on request

The right of Adrian McKinty to be identified as the author of this work has
been asserted by him in accordance with the Copyright, Designs and
Patents Act 1988

Copyright © 2006 by A. G. McKinty

First published in the USA by Scribner, New York in 2006

First published in the UK in 2006 by Serpent's Tail
4 Blackstock Mews, London N4 2BT

Website: www.serpentstail.com

Printed by Mackays of Chatham, plc

ISBN 1 85242 912 7
ISBN 978 1 85242 912 6

10 9 8 7 6 5 4 3 2 1

My sweet enemy was, little by little, giving over her great wariness... But Death had his grudge against me and he got up in the way, like an armed robber, with a pike in his hand.

—J. M. Synge, *Poems and Translations from Petrarch* (1906)

1: A RIOT ON TENERIFE

Dawn over the turquoise shore of Africa and here, under the fractured light of a streetlamp, brought to earth like some hurricaned palm, I woke before the supine ocean amidst a sea of glass and upturned bus stands and the wreck of cars and looted stores.

The streets of Playa de las Americas were flowing with beer and black sewage and blood. Smoke hung above the seashore and the smell was of desolation, decay, the burning of tires and fuel oil. The noise of birds, diesel engines, a dirge-like siren, a helicopter, voices in Spanish over a loudspeaker—all of it more than enough hint of the breakdown in the fragile rules of the social contract.

I was sitting up and adjusting to the light and the growing heat when a kid hustled me under cover and the riot began again.

Five hundred British football hooligans, three hundred and fifty Irish fans, all of them on this island at the same time for a "friendly" match between Dublin's Shamrock Rovers and London's Millwall.

A riot.

I wouldn't say I'd been expecting that but I wouldn't say I was that goddamn surprised either.

Some people go through their lives like a mouse moving through a wheat field. They're good citizens, they pay their taxes, they contribute to society, they have kids and the kids turn them into responsible adults. They create no stir, cause no fuss, leave no trace. When they're gone people speak well of them, sigh, shrug their shoulders, and shed a tear. They avoid chaos and it avoids them.

Perhaps most people are like this.

But not me.

You'd notice me in the wheat field. You'd notice me because the field would be on fire or the farmer would be running after me with a gun.

The Bible says that man is born to trouble as the sparks fly upward. Well, trouble followed me like sharks trailing a slave ship. Even when I tried to get away it was there swirling in a vortex around me.

Even when I tried to get away. Spain. Tenerife, to be exact, the largest of the Canary Islands off the coast of Morocco. It's a hell of a long flight from Chicago but the FBI won't let me go near Florida or the Caribbean. Seamus Duffy, the head of the Irish mob in New York City, has had a contract out on me for five years for killing his underboss Darkey White and testifying against Darkey's crew.

With that in mind you can't be too careful about where you take your vacation. So O'Hare, JFK, and seven hours to Tenerife for a wee bit of R & R and of course this is what bloody happens.

"Brian, are you all right?" the English kid asked. Pale skin, sunburned, wearing a Millwall shirt and white jeans.

I stared at him. My name had been Brian O'Nolan since I'd moved to Chicago in January. It still didn't seem right.

"I'm ok," I said. "I must have fallen asleep. What the hell is happening?"

"The riot's starting up again. Those Irish bastards have all gotten ball bearings from somewhere."

I gave him a look.

One of those looks.

My speciality.

"Oh, by Irish bastards, I meant, uh, I meant no offense by the way," he stammered.

I didn't say anything. I almost felt more American now than Irish. I ducked as stones and ball bearings landed in the shop fronts. Pieces of dark lava and Molotov cocktails flew back from the English side.

The London lads were drunk and the Dublin boys had taken off their shirts, looking like ghosts flitting nervously behind the barricades.

The riot progressed. A shop window caved in under a big rock, a roof collapsed, a car went up in flames. A big English bruiser trundled along a wheely-bin filled with gasoline and halfway down the hill, he burned some scrunched-up newspaper and tossed it after. The bin exploded and he caught fire. He rolled on the ground and the cops grabbed him and dragged him off to a police car.

Jesus.

The colors fused: green banana skins, inky smoke, crimson blood, the blue Atlantic and iodine sky merging in the west. Over by the dunes amazed surfers were wondering if the town was on fire, and later it was, as the hotel burned and the surfers and the other noncombatants decided to be long gone.

At dusk the Spanish police finally got their act together and turned fire hoses on the two sides. The Micks started an out-of-date football chant: "Francisco Franco is a wanker," and the English side trumped that with "What Happened to the Armada?" Singing was general over the lines now and each song was echoed back and as full night fell, everyone got teary-eyed and guilt-ridden and we had a truce, the impromptu leaders meeting up in one of the main squares under a flag of armistice.

The shadows lengthened and there was a toast. A drink. A parley. And it was agreed then that whatever differences existed between the Irish and the English soccer fans, here, fifteen hundred miles from the British Isles, the story wasn't terrorism or the Famine or Enniskillen or Bloody Sunday. It was August 1997 now, there was a new British prime minister, and a new IRA cease-fire brewing that extended even unto football hooligans. Aye, we could see that out here with our fresh perspective. Here in Tenerife under the black sky of

Creation, where Columbus set out to enslave half the world, where Darwin came on the *Beagle,* where Nelson lost his arm, and where they still made the same dark Canary drunk by Falstaff and Sir Toby Belch. Where we were all away from gloomy Albion and we could accept a new vision of a new Earth with sunshine and cheap food and Swedish girls and where we could see the folly of doing evil unto one's brother. The drunken leaders deciding that harmony would reign forever between kinfolk and that the riot between the Brits and Paddies was over; and from now on we would concentrate on the real enemies: German tourists and the Spanish police.

So began the second phase.

❖   ❖   ❖

This time, though, I wanted no part of it, especially when I saw the big NATO war helicopters landing beyond the cliffs and out of them pouring scores of paramilitary cops from Madrid—tough bastards who came with machine pistols and gas and billy clubs that they used up in the Basque country against the ETA guerrillas. Me and the kid, an eejit called Goosey, slipped away from the drunken insurgents under the cover of darkness. We negotiated our way through the abandoned holiday villas and the half-built outlying hotels and the pink-shaded small pensions where a few British expats hid in the dark, having retired to Tenerife to escape the bad weather and (ironically) the growing yob culture of England.

Goosey, it turned out, was a bit of a mental case from some East London shithole who wanted us to do a *Clockwork Orange*–style burglary on some of the pensions, nicking things and hurting people and generally raising a bit of hell, but I would have none of it. They might have shooters, I told Goosey, and Goosey thought this was entirely plausible and got discouraged from the idea.

Instead up we went into the lava fields and through the mangrove and the palm trees until we'd climbed a thousand feet above the town. We slept in a barn among guano and baked hay and the sleep was the best since the riots had begun two days ago when three Millwall supporters had attacked some guy from Dublin and the peelers had allegedly beaten the near life out of them down at the cop shop. It had grown like a tropical storm, stores being looted and cars set ablaze and the climax came when the local jail had been stormed and the Millwall boys and a team of time-share crooks were let out and one person got himself shot in the shoulder by a peeler.

The town beneath us five thousand feet and four miles to the west and the paramilitary police taking no prisoners, using dogs, whips, CS gas, and water cannon and this time the rioters were being rounded up like sheep. Fires burned and the helicopters came and went and it was ending now, we could tell.

"*Agua*," we asked a herder and he showed us a stream and we followed it another thousand feet up into the hills where, at a stone wall, it formed part of the boundary of a hacienda. We vaulted the wall, got about a quarter of a mile before a man in a suit appeared on a three-wheeled motorbike and asked us what the hell we thought we were doing. And not about to let Goosey do the talking I explained that we were innocent kids fleeing a riot down in Playa de las Americas. The man adjusted his sunglasses and said something into a walkie-talkie. He escorted us up to the hacienda, where a beautiful woman in her forties sat us down at an oak table under pine beams and gave us water and brandy.

"*Muchas gracias, bella señorita,*" I said and the woman laughed and muttered something to the man in sunglasses and he went back outside and then she said to me in English that she was married and was no señorita anymore and not even beautiful either. To which I sincerely disagreed and she laughed again and asked me what exactly had been going on at the beach and I told her, leaving out our part in the proceedings.

She fed us and gave us directions to the town of Guia de Isora.

By the afternoon our supplies were gone and we were lost in a region that had an uncanny similarity to the place the

NASA robots keep landing on the planet Mars. Rocks, stones, thin red soil. It grew unbearably hot. Goosey started swaying a bit, and all around us desert, black lava, and the baking sun. We sat under a rock and decided to move again at night. The sun set, it grew cold, above us we saw what God had made when he was getting things ready for the Earth. A million stars. A billion. Blue and red and Doppler-shifted ultraviolet.

I thought for a minute that we were toast, but we fell in the backbone of the night and its spell guided us safely through the wilderness. The sun rose over the sand hills and in the morning we were at a wire fence surrounding a banana plantation. We broke in and with comedy climbed a tree and gorged ourselves on green fruit. Nature was a civilizing influence and Goosey had given up plans for *Clockwork Orange* rampages and was now all for staying here forever in the great outdoors. We could build canoes and trade to Africa and be self-sufficient in meat, fruit, clothes. We could be outlaws and fish and roast our catch over charcoal fires. Live on the beach and dream our canoes out over the ocean. Steer by wave and swell and the stars like the Polynesians. His vision more *Coral Island* than *Lord of the Flies* and I said I'd write a letter to *The Times* suggesting a scheme whereby lager louts could be turned into Byronic pacifists just by letting them camp out a few nights in the wilds of Tenerife. Plutarch had called this place the "Fortunate Islands," Darwin had raved about it, and two hundred years ago Alexander von Humboldt had had the same thoughts: "Nowhere in the world seems more able to dissipate melancholy and restore peace to troubled minds than Tenerife." That's the real reason I'd come here. Five years in the purgatory of the Witness Protection Program. The FBI and federal marshals dogging my every movement. I needed a vacation. I needed out of North America. And I'd been to Tenerife before and liked it, it was mellow and I even spoke Spanish.

Nice move. I'd been deciding between Spain and somewhere completely off the wall like Peru. I'd flipped a coin. Heads.

A lot of people were going to get screwed because of

that coin flip.

Especially me.

There's only so many bananas you can eat and outside the plantation we flagged down a car which unfortunately had three undercover cops inside. Our football shirts and accents were a bit of a giveaway and before I could say, "I want to see the British ambassador," we were separated and driven to a cell block in an underground bunker near the airport.

The riot at Playa de las Americas all over now and the rioters being held under Spanish antiterrorism laws. A guard cheerfully told me that we were all going to get ten years.

* * *

The cell was deep underground, a yellow bulb in the ceiling giving off a little light. Cold, damp. Impossible to tell if it was day or night. But I'd been in worse. Much bloody worse. They fed you three times a day, there was a bog that flushed, and the fauna situation was manageable.

I was sitting on the cot reading *How Stella Got Her Groove Back* for the third time when the cell door opened.

I stood.

A man and a woman. A tall man carrying a chair and a water bottle. He was wearing a linen jacket, white shirt, Harrow tie. It was difficult to see in the dark but he looked about thirty-five, forty at the outside, hard-faced, blond-gray hair. He held himself like a high-ranking army officer: straight spine, shoulders back, stomach in. He unfolded the chair and sat down. A revolver peeked out next to his armpit. Interesting. The woman also had a chair. She was late thirties, wearing a sundress and sandals with red hair tied behind her in a ponytail. She was heavy but attractive—Rubens plump, not lesbian-biker plump. She took out a notebook and sat back in the shadows. He was the man and she was the assistant. They fell immediately into their roles, which wasn't smart, but despite that I still didn't like the look of either of them.

"You're British," I said to the man.

"That's right, old boy," he said in a plummy public school

voice. Not for him the attempt to tone down the upper-crust accent and give in to the increasingly common Estuary English pronunciation. It told me a lot about him—arrogant, proud, the Harrow tie not a joke but a reminder of a birthright. A wanker, more than likely.

"I suppose you're from the embassy," I said. "I'm completely innocent, you know. I wasn't involved in anything. I was on holiday. First bloody holiday in years."

"Beastly piece of luck, I'm sure. But the Spanish don't care, you will be tried, you will be found guilty, you'll get five to ten years, I suppose. The new prime minister, Mr. Blair, has said that he supports fully the Spanish government's intention of making an example out of the soccer hooligans who once again have blighted the good name of England," he said breezily.

"I'm not English," I told him.

"It doesn't matter," the man replied quickly.

"It matters to me."

"Well, it won't make any difference. You will be convicted," he said.

"Listen, mate, if you came here to give me a lecture you can piss off," I said, lifting up my trouser leg and scratching under the straps that held the artificial foot to my calf. I'd lost the foot five years before in a lovely piece of jungle surgery in Mexico. It had saved my life and I was thoroughly unself-conscious about it now.

The man smiled, picked at a piece of fluff on his shirt, looked behind him at the secretary, cleared his throat.

"I imagine, Brian, that you do not want to spend the next ten years in some ghastly prison on the mainland," he said softly.

"No, I bloody don't," I said, trying to conceal my surprise with passion.

He pulled out a pack of cigarettes.

"Do you smoke?"

I shook my head. He lit himself a cigarette, offered one to the woman, who also declined. But he had me now. It was an interesting situation and I had to admit that I was intrigued.

No guard had accompanied the two Brits. They did not appear flustered, angry. There was no pompous talk. Something was going on. Were they releasing me? Maybe Dan Connolly from the FBI had heard about my predicament and pulled a few strings.

"You've been living in America?" the man asked.

"What the hell is your name?"

"Jeremy Barnes," he said, blowing a Gauloise in my direction.

"Oh, and I'm Samantha Caudwell," the woman said in an even more upper-class accent than Jeremy's. The sort of snide Queen's English Olivia de Havilland used when she was badgering Errol Flynn in those films from the 1930s.

The smoke from the cigarette drifted over. Only pseuds and poseurs smoked Gauloises. Jeremy, however, seemed not to be either of these.

"You've lived in Paris," I said, surprising Jeremy with a good guess. Jeremy looked a little taken aback but quickly recovered his poise.

"Yes, yes indeed. They told us you were good," Jeremy said.

"Who's they?"

"The FBI. The U.S. Marshals Service. We've read your file, Brian, or should I say, Michael. We know everything about you."

"Aye?" I said, trying to appear casual.

"Yes. Shall I tell you what we know?"

"Maybe you should tell me a wee bit about yourself first," I said.

"No, I don't think so, old chap. Would you like a drink?" Jeremy asked and threw a flask onto the cot.

"I'd like water."

Jeremy tossed me the water bottle.

"Good idea. Water first, then the brandy," Jeremy said.

"Ok."

I drank the half-liter bottle of water, unscrewed the hip flask, and took a sip of brandy. I threw the flask back.

"Your name is not Brian O'Nolan. Your real name is

Michael Forsythe. You went to America in 1992 to work for Darkey White. You ended up killing Darkey White and wiping out his entire gang. You turned informer and the American government set you up with a new identity. I gather that recently you've been living in Chicago," Jeremy intoned placidly.

I said nothing.

"You speak fluent Spanish. That, and only that, can possibly account for your desire to take a vacation in the Canary Islands," Jeremy mocked.

"I'll ask again. Who the hell are you?" I demanded.

"Mr. Forsythe, I am the person who could get you out of this cell, today. Right now in fact. In the next five minutes you will have to make a decision. That decision will be either to come with me or stay here, get tried, get convicted, and then spend the next few years in the Columbaro Maximum Security Prison in Seville. Perhaps you'll choose the prison. Miguel de Cervantes began *Don Quixote* there. A fascinating place, apparently."

"Who do you work for?" I insisted.

Jeremy finished his cigarette. Slowly lit another.

"What do you see?" Samantha asked from behind Jeremy.

"What do I see?" I repeated.

"Yes. Tell us," Jeremy said.

I sighed. Leaned back. What game were they playing?

I looked the two of them over. They were relaxed, confident, obviously serious. This was a test.

"Ok, I'll play if you want to. I guessed Paris because of your fags. Easy," I said to Jeremy a little warily.

"What else?" he asked.

"You went to Harrow. Not on a scholarship, your father probably went to Harrow and his father before him. Your granddad probably used to tell you stories about how Winston Churchill was in the remedial class when he was there."

Jeremy laughed and choked on his cigarette. I continued.

"You're wearing a linen jacket. Expensive, but more than that, a kind of uniform. You knew you were going to have to go to Spain to see me, but you took the time to change from

English clothes into something more sartorially suitable. Why? Why not shorts and T-shirt, or a polo shirt, or a cotton shirt and chinos? Hmmm. You feel you have to wear a jacket because you're on duty. You look like an army officer but you're in civvies. Maybe you were in the army or maybe the RAF, you don't seem like a navy man anyway. . . . So why are you here? You work for the government. You and your wee secretary have flown all the way to Spain. You don't have a tan, you're not even red, you came here right from the airport. To see me. Huh. Why? A job. You need me for a job. You've come to make me a job offer."

Samantha whispered something to Jeremy. He nodded. I was impressing them with this bullshit.

"Who do I work for?" Jeremy asked.

"I don't know."

"Think about it."

"Why should I?" I asked petulantly.

"Why indeed?" Jeremy said, smiling.

"Ok, let me see. . . . Christ, I have it, it must be the Old Bill. You work for the cops."

"Not the police, why would the police want you?"

I sat forward on the edge of the bed. Yeah, he was too much of a patrician for the cops. He was a highflier, he worked for—

"British bloody Intelligence," I said.

Jeremy's jaw opened and closed. Samantha moved a little closer. Jeremy turned round to look at her.

And then I saw I was being dicked. I'd been wrong. Samantha was the superior officer. Jeremy was the underling. She was watching both of us, using him as a barrier to assess me, seeing if I was right for whatever it was they wanted me for.

Well, enough of that for a game of soldiers.

"Hey, Sammy, why don't you do us a favor, get your boy out of here and we can talk business," I said.

Jeremy looked startled. Samantha tried not to appear non-plussed.

"We do think we're clever, don't we?" she said, mispronouncing her *R*s in that way they teach you at only the most elite of English boarding schools.

I said nothing.

"You may leave, Jeremy. Please wait for me outside," she ordered. Jeremy stood, winked at me, and knocked on the door. The guard opened it and let him out. Samantha moved to Jeremy's seat and picked up the file he had left on the chair.

British Intelligence. Well, well, well. I suppose they wanted someone with insight into the workings of the rackets in Belfast. If the peace deal everyone was talking about came off, then they'd want to make sure all those bored paramilitaries in Ulster didn't move into organized crime and drugs. I could be very useful on that score. Or maybe they wanted someone to spruce up their training programs for undercover ops. I could probably do a job like that. I was army trained and I'd interrogated the shit out of people before. Might be a nice little earner if I played my cards right. The FBI kept me safe but they didn't exactly keep me flush.

Samantha skimmed through the folder, pretending to notice things for the first time.

"I don't have all day, you know. I'm very anxious to find out if Stella can learn to love herself again," I said, holding up my novel.

Samantha smiled and continued to thumb my file.

"You've been quite the naughty boy, haven't you, Michael?" she said, her tone as condescending as if she were a Victorian missionary and I, a recidivist cannibal chieftain caught with a hut full of human heads.

"Depends what you mean by naughty."

"Killing several unarmed people in cold blood."

"You want to tell me my life story or you want to get on with it?" I said, irritated.

"Don't get cross. I'm here to help you," she said.

"You're here to bust me out of this joint," I sneered.

"That's right," she said, crossing her legs and accidentally hitching up her skirt a notch.

Really not a bad-looking *chiquita* if you liked that sort of thing and, if truth be told, I did like that sort of thing. You could tell that underneath the prim, proper, repressed, King and Country exterior . . . the rest of the sentence is cliché, but I'd bet money it wasn't far off the mark.

"Michael, first of all, I feel that it's very important that I'm honest with you. You're obviously too smart to fall for a line, so I'll tell you how it is. Although it looks like we have all the cards, in fact I have a poor bargaining position. If time were not a factor, you would need us much more than we would need you. But, alas, time is a factor," she said in that round-about diplomat way again.

"Honey, if time is a factor, you better be a bit less oblique," I said, leaning back on the cot and noting that from this angle I could see right up to her panties, which were white cotton and soaked with sweat.

"I do apologize. Of course you're right. Let me explain, Michael. Jeremy and I work for MI6, British Intelligence overseas, which, in case you don't know, is the equivalent of the CIA and a—"

"I know who you are," I interrupted.

"Good. Well, I am in charge of a section within MI6 called SUU—the Special Ulster Unit. MI5 deals with Irish terrorism in the United Kingdom, but SUU looks at Irish terrorism in Europe and the Americas. We report directly to the home secretary. We largely bypass the MI6 bureaucracy. We have had many successes. Well, several successes . . ."

"Ok. Where am I supposed to come in?" I asked.

"For the last six months or so, Her Majesty's government has been in not-so-secret negotiations with the IRA to resume their cease-fire agreement. The election of Mr. Blair has changed little except for speeding things up. The negotiations have been going well. The IRA's Army Council is becoming convinced that this is the right thing to do at the right time. The Clinton administration has been helpful. Things are moving quickly now and the IRA seems to be on the verge of an-nouncing a complete cessation of hostilities and a resumption of the cease-fire."

"I read the papers," I said.

"Well, yes, it hasn't exactly been the best-kept secret in the world. And we're jolly well hoping that it's going to come off. The problem is that the IRA's Army Council is worried about causing a split in the IRA. IRA splinter groups are not uncommon. The council wants to eliminate the hard-line elements before they announce a cease-fire. We believe this announcement is going to come by the end of the month, perhaps even in the next few days. In Northern Ireland and in the Republic of Ireland, the British and Irish governments will turn a blind eye to a purge of IRA extremists. This is not the case in America. As you may be aware, the IRA has several well-organized cells in the United States. Most will abide by the Army Council's decision. Disband, disarm, sleep. But one, we know, will not. The IRA would like to wipe out the extremist SOC, Sons of Cuchulainn. The FBI and the American government will not permit such a purge to take place. They would rather go the legal route of evidence gathering and prosecution."

"Cuchulainn, love. It's pronounced KuckKulann, not Cush-coolain," I said with a smug grin. Samantha ignored me and soldiered on.

"It's a tiny group, almost a cell really, but, we believe, extraordinarily dangerous. And well off. Neither we nor the FBI have any agents at all with the Sons of Cuchulainn. None. We are desperately short of manpower. And for reasons I'll explain in a moment, time is of the essence. We have agents within the IRA, the INLA, the UVF. But we urgently need an agent, someone to go to America to join or spy on the Sons of Cuchulainn, to gather evidence and help in their prosecution, if of course they are doing anything illegal."

"I have an ominous feeling that I see where this is going. That someone, that poor bastard—let me guess who you have in mind."

"Michael, your folder only appeared on my desk the day before yesterday. It was handed to me by someone in the Foreign Office. But I have to say I was jolly impressed."

I wasn't really listening now. Whatever financial package they were going to offer wasn't worth the risk. An IRA cell. They had to be kidding. Samantha continued as I stared up her skirt and contemplated her oddly seductive voice.

"Yes, Michael, your handlers speak very highly of you and you were in the British army, which is good and although, um, unfortunately you were asked to leave Her Majesty's employ rather prematurely, you completed a reconnaissance course and received some special operations training."

"I failed that recon course, and the special ops course ended with me in the brig for assaulting a civilian," I said blithely.

Samantha was not to be put off.

"That's neither here nor there. The fact is you were in the army, which is good, and you were also a low-level gangster in Belfast, which is even better. And you worked for the Irish mob in America, which is best of all. You could be an ideal person to infiltrate the Sons of Cuchulainn for us. Dan Connolly of the FBI says that you're one of the best that he's ever seen. Proficient, merciless, bold, surprisingly disciplined."

"You talked to Dan, huh? Nice of him to sell me down the river."

"No, no, Dan was very complimentary. . . . Michael, I have to tell you, I'm going out on something of a limb here. Dropping everything, flying to Spain, talking to you. But now that I've met you I honestly think you could be the one to do this job for us. To infiltrate this cell and gather information and help put them away before they ruin everything. If they manage to do a bombing campaign in America, the Protestant terrorists will have to respond, the IRA will have to reply to that, and oh my goodness the whole cease-fire and all our hard work will be jolly well up the spout."

"How jolly sad," I said, irritated enough to take the piss.

"And naturally if you did do this for us, we would convince the Spanish government to drop all charges against you," Samantha said with a satisfied wee grin. She sat back in her chair, crossed her legs, blocking the crotch shot.

I also smiled. Who the hell did they think they were dealing with? Did they think I was some eejit Paddy just off the bloody boat?

"Why don't the FBI infiltrate this group of yours? It's their country," I asked for starters before moving on to the main course.

"The FBI won't touch it with a ten-foot pole," Samantha said, her eyes narrowing.

"Why?"

"Our plan is to insert an agent as soon as possible. *Before* the Sons of Cuchulainn begin their campaign, which we strongly believe will commence once the cease-fire announcement comes. In other words, we have to have an agent in their ranks in the next couple of weeks. The FBI feels that an attempt to hurriedly insert an agent in this manner and in this climate would be too rushed and too dangerous," Samantha said calmly.

"The FBI, in other words, thinks it might be a bit of a suicide mission," I said, my smile broadening.

"Er, yes," she muttered, embarrassed.

"And just to be clear, if the operation weren't dumb enough already, of all the people in the world, you want me—a man who has a contract on his head from the Irish mob in New York—to attempt to infiltrate an IRA splinter group," I said and laughed at her.

"Mr. Forsythe, I don't think—"

"Don't Mr. Forsythe me, Samantha; thanks for thinking of me, thanks for taking the trouble to fly out, but I think I've heard just about enough. Run along now. I'll do my time quietly in Seville. I've been in a lot worse places than that. Nice to have met ya," I said.

I leaned back on the cot and put my hands behind my head. I closed my eyes. Let them sweat for a bit. Let me think.

Samantha considered the situation.

"Perhaps I have oversold the problems. All we want you to do is gather evidence that would lead to a prosecution. The fact that you are from Belfast but have experience in America, the fact that you've been in the British army, the fact that you come highly recommended by the FBI. All this is to your advantage."

"I think, Samantha dear," I said with sarcasm, "you're barking up the wrong tree, love. As I've patiently explained, I'm already wanted by the Irish community in America. Seamus Duffy has a million-dollar bounty on my head."

"I am perfectly aware of that, Michael. But you must understand that the Sons of Cuchulainn are a separate entity from the Boston Irish mob. The mob dislikes and distrusts anyone whose motives are political rather than fiduciary. They have very little time for fanatics. And the Boston mob itself is a rival to the New York organization and they maintain few links. There will be at least two layers of separation between you and your former associates. You'll be quite insulated from Seamus Duffy and his agents in New York. And in any case, from what Dan Connolly tells me, Duffy is more than occupied with his own internal problems rather than looking to settle old scores. You're yesterday's news, Michael. It's been five years. No one remembers you. That's not to say that you won't be taking any risks. No, we must be clear from the get-go. Oh, good God, no. This will be extraordinarily risky indeed. Even if they never found out that your real name is Michael Forsythe, they would kill you at the drop of a hat if they discovered that you were linked to Her Majesty's government in even the remotest way."

She paused, ran her hand through that peachy auburn hair. No rings on any finger. Not married, not engaged.

"Did you hear what I said, Michael?"

"I heard. You're doing your case no good. What you're basically saying is I'd have to be mad to take this job, because I could get killed in half a dozen ways," I said, leaning back on the cot again and resting my arms over my eyes.

"Well, I'm not one for odds, but yes, I'd say that even a competently trained professional agent with years of experience would have a rather higher than average chance of being compromised in a time-imperative operation such as this one," Samantha said.

I yawned in the face of her candor.

"And compromised means killed," I said.

"I'm terribly sorry but I have to be frank. I feel it's only fair that you appreciate the risks. Of course I do not think you will be killed or compromised in any way. It's very unlikely that McCaghan would bring you into the inner circle. We just need tidbits of information, anything that will help prevent a potential bombing campaign. And yes, ordinarily, I'd do something dramatic, I'd leave the cell, give you a day or two to think it over, maybe get the Spanish to rough you up, hector you a bit, but as I've said time is a factor here. An ideal opportunity for an insertion has presented itself. If my plan is going to work at all you absolutely have to be in Revere tomorrow."

"Revere Beach, Boston? You must be joking, honey. If I go near a Paddy neighborhood like that, I'll be killed."

She shook her head and gave me a brilliant smile.

"No, you won't. I wouldn't send you if I thought that. The Sons of Cuchulainn are beyond the pale in Irish American republican circles and after the IRA hit tomorrow, they're going to be even more beyond the pale. They'll be pariahs."

"IRA hit?"

"Michael, please don't worry about your former problems. We'll dye your hair black, give you dark green contact lenses, something like that; that's not my field exactly, but we'll gussy you up so that your own mother wouldn't recognize you."

"Sure."

"You'll only have to be in Boston for one day. Then we'll fly you to an FBI field office in a secure location. And then in a week or so your formal assignment will begin. The most difficult part of an operation is the entry. Believe me, I've done dozens. And what we have going tomorrow is a perfect entry for you. It's an opportunity not to be missed. Instead of months of preparation, we can get you buckets of credibility in a single night. Indeed, if we pull this off, I'd say the risks of being compromised are considerably reduced."

"What exactly do you want me to do in Revere?"

"You're going to save a girl's life," Samantha said with a cough.

"What?"

"The IRA is going to try to kill her father, and you're going to save her," she said, looking at the floor.

"That sounds bloody risky to start with."

"Not really. Look, Michael, we need you. We had one other person in mind but . . ." her voice trailed off.

"Let me guess. He's turned you down," I said.

"Well, yes. That's why this whole Spanish angle has been particularly fortuitous for us. You know, not everyone agrees with me, I'm taking a bit of a risk flying here to see you. There are some within the department who don't agree with the idea of recruiting outsiders. Especially a potential loose cannon such as yourself."

I was fed up with her now and I'd thought about it enough.

"While I really appreciate the faith you have in me, Samantha, thanks but no thanks. Now I think I've been pretty polite with you; if you would do me a favor and tell your pal in the Foreign Office that I still haven't seen a lawyer and could they please arrange for me to see one ASAP I'd be much obliged."

She looked disappointed.

"A lawyer?"

"Aye. I want to plead and get this shit over with."

Samantha frowned, undid her ponytail, and let the hair hang down her back. She started doing her hair up again, glancing at me with what could almost be described as pity.

"Michael, obviously I haven't made the entire situation transparent. You're caught between a rock and a hard place. The Spanish government will see to it that you go to jail. And what's more, when your time is up, the Spaniards will extradite you to Mexico, where I believe you are a fugitive from justice."

That was her trump card. The one she'd been saving.

I sat up on the bed. Horrified.

I'd been arrested in Mexico on a charge of drug smuggling but I'd escaped from the remand prison before I'd come to trial. I could be looking at twenty years there for the drugs, plus God knows how much for bloody jailbreaking.

Cold fear ran down my back. I'd been so cavalier with Samantha because I knew the Spanish angle was bullshit. Who gets ten years for being a football hooligan? Even if I got convicted they'd sentence me to three or four and I'd do two at the most. Probably less. *The Sun* and the *Daily Mirror* would quickly be filled with horror stories about all the poor Brits and their mistreatment in Spanish jails. Even the worst offenders would never serve close to ten years. And me, a side player with zero physical evidence to back up the police case, I'd be out in easy time and probably well on my way to winning damages at the European Court of Human Rights.

But Mexico, that was another matter completely.

I was in a world of shit if I went back there.

"The FBI won't let you send me to Mexico. We have a deal. I'm a protected witness," I said, trying to keep the tension out of my voice.

Samantha read from the file in front of her and shook her head.

"You have been given exemption from the crimes you committed in the United States. You certainly could not have been given exemption for criminal acts committed in a third country. Last night I called up my counterpart in the Mexican intelligence service. He would be more than happy to have you back in Mexican custody and the Spanish government would be delighted to extradite you. They have excellent relations with Mexico, as you can imagine."

I stared at her.

Any residual lust evaporated, replaced pound for pound with enmity. There was no way I was going back to Mexico. The place where Scotchy, Andy, and Fergal all had died in horrible circumstances. The thought of returning to that prison at all was like an ice dagger in the heart. You know what they do to gringos in Mexican prisons? Let your imagination do the work and then add a little on top because I'd already goddamn escaped.

But I didn't want to work for her. Suddenly I felt trapped. Panicked. My mind sprinting through scenarios. Not Boston but not bloody Mexico, either.

Aye. Maybe there was another way.

What was it that Goosey had said? We could live out in the wilds of Tenerife forever. Fish, eat fruit, maybe escape by boat.

I formulated a tiny, desperate, pathetic plan.

Move fast.

Last thing anyone would be expecting.

Up, run at her, kick her off the chair, grab it, smash it down on that ponytailed skull. Jeremy hears the commotion, comes rushing in, let him have it with the goddamn chair too. Grab his piece, cock it, point it at the guard, put the gun in my pocket, but keep it on him, and get the guard to march me right out of the prison, telling everyone that I was being transferred or released. Walk right out, casual as you please. Take his money, steal a car, go back up into the volcano country. Wait out the search.

In von Humboldt's book I read that the indigenous people kept going a guerrilla war against the Spanish for over a hundred years. Easy, up there on the mountain fastness. Hunt out a cave, lay low until the heat cooled down, come back into town, find some drunken German tourist, mug him, steal a passport, money, plane ticket, Tenerife to Frankfurt, Frankfurt to New York. Get back to safety in the good old USA.

Not a great plan.

Not even a good one.

But this bitch wasn't going to threaten me.

"Since you put it that way, I suppose I have no choice," I said, readying myself.

"Oh, I am pleased. I'm sorry about the coercive aspect of all this, it's just beastly that Her Majesty's gov. has to be in the blackmail business, but there it is. Indeed, it couldn't have worked out better. Jeremy was right, what made you come to Tenerife in the first place, don't you know it's notorious for riots and disturbances? Vulgar, awful place," she said with an amused expression.

"I was reading Alexander von Humboldt and Charles Darwin and they paint it in a different light," I replied and offered her a conciliatory hand and a big broad smile of acceptance.

"Well, bad for you, but good for us, old boy, Sword of Damocles, Scylla and Charybdis, call it what you will," she said and gave me her hand too.

I grabbed it and pulled her violently off the chair, she screamed, dropping her pen, folder, and water bottle. I threw her to the ground, kicked her to one side, and grabbed the chair. I lifted it over my head and positioned it to bring it down on her spine.

A terrible pain in my right foot—which was not the one I'd left behind in a jungle village in the Yucatán. A searing explosion of nerve endings and when I looked down I saw a penknife sticking out of my Converse sneaker.

Jesus.

Before I could react, she'd kicked me behind the right knee and I fell to the cell floor, banging my head on the edge of the metal bed.

I groaned. Jeremy opened the door and looked in.

"Good heavens, what on earth is happening? Need any help, Samantha?" he asked.

Samantha picked up the dropped file, righted the chair, and sat down. She moved herself away from me so I couldn't pull the penknife out and threaten her with it.

"I'm fine, darling, but young Michael is going to need medical assistance," she said softly.

Jeremy called for the guard, produced his gun, and pointed it at me.

I pulled myself back up onto the cot.

I breathed deep, swore inwardly, pulled out the knife, and sent it clattering to the floor.

"What I'll need," I began between clenched teeth, "is a letter from the Spanish government stating that all charges have been dropped. So you won't be able to hold that over me indefinitely."

Samantha smiled.

"I'll get our lawyers working on it immediately," she said.

"And I'll want a document from the Spanish, British, and United States attorneys general that I will not in the future be extradited to Mexico under any circumstances," I said.

"I will get working on that, too," Samantha said. "Is there anything else?"

"Aye, a guy called Goosey who was picked up with me, him out as well," I gasped.

"I'll also see to that."

"I have your word?"

"You have my word," she assured me.

"Fine, in that case. I'll do it."

"Good," Samantha said and snapped my folder shut.

Within an hour, I was stitched, sutured, shaved, and sitting on a taxiing RAF Hercules transport plane that would be taking me to Lisbon. From Lisbon, the direct flight to Boston Logan.

Samantha sat beside me, organizing her briefing notes.

The big Hercules taxied down the runway. A military aircraft, tiny slit windows and you sat facing backwards.

Samantha passed me earplugs. I put them in. Looked out.

The harsh volcanic mountain, the outline of banana plantations, the aerodrome. The propellers turned, the transport accelerated, lift developed over its wings, and we took off into the setting sun.

The blue water. The other Canary Islands. Africa.

We flew west over Tenerife, and through the safety glass and smoke I could see what the hooligans had wrought on Playa de las Americas and what the concrete-loving developers at the Spanish Ministry of Tourism had done to the rest of the island. Humboldt for one would have been displeased. Samantha saw my grimace, patted my knee. Her big pouty red lips formed into a sympathetic smile.

"Don't worry, darling. It's going to be all right," she soothed and, of course, as is typical when someone in authority tells you that, nothing could have been further from the goddamn truth.

2: AN ASSASSINATION IN REVERE

The lough was dead and across the water I could hear jets land on the baking runways of Logan airport. The day dwindling to an end in heat and the ugly noise of massive tunneling machines in the vast scar of Boston's Big Dig.

Kids playing stickball. Old ladies in deck chairs on the sidewalk. Families heading back from the beach. It was August on Boston's North Shore. The temperature was hitting ninety degrees outside. Even the elderly mafiosi with thin blood and poor circulation had shed their jackets for a stroll along the sidewalk of Revere Beach.

I threw away my unsmoked cigarette, walked into the bar.

An Italian neighborhood but an Irish pub: the Rebel Heart. Tough one, too. Posters of old IRA men. Bobby Sands, Gerry Adams. *An Phoblacht* propaganda sheets. Guinness merchandise. The usual slogans: "Brits Out," "Thatcher Is a War Criminal," "Give Ireland Back to the Irish."

About a quarter full. Maybe thirty people. At least half a dozen of them, I assumed, were FBI men. I sat down at the bar. An aroma of spilled beer, body odor, and sunscreen.

The assassin came in two minutes after me and ordered a Schlitz Lite, which I took to be a sign of absolute evil. Anyone drinking lite beer is suspect to begin with, but this guy clearly had no depths to which he would not sink.

He was a hard bastard who'd entered with some kind of

automatic weapon under his raincoat, which he kept buttoned despite the heat. A dead giveaway. His face was scarred, his hair jagged, and either he was from Belfast or he worked twelve hours a day in a warehouse that got no natural light. Tall, stooped, birdlike. About fifty. An old pro. The dangerous type. Sipping the urine-colored Schlitz. Not nervous. Calm. Smoking Embassy No. 1 cigarettes, which I don't think you can get in this country, so that solved the nationality question. He caught me with my eye on him and I looked past him to the barman who said:

"There in a minute, mate," in the high-pitched tones of County Cork.

I gazed about to see if I could ID the feds but it was difficult to scrutinize faces. Too dark, too smoky, too many ill-lit spots. Loud, too, for such a small crowd. Keeping their voices up to talk over a jukebox playing Black 47, House of Pain, and U2.

I bit my lip. I'd check the crowd again in ten minutes to see who hadn't touched their beer, that would be a clue as to who was on a job or not.

Ten minutes.

Also my last chance to run for it. McCaghan was supposed to show up around six. 'Course, if I scarpered it would mean reneging on my agreement with Samantha. Undoubtedly she would see that I got shat on from a great height. They'd find me, eventually, and I'd be returned to Mexico to do serious time.

"What ya having?" the kid from Cork finally asked and he was so young, genuine, and nice I couldn't help but dislike him.

"What doesn't taste like piss in here?" I wondered.

"You're from the north?" he asked. Except in that Cork accent it was like "Yeer fraa ta naar?"

"Belfast," I said.

"Yeah, I recognized it," he replied. "I wouldn't try the Guinness if I were you. Get you a Sam Adams, so I will."

"Ok," I said.

The kid went off.

The assassin looked at me, nodded.

"You're from Belfast?" he asked, his eyes narrowing to murderous slits.

"Aye," I said, trying to keep the fear out of my voice.

"Me too," he mumbled.

"Is that so?"

"Aye, it is," he said. "Where ya from?"

"My ma was from Carrickfergus. I lived with my nan in—"

"Carrickfergus, like in the song?" he asked, suddenly interested.

"Like in the song," I agreed.

"Thought that was a Proddy town," he muttered, shaking his head.

"Not all of it is Protestant. Whereabouts you from?" I asked.

He put his glass of beer on the counter, lifted his finger slowly, and tapped it on his nose. In other words, mind your own bloody business. Which would have been fine if I had initiated the conversation, but he had, and now the big shite was making me look bad. Swallow it, I thought.

I adopted a *génération perdue* insouciance, which I think was rather lost on the hit man so I relented and grinned at him as my drink came.

"*Slainte,*" I said.

"Cheers," he said and turned away from me to scope the bar.

Looking for Gerry McCaghan and his bodyguards. Not here yet, still only six minutes to six. When they did show and he had a good angle, I knew the assassin was going to open his coat and gun them with that big muscle job he had under there. Or at least he was going to try to. For what he didn't know was that the man who had met him at Logan Airport two hours earlier was a stool pigeon working for the *federales* and had in fact supplied him with a weapon with its firing pin filed down, not enough to raise suspicion, but just enough to render it completely useless. Rules of evidence and lawyers being what they are, the FBI had to catch the assassin in the act and as soon as he brought out that gun with intent to murder, the peelers were going to order him to drop it and tell him that he was under arrest.

Samantha claimed it was all pretty simple. The gun didn't work, the assassin would be nabbed immediately, the place was crawling with FBI. It would pan out perfectly.

As perfect as Waco. As perfect as Ruby Ridge. I fidgeted with my shirt and trousers. Jeremy had bought them for me at Portela Airport in Lisbon while I changed in the first-class lounge. The white shirt was fine but the trousers were too loose. I had the belt on the last hole and even then I feared that they would fall down at a crucial moment, projecting an unwelcome element of farce into the proceedings.

Jeremy hadn't sat with us but I had gotten to know Samantha as well as one could on a transatlantic flight. She was surprisingly open. Born in Lincolnshire, her father a brigadier in one of those pretentious highland regiments. She'd read philosophy at Oxford and joined the civil service, before getting initially into MI5 and then MI6. She had never been married. No kids. But more important, I didn't know if she'd ever been a field agent because she wasn't allowed to talk about it. My hunch was no. As impressive as that little foot-stabbing incident had been, she should never have gotten herself into that situation in the first place. And it was a lucky stab, too; if she'd gotten my left foot—the plastic one—I'd be free on Pico de Teide and she'd be on her way to the indiscreet new MI6 building on the South Bank, trying to think of an explanation for the cock-up.

The flight was work, too. She'd passed me Gerry McCaghan's and his daughter Kit's police files, their FBI files, and the special file SUU had made for this op. Kit's was only four pages long but Gerry's could have been a PhD thesis.

I don't know about Gerry, but Kit's photograph didn't do her justice. A blurry mug shot from an RUC station when she was bruised, tired, dirty, and a little unwell.

The real Kit looked nothing like this. I knew that because she was here already. Gerry had a half share in the Rebel Heart and Kit worked bar every once in a while. I hadn't realized she'd look so young. Or so beautiful. Spotted her the moment I'd walked in. How could I not? Working with that big doofus from County Cork but not serving the likes of me, instead waiting tables with trays of drinks, from which she would get tips. Short spiky black hair. Big, wide, beautiful dark blue-green eyes. Pale cheeks, high cheekbones. Nose ring. Full lips painted with black lipstick. Cargo pants. Slender waist, small breasts. A Newgrange Heel Stone–style tribal tattoo on her left shoulder, just peeking out from underneath a green USMC T-shirt. Very attractive piece of jailbait you would have thought, but actually she was nineteen, nearly twenty.

I had memorized her full bio. The USMC T-shirt was a fashion accessory, but apparently she had taken part in one wee military operation. Not in America, of course. The Old Country. Born in Boston, but she'd spent a summer in Belfast, where Gerry had blooded her. In 1995 she'd been arrested for throwing stones at the police during a riot on the Falls Road. It wasn't remotely serious and she was detained for a day and deported. Still, Gerry's plans for her were clear—not exactly the crime of the century, but not a Swiss finishing school either.

She was Gerry's adopted daughter, but that didn't mean a thing, because she'd been raised in the cause and radicalized and if she was half as earnest as her da she was big trouble. For Gerry was an old-school hard man from the Bogside in Derry. He'd been interned by the British in the early seventies and had killed his way to the top of the North Antrim Brigade of the IRA. But Gerry was not as politically savvy as other brigade commanders and his bombings in Bushmills, Derry, and Ballymena had led to large numbers of civilian casualties, which did not play well in New York or Boston or indeed Libya, where the IRA's Czech explosives and Russian guns were coming from. Gerry had been asked to tone down his approach, focus more on military targets; he refused, dissented, argued, and finally was asked to leave Ulster, under sentence.

In the early 1980s he had come to Boston, started working as an IRA quartermaster channeling funds from the Bay State to Belfast. The IRA preferred him in this role and permitted him to set up his own shadow organization—the Sons of Cuchulainn—who ran guns and harried British interests in New England. Gerry prospered in America, got married, adopted a little girl, set up a construction company that initially began as a slush fund but then did very well for itself. Gerry had become rich. Things were going swimmingly until about the last twelve months or so.

In the last year the IRA had been in negotiations with Gerry McCaghan and his Sons of Cuchulainn movement, asking him what his position would be if the IRA's Army Council declared a renewal of its cease-fire. Gerry had said, in no uncertain terms, that he would not lay down his weapons for anyone.

But the Brits and Americans were close to a deal, a cease-fire was on the cards, and the IRA didn't need a Gerry McCaghan embarrassing them in front of President Clinton, so a decision had been taken to kill him. Indeed, to kill all the recalcitrant types who would be opposed to a resumption of the cease-fire. It would be a Night of the Long Knives. As well as this hit in Boston there were going to be two hits in Belfast, one in Dundalk, and four in Dublin. All the serious hard-line opposition would be taken care of in one blow. The IRA could then announce a cease-fire without fear of disruption from the radical element.

A good plan, but what the IRA did not know was that their main weapons contact in Boston, a weaselly little shitkicker called Packie Quinlan, had a cocaine problem. Packie had been caught buying an entire klick by the FBI and as a get-out-of-jail-free card had sold them the information about the upcoming Boston hit on Gerry McCaghan.

If this had been a whack in Belfast or Dublin, the British and Irish police would probably have let the assassin kill the bad guy first and then lifted him on the way out of the bar, but the FBI weren't like that. They wanted no violence at all, just a nice clean arrest. So some bright spark had come up with the idea of having Packie Quinlan give the hit man a doctored weapon.

Purely as a courtesy, the FBI had informed the British

consulate about the operation; the consulate had told MI6; and Samantha had asked the FBI (at least I hope she had asked them) if she could append a little operation of her own on to theirs.

That's where I came in.

The single most important part of any undercover operation is the insertion of an agent. The exit can be an extravaganza, hurried, broad, maybe involving helicopters, cops, or the bloody Green Berets, but an entry has to be of a different pitch. Clever. Subtle. Low-key.

Samantha's plan was breathtaking in its simplicity.

The moment the assassin was to pull out his machine gun, Samantha wanted me to throw myself protectively on Kit.

End of story.

That was the whole goddamn plan.

When Samantha told me this I looked out the airplane window, pretending to be fascinated by the cloud formations over the Azores and wondering again how I was going to get the hell out of it. But she had shadowed me all the way to Revere and now here I was, either about to attempt to carry out her harebrained scheme or run out the back of the pub into a new set of problems.

Samantha saw the op playing like this: The assassin pulls out the gun. People scream, I jump on Kit, throw her to the ground, shield her with my body, the gun fails, the assassin gets arrested, and I get up off Kit, embarrassed.

But Kit's impressed that someone has tried to save her life and asks my name and I say Sean McKenna from Belfast and she says she'll remember it and me, so that a week from now when she accidentally runs into me again at the End of the State Bar in Salisbury, Massachusetts, she laughs and tells her father that this is the Irish hero that saved her life and *he* asks my name and what I'm doing in America and I say, "Well, to be frank, Mr. McCaghan, I'm looking for a job."

And that would be that.

My way into their crew. Maybe first he'd put me in the construction company, but when he learned about my radical views he'd hopefully invite me into the Sons of Cuchulainn.

That's why I had to be here tonight. A golden opportunity to take a big leap forward in credibility. How else could you break into a cell as small and tightly knit as the Sons of Cuchulainn? Normally you'd need years of work. But Samantha saw this as a shortcut on the trust stakes. A moment of tension, a moment of embarrassment, and the good part was I wasn't going to try and ingratiate myself in one go. I wasn't going to be pushy or forward. Not too keen. Better just to make an impression tonight and then the real op could begin again in a week or so.

Besides, since I had no MI6 training this would be all I could handle. Playing this kind of role took caution, caution, and more caution and I would have to be fully briefed and trained before the real insertion came later.

Tonight it would just be: neat, clean, clever, out.

Only one small problem.

What Samantha didn't know, what I didn't know, what the FBI didn't know, what Packie Quinlan didn't know, was that there was a second assassin.

The IRA believe in redundancy and if an op like this is to go down right, there has to be two shooters, two chains of causation, two ways of getting the job done. The assassins would be on different flights, meeting different contacts, not even acknowledging each other at all until the target appeared.

Yeah, two gunmen, one with a gun that didn't work, but unfortunately one with a gun that did. None of us realized, not the feds, not Samantha, not me, that the arrest was not exactly going to be plain sailing.

Someone tapped me on the shoulder.

I turned round.

"I heard you were from Ireland."

"That's right," I said to a short, bald-headed man with a bicycle messenger bag and a beer gut barely contained by a *Star Trek* T-shirt.

"Take a look at this," he said and from his satchel he withdrew a plaster-cast Virgin Mary.

"Nice," I said, not sure how I was supposed to respond.

"Are you going back to the Old Country soon?" he asked in

a very heavy Boston accent.

"I might be," I said.

"Look, would you be interested in buying a batch to take back with you, five bucks each. You can mark them up to twenty punts when you get there," he said.

"I don't think so."

"What about a Jesus?"

He took a Jesus out of the bag. The problem with both votive statues was that they were incredibly lifelike. Thus his venture was doomed to failure because of the dark skin tone of both mother and son. I wouldn't say I was a keen observer of Boston's or Ireland's Catholic community but I do know that only Aryan-looking aspects of the Divine appear in Ireland; weeping Virgin Marys popping up frequently in the west of the country, tears running down their porcelain white skin and over the end of their retroussé noses. Whoever thought they could sell Semitic-looking biblical characters in Ireland had to be out of their bloody minds. I was not the bloke to disillusion the poor bugger.

"Sorry, mate," I said.

"Are you sure?"

"Not my racket," I told him.

"Ok."

He took his bag over to the next person at the bar, who happened to be the IRA hit man.

"Fuck off," the assassin said after listening to him for about three seconds.

The bald man got a bit intimidated by that and lucky for him he exited the pub only five minutes before the shooting started. Indeed, he left the bar after talking to only one more person, a short blond kid in the corner, who oddly enough wasn't touching his pint of Bass.

The blond kid also refused to countenance the possibility of selling the holy family to the Micks.

I laughed when the bald guy shuffled out.

I should have known better, for he had spoken to both assassins now, letting them know that McCaghan was coming and that the job was on.

❖   ❖   ❖

Kit came to the bar to pick up an order. She looked like a punk, but she smelled of—what was that?—sweet pea. I gazed at her and tried to figure out precisely how I was going to throw myself on top of her when the assassin was due to commence his work.

As soon as her da walked in, was I supposed to start following her around? What if the assassin took his time about it? Look a bit suspicious, me hanging off Kit's bloody shoulder the whole night.

Samantha had given me zero instructions on this.

I would have to come up with something. I took a sip of my Sam Adams. Nah, couldn't possibly tag behind her the whole evening. I'd just have to keep my eye on the door and when Gerry showed, I'd saunter over to wherever Kit happened to be. Until then, low profile, no fuss. If it didn't work, it didn't work. I could only tell Samantha I'd tried my best and she'd have to believe me. I looked at Kit. And really by now I wasn't contemplating the stupid plan. Two minutes staring at her was enough to get you.

Think Winona Ryder in *Heathers,* Phoebe Cates in *Gremlins,* Sean Young in *Blade Runner.* That kind of vibe. The dark eyes, the tubercular pallor, the thing on her head that had once been a Louise Brooks bob but now was teased and hairsprayed in all directions.

She leaned into the bar, picked up the order, and waltzed off with a tray full of black and tans.

Had she even noticed me? I wouldn't blame her if she hadn't. When we'd arrived that morning, Samantha and Jeremy had driven me to a safe house in Cambridge. A barber had shown up at four a.m. Obviously as annoyed about the hour as I was, he had savagely cut my hair to a number two and then dyed what was left a dark black. Previously, I'd had longish sandy-colored hair, and everyone in New York had certainly known me that way. Now I appeared quite different. Not a bad look for me. Little rougher, little tougher. But the jet-lagged eyes and nasty sunburn couldn't help.

"Get ya another?" the kid from Cork asked.

"Nah, still working at this one," I said.

"It's all right, is it?" the kid asked.

"Aye, it's fine," I said.

"One of this country's great patriots."

"Who is?" I asked.

"Sam Adams. He rode from New York to Boston to warn the people the British were coming. And he was the third president of the United States."

"And he made beer, too?"

"He certainly did now," the keep said and walked back to the bottles.

I looked at my watch, three minutes to six. I couldn't help but be a bit nervous. Quick time-out. I went to the bathroom and splashed some water on my face. Ok, take it easy, Forsythe, this is bloody nothing. Piece of piss, I told my reflection.

Nothing for you, buddy, remember you were in a riot a couple of days ago, my reflection said.

I splashed some more water and went back to the bar stool.

The assassin had ordered another Schlitz Lite. The blond kid in the corner hadn't touched his drink at all. And neither had a bunch of clean-cut men wearing board shorts and Gap T-shirts, sitting together, at two tables by the door.

Ah, the *federales,* I thought.

"So what you do for a living?" the assassin asked me out of the blue.

"Me, oh, um, I was a postman back in Ireland," I answered—the first thing that popped into my head.

"Fucking posties, bastards so they are, on the whole. Always bills, always fucking bills," the assassin said bitterly. The kid from Cork came over.

"Pushkin said that postmen were monsters of the human race, a bit extreme perhaps but you could see his point of view," he intoned, obviously attempting levity.

Both the assassin and myself turned the evil eye on him and he pissed off. We didn't need some know-it-all student showing us up.

"The Commie with the dogs?" the assassin asked me when the kid had gone. For a sec I had no idea what he was talking about.

"No, no, you're thinking of Pavlov, mate," I said and was about to explain but got interrupted by the assassin, who turned his full pale face and intimidating eyes on me.

"Look, maybe you should make yourself scarce, mister Carrickfergus postman," he whispered slowly, measuring out every word.

"I'm heading just as soon as I finish my beer," I said.

"No, no, maybe you should split right now, if you know what's good for ya," the assassin said.

I was touched. Fair play of him to spare me the coming unpleasantness, but I couldn't go.

"I'll be heading soon," I said.

The assassin opened his mouth to insist that maybe I should leave right now, but before he could the outside door opened.

In walked the bodyguards. The first one I noticed was "Big" Mike McClennahan. Of course, Big Mike was about five foot five. Bald, skinny, wearing a black polo shirt and blue jeans. He was from Boston, ex-cop, gunrunner, bookie. Next, Seamus Hughes—fifty-two, five nine, sallow-faced, wearing a tan jacket and a 5-0 shirt. Another Bostonian, another ex-cop in fact, twenty-five years, full pension, tough nut.

A heartbeat behind them, Gerry McCaghan.

Fifty-five years old. Six foot, a good three hundred pounds, pale, ursine, red hair, a really nasty smear of scar tissue under his left eye where he'd gotten hit by a rubber bullet at a riot in Derry. He was wearing sunglasses, blue corduroys, a Hawaiian shirt like Seamus's, black loafers, and rather surprisingly he had a gun showing in a holster on his left hip. The gun visible only for a moment as the draft from the door wafted up his shirttail.

"Mr. McCaghan, the usual?" the kid behind the bar shouted.

Kit looked over, smiled at her dad, and waved.

The feds tensed.

The assassin put down his pint. Too late now to warn his compatriot about the upcoming slaughter.

I got off the bar stool, began walking toward Kit.

Here goes, I thought. She was hovering over a table, clearing away the drinks. The table was between the exit and a toilet, so I could always say I'd been heading for the toilet if she ever asked why I had suddenly started walking toward her when all hell had broken loose.

About fifteen paces from me to her. How long did I have? A few seconds?

Three paces, four, five, six, seven.

I knew it was the wrong thing to do but I couldn't help but half-turn and look at the assassin. His pint was on the bar now, his cigarette in the ashtray, both his hands free. He slid off the bar stool, stood, legs apart, steady.

Nine, ten, eleven . . .

Gerry, slightly behind Hughes and McClennahan, nodded at someone in the far corner of the room.

Kit picked up an empty glass, put it on her tray.

Twelve, thirteen, fourteen . . .

The assassin reached in his coat, pulled out a sawed-down AK-47 assault rifle. He hooked in that big curved magazine, lifted the gun, and aimed it. I leapt at Kit just as someone yelled:

"He's got a gun."

My hands reached Kit's shoulders.

Seamus went for his revolver. McCaghan reached for his pistol.

The assassin leveled the AK at McCaghan, pulled the trigger.

Nothing.

A blank look on the assassin's face.

I hauled Kit to the floor. Her body warm, slender, slight. A pint glass fell out of her hand and I pushed it away in midair before it smashed on top of her.

"What the fuck—" she began saying to me while her father ducked and the assassin, looking baffled, pulled the

AK's trigger again.

Then a dozen people stood and yelled "Drop your weapon" and "Put the gun down" and "This is the FBI."

And at the same time, the blond-haired kid in the corner took out a 9mm pistol, leveled his arm, took aim, and fired two quick rounds at Gerry McCaghan. Put off by all the noise, confusion, and yelling, he missed Gerry by ten feet and the bullets sailed through the upper windows and out into the back bay.

Panicking, one of the FBI agents fired his weapon, hitting the effectively unarmed assassin at the bar, nailing him in the left shoulder.

The blond-haired kid fired again, almost getting McCaghan this time, missing him by a few inches, hitting a bell hanging from the ceiling just above his head. Seamus spun round and shot twice at the kid in the corner. Bullets ripping up a Boston Celtics wall hanging above his booth. The kid shot back at Seamus and, seeing that the situation was untenable, began making a break for a side door. Underneath me, Kit writhed and called out, "Daddy, Daddy, oh Daddy" while the FBI men were screaming: "Everyone drop your weapons, cease fire, this is the FBI."

The kid shot a round that thumped into a Guinness mirror just to the left of us, shattering it. Three seconds of everything happening at once: Kit howling, the FBI yelling, Seamus shooting at the kid, the kid shoot-ing at Seamus, Gerry completely safe, crouching behind Seamus and McClennahan. The other patrons lying on the floor, absolutely terrified.

An FBI agent jumped unnecessarily onto the first gunman, crashing him over the bar and into the Cork barkeep. Two other agents fired at the blond assassin, missing but almost killing an innocent tourist who had wandered in off the street to see what all the commotion was. Smoke, cordite, chaos, and Gerry's bodyguard, Seamus, keeping the coolest of everyone, crouching, taking good aim, firing just to the left of the kid's determined face.

It had lasted almost fifteen seconds, but it couldn't last much longer.

The kid fired the final bullet in his clip, hitting an FBI guy right in the center of his Kevlar vest.

And at that, a senior FBI man with a mustache stood on a table and screamed to make himself heard: "Everybody fucking freeze. You're all under arrest. This is the FBI. Stop shooting. Drop your guns, drop your guns, drop your goddamn guns."

The blond-haired kid finally saw sense and put his hands up. Seamus dropped his gun and put his hands up too.

Kit, writhing, turned round to look at me.

"Let's get out of here," I whispered. "Away from the bloody peelers."

"How?"

"Stairs to the basement and up through the barrel hatch," I said, wildly improvising.

"My dad?" Kit whispered.

"Is going to be arrested, everybody is, let's go," I said. "We can slip out through the smoke."

The senior FBI agent yelled commands over the ringing in our ears: "Drop those guns on the floor and put your hands on your heads. Everyone else freeze. This place is surrounded by the FBI."

The blond kid put his hands on his head and two agents knocked him to the floor, pinning him. They grabbed Seamus and Gerry and attempted to render assistance to the injured assassin.

"This is our chance, in all the confusion," I whispered.

"Ok," Kit said.

We slipped down the steps into the basement. I didn't know if they even had a hatchway for delivering the kegs, but Kit did.

"It's over here," she whispered. "There's a stepladder against the wall."

I grabbed the ladder, climbed it, and pushed open the hatch into the glare of the sun setting over Boston Harbor. I clambered onto the sidewalk and helped Kit up.

"What about my dad?" Kit asked.

"He's fine, he'll be going downtown for having that gun,

though," I said.

"Who are you?"

"I only came for a bloody drink."

"Who are you?"

"Sean McKenna."

"You two, you better hold it right there," a Boston cop yelled from behind one of the trash compactors.

"We're FBI," I said and reached in my pocket for my driving license, which I couldn't let Kit see because it was still for Brian O'Nolan.

The cop walked over and when he was close, I lowered the license, let him bend down to look at it, smashed my fist into the side of his head, kicked his legs from under him, and kicked him twice on the ground, blows that probably hurt me more than him—with my stabbed foot—but which rendered him briefly unconscious.

Kit looked at me, appalled but also excited.

"Let's go," I yelled, and we ran down an alley into the back streets of Revere.

Within a minute we had disappeared into the holiday crowd, but just to be sure, Kit found a parked Toyota Camry, wrapped her jacket round her arm, broke the side window with her elbow, yelled in pain, opened the door, kicked the plastic off the ignition system, sparked the starter, turned to me, and said:

"I'm a little bit . . . um, can you drive?"

"Ok, honey," I said and drive I did.

❀   ❀   ❀

Route 1 out of Revere. Kit distracted, on the mobile phone, trying time and again to call her dad and her dad's lawyer and finally getting through to Sonia, whoever Sonia was, explaining what had happened and asking Sonia to call her back.

Kit ignoring me completely. Not that I cared—I was focused on not getting us killed in the hellish evening traffic heading out of the city.

"Where are we going?" I asked when she finally seemed

done with her phone calls.

"Plum Island."

"Can we drive there?" I asked, remembering that this was also the name of one of those islands in Long Island Sound.

"Of course. Forty-five minutes."

"Where is it?"

"Route 1 to 133 to Route 1A, it's at the mouth of the Merrimack River."

Kit's mobile rang.

"Dad, Daddy, is that you? Oh my God. Ohmygod. Oh my God."

Apparently it was. Kit started to cry, and I gave her a tissue we'd found in the glove compartment. She blew her nose. Wiped her eyes.

"Daddy, where are you?" she asked into the phone.

Gerry told her and Kit seemed reassured.

"I'm going back to Newburyport; a nice boy called Sean is driving me, he sort of saved me, he's from Ireland."

Gerry must have been suspicious, because Kit gave me a winning smile.

"It's ok, Daddy, I'm totally fine. He's nice. We're heading home. What about you, are you hurt? Did you tell them about your blood pressure?"

Gerry said something and Kit laughed. She put her hand over the receiver.

"He's fine," she told me.

"Good," I replied.

Gerry said something else that sent her into hysterics. She put her hand over the mouthpiece again.

"He says he'll be out tonight because he's got something rarer than a tap-dancing dodo," Kit explained, the tears gone from her eyes now.

"What's that?" I asked.

"A Massachusetts concealed carry permit," Kit said and chuckled at her father's unfunny remark.

Gerry gave her a few instructions and told her he loved her.

"I love you too, Dad," Kit said and hung up.

Kit turned to me and smiled.

"They're all ok," she said.

"Ok, good. I'm glad," I said and gave her a quizzical look.

"What's that expression about?" she asked.

"Well, this may be a perfectly normal event to you but I'm a stranger in these parts, so you wanna tell me what the fuck happened in there?" I asked.

"I don't know, I suppose it was a gang thing," Kit lied.

"A gang thing? Jesus. Does that happen in Boston a lot?" I asked.

"No, not really, but sometimes it does. It doesn't usually come down to violence."

"How come your dad had a gun?"

"Oh, he, like, runs a construction company, gets a lot of threats from the mafia and stuff, he's allowed. But I don't think this was anything to do with him. Just wrong place, wrong time."

"Well, I must say you're taking it pretty well, been in anything like this before?" I asked.

Kit said nothing but her face was hard and wary.

"It's certainly a first time for me," I said, as gentle a probe as I dared.

"First time for me, too," she said and patted me on the leg. She was being comforting but also taking the piss. Still, the physical contact was welcome. A lot of attractive women were finding me extremely tactile these days. That unwashed combination of prison cell, banana plantation, riot, sunblock, and cheap beer must be an irresistible mix.

"Terrifying," I said, and Kit nodded. "I mean, Jesus, it was terrible, oh my God, it was really terrible," I added, hamming it up.

But Kit was bored with me. She didn't want to pretend that this was her virgin encounter with serious violence. She tried to look away. Her lip began to quiver and she looked for her fags. No, not bored, it was all just too much to deal with right now.

A good idea to change the subject.

"Well, you're not going to tell me that that was the first car you ever broke into," I said.

Kit pressed the button to open the Camry's sunroof.

The scent of pollen.

The night air smeared with stars.

"No, I'm not going to tell you that," she said softly and with a nervous laugh. "Let's talk about you, though. Why are you over from Ireland?"

I had to be quiet now as I exited Route 1 and joined the 1A, via the 133. The 1A was a narrow two-lane road, not much traffic, that made its way through little white clapboard towns, swampy grasslands, boggy woods, and big wet marshes near the tidal shore.

"What are you doing in America?" Kit asked me again.

"Apart from beating up cops and saving girls?"

"Yeah, unless you do that full-time? You're not Superman, are you?"

"Superman digs the police. I'm here just the same as everybody. Looking for work. Someone told me this morning that I might have a job opening up in Salisbury Beach, Massachusetts," I said, hastily recalling what Samantha had told me of the second part of the plan.

"Doing what?"

"I'm not sure what exactly, probably bar."

"Salisbury? Well, I don't think you'll have a problem with gunplay up there, it's not exactly the most happening of places."

"Hope not. Christ, twenty-five years in Belfast and I'm safe as houses, a week in America and I'm in a bloody gun battle."

Kit said nothing. She rummaged in her bag and found a cigarette.

"Smoke?" she asked.

I shook my head.

"Filthy habit," she agreed and lit herself one.

"Not so much that, I had a hard time quitting; I was addicted and I don't want to start again," I said.

"I'm just a social smoker. Addictions are for the weak," Kit announced with condescension.

I grinned inwardly and said nothing.

"At least everyone's ok," Kit said more to herself than me, and out of the corner of my eye I noticed that now her hand was starting to shake.

Well, yes, it had been scary, and after all she was little more than just a kid. No Mexican prisons on her résumé.

"Yeah, everyone seemed fine," I agreed.

The woods thinned and the road went over a narrow perfumed river winding its way uneasily into the black sea.

"The feds had it all staked out," she muttered to herself.

"I suppose so," I concurred, staring at her.

"I should have known those guys were feds, they didn't tip," she said.

"And I was suspicious of that guy with the assault rifle from the start," I said.

"Why?"

"He was drinking lite beer," I said. "Don't you find in your professional capacity that lite beer drinkers are generally wankers?"

"Now you come to mention it," Kit said, drawing in the tobacco smoke and relaxing a little.

We drove in silence and she smoked her cig, lit another, and was soon chill enough to become the proud amateur tour guide.

"See the road to that beach?"

"Yeah?"

"That's where they filmed a Steve McQueen movie, the one with Faye Dunaway and he's a bank robber."

"Don't know it but it sounds good," I said.

"And down there is where the famous writer John Updike lives."

"John Updike? Sounds like a porn name," I said.

"Joan Updike would be more appropriate. . . . Oh, and see over there, that's where Jackie did a hundred and five in the Porsche and got caught by the state police."

"Who's Jackie?"

"My boyfriend," Kit said breezily.

"Nice boy?"

"Who cares about nice?" she said in her best Madonna.

"Well, I'm sure he's perfectly charming, but I can tell you one thing about him that you don't know."

"What?"

"He isn't good enough for you," I said.

Kit turned her head slightly and looked at me.

"Are you making a pass?" she asked with a smile.

My lack of an answer was my answer and it unsettled her in a way I found I liked a lot.

At Ipswich we approached a well-lit place called the Clam Box, where you could smell fried fish through the Toyota's sunroof and broken window. Dozens of cars. Perhaps fifty people waiting outside.

"Look at that place, it must be good," I said. "I'm hungry. You wanna pull in?"

"Best fried clams in New England," she said.

"Really?"

"You ever have a fried clam?"

"No."

"Well, that's the best. Huge lines all summer. Ted Williams goes there."

"You want me to stop the car?" I asked, slowing down.

Kit shook her head.

"I should get home," she said.

We drove on and as we got closer to Newburyport, farther from Boston, she regained more of her composure and beamed at me.

"Not good enough for me," she mused. "Who do you think you are, mister?"

She seemed happier. I patted her knee and she didn't seem to mind. I was impressed. I mean, I don't how I would have taken it if someone had tried to assassinate my da half an hour ago, but I doubt I could have been as cool as this. Clearly, a tough wee soul lived under the late-teen veneer.

"Where you living in Salisbury?" she asked.

"Not sure yet, everything's a bit up in the air."

"How old are you?" she asked.

"I'm twenty-five, twenty-six in a month or so."

"Twenty-six? You're, like, seven years older than me."

"So?"

"You're totally an old man," she mocked.

It made me wince a little. No one wants to hear something like that from a pretty girl and this girl was very pretty.

"How old are you? Nineteen?"

"Nearly twenty," she said.

"You're a mere child," I mocked back.

She looked at me with fake annoyance.

"What's your name? I know you said it but I forgot."

"Sean."

"No, your second name, I remembered the Sean."

"Sean McKenna. Oh my goodness, what's yours? In all the excitement I forgot to ask."

"Katherine, but everyone calls me Kitty, or Kit; I used to hate it, oh my God, I used to hate it, but I kind of like it now. Kit, I mean."

"I suppose it's because of Kitty O'Shea," I said.

"Who was that again? The name's familiar," Kit asked.

"You don't know who Kitty O'Shea is?"

"No."

"That's what I was about talking about when I said you were a mere child," I said.

She wanted to ask but she was too pissed off and I enjoyed watching her fume. We came to a road junction in the small town of Rowley. We could either go left or straight on.

"Where to?" I asked.

"Straight on, oh wait, I can hardly bring you home, Dad wouldn't like that. What are we going to do with you? Where are you staying, in Salisbury?"

"Nah, for the moment I'm still back at the youth hostel in Boston."

"I'm sorry, Dad wouldn't like me to bring you home. Do you want to drop me and then you can take the car back to the city?"

"I don't want to drive a stolen car, it's freaking me out a bit, to be honest. I don't want to be deported after my first week in America."

"Ok, then, we should go straight on, we'll go to the bus

station in Newburyport. I definitely can't leave this car at Dad's house. Sonia can pick me up and you can get the bus back to Boston. I can't drive you, I'm pretty messed from when you fell on top of me," she said and winced at her own lame excuse.

"You don't have to say thanks or anything," I said.

She fought the urge to thank me, her punky little pride unable to accept the fact that she had been in danger and I'd helped get her out of it. We drove in complete silence for the next couple of minutes. Dark now, but I could tell that the landscape had become swampy. It smelled of marsh gas and seawater.

Mosquitoes and a million types of fly bouncing into the windshield and a sign that said "Newburyport, Plum Island— 5 Miles."

"So who's Ted Williams?" I asked, to resume the conversation.

"Are you joking?"

"No."

"Only the greatest baseball player ever. The last man to hit over .400, war hero, batting champion again and again."

"I thought Babe Ruth was the greatest player," I said innocently.

Kit looked at me as if she were having a fit. Her nose had wrinkled up and she was plucking at the pointy strands of hair over her forehead.

"Are you trying to rile me up?"

"No."

"This is a Red Sox town," she said.

"So?"

"You don't know about the Red Sox and the curse of the Bambino?"

"No."

"Well, anyway, it's a long story, *No, No, Nanette* and all that, suffice to say, we don't talk about Babe Ruth. We don't, in Massachusetts, talk about any Yankees players. It's a rule."

"Sorry, I don't know much about baseball, nothing actually. We don't play it in Ireland. I've only heard of Babe Ruth, oh,

and Joe DiMaggio of course, because of Simon and Gar-
funkel, and yeah, Lou Gehrig because of the disease. Oh aye,
and Yogi Berra, you know because of the cartoon."

"What did I tell you about Yankees players?" Kit snapped,
her face turning bright red. She was working herself up into a
little bit of a state. More of a state than immediately after a
man had tried to bloody kill her da. Odd but a good thing perhaps—you keep your calm for the dangerous things, you lose
your cool over the trivial.

"They were all Yankees? Jesus. Sorry. Who are the famous
Red Sox?" I asked.

"I don't walk to talk about it now," Kit said, still a little
ticked off. Petulant and furious, she looked even more fetching.

"I was just asking," I said.

"Obviously you're, like, totally ignorant about the whole
business," she said.

"I just said I was," I protested.

"And you fucking are."

"But that's what I said."

"And you were right."

She turned away from me, so that I couldn't see that she
was laughing. I wanted to pull the car over, grab her, and kiss
her.

It was completely the wrong thing to do, but also . . .

"Why are you slowing down? The bus station is still a couple of miles, come on," Kit said.

True enough, we were getting close to civilization. A big
town. The trees giving way to houses. Old wooden homes,
some with signs saying that they dated back to the 1630s. Traffic started to increase and I could definitely smell the sea. We
stopped at a red light. A sign to the right pointed to Rolfe's
Lane, Plum Island, and Plum Island Airfield.

"This is where you'd turn to take me home but Daddy
really wouldn't approve of me bringing you to the house, he
just wouldn't. Sorry," Kit said.

"It's ok," I said. "So what do I do?"

"Go straight through town and then turn right at the bus

station. There's a big parking lot, we can dump the car, you can get a bus back to Boston, I'll phone Sonia."

"Who's Sonia?" I asked.

"My dad's new wife. I guess my stepmom now. My mom died two years ago. Well, not my real mom, my real mom is out there somewhere, it's complicated."

"Is she a wicked stepmom?"

"No, she's nice. She doesn't like Jackie very much, though."

"Jackie—the boyfriend, right?"

"Yeah."

"I like Sonia, sounds like she has good horse sense. I want to meet her."

"No way, Dad wouldn't like it."

We drove along High Street. Enormous mansions to the left and right built during Newburyport's boom times in the nineteenth century on profits from the whaling and the China trade.

We turned into the parking lot at the bus station, got out of the car. I started walking away.

"You really are naive, aren't you?" she said, took off her jacket, and wiped down the steering wheel, the gear stick, the dash.

"Can't leave prints," she said.

I nodded, slapped my forehead.

We walked to the bus station.

A lovely night. Warm and the heavens packed with constellations and a waxing moon. We walked in silence across the parking lot and she led me into the station entrance. Not much of a bus station, more of a halt, a desk, a guy, a phone, a Coke machine, half a dozen chairs. She phoned Sonia while I asked the man at the desk about the next bus to Boston.

"Ten minutes, Boston and Logan," he said, though it was more like *tea meen, bosson, logue.*

We went outside. Moths bewitched by the big arc lights over the car park, crashing into them and falling stunned to the ground.

"Let's get away from shere," I said and led her away from the lights and under an oak tree. We sat on one of the enormous roots. Kit's hand reached round to mine. Her fingers were cool and delicate. She turned me to look at her.

"I'm like totally dating someone, you know . . . Jackie, but, but I want to give you this in case I never see you again," she said.

She pulled me toward her and kissed me on the lips. I opened her mouth with mine and I found her tongue and we kissed there in the night under the moon and the arc lights. She was young and beautiful. So alive. I kissed her and held her and put my hands on her bum, squeezed her ass, and ran my hand up her back and leaned down and kissed her small pert breasts.

A car honked.

"Sonia," she said, gasping.

She broke away and stood and then came over and kissed me again.

"I never thanked you," she said.

"You just did."

"Yes," she said, blushing happily.

"Will I see you again?"

"Sean McKenna from Ireland, I'll remember that."

Sonia honked the car horn again.

"I have to go. Sonia's not one to gossip, but Jackie, you know, he can be a bit jealous. And I don't want him to go after you. I don't want you to get hurt."

"Don't worry, I avoid hurt," I said.

She kissed me on the cheek.

She signaled Sonia, ran to the car, climbed in. Waved at me as she drove past.

I avoid hurt, I said to myself with a thin smile. Of course. I'm at the other end of the stick. I'm the hurter. I'm the goddamn nimrod that could destroy all of them. Jackie, Gerry, Sonia, Seamus, and even the famous Touched McGuigan. And you too, Kit. You too.

Aye.

Stay young, stay beautiful, stay away if you know what's good for you.

I walked into the bus station, put fifty cents in the pay

phone, and called Samantha at the safe house. Jeremy answered and told me to hold on.

"Are you ok?" Samantha asked. "How did it go?"

"Better and worse than we could have hoped," I said. "I drove Kit home, but the bar was a disaster. For a start there were two assass—"

"Not on the phone," Samantha snapped. "Where are you?"

"I'm in Newburyport, at the bus station."

"Newburyport. Ok, let me think. Ok, we want to get to New York. What's the number there?"

"Let me see, Newburyport 555-9360, the area code's 978."

"I'll call you back in five minutes."

"There's a bus going back to Boston right now, do you want me to get on it?"

"I'll call you back," she said.

The bus came and went and the man behind the desk gave me a hangdog look.

The phone rang. It was Samantha. I was pissed off.

"Yeah, well, now we're screwed, I just missed the last bus to Boston," I said.

"No, no. This is what I want you to do. Get a taxi to the airport at Portsmouth, New Hampshire. There's an 11:50 flight to New York. I will meet you there. Is that clear?"

"It's clear," I said, rubbing the tiredness from my eyes and hanging up.

The cab ride took an hour and cost seventy bucks. Samantha arrived at the airport the same time that I did, landing in a helicopter.

She bought us tickets for the last flight out to New York. She found a quiet corner of the almost deserted airport and debriefed me.

"I heard all about it," she said, shaking her head. "The FBI cocked it up. But at least you met Kit? Didn't you? Our plan worked."

"I suppose so," I said. "I drove with her all the way to Newburyport. I think she liked me."

"Excellent, it's our way in," she said. "And as expected, take a look at this."

She handed me a faxed copy of tomorrow's *Irish Times*. The banner headline occupied the whole front page: "IRA Announce Unilateral Cease-fire. Protestant Groups to Follow."

I gave her back the fax and frowned.

Something didn't sit right. I examined my feelings and found that I resented her for making me use Kit in this way. Regardless of what her father represented or what he'd done, I liked the girl.

"Come on, then, we're going to a bureau training facility in New York," Samantha said.

We boarded the plane. A Short 360 with the two of us and a couple of tired businessmen as the only passengers.

First class was empty and I switched to the right-hand side of the aircraft so I could follow the coast as we headed back down the Atlantic.

We took off steeply. The plane reached ten thousand feet.

Portsmouth lit up and very clear.

The harbor, the river, the highways.

Below us, farther down the coast, a long barrier island. I found a stewardess.

"Is that Plum Island, Massachusetts, down there by any chance?"

She called the captain on her little phone.

"Yes, it is," she told me.

That's where she lived. And Samantha was right—she was the way in. But the way had a name and she was beautiful and quick and I doubted that she was and ever could be my enemy.

3: BACK TO THE BIG A

New York City. Overdescribed. You know what it's like even if you've never been. This was August in New York so it was all that and more and you couldn't get a doctor, electrician, or plumber on the weekends.

Dan grinned.

Manhattan behind his head. The Twin Towers, the Chrysler Building, and the Empire State blurring in the heat haze. We were out in the wastelands of Queens, where the subway lines used letters from the end of the alphabet and the video stores had an Urdu section.

He sipped his coffee.

"You're pretty much fucked, Michael," he said with more than a hint of gleeful schadenfreude. It wasn't contempt. Dan liked me, but he sometimes felt that I was more trouble than I was worth. Dan was my FBI controller who liaised with the U.S. Marshals Service and the Witness Protection Program. It was Dan's job to make sure I didn't get killed. As I saw it, he was letting me walk into a snake pit, without raising too much of a stink about it. He said it was over his head, but everyone always says that when they're scared or they can't be arsed.

"You'll be fucked if I die," I said.

"You won't die," Dan assured me. "At least not on my watch."

I didn't say anything. I needed a lot more convincing than

this. Dan rubbed his cheeks, smiled.

"I like what you've done to your hair, it's very contemporary. Now that Cobain's dead that whole look you used to have is on its way out. If you were a bit more tanned you'd look like an Israeli commando," he said.

"They did it to me. It's their idea of a disguise."

I took a sip of the coffee, too. It was from the deli round the corner, made, no doubt, by a recent immigrant who knew the ingredients and the method for making coffee but certainly not how it was supposed to taste.

"I can't drink this. What are we doing out here?" I asked.

"You're lucky you're not in Union City or Weehawken. The lower echelons of the bureau got priced out of Manhattan a long time ago. Count your blessings, buddy."

"Count my blesssings? Dan, they want me to infiltrate a rogue IRA splinter group. What exactly is the blessing aspect of that?" I asked.

"Well, you're not back in Mexico, which, as I understand it, is the alternative," Dan said with complacency.

"True, but I'm worried about being shopped to Seamus Duffy. And that, pal, is your department. If I was you, I'd be on the phone to Janet Reno telling her that as a matter of policy I have to be protected from these Brits who are doing their damnedest to get me killed. I am very disappointed in you, mate."

Dan looked hurt. He was a big guy, chubby, blond hair, about thirty. He had a penchant for wearing polo shirts and golfing gear. It only made him seem fatter. And when he looked sad, it was all the more pathetic. He tapped his chin nervously.

"Michael, I know you think that you're the center of the world but you ain't. Janet Reno? Come on. You got yourself into this mess and you'll have to get yourself out of it. Our job is to make sure you don't get killed by the people you ra—, er, the people you helped put behind bars. If you messed up in Spain, that's your own problem. I think, if you recall, I warned you not to go abroad."

"I needed a vacation."

"Try Disney World next time."

"You wouldn't understand. You don't know what it's like to be in my shoes with a bloody contract on your head," I said.

He rolled his eyes.

"As to that—" Dan began, but before he could continue Samantha popped her head round the door.

"Is everything going all right?" she asked. "We really have to get back to business, Michael, time is of the essence."

"Everything's not going all right, actually, Samantha. Dan is refusing to help me get out of this bloody Faustian bargain."

Dan looked at me cross-eyed, knowing that he should have gotten the reference but he just wasn't quite smart enough to remember it. Dan would be the guy on *Jeopardy* who wouldn't get to play the final game because he had a negative score. Samantha, though, considered it an insult, for if I were Faust she was Satan. She stepped completely into the room. She was wearing a fetching yellow sundress that was see-through from certain angles.

"We have a deal. Don't make me cross this early in the day," Samantha said.

"Why don't you come over here and tell me that," I said with mock aggression that she took to be real. Samantha was not one to be bullied. She thought stabbing me in the foot had already established that but clearly she had to do more. She walked right up to me and stared. All five foot six of her glaring at me. I moved back a little and sat on the edge of the table. The angle was now perfect and I could see the outline of her breasts. I don't know if it was an English thing or the humidity but whatever the explanation Samantha sometimes did not wear a bra. Her breasts were pale, very large, and inviting. And there was no getting around the fact that she was an attractive woman. A beautiful face, seductive, heavy-lidded eyes, a cleavage that would have fitted snugly in the court of Louis Quatorze. Even Dan was impressed and had to look away, a big grin spilling over the edges of his face.

"You are not getting out of this, Michael. The FBI and the United States government are fully on board. The only way you'll get out of it is if I say that your services are no longer required," Samantha said, those eyes flashing imperiously, the voice that of Thatcher about to invade the Falklands.

"Or I get killed," I muttered.

"Quite," she said, indifferently, and the coldness in her face repelled and aroused me in confusing ways.

"Well, comforting as always. Now if you'll excuse me, I'd like to talk to Dan alone, please," I demanded, flitting between an urge to either throw the scalding coffee at her and push her out the window or squeeze her bum.

Samantha said nothing, nodded to Dan, and exited the room, closing the door gently behind her.

"I like her," Dan said. "They say she sleeps with her agents. Jeremy told me something about a Stasi colonel."

"Is that so?"

"Apparently. Word of advice. Don't do it. It's not good for anybody. Get emotionally involved and all that."

"Aye, that would be terrible, if she got overly concerned about me getting topped."

"You're not going to get killed."

I stood up, walked around the room, and gazed through the window at the godforsaken flatlands of Queens Boulevard. Manhattan was a distant dream. Out of the question with all the goons and ex-goons that I knew. I sipped some more of the rancid coffee and sat down again.

"Please, Dan, as a friend," I said as a jet on its way to La Guardia shook the building. Dan groaned and closed his eyes.

"Michael, all this is bigger than you or me. If those idiots up in Massachusetts manage to blow up a British consulate or kill an ambassador or something it will jeopardize the entire peace process in Northern Ireland. With things screwing up in the Middle East, with the president stuck with an angry Congress, rumors about his sexual activities, basically, apart from the economy, the Northern Ireland thing is the only card Clinton has left to secure his legacy in history. There's no way I can pull you out of a well-thought and well-planned operation run by the Brits and the bureau to get at least an insight into this group's activities. There's nothing I can do to extricate you from this. My job is to make sure

Duffy doesn't kill you, that's all."

"Listen, Dan, me old mate, if you let me go back to Chicago, I won't get in any trouble again, I promise. I'll live a quiet life within my means."

Dan blinked with a tired melancholy, shifted his weight, and wiped the sweat from his forehead.

"Sorry."

"Duffy will find out and he'll kill me and your career will be over," I tried, on a different tack. And I had a flash of that evil old man on his huge Port Jefferson estate casually ordering a couple of driller killers from West Belfast to keep working me over while he sipped Bushmills whiskey and watched his new Lord of the Dance tape.

"You don't need to worry about Duffy. Duffy is on his way out. He's seventy years old. You think he thinks about you ever? You don't have to worry about him. That contract has long since lapsed. You practically did him a favor getting rid of a power-grabbing maniac like Darkey White."

This was news to me.

"Are you sure about that?"

"Duffy was never serious about going after you. He had to do a big show, issue the contract. It's irrelevant now in any case. Duffy doesn't even have close to a million in ready money anymore. We've been closing down his operations one by one. Not just him. They're all on the way out. The Italians, the Irish, the Russians. The bureau has broken them all. They have a lot more on their minds than old scores."

"Dan, do you really believe this or are you telling me what I want to hear?" I asked.

He looked at me and I saw that he wasn't lying, or if he was it was a new skill.

"It's the truth, Michael. Darkey White is old news. You destroyed his crew completely. You weakened Duffy and now he's down and soon he'll be out. There is a contract on your head but Duffy won't pay it and no one else cares enough to collect it. You can go to northern Massachusetts and you can fly with these fanatics and they won't know you from Adam. I guarantee it. Even if it was South Boston, I'd say go. Five years is a long time, my friend. And you *are* my friend, Michael, and I do look out for you, don't think I don't."

He inched closer to me, threw his empty cup in the bin.

"Look, Michael, I'll keep my eye on this English bitch, this whole op. If it don't look kosher, I'll send in the Seventh Cav."

"How will you keep an eye on it?"

"We got a good guy as liaison. Harrington. I know him from back in Virginia. If he doesn't like it, or one aspect of it, I'll make sure you're pulled out. I'll go against the AG and the whole State Department to pull you, Mike. I promise."

I smiled.

He'd made me feel better. Just to know that there was someone, anyone, on my team helped a great deal. He passed me a box of cigarettes but I declined. He lit one himself.

"Anyway, I have news about your old friend Scotchy Finn," Dan said, smoking his cigarette.

A dead hand grabbed my heart.

"Scotchy Finn?" I asked incredulously.

Scotchy and I had broken out of that Mexican jail five years ago, except that I had made it and he hadn't. He'd sacrificed his life for mine, dying there on the razor-wire fence that went around the prison. I still had nightmares about it. Scotchy falling through the razors, urging me to go on, screaming . . .

Dan slapped his forehead.

"What am I talking about? Scotchy Finn, no, no, no, he was an old pal of yours, right? I must have read that name in the report. Er, no, Sandy Finney, that's who I meant. Sandy Finney."

I looked at Dan suspiciously.

"I don't know any Sandy Finney."

"Sure you do, you called him Shovel."

"Oh aye, I remember him," I said. I had kneecapped Shovel and banged his old lady while he was in the hospital. One of my more charming moments as a gangster.

"What about him?"

"He was murdered last week."

"Sorry to hear it," I said.

"More than just a murder, Michael. Much more than that.

Ever since Darkey's death there's been a power vacuum in the west Bronx. The Dominicans, the Irish, the Russians. It's been crazy. Shovel had risen to the top of the new Mick crew. But now he's dead. An internal feud. A whack. It's hard to tell for sure but we think the new underboss for the Bronx is someone who you will definitely remember," Dan said and licked his lips.

"Oh, the suspense," I said sarcastically.

"I won't tell you then," Dan muttered, his eyes wide with delight.

"Tell me."

He blew out a line of smoke.

"Bridget Callaghan."

"Darkey's Bridget, my Bridget?" I asked, amazed and excited.

"Yeah, Bridget. She's only a small-time player but she's going places. Protecting herself, protecting her family, by rising up."

"She's married?"

"Nah. Doesn't need to be. Not just a man's game anymore. She's the business. If I was the worrying kind, Michael, she's the one I'd be worried about. Not now. She ain't got it now, but in a couple of years."

Bridget, a player? Sweet, adorable Bridget, my ex-girl, Darkey's ex-girl, who had shot me in the stomach, would have shot me in the head, and now was looking to take over her late fiancé's operations. I wouldn't put it past her. I wouldn't put anything past her. She was a rare bird.

"Tell me everything," I said.

Dan and I talked some more and I blew off my schedule for the rest of the day and he took me out to a bowling alley round the corner where I let off some steam and had a few drinks. Dan and I were to bowling what Laurel and Hardy were to competent piano delivery but we drank a lot and we nearly got into a ruck with a Polish short-order cook over the tactics of the Polish football team. The cook denigrating Ireland's approach as unglamorous and cowardly and praising Poland's much freer passing game. The dispute had then degenerated into a slagging match over the two countries' landscapes, women, and finally, Second World War record. The Pole threw a punch, missed, and Dan hustled me out of there before the altercation progressed to international incident.

Instead we bought cheap vodka at a liquor store and drank it in the safehouse. And I felt better. I knew Dan and I trusted him. And if he said it was going to be ok, I wanted to and I did believe him, at least while the vodka lasted and that early August daylight kept away. . . .

Training days.

Jeremy made me watch dreary British civil service–produced videos from the early 1980s on how to do a drop safely, how to contact your control, emergency techniques, the Official Secrets Act, my rights under the Geneva Convention and the United Nations Covenant on Civil and Political Rights.

Then I got briefings on Gerry McCaghan, Touched McGuigan, and the other players in the Sons of Cuchulainn. Following the hit, Samantha said that two of them had already defected back to the IRA. In other words, left Gerry and run like the blazes. Samantha reckoned that the SOC were down to a rump of perhaps seven or eight, maybe not the biggest terrorist organization in the world, but Timothy McVeigh had already shown what a dedicated team of just three could do.

Back in the OC, Touched and Gerry had killed at least a score of people between them and of course those were only the ones we knew about.

After the morning briefings, Samantha took me to the big loft room and questioned me on every detail of my new identity. My name was Sean McKenna. A good name, because it could be Catholic as well as Protestant and there are thousands of the buggers. Sean McKenna, though, was a Catholic. Like me, he grew up in Belfast. He went to Belfast High School (a file had been created and placed in the school's database), he worked construction in London with the MacLaverty Brothers (two unimpeachable MI5 contacts), he lived in Spain for a year and worked bar. In Spain he made some money and traveled the world for a couple of years. A nice clean bio that kept me away from any connection with the British government, the police, or the centers of the establishment. Also, it was vague enough (Spain, traveling the world) not to tie me down to anyone that the lads in the Sons of Cuchulainn might know.

As for the radical element, an arrest record had already been created for me—vandalism, petty theft, jail time in Manchester—and the big story was that when I was sixteen I had the shit beaten out of me and got charged with rioting by the Northern Ireland cops for throwing a petrol bomb at a police Land Rover. Again they put all this on file and backdated the records. If, as Samantha suspected, Gerry had a contact in the Boston PD, they could look me up in Interpol and there would be my rap sheet.

Sean's parents were conveniently dead and he was an only child, but so that he wasn't lonely he had a host of cousins in County Cork. Just like every other Mick in the world.

Samantha was thorough. Questioning me again and again, asking about every month of every year of my fictional life. She got me tired, tried to catch me out, called me Brian, Michael, interrogated me, woke me at night to question me, sleep-deprived me. Every trick in the goddamn book. It was a new game for me. You'd think the army training would all have come back with a vengeance but it didn't help for shit. In the army you learn the application of deadly force, how to wait between bouts of deadly force, and how to clean boots. They don't teach you this kind of thing, unless you're in the Special Air or combat intelligence and I certainly was never a good enough soldier to be asked to try out for those boys. And that special ops course on my résumé that Samantha thought so highly of had really been an SAS staff sergeant and a dozen of us getting drunk and trying not to fall off the windy cliffs of Saint Helena.

But I remembered the discipline, and learning a new identity was easy for me. I'd played many roles in my quarter century on planet Earth. This was just another one.

I had to trust Samantha, though, because her role was crucial.

She was my control, my contact on the ground.

They were going to put her into a British food and merchandise store in Newburyport, Massachusetts. The owner
was a man called Pitt, an old Foreign Office hand, who had
been contacted and asked if he wouldn't mind taking a vacation for a couple of months. Pitt's supposed cousin Samantha
was going to run the store while he was away. She'd been up
there once already to meet the man and learn the workings of
his shop. He was happy to be doing something hush-hush for
Her Majesty; and after all, MI6 was compensating him well
for his cooperation.

Any time I wanted to talk to her all I had to do was walk
right into the store. Easy.

I was to be based in the town of Salisbury Beach, about
five miles away from Newburyport, but they hoped that would
only be temporary until I made contact with Kit again. I was
going to be sharing a flat with a Six agent called Simon Pre-
ston that Jeremy had recommended for the job.

With me, Samantha played it both ways. Keeping me
sweet, keeping me off balance. I don't know if it was a tactic
or just her approximation of a happy medium.

Trying to calm me: "You've done well, Michael. Jolly well.
As good as I've seen. I've run twenty-year veterans behind the
Iron Curtain that don't have it down as good as you."

Trying to scare me: "Oh yes, Michael, you're going to have
to be careful. McCaghan will be like a wounded bear now following the assassination attempt. We don't know what he's
capable of. He's already killed scores in Northern Ireland.
He's ruthless. Cold-blooded. He could do anything. . . ."

But this talk was unnecessary. I already knew the stakes
and I was already scared enough.

✳   ✳   ✳

A Friday night. A going-away party that had the uncomfort-
able feeling of a wake. A long evening of drinking with Dan
and Sam. Dan drunk in two hours, Samantha sober enough to
order me to bed.

The next morning she woke me before dawn and said that

we were ready for the drive up to Massachusetts. She looked terrible, and I got the impression that she had stayed up drinking all night after I'd gone to bed.

It made me nervous.

"Rough night?" I asked. She grunted a response.

I went outside and bummed a cig while everyone got their keek together.

I smoked the fag and looked at the predawn activity in the borough of Queens. No one was watching me. I could run now.

Bolt into the street, hit the subway, and they'd never bloody
find me.

I shook my head. Pure fantasy. I wouldn't run. I needed their help, I needed their protection, even if it meant risking my own life to get it.

Jeremy pulled up outside the safehouse in an old Jaguar Mark 2 from the 1960s. Burgundy or plum with sparkling chrome. I don't know where Samantha got it from but you wouldn't call it discreet. And that also disturbed me. The thing you had to remember when dealing with these people was that the Britain of the Empire was long gone. The Brits may have conquered India and won two world wars but they also had a complacency and an incompetence that had gotten many people killed. Jeremy and Samantha were the descendants of the people who had been responsible for the disasters of the Somme and Gallipoli in World War One. The people who had tried to walk to the South Pole instead of taking dogs, who had built the unsinkable *Titanic,* who had lost America, surrendered at Singapore, starved Ireland, appeased Hitler. And now that I thought about it, wasn't it MI6 that had been so thoroughly and completely penetrated by the Russians that the KGB were practically running British Intelligence for a time in the 1950s?

And the FBI wasn't that much better. What the hell was I doing with these people?

"Ready for the show?" Jeremy asked, getting out of the car with a stupid grin.

I ignored him and let the gloom take over again.

Go for it, Michael. Punch Jeremy and run. Live on the lam. By your wits. Like the old days. Except that in the old days I didn't have a contract over my head and an arrest warrant waiting for me in the Republic of Mexico.

"Take a puff?" Jeremy asked.

I passed him the cigarette.

"Keep it," I said.

Samantha appeared outside and my mood flipped yet again.

From mousy Diana Prince to Wonder Woman. Green eyes, Roman nose, crimson lipstick, acherontic hair tied in a severe plait behind her head. A sharp black business suit, pumps, powerful hips; she seemed slimmer, ten years younger, and the heels brought her up to about five nine. She looked corporate, competent, professional.

"Do you like the car?" she asked.

"It's a bit bold, don't you think?"

"Not really. I'm Pitt's rich country cousin. Of course I would drive a classic car. It's part of my character," she said.

I didn't say anything.

I got in the passenger's side.

Jeremy slid into the back next to a sallow-faced, bald man called Harrington, who was to be the FBI liaison. They didn't exactly inspire confidence either. Harrington was listening to a Walkman, Jeremy staring gormlessly into space.

"So basically there's only going to be four people watching me," I said to Samantha while she fiddled with the radio.

"Who's the fourth?" she asked breezily.

"Simon. The guy in Salisbury."

"Oh, he'll be flying back to England as you soon as you make contact with the Sons of Cuchulainn."

"So, the three people in this car," I said in as neutral a voice as I could.

Samantha sighed.

"I have to warn you, Michael. We are here under sufferance. You can't just go around running foreign agents in a host country without conditions. This has to be a low-key affair.

The administration is keeping a tight rein on things. Simon will be your contact in Salisbury, but I'm afraid after that we'll have to lose him. But don't worry. I'll be your control in Newburyport and Jeremy and Harrington here will be in Boston waiting to bring the entire resources of the FBI to our assistance if we need them."

And there's also Dan, I thought to myself. Dan says he'll keep an eye on things.

"You should give him the speech, Samantha," Jeremy said from the backseat.

Samantha nodded at him in the mirror.

"In your case, Michael, it probably won't be necessary. But sometimes I've had to restrain my more enthused agents," she said.

"Oh no, I'd love to fucking hear it," I said.

"Well, maybe I'll give you a précis, Michael. Basically, I tell anyone I'm running that there's to be no silly heroics. No theatrics, no diminishing of the problems. You see, some people can get carried away, they don't want to let me down, let the side down."

"So what does that entail?"

"At the first sign of trouble, darling, you really have to let me know. You should remember it's my safety too. God forbid they suss you, grab you. They'll make you talk. They'll make you talk and then they'll come for me. So at the first inkling that you may have slipped or done something, or someone has rumbled you, you come to me, we'll talk it over. And if things haven't gone as planned I'll make sure you're out with an honorable discharge and all threats dropped."

"No extradition?" I asked.

She nodded. Maybe she wasn't such a cold-hearted cat after all. And I found myself fighting two contradictory impulses. The first, to find a way out of the assignment and my association with these people. And the second, a desire to do the job, to get it right, to please Jeremy and Samantha and Dan. The second I had to battle against.

In Cambridge we dropped Harrington and Jeremy at another nondescript FBI safehouse on Harvard Square, and

after an enormous traffic jam on 98 we didn't get into Newburyport until close to midnight.

We quickly found the All Things Brit store on State Street.

A twee, quaint, touristy street with a Celtic imports store, a
sewing shop, a chocolate shop, an antique maps store, and
three ice-cream parlors.

The place was quiet. The kids were in Boston and the
tourists were in bed.

"We shouldn't really be seen together, darling, but it looks
as if there are no witnesses. Come on in and I'll show you the
shop," Samantha said.

She parked the Jag and found the keys to All Things Brit.
We went inside. It was the usual collection of tat. British
foods, Barbour jackets, pipes, hats, damp-looking woolen
things. The decor that of an old vicarage that would appear
complete only with a spinster lady shrieking over the body of a
poisoned industrialist.

I thumbed through a selection of *Masterpiece Theatre*
videotapes while Samantha hung up her coat.

"Let me show you the upstairs and then I'll drive you up to
Salisbury, it's only about fifteen minutes away. McCaghan
takes his family up to Salisbury Beach every Friday night in
summer. They have a fireworks show just over the state line.
That's why we picked it as a place for you to be. You're not following him to his home on Plum Island, you're not showing
up on his doorstep asking him for a job. You're just accidentally bumping into Kit at the fireworks display. It won't seem
strange at all. I expect Kit will be happy to see you."

"I expect so," I said sourly.

"Hopefully, Touched will have you checked out and they'll
ask you to join them down at their rather palatial home on
Plum Island, which is only a mile or so from here. It's an actual island, by the way—a barrier island, quite nice, I went
there bird-watching with Pitt, the whole bottom two-thirds is
a wildlife reserve. I think we saw plovers, egrets, that kind of
thing."

"Fascinating."

She led me upstairs to Pitt's flat. A poky affair. On one side of the stairs, a bathroom and a den that barely had room to squeeze in a sofa, drinks cabinet, and bookcase. On the street side, a tiny kitchen and a bedroom dominated by a big cast-iron bed with red silk sheets and pillows. Above it, an enormous skylight that let in the heavens.

"I am going to have this completely redecorated. I think a Mediterranean theme will work very well here. We're near the sea and this is a working fishing port. What do you think?" Samantha asked.

"You think we'll be here long enough to bother about that?"

"Oh good Lord, I have no idea. Could be weeks, could be months. Would you like a drink? Pitt's got an excellent Scotch collection. All island single malts, wonderful, I promise. And the brandy is to die for. He really is a very resourceful and charming man."

She went into the den.

"He used to be in the civil service or the Foreign Office or something, did I tell you that?" she shouted in.

"You told me that," I said, unable to shake the somber feeling that had been following me round all day. The feeling that Death was making his way back into my life again after five long, lean years.

She came back with the drinks. I sat on an ottoman and she sat on the bed. She kicked her shoes off and let her hair down. She had poured two generous glasses of a sixteen-year-old Bowmore and brought the bottle, too. She knocked hers back in one. I followed suit and she poured us both another. Again she scooted her drink. This time I sipped mine.

She undid the top button of her blouse.

"How nervous are you, on a scale of one to ten?" she asked. I held up five fingers.

"That sounds about right. The Greeks tell us. . . . well, never mind what the Greeks tell us. Finish that and let me go to the loo and I'll drive you up to Salisbury. Simon will be dying to meet you."

I finished my glass of whisky. She retired to the bathroom.

"I've been thinking. You know what your problem is,

Michael?" she said through the bathroom door.

"No. What?"

"Men will always hate you and women will always love you."

"Is that a fact?"

"Pour me another drink," she said.

"I thought you were going to drive me."

"Pour me another drink," she insisted.

I poured two more whiskies. She came out of the bathroom a little unshaky on her feet, with her blouse completely off and draped over her shoulders and her beautiful, voluptuous body stunning me under the stars. She took the glass and drank the whisky and lay down on the bed.

"Kiss me," she said.

I kissed her. I removed my shirt and sat beside her, and she put her arms round me and I kissed her neck and ran my hands down her back. I stood to take off my trousers and when I lay beside her again her eyes had closed and her breathing had eased and she was asleep.

I stood there for a minute and then lifted her onto the pillows and placed the silk sheet over her.

"I suppose it's the sofa for me," I said to myself.

But I sat on the ottoman and watched her for a while. Her eyes fluttered, and when she was deeply asleep I lay down on the other side of the bed and wrapped myself in the blanket and closed my eyes.

And there we were, chaste and together in this big bed. A bed where, perhaps inevitably, Samantha and I would finally make love immediately after my first harried and traumatic contact with the Sons of Cuchulainn.

A bed where Samantha would get no sleep at all as the operation she was running gradually spun out of control.

A bed where Touched McGuigan would stand and admire his handiwork and I would gasp in horror at a scene of murder, torture, and a body bleeding slowly to death in those red silk sheets under a bright blue and endless sky.

4: TROJAN HORSE

On the sand at Salisbury Beach, in the far north of Massa-chusetts, a Greek and a Trojan battling it out over the upturned hulks of the Greek ships.

It was warm and the sea breeze was only enough to ripple the hair on my arms and make a slight sound on the clandes-tine greenness of the waves. We skirmished, sweated, and our swords caught the light from the last of the dog-day sun set-ting slowly over the blurred headlands of Maine and New Hampshire.

Everything in silhouette.

The dome of Seabrook Nuclear Power Station, the crowd of onlookers, the children screaming as the whirligigs of the amusements tossed them in the air and turned them to the wide expanse of sky and brought them down again.

We hardly noticed as we moved over the upturned gun-wales, a mainmast, and the tattered remains of an anchor chain, following a motion of rehearsed delirium. Bronze clanging off bronze and the sand becoming wet with the turn-ing of the tide. Lunges, ducks, parries—an exotic play of shape and form in the living grease of the sea air and the sun.

The sky aquamarine and the Atlantic heavy and distant in the violent beginnings of the summer dusk.

My opponent seemed to have the advantage, using his shield to force me into defensive postures. He was playing

Achilles and he was bigger than me. I suffered under his pushing and shoving for a while and then, in a moment of drama, I leapt over the carved prow of the boat and made a run for it across the sand.

The crowd booed.

I turned and ducked as a javelin came screaming at me.

"Jesus H. Christ," I said under my breath.

I stood my ground and Achilles drew his short sword, spat.

Lights appeared on the Ferris wheel. Faces. They might be watching us, but the view was so good up there you could see the Isles of Shoals and Cape Ann and if you were really lucky, Mount Washington, way up in the White Mountains. Achilles caught his breath and approached, lifting his sword for the killing stroke. He was an English guy called Simon. He'd been in the RADA briefly and had also done summer stock. If he'd stayed in acting rather than joining MI6, this, he said, would definitely have been the low point of his career. You could tell he was pissed off. That bloody javelin had nearly killed me.

I'd known him for eight days and we both worked for Salisbury Beach's Department of Tourism. As a tourist town, Salisbury Beach was down on its luck. Everything had an old-fashioned, seedy, worn-out feel to it—think Blackpool, England, or, I guess, Coney Island, New York, on a bad day in 1977. If Martha's Vineyard and Provincetown are your archetypes for the Massachusetts seaside, you should probably avoid Salisbury Beach. And the people who came here weren't exactly flying in from the Riviera; a condescending wanker would say they were fat, Kmart-clad white trash who smoked cheap cigarettes, drank Old Milwaukee, and lived in trailers.

In this part of Massachusetts, it wasn't Congregationalists, East Anglians, old money, and Puritans. Here it was Portuguese, Italians, bog Irish, and Greeks. The latter particularly relevant for us, since as part of their sponsorship of the Salisbury Beach Summer Pageant, the Greek community put on the Trojan War, specifically the death of Hector, every day at six o'clock. Except that after eight repetitions of this shite, today I didn't feel like cooperating.

I lunged at Simon and seemed to slip a little on the sand.

Simon seized the moment and raised his sword to plunge it into my back. The crowd oohed. It was a second before Simon realized that it had been a ruse. I came up underneath him, hooking his parried sword and swinging it harmlessly through the air. I hit him on the back between the folds of his leather armor, and Achilles, son of Peleus, went down into the sand cursing while I applied the coup de grace and took applause from the dour Massachusetts crowd. I helped Simon up.

"One in the eye for the invading Greek dogs," I said.

"You'll get in trouble for this," Simon said.

"Who from?"

"Cleo, for one," Simon said.

"Who's that? That hatchet-faced woman on the Chamber of Commerce?" I asked.

"The muse of history, you ignorant Paddy," Simon said.

We walked back across the sand.

The crowd took some photographs and drifted away from the performance, moving back towards the fair, where they bought Cokes and cotton candy and the more adventurous sampled the local delights of dulse and saltwater taffy. I helped Simon with his gear.

"You'll be sorry when they hear about your little stunt. The Greeks see Hector as a Turk, they won't stand for this, they'll do you, mate," Simon said.

"They won't fire me, no one else would take this gig. By the way, every day you're closer with that bloody javelin."

"Sorry about that. Come on, we'll go to the pub, check out the talent," Simon said.

"If there's gonna be girls, shouldn't we shower first?"

"Nah, the lure of show business will impress the babes. You wanna hit the pub or not?"

Of course I wanted to hit the pub. It was Friday night. My second Friday night here. Last Friday, Kit, Gerry, and the whole Sons of Cuchulainn had singularly failed to show up at the End of the State Bar for the fireworks show, despite the fact that Samantha Caudwell had assured me that they came each and every Friday. Bloody British Intelligence. Going to be the death of—

"Quite the display there, macho man."

I looked over. A girl in the crowd: pretty, Daisy Dukes, high-tops, a pink shirt showing her shoulder tattoo and the dark outline of her nipples. My heart danced a jig. Kit. Simon nudged me in the ribs.

"I think you have a classical mythology groupie over there, mate," he said.

Kit came over and shook me civilly by the hand. She seemed older or more tired than a little over a week ago, when I'd seen her last. What fresh nightmares were Touched and Gerry cooking up that were disturbing her sleep?

"I've been looking for you for a while. I thought that was a line you told me about Salisbury. It's good to see you again," she said.

"Good to see you, too," I said and I meant it.

"But Sean, what the hell are you wearing?" Kit asked, suddenly taking me in.

"You like my summer wear? I'm setting the fashion. Seriously, Trojans are in for '97," I said.

"In America that's a brand of condoms," Kit said soberly.

"You think I didn't know that," I said, over the top and saucy.

Kit laughed.

"Are you going to introduce me?" Simon asked.

"Aye. Simon, this is Kit; Kit, this is Simon."

The two of them shook hands.

"How do you know Sean?" Simon asked Kit.

"Sean and I go way back," Kit said with a beautiful, sweet smile.

"Yeah, we do," I agreed. "We backpacked around Africa together. Boy, we had some times. Remember Clarence from Australia? Eaten by a lion."

"It was shocking," Kit agreed. "It only left the head."

"No way," Simon said, pretending to believe us.

"Way," Kit assured him.

Simon looked at the pair of us. Kit could barely contain her giggles.

"You're having me on," he said.

Kit burst out laughing. Slapped Simon on the back.

"Got ya," she said.

By this time we were up off the beach, walking along the seafront in the direction of the End of the State Bar.

The town sprawled in a long line all the way from the Merrimack River to the New Hampshire border. But the beach strip was the worst. A desperate air hanging over everything. A grim, worn sadness that coated the half-drunken people in their shapeless T-shirts and denims. I tried to ignore it all as we walked toward a fish-and-chip stand.

"Are you hungry?" Simon asked Kit.

Kit nodded, which was a relief because Simon and I were famished. In the mornings we did beach clearance, picking up rubbish and the occasional dead thing, and in the evenings we performed the pageant for the Greek Fair. It was hard work for shit pay and we hadn't eaten anything since lunch. We stopped at the fish-and-chip stand and I bought her a cod.

"Our first meal," she said coyly. She ate and the food perked her up. Now she looked healthy, happy, pleased to see me.

"You mentioned that you were looking for me," I said between mouthfuls.

"I was. You told me you were working up here, you didn't tell me what you were doing."

"Would you?"

"No, I suppose not," she said, looking at my outfit.

"What are *you* doing up here?" I asked, and she explained to me that her dad and her stepmum, Sonia, were at the End of the State Bar. She'd come with them, but it was karaoke at the moment, so she had decided to go for a walk and accidentally caught our act on the beach. Not, of course, knowing that I was Hector until I took my helmet off.

Simon asked her about the nuances of our performance. Kit, being polite, told him it was a terrific show.

"You know, when Sean got the job of Hector he knew next to nothing about sword fighting; there's a technique to the stage fight, choreography, much more difficult than you would think. I taught him everything he knows," Simon said.

"It's true," I admitted.

"Well, it was very impressive, I liked the javelin bit," she said. "It seemed to get very close."

"Oh, that was improvised," Simon said proudly.

"Yeah, you nearly improvised me into the emergency room," I said and winked at him, nodded at Kit, and somehow made clear that now was the time for Simon to make himself scarce.

"Oh yeah, well, Sean, I must be heading along, see ya in the pub," he said and scarpered with a look of ironic jealousy playing across his face.

I binned the rest of my dinner and walked with Kit a little farther along the strand. The End of the State Bar was a good mile up the beach and we had to thread our way through the amusement arcades, go-cart tracks, taffy stands, fortune-tellers, cotton candy sellers, and a plastic-duck shooting range. A lot going on but Kit wasn't talking, there was something on her mind. I tried a few conversational openings and got mono-syllabic answers.

"Ok, go on, just say what's cooking in that brain of yours. You're plotting something," I finally demanded.

She stopped, looked at me, and nodded.

"Sean. I've been thinking about you. And, like, this is the deal. I think you should meet Dad," she said.

"So I can ask his permission for your hand?"

"Jesus, Sean, be serious for a minute," Kit demanded, blushing in a way that Winona Ryder would have killed to be capable of.

"I am being serious," I said with increasing gravity the more I looked at her. Her blush deepened and Winona, to extrapolate the analogy, would have been well on her way to the electric chair.

"No, I want you to meet my dad. It's for your own good. But you can't go like that. You're going to have to change into your regular clothes. He and Sonia won't mind, but Jackie and Touched are going to be with him and they'd take the piss out of you," Kit said without any levity at all. I smiled at her. Her lips narrowed.

"Good news and bad news. The good news is that I'd love to meet your dad. The bad news is these are my regular clothes. The costume was the gear I had on in Revere. I dress like this all the—"

"Sean, stop fucking around, I'm not kidding," she interrupted, starting to get exasperated. I leaned back on my heels and smirked at her. She was fuming a little and her face had transformed into a delicious pout.

"So you've been looking for me and thinking about me. Can't get me out of your head, huh?" I declared.

"Don't get ideas. I wasn't thinking about you in that way. I just want you to do well in America. My dad could really help you out. If you want to make a good impression you're going to have to change your outfit. Look at the state of you."

"And now you can't keep your eyes off me."

"Stop saying that."

"I'll stop saying it but I won't stop noticing it."

"Come on, Sean, they're going to be waiting at the End of the State, you won't get an opportunity like this again," she pleaded.

"Ok, fine. I'll change. No big deal. Why don't you come back to my flat; I'll shower, get dressed, you can look through my CD collection and make snotty remarks about it," I said.

"Sounds like fun," Kit replied.

"Everything we'll do together is going to be fun," I said, and if that wasn't the lie of the year I don't know what was.

✿　✿　✿

In the time it had taken me to shower, a thunderstorm had rolled down the Merrimack River valley. A common occurrence in the week I'd been here. Hot during the day, thunderstorms at night. Sometimes Simon and I would go on the roof, drink Sam Adams, watch lightning hit the dome of the nuclear power station and half hope for some kind of atomic emergency to relieve the tedium.

I toweled off, changed into a shirt and jeans. Kit was looking at my bookshelves. She ignored the books, barely pretending to skim through them, but she couldn't conceal how much she coveted my CDs, which were cool English music, a year or two ahead of similar American trends. The covers she found to be fascinating objects. I stared at her for a minute and she caught me looking. I pretended to be checking out the weather behind her head.

"It's raining," I said.

Kit hadn't noticed. She peered out the window, nodded absently.

The apartment was small. Two tiny bedrooms, a living room that connected to a minute kitchen. A sofa, a couple of deck chairs. No air-con but a bit of a breeze from the Atlantic out the window.

"What are these like?" she asked finally, holding up a handful of the CDs.

"They're good," I said.

"What type of music?"

"It's a thing called Britpop, somewhere between pop and rock, I don't think there's really an American equivalent. I suppose REM would be the closest thing," I said.

"I like REM," she said, her big eyes shadowed black, blinking slowly, seductively, without meaning to be seductive.

The blue of cornflowers in a black orchid bouquet, you could say, if you were so inclined. And I wasn't. It wouldn't do to get carried away.

"Who else do you like?" I asked, to break the silence.

"Nirvana, Pearl Jam, that kind of thing," she said.

"You might like Oasis," I said. "Take the CD with you. You can borrow it."

"Is that your favorite?" she asked.

"Nah, Radiohead is what's happening at the moment," I said.

"Can I listen?" she asked.

I put on *OK Computer,* which had just been released that week. After only a few tracks I could tell that Kit loved it. I was pleased. She'd already called me an old geezer once and I wanted her to think I wasn't completely unhip. I brought a couple of Sams from the fridge. We drank, listened to a bit of the record, and watched the rain. Kit found herself edging towards me on the rattan sofa, realized what she was doing, stopped herself, shifted away. She made an obvious play of looking at her watch.

"Oh, we better head up to the bar," she said.

I pulled on a pair of socks and grabbed my Stanley boots. After Samantha's foot stab, I found that I felt safer in shoes with steel toe caps even despite the god-awful heat. Kit watched me pull the boot on over my plastic left foot.

"What happened to your foot?" she asked. "I noticed when you were wearing that skirt that you have a pro, pro, what's it called?"

"Prosthesis," I said unself-consciously. I was used to it by now. I didn't even think about it anymore.

"*Prosthesis*. That's a good word. What happened to you?" she asked, her face radiating concern and curiosity.

I smiled at her.

"Motorcycle accident when I was nineteen. I was going way too fast, I fell off, the bike came down on top of me, my left foot went into one of the wheels. It was my fault, I was speeding, the road was slick, and no one else was involved," I said.

A nice wee invention with just a little bit of gore and not one-tenth as bad as the real story, of horror piled upon horror down in the gothic badlands south of the border.

"Does it hurt?" Kit asked.

"Now, you mean?"

"Yeah."

"No, it doesn't hurt."

"You moved pretty good down there on the beach, with your sword and all, I wouldn't have known otherwise."

"I can run on it too; I can pretty much do everything except swimming. I can't get the hang of swimming."

"You could just use your arms," Kit said helpfully.

"I know. It's not that, it's just, well, I don't know what it is."

"I'll take you swimming with me, you can use the surfboard to keep you afloat. It'll be easy."

"You surf?"

"Of course. You?"

"No."

"You can learn. I'll teach you. We'll get you over this swimming thing and I'll teach you to surf. Your foot might make it a little harder but I'm a good teacher and the break on Plum Island is pretty easy."

I wanted to change the subject because I didn't want the focus to be on me and my bloody handicaps.

"You look nice," I said. "You did something to your hair."

She blushed again. She wasn't used to compliments. The atmosphere of the Sons of Cuchulainn was probably one of matey blokishness, and that pleased me too. It would give me an angle.

"Yeah, got it cut, less of a bob, more of a pageboy," she explained.

"I don't know what that means, but it looks good," I said.

"I got rid of the hairspray, too. It was too 80s, too glam, too New Wave."

I nodded to show that I got her pop culture references.

"Too much of a fire hazard as well. One loose cigarette and you would have been up like Michael Jackson."

She looked puzzled.

"What do you mean?

"Michael Jackson set his hair on fire during a Pepsi commercial. Remember?"

"That must have been before my time," she said, again making me feel like an old git. I was too ticked off to think of a response.

"Anyway, Sean, I'm glad you've changed out of your centurion uniform, you look much better," she said.

"Thanks. But tell me again why precisely I have to dress up for your father?" I asked.

"Because, Sean, my father is, like, a very wealthy man who runs a construction company and can get you a job which would not involve you having to wear a ridiculous costume and fight some English dude for a pittance."

"How do you know it's a pittance? And how do you know that I would want to work for your da?"

"Simon said you were getting like six dollars an hour," she said.

"How much your da pay?"

"Twelve skilled, nine nonskilled. Really, like, twelve if you're Irish, nine if you're Mexican or Portuguese," she said.

I looked at her to see if she was joking or being sarcastic, but apparently not. Her dad was an institutionalized racist and she wasn't that concerned about it.

"And it wouldn't look good if I was to say, 'Dad, here's this Irish guy you might want to hire,' and you come in looking like Julius Caesar," she said.

I stroked my chin, nodded.

"Kit. Why do you want to help me?" I asked.

"'Cos you tried to save my life, 'cos you're Irish, 'cos you look like a total idiot in that Roman getup. I wouldn't wish your job on my worst enemy," she said.

"Not Romans, Greeks and Trojans," I said.

"What?"

"We were supposed to be Greeks and Trojans. You know, hence the bronze sword, rather than iron; they really paid attention to detail."

Kit looked at me skeptically. Biting into her lip in a way that was completely captivating. She had no idea what it was doing to me. I had no idea what she was doing to me and since she was doing it so effectively I hadn't even put up any defenses until it was too late. She was across the moat and over the wall and I had left the keep doors open for her too.

"Well," she whispered huffily, "I didn't know you were, like, so enthusiastic about it. If this is what you want to do all summer, I won't try to help."

"No, no, I'll meet your da," I said, smiling as if I were making a concession.

"Good," she said, pleased with herself.

It was completely dark outside now and the rain was ending. Kit stood. She looked at me with a little impatience.

"We should head up. Jackie will be wondering where I am. You don't mind meeting everyone, do you?"

"No, who's everyone?"

"Touched, Sonia, Jackie."

"Touched is?"

"My dad's old friend from Ireland."

"I take it that's a nickname, right?"

"Yeah, supposedly because he's crazy, but he seems ok to me."

"Sonia is your stepmom, right?"

"Yeah. My mom's dead. Well, technically she was my adopted mom but you know what I mean," Kit said.

"Yeah, you told me that. You said that your real mom is still alive somewhere?"

"That's right."

"Do you ever—"

She put her hand up to cut me off.

I stopped speaking.

She closed her eyes and when she opened them she looked pissed off.

"Sean. There's one ground rule with me. You can ask me anything, talk about anything, but just don't ask if I ever want to meet my real mom or dad someday. Everybody always asks that and it's really irritating. My dad is my dad and he's a great man and as you saw yourself a brave man, too. And my mom was my mom, too. And that's it. I don't know who my real mother or father were and I don't care. My real dad is Gerry. End of story."

Kit looked flustered. She'd said all this to stop me digging a potential hole for myself and, if truth be told, I probably would have asked her if she'd ever considered looking for her "real" mom or dad someday. Clearly, many people had made that gaffe in the past and she didn't want me to be one of them.

"He'd probably be a jerk anyway," Kit continued. "I always think of him as one of those idiots who tries to do kung fu on the lions at the zoo or falls into a vat of molten chocolate or dies from urinating on the third rail," she said with a laugh.

I laughed, but I found her examples of stupidity disturbing, not amusing. There was a hardness in Kit that she got from her adoptive da.

"Ok, so who else is going to be there tonight?" I asked.

"Just Jackie. You know about him. He's my boyfriend," she said, playing it straight.

"He's still your boyfriend?" I asked innocently.

"Yeah."

"I thought I told you he wasn't good enough for you."

"You're wrong. Jackie is really nice and you'll like him."

"Sure," I said, trying to sound disappointed but not obsessively disappointed so she didn't think I was a perv already in love with her or something. Hard to convey all that meaning in one syllable, but I did my best.

"He's a bit like you," Kit said almost defensively.

"Handsome, smart, funny, and brilliant, you mean?"

"No, he's Irish, real Irish like my dad. He came over to South Boston about five or six years ago."

"South Boston. Yes, I've heard about that place. North of the river is Cambridge, racially tolerant, attractive, full of geniuses, and South Boston's the counterweight."

"Who told you that?"

"What I heard."

"It's not true. I have a lot of friends from South Boston and they're smart and they're not bigots. At least not all of them."

"I stand corrected. Where's he from in Ireland?"

"I think he said Sligo."

"Oh dear, well that I do know about, they're all cow fuckers over there."

Kit punched me on the shoulder.

"Ok, that's enough," she said, laughing.

I sat back on the sofa, edged my arm towards her, rubbed my lip. Considered a move right here and now.

"Come on, dude, tie your shoes up," she said, interrupting my schemes.

"Ok. Well, look, one more track, the next one's 'Karma Police,' you'll really like it," I said.

"Karma Police" came on. Kit really liked it. She made me play it again. Not that surprising. Many magazines would vote it the best track on the best album of the year. I was starting to get nervous so I finished the Sam Adams and popped the last one in the six-pack, chilled, listened to the track, and sat with Kit. These were the moments you lived for. A beautiful girl, good music, good beer. As she watched the sun set, I studied her until I feared she would catch me at it again, so I looked out the window too. The sun completely gone now and the sky amber and gold all the way west into the Berkshires and Vermont. Oystercatchers and gulls on the bay. Kites down at the headland and higher up a light plane skating along the coast, a white single-engined craft with a trailer on the back of it that read "NH Fireworks Shack—Sail Sail Sail This Sunday." A bad speller but a good pilot. He did a final spectacular dip over the beach and banked the plane lazily towards the New Hampshire border.

We watched the plane until it was a mere speck in the opaque sky, lost in the pattern of cirrus clouds and the regular plough lines of the high jet vapor trails. Its engines long gone in the soporific drone of the fairground generators and the light booming of the water against the seawall.

The music faded. Silence. I turned off the stereo. We looked at each other. We both knew what was going to happen, but I had to ask.

"Why mention the boyfriend?" I asked.

"Just, like, so you know," she said.

"Is it serious?" I asked.

"As serious as you can get at my age," she said, grinning, and leaned over and kissed me on the cheek to let me know that that was all it would ever be. Another thank-you for Boston. She had her boy and I wasn't him and she was just happy to see me.

But she wasn't going to get away with that.

I took her face in my hands and kissed those soft pillowy lips and pulled her down beside me. I ran my fingers down her back. Her skin was smooth and electric. She was gorgeous.

She put her arms around me and held me tight. I wanted her to touch me, I wanted her to hold me. And I wanted to possess her.

We kissed and when she was out of breath and her mouth

was opening and she caught herself pushing her crotch onto my leg she froze, opened her eyes, and pulled on the hand brake. Stopped herself. Moved back.

"I'm serious, I have a boyfriend," she whispered, like a mantra.

I didn't say anything.

For once I was utterly speechless.

Kit stood.

"Come on, we really should go."

I nodded.

"We'll go."

She must have remembered about my foot because it drew the mothering instinct out of her and she gave me her hand and pulled me up from the sofa. She let go immediately I was up.

"Thanks," I said.

"You're welcome."

And I looked at her. Drew in every essence of her. And oh my God. She was beautiful and charming, and I knew, goddamnit, that because of her the mission was going to be much harder, much more complicated, and ultimately much more dangerous.

5: SALISBURY MISTAKE

Salisbury was the very last town in Massachusetts and the End of the State Bar was actually just over the state line in New Hampshire. Massachusetts had strict gun controls, bans on fireworks, high taxes on cigarettes, blue laws, and other regulations. The "Live Free or Die" state had none of these things. Booze was cheaper, you could drink all night if you wanted, the blood alcohol limit was higher, and if you were driving home drunk, smoking your cheap cigarettes, and letting off fireworks, you weren't even required to have car insurance.

The pub was packed full of youngsters with fake IDs, as well as fishermen, illegal immigrants, frat boys, tourists, and the regular town drunks. The lighting was poor, the ventilation nonexistent, and the jukebox would have you believe that the greatest epoch in popular music was the era of hair bands and Englishmen playing synthesizers.

I spotted Simon at the bar, talking to some girl, and I saw Gerry McCaghan up in a corner booth that had walls on two sides and afforded a view of the whole establishment. He was with Sonia McCaghan, Touched McGuigan, and Jackie O'Neill.

People Kit thought I had never seen or heard of before, but already I was pulling up the briefing notes on all of them.

Kit let go of my hand and waved at Jackie.

"When you meet everyone don't, like, go mental if Dad winds you up a bit, and whatever you do, don't fuck with Touched. You'll like him but seriously don't mess with him," she said, concern dripping into her voice and those cornflower blue eyes taking on an anxious iodine tint.

"Understood," I said.

The Sons of Cuchulainn had never been a big group. About nine or ten "volunteers" at its greatest extent. Samantha said that following the hit on Gerry there had been several defections and that now she thought it was down to a rump of about six or seven. Kit, Gerry, Sonia, Touched McGuigan, Jackie, Seamus (one of the two bodyguards I'd seen that night in Revere), and possibly one or two others. But Touched and Gerry were the only two I was concerned about.

Gerry, fifty-five, an old-school hard-nosed Provisional IRA man from Derry. Violent, clever, charming, unpredictable. In the 70s, responsible for more than a score of bombings and attempted bombings. British Intelligence couldn't be precise about these things but they reckoned he'd killed and maimed at least three dozen people in his career.

Gerry wouldn't hesitate to cut out the cancer or risk civilian casualties, and you couldn't be fooled by his girth—you didn't need to be a lithe man to pull a trigger or push the button on a radio-controlled bomb.

But as much as Gerry put the fear of God in me, it was Touched who worried me most. Davy "Touched" McGuigan, forty-nine, Gerry's second-in-command, was a gunman from Belfast exiled from Ireland by an IRA tribunal. Quick tempered, violent, and even more unpredictable than Gerry (hence the nickname Touched, i.e., crazy). He looked and dressed like an aging rock star. Black jeans, white embroidered shirt. He was tall, well built, square-jawed, and quite the handsome devil if you didn't mind the ear that had been partially burned off in a premature explosion, an ear that Touched covered with a long mane of partly graying hair.

Touched had committed at least six murders that we knew about. Two cops, a guy he thought was having an affair with his fiancée, a man he stabbed in a bar fight, an eighteen-year-old who had stolen Touched's car (Touched finding him three days later, beating him, tying him into the car, dousing car and kid with petrol, and torching the pair of them), and an IRA informer that Touched grabbed from a Glasgow Celtic social club in broad daylight, bundled into a van, drove to a safehouse, tortured for two days, and finally shot, after he had revealed everything that he knew.

Touched had known Gerry since the old days and had been living with him at the house on Plum Island for the last year, ever since he'd screwed the wife of a comrade who was doing fifteen to life in Belfast's Long Kesh prison. Touched would have been given the death sentence if they'd had anyone with the bottle to kill him. Exile for life was the safer alternative for all concerned.

So both Gerry and Touched had been expelled from Ireland and both had an axe to grind. The other two people at the table were nothing to worry about. Sonia was around forty years old, from Portland, Maine, and for the last year, Gerry's wife. She was a history professor at UNH, a Marxist, anticolonialist Edward Said type who almost certainly knew about Gerry's activities but probably saw him as a romantic hero. Sonia was pretty in a skinny, blond, washed-out kind of way. Harmless, I suppose, but you never knew, sometimes the quiet ones were the ones who'd fucking cut your throat in your sleep. The FBI didn't have much on Sonia, she was too young to have been a sixties radical, she hadn't been to Ireland with Gerry on his trips, and since the SOC had more or less been a sleeper cell for the last five years, it was unlikely that she had done any mischief.

In fact, none of them had carried out any recent terrorist activity and it was only the IRA's tip-off that the SOC was reactivating its operational command that alerted MI6 in the first place. Still, Gerry was not a stupid man and he was bound to know that the FBI was probably watching him. Maybe the hit, the FBI interest, and his advancing years would be enough of a deterrent, and the SOC really was going to disarm despite Gerry's defiant communications to the IRA's Army Council. My job was to find out. 'Course, it was much harder to prove a negative, but it was still my job.

The final person at the table was Jackie O'Neill. The file on Jackie was only a couple of paragraphs long. Born in County Sligo, he had run away from home, lived in Manchester, England, for a while, and had moved to America when he was just fifteen. He'd spent the last five and a half years Stateside cutting his teeth terrorizing black and Latino kids out of his old neighborhood in Roxbury. He had a few convictions for vandalism and theft but nothing to write home about. He'd met Touched at a Troops Out rally and Touched had offered him a job working for Gerry. He'd been in the construction company for about a year. Hard to say how long he'd been in Sons of Cuchulainn but probably the same amount of time.

Jackie was clearly going for the bad-boy look. Leather jacket, white T-shirt, hair gelled back like Brando in *The Wild One*. Long-nosed, sallow-featured, slightly pigeon-chested— the T-shirt sagged and the jacket was too big.

Still, this was the boyfriend Kit had been talking about. And I liked Kit and I felt she had good judgment about people, so there must have been something about Jackie, some redeeming attribute. Maybe he had a great fucking personality.

The rest of the group wasn't there. But Touched and Gerry were the players. Get something good on them, send those boys to the chokey, and the whole organization would fall to pieces.

Kit prodded me in the back. We walked across the bar and stopped in front of the booth.

"Hello, my dear," Gerry said, and I was struck immediately by his ease of bearing and his ursine confidence.

"Hi, Dad," Kit said.

They were all drinking from a pitcher of Budweiser, except for Sonia, who had a glass of sparkling water. Touched and Gerry looked relaxed. Jackie was pissed off.

"Dad, I'm really sorry I'm a bit late," Kit said.

"It's ok, but punctuality is a sign of respect, Kit, honey," Gerry said. He had lost some of his Irish country accent and now had a slightly pompous NPR-ish voice. It was interesting.

I wondered if it was a cultural cringe—a reaction to his humble beginnings and newfound wealth. Or perhaps it was his wife's recent influence. Sonia was old money and old New England.

"Sorry again," Kit said, looking at me.

"Where have you been, Kit?" Gerry asked.

"Aye, where the fuck have you been?" Jackie asked in a distinct South Boston drone. It threw me a bit and Kit had already answered before I had understood Jackie's question.

"Nowhere. Anyway, I want you all to meet someone," Kit said.

"You must have been somewhere?" Jackie asked, reddening with anger.

"Nope," Kit said.

I shuddered involuntarily. Yup, this fine specimen was definitely the boyfriend.

"Who's this?" he asked Kit while looking furiously at me.

"This is Sean," Kit said.

I put my hand out.

"Nice to meet ya," I said.

Jackie had no real option but to shake my hand. His touch was cold, clammy, sweaty. As he leaned across the table and into the light, I saw that he was a thin but sinewy wee shite, with a weak attempt at a mustache on his upper lip. Bit of a pong off him too. Nice.

"I'll introduce everybody," Kit said, not in the least nonplussed by Jackie's rudeness.

"My dad," Kit said, beaming.

"Nice to meet you," I said.

"The same, I'm sure," Gerry replied with some diffidence and gave me his left hand. For his visit to the End of the State Bar, Gerry was wearing a green polo shirt and enormous white shorts. He seemed mellow, at ease, happy. Christ, if the Provisional IRA had me on its death list, or at least had attempted to kill me, I'd be squatting in a cave in Patagonia, not having a few beers down the local pub. It impressed me, and I shook his proffered hand with something approaching genuine admiration.

Kit leaned over and whispered something in his ear. A big un-Belfast smile broadened across Gerry's face. Un-Belfast because the teeth were white, capped, straight, and symmetrical. Gerry transferred his cigar from his right to his left hand and offered the right to me. This time his grip was powerful and enthusiastic.

"You're the hero that saved my daughter's life," he said, laughing.

"Hardly that," I said.

"He was totally heroic, he jumped on top of me," Kit said with a grin.

"Oh aye?" Jackie said, his face contorting as if he were in a high school production of *Othello*.

"Steady on there, big fella," Touched said. Jackie looked at him for a second, nodded, and forced a grin.

"Allow me to present Sonia, my better half," Gerry said.

"Nice to meet you, Sonia," I said.

She smiled demurely.

"And over here we have David McGuigan and Jackie O'Neill, my associates, confederates, and all-round comrades-in-arms," Gerry said again in this florid style that he definitely must have picked up in America. No one ever spoke like that in Belfast, where Laconian immigrants would be known as chatterboxes.

I sat down next to Kit.

"Nice to meet you all," I said.

"Charmed," Sonia said.

Touched and Jackie kept their own counsel. Touched merely nodding, Jackie pretending not to see me.

"Can I offer you a drink?" Gerry asked.

"Whatever you're having," I said.

Gerry poured me some Budweiser.

"Kit told us about you," Touched said. "You helped her out in a big way."

"Aye."

"And what exactly were you doing in the bar that night?" Touched asked, raising his eyebrows slightly.

Gerry looked at Touched as if he had committed a social

faux pas by being so impertinent, but he let the question stand, so I had to answer it.

"Well, I was itching to be in a gun battle and that looked like just the right place," I said.

Touched grinned and his penetrating eyes bored into me for a moment.

"And the real answer?"

"Looking for a job, really," I said.

"A job. I see. And where are you from again?" Touched asked.

"Belfast. Ma was from Carrickfergus."

"Thought that was a Proddy town."

"Everybody thinks that. Not all of it," I said.

"There's a song about it, isn't there?" Gerry asked with a smile.

"Aye, there certainly is. Dreary, bloody awful song it is, too," I said.

"Family still over there?" Touched asked.

"Cousins in Cork but my ma and da are both pushing up the daisies," I said.

"Sorry to hear that," Touched said with no sorrow at all in his sleekit, suspicious face.

"How long you been on the fair shores of the New World?" Gerry asked.

I looked at Touched. How could he stand to listen to Gerry talk like this? Kit and Sonia would be indifferent but Touched was an old guerrilla buddy.

"I've been on the fair shores about a month," I said with slight sarcasm and a straight face.

"Doing what precisely?" Touched asked.

"Anything. Christ, you should see what I'm doing now. Kit'll tell you, bloody embarrassing," I explained, trying to get Kit back into what was becoming a difficult one-sided conversation.

"Oh, Daddy, he's a gladiator on the beach, fighting the Christians or something, isn't that right, Sean?" Kit said.

"Sort of."

"I've heard about that, it's the Greek festival, isn't it?" Sonia asked, suddenly brightening.

"Yes, we're dressed up as Hector and Achilles," I said.

"Aye, I seen that too, pair of you dressed up like a couple of fruits, skirts and everything," Jackie said.

Well, Achilles was passionately in love with Patroclus, I nearly said to tweak Jackie, but I remembered that Sean McKenna would probably never have heard of Patroclus, so, alas, Jackie's remark went untweaked.

"I think it's a very good idea to boost our cultural heritage like that," Sonia said.

I smiled at her. Not a bad-looking lass really. If she gained a few pounds, saw a bit of sunlight now and again, and renounced the dark side, she might just be an acceptable piece of ass.

"And are you happy in your job?" Touched asked.

"It's ok," I said.

"You like the fucking skirts?" Jackie mocked, laughing as heartily as if he had just cracked a devastating Wildean bon mot.

"They are popular among the warrior peoples of the Celts. But I can tell you don't know much about warriors, Jackie," I said with a twinkle in my eye.

Jackie started going for me, but Touched put a hand on his shoulder. Light aphorisms were clearly the way to get to the wee shite. Have to remember that one for the future.

"Well, I, for one, am very happy to have met such an enterprising young man, it's not easy to be *magnas inter opes inops*," Gerry said, pleased with himself.

"His name's Sean, not Magnus, Daddy," Kit said.

I would have loved to be able to source Gerry's remark to impress him but that probably would also have been a mistake. Besides, I had no bloody clue what he was talking about.

Gerry struggled to his feet, pulled his polo shirt over his enormous stomach and holstered gun, and gave me a wink. "If you'll excuse me, I have to make use of the facilities."

Touched nodded at Jackie. Jackie stole a look at me, got up, and followed Gerry out of the booth. He was protection tonight, which meant that he also had a piece on him.

"I'll take the opportunity too," Sonia said and looked at Kit.

"Me, too," Kit said in that bubbly voice of hers.

"Fucksake, are they giving out twenties for turds tonight?" Touched said, laughing. But I could see that they were giving him five minutes alone with me. It was a bit obvious, but I'm sure they were thinking, you can't be too careful these days.

"Because of the incident. Jackie or me go everywhere with Gerry," Touched said when they had gone.

"You're both armed," I said.

"Aye."

"The incident," I mused.

"The incident," Touched said without inflection, his eyes narrowing.

"Kit said her da got caught up in that shooting by accident," I said.

"But you don't believe that, do you?" Touched asked.

"No," I said.

"Tell me what you know," Touched said.

"I asked around. Kit's da was a player back in the olden days. So I reckon it wasn't an accident at all. I reckon the hit was on him," I said.

"Why would the boys want to hit an old pal like Gerry?" Touched asked.

"A million reasons. He wasn't making his payments, he pissed off the wrong guys, or maybe he didn't like the new direction the movement's been taking recently," I said confidently and took a sip of my beer.

"By direction you mean what?" Touched asked.

"The bloody cease-fire, what else? Fucking capitulation, if you ask me."

Touched nodded, lit himself a cigarette.

"When you were doing your snooping, did you ask around about me?"

"First of all, mate, I wasn't doing any snooping. Just asked a few questions. Second of all, I never heard of you until five minutes ago. You weren't there that night," I said.

"Aye, more's the pity," Touched said and rubbed his chin. We sat in silence and I took another sip of beer.

"So," Touched continued, "you have Gerry pegged as an old Provo that the Ra either wanted rid of or scared into toeing the party line. Am I right?"

"Something like that."

Touched nodded and shook the hair out of his face.

"What do you have me pegged as?" Touched asked.

An aging nutjob who looks like a roadie for the Grateful Dead.

"I don't have you pegged as anything yet," I said.

Touched sat back in the chair.

"You're a keen guy," Touched muttered.

"I just read the papers like everybody else," I protested.

"Where did you go to school?"

"Didn't really. Bounced around. Belfast High School for a few years, then I left."

"What did you do after?"

"I was a brickie in Spain, dicked around London for a while."

"You're not one of those fucking illiterate Paddy navvies, are you? You can read and write though, can't you?" Touched asked with disgust.

"Of course. I'm a big reader," I said indignantly, maybe a bit too indignantly.

"Ever been inside?"

"Never."

"Never?" Touched persisted.

"Well, do you mean jail or prison?"

"Prison."

"Never. Couple of overnight bins here and there, police lockups, never what you might call real prison time," I said.

"That's good, the smart ones never do a day's time in their lives," Touched said, beginning to warm to me. He took a knot out of his gray hair and wrinkled his brow, maybe remembering his own numerous stretches in joints and lockups all over the British Isles.

"Can I ask you a question?" I asked.

"Aye," he said cautiously.

"What happened to the two geezers who were with Gerry

that night in Revere Beach? Are they still inside? I know they shot their guns and I'm sure the peelers lifted them."

"No, no, both made bail. It was a real fuckup, though. The serious charges are against Seamus. Worried about him. They're charging him with attempted murder. Even though it was obviously self-defense. He doesn't want to plea, wants to fight it, and Gerry says ok. Seamus is a good bloke."

"What about the other guy?"

"We won't talk about Big Mike. That weasel went yellow on us, heard nothing from him since we paid his bail, fucked off the next day, didn't even leave a place where we could forward his wages. He's gonna cost Gerry fifty thousand if he doesn't show for court, which he won't."

"Don't blame him getting scared, it was pretty intense. Local, was he?"

"Aye, ex–Boston PD."

"There you go, he didn't grow up with it," I said, hinting that I, by contrast, had grown up with it.

"I should have been there," Touched said, clenching his fist at the thought of the assassination attempt.

"I wish I hadn't been there, except for being able to help Kit," I said and took a long drink. Touched smiled.

"You did well, anyway, for a civilian," he said and slapped me on the back.

"It was just something I had to do, get the wee lass out of there," I said.

Touched leaned over, grabbed my hand, shook it deliberately.

"Well, we're all happy that you did," he said.

"Don't even need to say it, mate."

Touched reflected for a few seconds, tapped his nose, and pulled his shaggy locks into a ponytail. He tied back his hair and looked at me.

"What do you make of this?" he asked and rolled up his sleeve to reveal a tattoo of the legendary Irish hero Cuchulainn, the Hound of Ulster. Except that the Cuchulainn of the tattoo did not resemble the famous statue in the GPO in Dublin. This one had been done in prison with a needle and smuggled ink by an artist of questionable skills. With big hair and equine features, he actually bore a strong resemblance to the queen of England—an unfortunate circumstance for Touched, a staunch Republican and anti-Royalist.

"What's that mean to you?" Touched asked, pointing at the tattoo.

"It's not Queen Elizabeth, is it?" I couldn't resist asking.

"What the fuck are you talking about?" he said furiously.

"Looks like her, or some member of that selective breeding program they have over there for picking the royals. Wait a minute, it's not the Queen Mother, is it?"

Touched was boiling with rage. I'd pushed him too far. He let go of my hand.

"For your information, mate, that is Cuchulainn, hero of the *Táin,* Hound of Ulster, greatest Irishman since Finn McCool. Clearly, you are one very fucking uninformed bog Paddy."

"Sorry, no offense meant, I'm just not a big history buff," I said.

"Aye, well I can see that," Touched said, finished his drink, and poured another from the pitcher.

"So in school you never even read the *Táin Bó Cúailnge*?" he asked after a long pause.

"Sorry, no," I said.

"Aye, I forgot you said you were a laborer, despite your protestations you probably didn't learn your letters at all, did ya?"

"I read just fine," I said angrily, letting him see that I had limits too.

We sat in silence for a minute, Touched glaring at me and shaking his head. I took a big drink from my glass.

But then his anger began to slip and he looked at me and suddenly laughed.

"Well, I suppose it *is* a bit of a fucking shite tattoo," he said.

The break in the tension made me laugh too.

"No, it's good," I insisted.

"It's shite. The guy who did it, did a lot of murals but he couldn't work in miniature. He bollocksed it up."

"I was only joking with that queen remark. I knew it was Cuchulainn, sure I seen that statue of him on O'Connell Street," I said.

"Taking a hand out of me were ya, ya wee shite," Touched said with a huge attractive grin playing over his face.

"A wee bit," I said.

"Jesus, have to watch you. You've got back doors to you, haven't you? Well, ok, Sean, we'll drop it now. Change the subject, bit of a sore topic for me and I'm trying to fucking relax."

"Are you into music?" I asked, trying to think of some other conversational opening.

"Nah. Not really."

"What do you like to do?"

"You like to gamble?" Touched asked. Touched, I recalled, grew up near Down Royal racetrack. Maybe this was a place to butter him up.

"Well, I haven't really had much opportunity, but I have bet on the gee-gees now and again. It's fun," I said.

"Oh aye? What do you prefer, flat or the fences?"

"Flat," I said. "Fences is too much of a lottery. Jesus, any punter could win the Grand National, but the Derby or the Triple Crown, that's more of a science."

Touched liked my answer.

"Aye, you're right there, Sean," he said. "I used to go over to the Cheltenham Gold Cup all the time and then sometimes the Derby. I went to Ascot one time; Jesus, do you know they don't search you going in there? Talk about the queen. I swear to God, if I'd brought a wee revolver in there with me I could have bloody assassinated half the British establishment."

He waited to see what my reaction would be. I didn't hesitate.

"Aye, and half the world would have thanked you," I said.

He smiled. His large gray-blue eyes relaxing, radiating genuine affection for me.

"I couldn't then, you see, didn't have the authorization. Actually had a few problems back in the Old Country. Little local difficulty, had to come to America, you know."

"What was the problem?" I asked, to see how far he was going to trust me on a first meet.

"Well, since you've asked, mate, it was fucked up for a start, totally fucked up. I was sent out here under sentence. Told not to come back," he said bitterly, his face growing white with anger. I let the rage boil in him for a while and decided to probe a little deeper. I knew the story but I wanted to see how much he would give me.

"Why?" I asked.

"You heard of Corky Cochrane?"

"Yeah, IRA man in South Armagh, everybody's heard of him. He's inside."

"Aye, hardly the most bloody discreet of characters; anyway, I was doing Corky's ex. Divorced. All legal like and everything. Seeing her. All aboveboard. Jesus, one night, dragged me from my bed down to Corky's house. His two brothers there waiting for me. Went at me with pistol butts, the bastards, said I'd raped Corky's old lady or something. Anyway, long story short, either I go to America or England or I was going to get a bullet in the fucking brain."

"Jesus."

"Aye."

"So you came here and started working for Gerry?"

"Nah, I see it more like working with Gerry, subtle difference," he said.

"I see that," I agreed.

Across the bar I spotted Gerry and Jackie coming back from the toilet. They were having a heated discussion about something. Gerry looked pained. Jackie, animated. They had to be talking about sports or kung fu movies or some other tedious thing in which Jackie considered himself an expert.

"Believe me. I'm telling you, corned beef in Ireland comes from Brazil or Argentina," Gerry was saying despairingly.

"Saint Patrick ate corned beef, cabbage, and potatoes," Jackie was insisting. "That's why you eat it on Saint Patrick's Day."

"Hardly likely, since potatoes are also from South America. There wasn't a potato in Ireland before the seventeenth xcentury," Gerry said as he sat down next to us. A look passed between him and Touched that I couldn't interpret.

"Saint Patrick ate potatoes," Jackie muttered as he slunk down in his chair and knocked back his beer in one.

"What's your opinion, Sean?" Gerry asked me.

"What's the debate?"

"Jackie, bless his heart, believes that you eat corned beef, potatoes, and cabbage on Saint Patrick's because that's what Saint Patrick himself ate as he wandered round the emerald isle."

"Well, I'm no history expert." I nodded at Touched and he nodded back. "But I thought Walter Raleigh brought back the spud from South America and that was a good bit after Patrick, I believe," I said.

"You are absolutely right, Sean. And you are put in your place, Jackie," Gerry said and turned to Touched. "Now let me hope that your conversation with young Sean here was more riveting than mine."

"We chanced over many subjects, Gerry. I was just finished telling Sean here about me and Corky Cochrane's old lady," Touched replied.

"Oh aye, I remember her, she has the MS now, doesn't she?" Gerry said.

"No, no, not MS, she has lupus, early-onset lupus," Touched said. "Funny story, actually. Tell you, Sean, just before I had to, uh, gather up my stakes, shall we say, she tells me she has lupus. Right, well, I'm a good Catholic and I did Latin to A level, and I never heard of lupus before and I think bloody hell, lupus, she's been bitten by a werewolf."

Gerry and Touched both laughed. Jackie did not and I knew that this was a good opportunity to establish a bit of character. It might have been a bit much rubbing it in his face with that Walter Raleigh line.

"I don't get it, sorry, David," I said to Touched.

"Lupus, lupin, the wolf, you know? You see, I got it mixed up with lycanthropy," Touched said.

I looked at him blankly.

"Do you get it now?" Touched asked.

I shook my head.

"Well, it's not important," Touched said and raised his eyebrows at Gerry as if to say, nice kid, but bloody hell, could be a bit of a dumbass.

Sonia and Kit appeared, sat down. With the women among the men, the mood changed completely. Gerry became more gregarious, Touched less suspicious. The subject changed to what was playing at the cinema.

We chatted and drank.

I was the last to arrive, so I knew it would be my shout next and when Jackie finished the last of the beer I went to the bar to get a pitcher of Sam Adams. And suddenly, of course, *she* was there. I hadn't seen her before, but obviously she'd been there all evening. Watching me. She was wearing skintight black jeans, a black silk blouse, and high heels. She was deliberately, overly made up, but the fake glamour couldn't hide her good looks. Her shock of red hair and those proud crimson lips that were sipping gin. She saw me but she didn't acknowledge me. She was talking to a surfer boy and had positioned herself so that she could see McCaghan's booth quite clearly. I didn't know how long she'd been there but Simon must have given her the heads-up.

Our eyes met briefly. She looked away and laughed at something the surfer boy said and her laughter came across the room delicately, like a waterfall breaking over the edges of the rocks. I took the pitcher back to the table, more confident and reassured. My guardian angel was on the case, a step ahead, as all guardian angels should be. And when I sat down, Gerry, Touched, and Jackie were all eclipsed. Diminished. They didn't know who they were dealing with, with their foolish talk of the Cuchulainn of the Uladh and Patrick and potatoes. She was the brains, the spikenard, the white-shirted predator among the thistles. And I was no mean boy. I had been there. To the depths. Mastering the hard places of the nocturnal world. I had brought destruction on greater men than these. Darkey White, Sunshine, Big Bob, all the while careful, professional, ice cold, singing happily the sweet songs of the hammer of retribution.

I was not afraid of them. If anything it should have been the reverse.

* * *

The evening was drawing to a close. I was comfortable and relaxed. Kit, unfortunately, was wedged between Jackie and her da but the center of gravity was at my end of the table.

The conversation drifted among music and movies and television. I contributed now and again but the interrogation phase was over.

I excused myself to go to the toilet. I didn't need to go to get my shit together or calm my nerves. Gerry was fine and Touched wasn't the monster of the Six report. Nah. I just needed to take a piss.

This was a scumball bar, but they had tried to gentrify the toilet by putting in electric hand dryers, burlesque prints, and a chalkboard above the urinal for graffiti. The graffiti was stuff about surfers and the Red Sox and there were a few anti-Mexican comments. Above the board and deep into the wall someone had scrawled "Fuck your chalkboard, you yuppie fucks" in six-inch-high letters. I'd bet money it was Touched. I'd have to ask him about it, I was musing, when, without looking round, I knew Jackie had come in behind me. The kid had a presence and a distinctive smell. Old Spice, surf wax, and zit cream. He was standing there, thinking he was invisible, trying to decide what he was going to say or do.

I took a piece of chalk and wrote: "You like staring at my cock, Jackie?"

I zipped up, turned.

"So you *are* fucking queer then, are you?" Jackie said, sneering.

"You'd like that, wouldn't you?" I said, neutral, calm.

"Wipe my name off that fucking board," he demanded, his pupils dilated, ready.

"You wipe it off," I said with a smile.

"Wipe it or I'll fucking make you wipe it."

I let the tension fall from my shoulders and waited for him

to come at me. He'd swing first. He'd had about six or seven beers. He'd be slow. I stuck out my jaw to give him a target. He'd come at my head with a big right hook. Just needed a wee bit of encouragement.

"Now you're starting to annoy me," I said. "Why don't you piss off before I have to teach you how to act around your elders."

"Aye, and before I brain you, you better tell me what you think you're fucking playing at with Kit," he snarled.

"I don't know what you mean, pal."

"You were all over her, don't think I couldn't see it. She's my girl. You fucking lay off. Ok? Unless you're looking for trouble, that is."

I took a breath. What was the right thing to do? What would Samantha want me to do? What would Kit want me to do? Of course I knew. Taking him would be fun but bad form.

"Listen, mate, I don't know what you're talking about. Kit is a nice girl, but she's not my type. I just want a job and a quiet life," I said, figuring that defusing the situation was probably the better way to go. I stepped backwards to give him more psychic space to think.

Jackie, however, was spoiling for a fight. His blood was up and he was not going to be denied.

"I seen you looking at her, I'm gonna have you, fucker," he said, squaring up to throw that obvious opening punch.

I backed off again.

"I'm not going to fight you, it's ridiculous, I don't want to fight you."

"Chickenshit," Jackie said.

"Aye, call me what you like, I'm leaving," I said.

I washed my hands and headed for the door.

"Wipe my name off that board."

"Piss away off, you wee shite," I said.

Jackie lunged at me. He did indeed lead clumsily with the right and, in his haste, he caught one foot behind the other and practically fell on me. I stepped to one side and let Jackie's momentum carry him into the hand dryer. His head banged into the swivel head of the blower and he collapsed to the floor. He scrambled away from me, blood oozing into his left eye from a two-inch cut above the eyebrow.

"Now you've done it, you're in big trouble now, you fucking bastard," Jackie said and then muttered something in that South Boston dialect I couldn't understand at all.

He reached in his back pocket and pulled out a flick knife. He pushed the button, revealed the blade, and locked it into place. He staggered to his feet. His jacket was open and I could see that, as I'd suspected, he was packing heat. A little .38 Saturday Night Special, but he was going for the knife, not the gun. Not even Jackie was that stupid. Even drunk he had his limits and this was not meant to be a fight to the death. He just wanted to hurt me. He'd probably try to slash out with the switchblade rather than try to grapple me and stab me. It was good to know.

Jackie was between me and the door, so I was going to have to deal with him one way or another. To give myself more room I backed into the center of the toilet, away from the cubicles.

"Aye, you can run but you can't hide," he said, an ugly little grin appearing on his face. His eyes squinting from the blood dripping into them.

"I don't know what Kit sees in you," I said, articulating a thought I had been pondering for at least the last couple of hours. And he really was an unattractive creature. Pale, skinny, and not exactly endowed with brains.

Jackie attacked with the knife. He was faster than I'd been expecting and the blade nicked my shirtsleeve. He laughed.

"Have you now," he sneered.

I moved towards the rear wall. He had a knife but I had all the advantages. He was drunk, I was sober. He was clumsy and I was poised. He had no idea what he was doing whereas I had been bloody sword fighting for a week, had been trained by the army in unarmed combat, and had been boxing shites like him since I was fifteen.

I remembered a move from this afternoon.

I pretended to slip on the bathroom floor.

I half went down.

"Gotcha," Jackie said gleefully. He bent down and swung the blade in a big arc, trying to cut me on the left arm, which I'd raised in a defensive posture. I dropped my hand so that the edge of my palm caught him on the forearm. I tugged him towards me, kicked at his feet, and hooked my thumb into the nerve bundle on his wrist. He let go of the knife and lost his balance. I wrenched him to the floor, pushed his head down, got up, snatched the chalkboard from above the urinal, and smacked it down on the top of his skull. Jackie yelled as the board broke in half and I smacked him again with one of the pieces, knocking him spreadeagled to the floor.

Blood drooled out of his mouth and he groaned incoherently.

I picked up the knife and began walking it across the room to the nearest trash bin.

That was my only mistake.

I'd thought he was out for the count and I'd forgotten about the firearm.

Jackie was now so enraged that any notion of proportionality had long since departed his dazed consciousness.

He sprawled on the floor, rolled to one side, and tried to pull the revolver out of the shoulder holster under his jacket. He got the gun into his hand. I turned round, saw what he was about, ran at him, and jumped. My big Stanley boots landed on his back, knocking the wind clean out of him.

I placed one knee on his throat, pushed the other hard down on his wrist, bent over, removed the gun from a hand already turning purple.

I squeezed his throat with my knee until his face reddened and he began to pass out.

"Will I kill ya, Jackie?" I asked.

The fight was out of his eyes. He was frightened.

"Nah, I won't. At least not today," I said.

I stood, emptied the shells from the revolver, and dropped knife, gun, and shells into the nearest toilet bowl.

Jackie was only semiconscious now.

"Fugga, have you, keep fugga mits off her."

But the adrenaline was pumping through me, so maybe

that was my excuse for piling on. I pissed onto the gun, knife, and bullets, zipped up, washed my hands, kicked Jackie in the stomach for good measure, and exited the men's room.

I fixed my T-shirt, wiped his blood off my steel toe caps, and walked back across the bar.

Back at the booth, they'd been talking about me.

"What took you so long?" Kit asked as I sidled in next to her.

"In one of the toilet cubicles there's a portal to the land of Narnia. I went through, got married, met Aslan, became a prince, and had fifteen kids; of course, only minutes passed for you, that's because of the time-dilation effects off General—"

Kit grabbed my leg to shut me up.

"Dad wants to say something to you," she announced significantly and looked at her father.

Gerry cleared his throat.

"Yes. Kit tells me that you're a very hard worker and she mentioned that you're looking for a new job," Gerry said.

I faked an aw-shucks and stared at Kit.

"Well, I suppose so," I said, as diffidently as I could.

"Have you done any construction before?" Gerry asked.

"Oh aye, sure enough, hod carrying, mixing cement, brickie stuff," I said.

"In this country the dwellings are made of wood, so that won't be much good to you here," Gerry said sternly.

"Ach, Gerry, stop teasing him, offer him the fucking job," Touched said, winking at me.

"Would you like gainful employment?" Gerry asked with a grin.

"I certainly would," I said.

"Then it's yours, my young friend," Gerry said, stretching his big paw across the table. I shook it and said politely:

"Thank you very much, Mr. McCaghan."

"Gerry, call me Gerry, the only one that calls me Mr. McCaghan is the bloody magistrate."

"Thank you, Gerry."

"Come by tomorrow, I'll fix you up and give you a place to

stay, rent-free if you want it," Gerry said.

"That's very generous," I said.

"No, it's not really, you'll stay in one of the premises we're renovating; it means I can rise you earlier and work you longer," Gerry said and started to laugh, his big body shaking with unaccountable mirth.

We talked a little about construction and Gerry launched into a story about a Portuguese man who fell into a cement mixer, Touched hinting that he had pushed him in as a practical joke. At the end of the story Sonia yawned behind her hand. Gerry took the sign and got slowly to his feet. When Gerry stood, everybody stood, and such was his presence I found myself getting up as well.

"Look, we better head on to pastures new. Come by the company tomorrow. It's on Plum Island. You know how to get there?" Gerry asked.

"Aye," I said.

"Where's Jackie?" Kit asked.

"Last I saw he'd collapsed in the toilet, think he was the worse for drink," I explained.

Touched looked at me, at first with suspicion but then a glimmer of understanding came into his eyes.

He'd been watching Jackie and he was astute. He reckoned he knew what had transpired in the bog. He pushed hard on my shoulder as Gerry and Sonia started putting on their jackets. Touched leaned in to whisper to me, all the while keeping his eyes on the bar.

"Jackie's my boy, he won't bother you again, I'll see to that. But, just so as you know, if you lay a finger on him one more time without my say-so, I'll fucking kill ya. Savvy?" Touched said.

He squeezed a little on my shoulder to emphasize the point.

"If he doesn't bother me, I won't bother him," I said.

Touched nodded. "Good," he said. "We understand each other."

"We do. Make sure Jackie understands too," I muttered, glad that I'd gotten the last word.

Touched turned to Gerry and led him towards the toilets to gather up their fallen comrade.

"Bye," Kit said happily to me, catching her dad and looping her arms between him and Sonia.

"Bye," I said.

Touched went in to get Jackie, leaving Gerry with the two women in the wide blue yonder, without a bodyguard, for nearly five full minutes. Not the sort of thing I would have done even if my boss hadn't been the victim of an assassination attempt a few weeks before. Touched clearly had a soft spot for his young apprentice. This made him vulnerable and in my eyes weak. It was good. Gerry was careless, Jackie was unpredictable, Touched had mellowed. The Sons of Cuchulainn were on the skids. That suited me just fine. The more cracks, the more fault lines, the better. Easier for me to slip between them.

Even so, I was a little nervous for Kit until Touched came out again. Without a piece I couldn't have done anything to stop a hit, but by God I would have tried.

When Touched did finally materialize, the protégé was cleaned up and appeared half-respectable. Still, a look of disgust passed across Gerry's face. Hmmm, maybe the time was ripe to move someone else into the role of junior bodyguard.

"Bye," Kit yelled across the room.

"Bye," I said.

Jackie didn't look at me but Kit did and with a final wave from her they left the bar. I finished the rest of my pint, well pleased with a very successful night's work on every conceivable front.

❋   ❋   ❋

Drizzle. Cold for summer. The amusements deserted. The sound of generators guttering off, stalls being closed, people leaving.

Someone pulled the master switch and the colored lights swayed on the cables for a moment and went out.

Her eyes were dark. Her skin alabaster.

She'd been waiting for me.

"Spare a couple of hundred?" a homeless man asked and I gave him a buck.

We crossed to the ocean side of the road. The town like a deserted film set. Oppressive reds and a frail green light bobbling on the concrete.

"This is how every episode of *Scooby-Doo* starts," I said to lighten the mood. "An abandoned fairground, a dark and stormy night."

She smiled and looked confused.

"A TV show," I explained.

The rain ceased.

A few insects, a few seabirds. Quiet.

Her tousled hair falling beneath her hood. She was wet, younger now. Her legs a wee bit unsteady in heels and tight black jeans. I'd heard her murmur something to herself. She was a little tipsy and it was almost as if I were the older one.

Novice and initiate.

The field agent and his control.

"You made a successful contact?" she asked finally.

"Yes."

"We'll talk in my car."

"Are you sure you should be driving?"

"Don't make me cross, darling. I had to have a couple of G&Ts to keep up the act of the desperate woman on the prowl. But I'm fine."

The big plum-colored Mark 2.

"You met them," she said when we were inside.

"Yeah."

"Did you make a good impression?"

"What do you think?"

"I think you did," she said, grinning.

"Gerry offered me a job, I said I'd take it."

She nodded, drove south. She opened the sunroof and wound the windows down. Not for mood, but to clear her head and help her drive. She was slightly more intoxicated than she was letting on.

I knew enough not to ask why we weren't going to my

apartment in Salisbury. She drove over the Merrimack bridge and into Newburyport.

She parked the car in the lot behind the All Things Brit store.

"What about Touched?" she asked as she turned off the ignition.

"What about him?"

"Did he frighten you?"

"No."

"That's what I was afraid of, dear. Well, we'll talk about that."

"I have to say, I'm not impressed. The Provos have put the fear of God into them. I met most of the whole crew. Can't be more than five or six of them."

"I saw that, too."

"Six people. Come on. All this for six people?"

"That's the definition of a cell, darling. Now save your breath just for the moment while I look for the keys to the . . . I suppose I should have put them on the same ring as the car key, I hope I haven't left them back in . . . no, there they are. Thank goodness. My ability to retain keys is not my best virtue."

She walked me to her flat above the All Things Brit store.

She'd painted it Mediterranean blue and filled it with numbered Picasso prints and Andalusian pottery. There was a Moroccan throw rug and of course that skylight that let in half the galaxy.

The air-conditioning had cooled the apartment to fifty degrees.

She removed her coat. She'd been watching me all night. Watching me with Kit. I may not be an expert at intelligence but I can read a situation.

Of course she was beautiful. Seductive. Almost the polar opposite of the way Kit was beautiful. This was a woman, not a girl. A poppy bloom, not a daisy.

Her hair wild and wet. Soaked dark strands plastered inside her blouse between her breasts.

She unbuttoned the blouse, removed her watch and a pearl

necklace. She sighed as she kicked off her shoes.

"What else do you want to know?" I asked.

She leaned over the bed.

"Help yourself to a drink, darling," she said, her breath carrying the scent of juniper.

"Uh, where is the booze again, over in the—"

"In the little study. The drinks are in the bloody globe, if you can believe it. I know it's terribly bourgeois but it came with the place. Have a drink, I need to freshen up."

She went to the bathroom. I opened the globe. A twenty-five-year-old Glenfiddich, a thirty-year-old-Bowmore, and a venerable bottle of brandy that looked as if it had been laid down to celebrate one of Napoleon's more famous victories. I helped myself to a full glass of the brandy but before I could sip it she came out of the bathroom in only the high heels. She marched across the room, took the glass out of my hand, knocked it back, and lay down on the bed.

"Fuck me," she said in an imperative tense that was impossible to refuse.

I took off my T-shirt and jeans, dimmed the light.

Her body was ruddy and pale and her breasts were huge and perfect. I climbed on top of her. Her lips like a dollop of strawberry jam on a cream scone. I kissed her. She was hot, aching with desire, her body bending up to meet mine.

"Don't think I'm always this unprofessional," she said.

"Of course not," I assured her.

"I don't screw all my agents. Not even all the good-looking ones."

"No."

"Clouds the judgment."

"Yes."

And I laid her down, and eased my body on top of hers.

I was an amputee but it meant nothing. Not to her, not to me, and I could do wet work just as well with a prosthesis as your average bloke.

Her hands stroked my back and pulled me close. I kissed her breasts and her neck but she was impatient for sex. She pushed me off her and kissed my belly and stroked my penis and sucked it till it was hard.

She smelled good.

And we kissed and I thrust my way inside her and we made love, our bodies moving together like singers in a duet, a new song, but one, somehow, that we knew by heart.

And I forgot Kit.

And I thought only about her.

Her snowy English arms and thighs, hungry lips, and assassin's eyes that were warmer now, burning and alive. The only sound, the harbor boats; the only light, the rotating galaxies and nebulae and stars. We made love until Orion set and the big bear rose. The heavens peaceful, silent, and fair; and, for once, here on Earth, we were in perfect symmetry with the world above.

6: A HEIST IN NEW HAMPSHIRE

Four days of this. Seagulls. Heat. Midges. Greenhead flies. Blackhead flies. Mosquitoes. The stink of marsh gas and a broken sewage pipe. Sand fleas, no fresh water, hundred percent humidity, a dozen men grumbling in Portuguese.

It was noon. Ninety-two degrees and the flies liked the taste of a Belfast boy.

The cool blue waters of the Atlantic a few feet away. Instead this.

"So it's bloody mutiny, is it?" I asked the leader of the Portuguese insurrection, who wagged his finger in my face and accused me of being the offspring of Satan and either a kind of donkey or, more likely, a prostitute. At least that's what I gathered from my shaky command of the Romance languages.

"You listen to me, you fool, I am at my wits' end, you either start digging or it's back to the Azores," I told him in broken Spanish. The Portuguese looked at me with disgust.

Seamus lay snoozing in the hammock. Seamus was supposed to be the foreman but when he had shown up for work, all he'd done was sleep off his hangover and tell me to get the "dagos" back to work.

It all began so promisingly. The day after I met the crew, Seamus and Touched came to see me in Salisbury. They formally offered me a job in Gerry's construction firm. I packed my bags and drove with them down to Plum Island. They introduced me to a bunch of Portuguese guys and said I'd be living with them in a house Gerry was renovating. The house was the first bad sign. A timber-frame sweatbox with mattresses on the floor, no ventilation, poor plumbing, and also apparently the major breeding ground for every type of bloodsucking insect in New England. The job itself was a piece of piss. Twelve bucks an hour and uncomplicated and anyway I figured it wouldn't be long until Touched checked out my rap sheet with the Boston PD.

But then nothing after that.

No contact, no pledge of loyalty to old Hibernia, no secret torchlight induction ceremony à la Riefenstahl. No news of any kind. Just getting up and working all day in the hot sun, liquid lunch with Seamus, more work, a quick dye job on my hair, and going to bed in the fly-ridden hell house full of drunk Portuguese men all of whom, it transpired, hated me.

I'd been to see Samantha once at her lair in the All Things Brit store, ostensibly going in to buy English candy; but she had been aloof and very unhelpful. "Just keep at the job and sooner or later they'll swing by and recruit you. They're desperate for manpower, bound to be what with the defections they've had."

"What if, Samantha," I said bitterly, "the Ra has scared the shit out of them and they have decided to pack in the life and disband their organization? How long am I going to have to do this sweaty, annoying job before you tell me that I've finished my bloody assignment and can go home?"

"Oh, we're not close to that time yet," she said. "Now if you don't mind I have to get back to the shop. I'm quite enjoying working here. I might take early retirement and open a place like this for myself," she said, arranging a box of tea towels.

No erotic fumbling, no swooning looks. All bloody business.

No joy from Samantha, and I hadn't even seen Kit at all in the last four days. Four days, seemed like forty.

August had ended and it was now September. Princess Diana had died in Paris, not that the Portuguese or Seamus gave a shit, but Samantha had put black drapes in the windows of All Things Brit and, in a canny business move, doubled the price of the Princess of Wales mugs and commemorative wedding plates.

I've described Seamus once before, but I'll recap. He was the one that did the shooting in the Rebel Heart back in Revere. His pal, Mike, as Touched had explained, had the be-jesus scared out of him and left Gerry's employ, but Seamus was seeing it all through at least until his trial, when he'd be convicted of assault or attempted murder, probably the former, and get a couple of years inside. Serve him right.

Seamus was a disillusioned beat cop, about fifty-five. An old-school racist, with gray skin, salt-and-pepper hair, and a body wrecked by his sixty-a-day habit, which he'd been maintaining through thick and thin since he was fifteen years old. In a series of depressing lunchtime conversations, I quickly ascertained that the highlights of Seamus's life had been the assassination of Martin Luther King, Jr., the abandonment of court-ordered busing in the 1980s, the blowing up of Mrs. Thatcher at the Conservative Party Conference, and the glorious run of the Celtics under Larry Bird. The low light: game six of the 1986 World Series. I suppose his loyalty to Gerry was less ideological and more an attempt to give his pathetic and useless existence some meaning.

I'm being hard on Seamus, partly as a defense mechanism, because a week after I met him for the first time, in circumstances that were less than pleasant, I had to shoot him in the head from three feet away with a whopping Colt .45 hand cannon, the round at that range blowing his skull apart and sending his brains, blood, and bone all over me and a hapless squaddie standing nearby.

But we'll get to that.

Seamus lying there in the hammock, snoozing while greenheads and horseflies sucked the blood out of his pasty legs.

But for the Department of Fish and Wildlife's bird sanctuary (and that do-gooder DFW alum Rachel Carson), they would have nuked this whole island with DDT years ago and made it bearable for thin-skinned Paddies like Seamus and me.

"Seamus, are you awake?" I shouted.

He didn't budge.

"Seamus, the Ports are saying they're on strike," I tried again, but Seamus was in a deep drunk sleep.

"Get your bloody backs into it," I said to the Portuguese men, but none of them moved a muscle. I didn't blame them, really. Our job itself was a KKK dream or a good Catholic's nightmare. Demolishing Plum Island's small Roman Catholic church to make way for housing. The church had suffered declining attendances for years and the land was worth a couple of million, so the diocese must have thought, what the hell, it's coming down.

McCaghan's firm had been contracted to do the demolition and the Church had already sold the lots for three five-bedroom houses to be built on the former hallowed ground, the prospective buyers obviously having learned nothing from countless Stephen King films. Not so the Portuguese navvies, who were all superstitious illegals from the Azores. To say they didn't like demolishing a Catholic church would be understatement, and for days they'd been working slow and acting stupid.

They were supposed to be shoveling a straight path through the sand, the loam soil, and the concrete foundations to let the bulldozer in to demolish the church. A nasty job but one that could be done in a day if everyone's heart was in it.

The Portuguese rebel stood on his pickaxe and mumbled a remark about my mother, which, if he had but known, was remarkably accurate.

I walked over to Seamus, who was still snoring in the hammock slung between a generator and a portable toilet.

"Seamus, wake up, they're on strike. They're refusing to budge," I told him with a kick in his arse.

Seamus groaned, slapped at the flies on his ankles, and looked at me with annoyance.

"Why did you wake me? You total bastard."

"Now that we're close the Portuguese are refusing to dig the final bit of the path. They think it will bring down a rain of curses on them."

"You speak dago, tell them to get a fucking move on. Touched won't stand for it."

"Why don't you call Touched and tell him to come over here."

Worry slipped across Seamus's face.

"Nah, he won't like that."

"Well, you get them to bloody move, I've had it," I said and slumped down in the shade next to the chemical toilet. Seeing me sit, the Portuguese all found places to sit too. Seamus lit a cigarette.

"Ok, suppose I better take care of it. Help me out of this thing."

I helped him out of the hammock and he walked over to the Portuguese. I stood behind him.

"You won't work?" he said to the lead rebel. The man shook his head.

"You're fired."

The man stared at him.

"You're fired. Get the fuck out of here. Translate, Sean."

I told him in Spanish that he'd been axed and someone translated my Spanish into Azorean Portuguese. To further make things clear, Seamus slapped him in the head and kicked him off the building site.

"Who else won't work? You?" he asked, pointing at one of the youngest men on the crew. "You're fired too, get out of here. Anybody else?"

The rest of the men picked up their tools and got their backs into it. Seamus looked at me, satisfied.

"That's it, Sean. Break the will of the leaders and the rest fall into line. That's the dago mind-set all over. Now don't fucking wake me again, or you're on the chopping block yourself."

An hour later. The boys had carved out two shallow ditches, three feet wide by ten feet long. The bulldozer path was complete.

"Señor, por favor . . ."

I shook my head.

"Sorry, lads. But if the bishop has given the ok—" I was

about to explain that this was no longer God's house when I noticed Samantha, ostensibly coming up from Plum Island beach carrying an umbrella, wearing outsize sunglasses and a big floppy hat. She was sauntering past the construction site and paying no attention to any of us. You could tell she was English: the last thing this big and this white in Massachusetts was Moby Dick. She washed her feet with a water bottle and walked to the car park at the lighthouse. No signal, no acknowledgment, nothing. But I knew this wasn't a casual beach trip. She hadn't been to the sea at all. She'd wanted me to see her, to let me know that something was happening.

She drove past in the big Mark 2 five minutes later, with the sunroof down, blaring "Like a Virgin" from her car stereo.

It was a very un-Samantha piece of music. She, who hadn't heard of Scooby-Doo, liked Madonna? It made me think. Like a virgin . . . Of course.

"Touched for the very first time" was the second line of the chorus.

Jesus. Touched was up to something. Dan Connolly, who was a big Madonna fan, must have given her the idea.

I grinned.

Maybe those eejits weren't so dumb after all.

I'd have to find an excuse to go into Newburyport later.

But for now the job at hand. I climbed into the big yellow bulldozer, turned the key in the ignition, and pushed the red starter button. The bulldozer growled into life. I lifted the massive steel-toothed bucket to about three-quarters elevation and drove the machine down the path that the Portuguese had cleared.

The church was a wooden single-story structure, simple, beautiful in a very un-Catholic, Puritan kind of way. I edged the bulldozer gently into the porch and pushed with the grabber. The entire edifice buckled.

The bulldozer had a fully enclosed cabin and I was wearing a hard hat but even so I ducked as the roof wobbled, the back wall caved in, and the church began to fall to pieces with an enormous crash. When the cross from the spire came tumbling down and smashed on the ground the Portuguese

howled a few incantations to the Holy Ghost and Seamus gen-
uflected when he thought I wasn't looking. I reversed the bulldozer, lowered the grabber, and drove into the remaining wall
and support beams.

The site was leveled in under ten minutes. The Portuguese
men crossing themselves and muttering Ave Marias. No one
on Plum Island seemed to care, no protests and no gawkers. I
got out of the cab and brushed the debris off my white T-shirt,
cargo pants, and Stanley work boots.

However, through the spirals of dust I noticed that there was
someone who *had* seen and had come to see me. Aye, something was up.

"Well done, Sean," Touched said and offered me his hand.
Touched must have been watching from McCaghan's house,
which was about a quarter of a mile farther up on Plum
Island's Atlantic side.

"Thanks, Touched," I said, trying out the nickname to see
how it would play. He wasn't fazed at all.

"Gerry will be pleased. Hell of a job, we can work on building those houses now," he said with a distracted air.

"Ok."

He put his hand on my shoulder and a gleam came into his
eye. A gleam that could mean anything on that handsome,
generous, psychopathic, murderous face.

"But not you though, Sean."

"Not me?"

"I've been checking you out, mate," he said. "Checking you
out. Got something special lined up for you, if you're up for
it."

Checking me out? So that's what Samantha was trying to
let me know. He had accessed his buddy on the Boston PD
and run the files on Sean McKenna. Well, well, well.

"Something special? Will there be more money in it?" I
asked.

"Could be."

"Ok, then. I'm in."

❖   ❖   ❖

Short walk to Touched's car. Me, Touched, Seamus. A big Toyota Land Cruiser that he'd obviously just stolen because it was still full of toys, a box of diapers, and wipes.

Touched handed Seamus and myself a pair of gloves. We put them on without asking why.

I got in back. Kit sitting there, smoking a cigarette. She was also wearing gloves, black tank top, black jeans, no bra. The nipples on her small breasts were erect because of the Land Cruiser's powerful air-conditioning.

"Hi," I said.

"Hello. We saw you, like, totally bring down that church. Dude, that was pretty awesome," she said. "I didn't know you could drive one of those things."

"One of my many hidden talents," I said.

Touched and Seamus got in the front.

"How's your boyfriend, Jackie, I believe he had a bit of an accident?" I said innocently.

"Yeah, that graffiti board in the End of the State totally fell down on him while he was peeing. He's thinking of suing, you know?"

"Is that what happened?"

"Yeah."

"Well, he should sue, open-and-shut case, I would have thought."

"How do you like living on PI?" she asked, to change the subject.

"Nice place if you don't mind getting eaten alive. The Pilgrim Fathers were on to something when they decreed that no flesh should be exposed. Sound religious reasons, possibly, but certainly practical common sense in the boggy, marshy coast of Massachusetts."

"The pilgrims didn't come up here," Kit said.

Touched turned round to look at us.

"Listen, you two. Enough of the chitchat. This is serious. If you don't want to go, now's the time to opt out," he said.

Kit shook her head, her eyes wide, slightly frightened, her chin jutting out with determination.

"Might help, Touched, if I know what I was opting out

of," I said.

Touched looked at Seamus, who nodded.

"What do you think? Is he one of us?" Touched asked.

"Seems ok to me," Seamus said.

"What I say in this car is totally between us, if you're not interested, you keep your fucking mouth shut and we'll forget the whole thing, ok?" Touched said to me.

"Ok."

"Aye. Sean, I heard that you were lifted in Northern Ireland for attacking a police car. And I heard that the peelers knocked the shite out of you. Heard you were a bit of a wee rebel when you were a kid," Touched said cautiously.

"Where did you hear that?" I barked, trying to sound pissed off.

"Don't fly off the handle, Sean, I don't want to cause you any trouble, in fact quite the reverse. I had to check you out. These are very difficult times that we're living in. It's quite possible that Gerry is being watched by the cops or the FBI, although I think we might have heard about it before now. But that's neither here nor there. The thing is, Sean, I have a wee contact in the Boston pigs and I got them to run you on the computer. I read about your past and I know where your sympathies used to lie, and I want to know if you still feel that way?"

Kit looked at me, her gloved hand patting me on the leg. She smiled. Her eyes the color of a glacial lake. Not a cold, uninviting glacial lake. More of a cool lake on a warm day. Let's say it's summer in the Alps and you're sweaty and hot from hiking and you—

"Sean, did you hear what I said?" Touched asked, shaking me out of my reverie.

"You want to know how I feel about the Brits in Ireland?" I muttered, snapping my head away from those hypnotic peepers.

"Aye."

"I think the Brits should stick to their own country and get out of Northern Ireland. And if the bloody Protestants don't want to live in a united Ireland then they can fuck off back to

Scotland where they came from," I said with just enough but not too much passion.

Touched nodded and put the car into gear.

He accelerated away from the remains of the church and we drove over the metal swivel bridge and off the island. To the left was the swampy Parker River National Wildlife Refuge, to the right Joppa Flats and Newburyport Harbor. Touched lit a cigarette, began another little speech.

"Sean, apparently you did wonders in Revere, but I have to see for myself. This is going to be a test. This isn't going to be your only test. But if you don't do well today, you're out. Generous redundancy package, couple of handshakes, no hard feelings. If you do well, I'm going to recommend you to Gerry. Simple as that. There's going to be four of us. Me and Seamus will run the show. You and Kit just shut the fuck up and do nothing. I'm not even sure I agree with having Kit here but—"

"We're not going to get into that again, Touched, like, come on," Kit said, interrupting him angrily.

Touched coughed on his cigarette. If this was any other wee girl but Gerry's daughter he probably would have turned round and slapped her.

"Ok, Kit, keep your fucking hair on," he said and threw his fag out the window and angrily lit another.

He put the radio on and flipped through the stations, looking for one playing country, not an easy task in Massachusetts. Finally he dug one up on the AM band and, more relaxed, winked at me in the rearview mirror.

The drive.

Nobody talking.

Touched singing along to the radio. The ocean on our left, North America on our right. Swamps, mudflats, marshes. Kit looking out the window. Touched packing heat. Seamus, too. Slowly down route 1A. Many places along the way with pull-offs, deserted little lay-bys. Easy for Touched to stop the car with any kind of excuse. A play like this:

"I just need a quick piss," Touched says.

Suggests we all get out. I have to get out too, or it will look suspicious. As soon as I'm out of the car, Touched checks the highway, looks left and right, pulls his piece, shoots me in the belly to put me down. Shoots me in the head and then another one right in the eyeball to be on the safe side.

Kit's screaming. Seamus holding her back. He explains it to her or tries to. They search the body but they don't find anything. They fill my pockets with gravel, stones, anything really, take me to the swamp and dump me in.

Kit gets in the car, sobbing, hysterical.

"Why, why did you kill him?" she asks.

"Fucking British agent, Kit," Touched says. "I could tell immediately. Your da thought it was important that you were there to see me top him."

"Oh God," Kit says. . . .

I looked out the window, waited for the car to slow, for the indicator to come on. But it didn't. We drove through Rowley, over the Parker River bridge, and down to Ipswich. Some of my fear had gone, but the adrenaline pumping through me still kept me off kilter and alert.

"I'd like to tell you a little about what's happening, Sean," Touched said from the front as he tried to drive round a slow-moving RV.

"Tell away."

"First of all, we're going to go get some ice cream and then we are going to go to a town in New Hampshire called Derry. There's two towns in New Hampshire right beside each other. One is called Derry and one is called Londonderry. As you know, Sean, but Kit and Seamus don't, back in Ulster the Prods call Derry 'Londonderry' and the Catholics call it 'Derry.' So obviously settlers from there came here and they couldn't agree what to call their new town and so both Derry and Londonderry are right next to each other. Interesting places, I was up there yesterday."

So what? I was thinking but Touched came to the point.

"As a spite to the Protestants we are going to rob a bank in Londonderry, New Hampshire. Recon on it for the last week. It's 1950s America. One security camera. Rush in the morning, very slack in the afternoons. Two part-time clerks and a manager. After we get our ice cream I am going to give you all one more chance to back out. And that's it. Ok?"

I nodded. Kit nodded. Touched looked at us in the mirror.

"By the end of the day, both of you are going to be men," Touched growled as he pulled into the White Farms Ice Cream stand that Kit had pointed out the night of the hit on her da.

"All right, Seamus, you go up and get us four butter crunch with chocolate sprinkles. Here's a twenty, if she's nice give her a two-buck tip, got that?"

"Four butter crunch with sprinkles, two-buck tip. I'd rather have rocky road if that's ok?"

"Butter fucking crunch," Touched insisted.

Seamus slunk out of the car and walked up to the ice-cream stand. There was a queue of about a dozen people ahead of him, so it might be a while. Touched turned the car and the air-conditioning back on.

He turned to face us.

"Seamus is ok. Don't worry about him. He's been a bit shaken up since the attempted hit on Gerry, but he's ok. You saw him that night. Fucking outstanding. He's solid. Not like some others I could mention."

"He seems fine to me," I said.

"I've had him teasing info out of you, and I've asked around. You're ok, Sean, and I think your heart's in the right place. I want you, Sean. I like you. I think we could use you. Your country could use you."

I looked at him. His eyes were cold now. Serious. How stupid was I supposed to act? Would Sean know what Touched was asking him to join?

"Will it mean killing people?" I asked.

"For you it will not. Not you. Certainly not initially. British companies, businesses. Maybe military or governmental officials, and you won't be involved in that unless you're completely comfortable. Me, Gerry, and Seamus will take the high-risk assignments. Maybe Jackie later."

"You're not the Provos, are you?"

"We're not, we're our own group. The Sons of Cuchulainn. Back in the heyday there used to be about a dozen of us in two cells. Now it's basically Gerry's family and a few others. We're down in numbers but not in clout. I really think we can make a difference. Gerry is fucking loaded. We have resources up to the roof, we just need young guns, new blood. The IRA have never even tried a campaign in America. Chickenshit traitors that they are."

"They tried to kill Gerry."

"Aye, but they won't try again. They're on cease-fire now, so they can't."

"So who's your enemies?"

"Nobody knows about us yet. Probably only a couple of files in the FBI. Those files will get bigger. The Brits will get involved. But we're going to be smart. Cell structure, untraceable. Even if the FBI are doing surveillance on Gerry, none of it's going to get back. Hoping to have two or three cells in place by Christmas," Touched said.

"What's the point, what's the goal?"

"The point is to take the war to the enemy. What I'm going to tell you is very confidential. This goes for you too, Kit, no blabbing."

"Of course not."

"In the next week or two a new organization is going to be announced in Dublin called Continuity IRA or Real IRA. They're opposed to the IRA cease-fire. So we won't be alone. If we can impress Real IRA with a few spectaculars, I'd say we'd be quids in with them. We can have a formal alliance or we can be co-opted. Either way we won't be alone, not by a long shot. It'll mean money, influence, power, and history's going our way, Sean. And Mr. Blair and the Labour Party are for a United Ireland anyway. We hope to give them the boost they need to withdraw."

"By?"

"Making life impossible for British companies, consulates, and so on in the United States of America. Hurt them economically. Way to their heart is through their wallet."

"So no killing?"

"If you're squeamish about that you should turn me down now, because killing is unavoidable in any war," Touched said, and to impress the seriousness of his point, he smacked his fist into his palm. I looked at him, thought for a moment. His face had lost all of its levity. This was one subject not to be taken lightly.

"I hate the fuckers, but it's just not something I personally have had to do before," I said.

"I know, Sean. It's hard. The first time is hard. Look at Kit there beside you, she knows," he said somewhat surprisingly.

Kit nodded.

"You've killed someone?" I asked her, shocked.

"No. That's not what he's talking about. But I know it might be necessary. If you don't think you have the nerve . . ." Kit muttered, trying to appear steely and composed. Touched nodded grimly, his face a mask of certainty.

"I have the nerve, sister, don't worry about that," I said.

"Good," Touched said, reaching back and clumsily punching me on the shoulder.

"The ends will justify the means," Kit said dreamily, as if that explained anything.

"I'm in," I said.

Touched grinned, grabbed my hand, and shook it.

"I knew I could depend on you, Sean. Not so fast, though. You have to prove you have the bottle. What you did when you were sixteen was one thing, have to see if you have the balls right now. Today will be the first test; but we need you, Sean. I'm not telling tales out of school if I admit that what happened in Revere was a big setback. Nobody got hurt, but as I've already told you, Mike has split. And we lost two more, old pal of Gerry's called Tommy O'Neill and a wee kid called Jamie, thought he was coming along, we all liked him, but he's scarpered too."

"He was a nice boy. Jackie taught him to surf," Kit said sadly.

"I'm in if you'll have me," I said.

"We'll have you if you do well today and the next and . . . Here comes Seamus with the ice creams and oh my fucking Christ, he got the rainbow instead of the chocolate sprinkles."

*　*　*

The National Independent Bank of Londonderry, NH, was in a little patch of land cleared from the thick woods off Route 128. It hardly resembled a bank at all. More like a settler's cabin with a tiny car park next to it. It was the sort of place Robert Frost might have written about, juxtaposing the capitalistic rudeness of the bank with the loveliness of nature. Some sort of shite like that.

Touched drove past it once and pulled the Toyota into a lay-by about fifty yards up. I would have parked closer, in case we had to run out of there, but I didn't want to mess with Touched's arrangements. Presumably he knew what he was doing. Besides, if we were caught, they'd all go to jail and I'd be out of the op. Though getting shot by the cops or a security guard was a different matter.

Touched reached in the glove compartment and gave us each a ski mask to pull on. From his jacket he produced a couple of .38 revolvers, gave them to Kit and me.

"You fired a gun before?" he asked, a fine time for a question like that.

I nodded. Kit shook her head.

"I thought your da took you to Bob's on Route 1?" Touched asked.

"He—he said he was going to but he never did."

"Jesus. I should have done it before now. Ok, well, can't be bloody helped. You wait in the car, Kit," Touched said.

"I'm not waiting in the car," Kit said angrily. "I'm going."

"You're not going anywhere if you can't handle a firearm."

"I'm fucking going, Touched," Kit said.

Touched looked at her. She wasn't budging. He liked that. A grin spread across his face.

Touched took the gun back, emptied out the shells, and handed it to her again.

"Just look threatening," he said to Kit.

"Ok," she replied.

"Last chance to pull out," Touched said to the pair of us.

"I'm in," I said.

Kit thought for a moment. "Me, too," she said finally.

"Ok, leave it all to me, not a word from either of you and do everything I say, understood?"

We both nodded.

"Seamus, are you ok?"

Seamus nodded, produced his own .38, spun the barrel, snapped it in his hand. Seamus was pretty confident with a pistol, I remembered.

We put on our ski masks, got out of the car, and walked through the woods to the back of the bank.

There were two cars outside. Route 128 was quiet.

"Me first," Touched said, adjusting his ski mask.

He walked into the bank. I heard Kit behind me, gagging back vomit.

The bank was tiny.

One woman clerk behind the counter, one man helping her in the back. No customers. Fan in the upper left of the room. Desk for filling out forms. Handmade posters advertising yard sales and a stock show. Glass partition between customers and tellers. A smell of resin, wood glue, and coffee. And as Touched had told us, one big old-fashioned surveillance camera.

Touched walked up to the woman teller. She saw the four of us, the guns, the masks.

"Can, can I hel . . ." she said, her voice trailing off into a whisper. Betty, according to the nameplate in front of her, was an older woman, with dyed red hair and a perma tan that actually suited her. She was dressed in a garish yellow frock she must have bought at Woolworth's in about 1971.

"It's like this," Touched began calmly. "We plan to be out of here in two minutes. No one is going to get hurt. What you're going to do, love, is fill this bag full of money and then we're going to go and when you've waited for twenty minutes you're going to call the police."

Touched pushed a black bag under the six-inch gap in the glass partition. The woman picked it up absently.

"Harris, we're being robbed," she said, and finally the man behind her looked up from whatever he was doing. He was also elderly, in a gray shirt, black woolen tie, and glasses. He looked the flighty troublemaking type to me. I kept him between me and Kit in case he was going to try anything.

"Oh my God," Harris said.

"It's ok, everything is going to be fine," Touched said.

"Mr. Prescott isn't here yet today. Of all days, why today? He's not here, he's still in Manchester," Harris said in a voice trembling with panic. The woman looked at Harris and then at Touched.

"Fill the fucking bag," Touched said, and for the first time he raised his pistol to the horizontal and pointed it at her. She froze.

"I think we should wait until Mr. Prescott comes back," Harris said.

Touched was getting angry now.

"If you don't start filling that bag with money, I am going to fucking butcher the pair of you," he yelled.

Betty started to tear up and let the bag drop on the floor.

"Please go away," she said.

Harris put his hands over his head.

"Mr. Prescott should be back in half an hour, please, can you not wait, or come back then? We won't tell the police. I give you my word as, as an Elk," he pleaded, sweat shining on the bald spot on his head and appearing under the arms of his polyester shirt.

Touched clicked the hammer back on his revolver.

"One more word out of you, mate, and you're going to be fucking toast," he growled.

Betty began to sob. Harris began to hyperventilate and backed away into a filing cabinet, which banged shut. Touched turned to Seamus, Kit, and myself.

"We're going to have to shoot through the glass," he said. "You two stay back. And can someone take out the bloody camera?"

Seamus shot the surveillance camera, something he should have done as soon as we'd walked into the bank.

The noise was deafening.

Betty began to sway.

This was all spinning out of control. Bank tellers are

trained to give you the money. They want to give you the money. This should be easy.

I put my hand on Touched's shoulder and whispered: "Let me try."

Touched was about to say something, changed his mind, nodded. I walked as close to the glass as I could and put the gun down on the counter so that Betty could see I was not pointing it at her.

I spoke gently: "Betty, please, pick up the bag, if you put some money in it we'll be gone and out of your life forever and this will all be over."

"I, I, I dropped it," she said.

"That's ok, you're bound to be nervous. But don't worry about it, you're really doing very well. Mr. Prescott is going to be very proud of you. Now pick up the bag and fill it with money."

She looked at Harris. He nodded.

"Come on, Betty. It'll be something to tell the TV news and your grandchildren," I said as kindly as I could, but hoping that mentioning the grandkids would also remind her that this was life or death.

Touched seethed impatiently beside me.

Betty looked at me for a moment, picked up the bag, opened the drawer for the twenties, and threw in all the stacks. About a dozen in total.

"What about the other drawers?" I asked.

"Mr. Prescott has the keys for those, but, but he should be back directly."

"That's ok, just give me that bag," I said.

Seamus suddenly came to life.

"There's someone coming in from the parking lot," he yelled, eyeing the door.

I looked at Betty and Harris.

"No silent alarms, no tricks, you two just do your job and give me the bag," I said to Betty.

She flattened the bag and calmly pushed it under the glass. I picked it up, chucked it to Touched.

"He's definitely coming in," Seamus said, peering outside.

"I can't believe this, they usually get one customer an hour," Touched growled nervously.

Kit was rocking back on her heels, looking like she might be about to pass out. I reached over and steadied her shoulder.

"What's he look like, Seamus?" I asked.

"Old guy in a red cap," Seamus hissed.

"Let him come in, smack him on the head as soon as he's through the door," I commanded.

"I'll do it," Touched said, trying to assert some of his authority.

Touched walked to the front of the bank and almost immediately the door opened. An old woodsman came in out of the bright sunlight and before he had time to adjust to the interior dimness Touched had savagely clobbered him with the butt of his pistol. He went down like a puppet with the strings cut.

I turned to Betty and Harris.

"Thank you, Betty, now make sure you give us twenty minutes to get away before you call the police, because if we're captured before then, we'll make sure our associates kill you and Harris before the trial. They'll torture you with arc welding gear until you're begging for death. A good twenty minutes, do you understand?"

Betty's eyes widened and the color drained from her cheeks. She nodded and tried to speak but could not.

"That's about the best we're going to do," I said to Touched. "I think we should head."

"Aye. Let's go," he said.

We ran out of the bank and into the sunshine. We sprinted through the woods and climbed into the Toyota. Ski masks off.

Kit was breathing hard and her face was white. Touched drove us up 128 like a goddamn maniac, hitting a ton before he came to an intersection. Kit threw up into her ski mask. She opened the window to dump it out, but I shook my head.

"No, just wait," I said.

At the intersection, Touched headed us south back towards the Massachusetts border along the Alan B. Shepard Jr. Highway.

When he reckoned we were safe, Touched playfully slapped Seamus on the back of the head and looked at Kit and myself in the rearview mirror.

"You did well, lads. Did well. We did it. We fucking did it. Yeah. Jesus. Sweet and fast. Shit, yeah," Touched said, driving now at a more sensible speed.

"Went pretty smooth," Seamus said.

"Oh my God, yeah. So quick. Under two minutes, I reckon. Dead impressed. You all did very well. . . ."

We drove to Route 1 and pulled the Toyota onto a swampy piece of land where Touched had left his own car, a green Mercedes, behind an old ruined factory or warehouse. We got out of the vehicle. Touched collected the ski masks and the gloves, put them in a bag and threw them in the swamp. Kit had left vomit on the floor of the Toyota.

"What about the vomit?" I asked.

"What about it?"

"Can you trace DNA through vomit?" I asked.

"Better scrape it up, Kit," Touched said.

"I'll do it," I said and used the baby wipes to clean up the mess.

We got into the Mercedes. Seamus in the front, very quiet now. Touched, exhilarated, flipping through the rock channels until he found Garth Brooks. Kit looking like one of the undead, all the color gone from her cheeks and pale lips. I put my hand on her neck, rubbed the tension out of it, smiled at her. She put on a brave face and smiled back. I took her hand and held it. She'd been a lot more terrified about this than she'd been the night her father had been shot at. I suppose she'd known about this plan for a while and had been dreading it all morning.

"You did great," I whispered.

"I didn't do anything," she replied.

"No, you were fabulous," I said.

Within fifteen minutes of getting in the Mercedes we were pulling up to Gerry McCaghan's enormous house on Plum Island. Kit held my hand all the way to the front door. I squeezed it and let go only when Gerry came in sight.

* * *

The house sat above the dunes right on the Atlantic Ocean. The previous owner, Gerry proudly told me later, was a vice president of the *Penthouse* company and before that it had been the summer retreat of a New England shipping family.

Gerry had extended the already "improved" *Penthouse* dwelling both laterally and vertically and now it was an eleven-bedroom mansion with a five-bedroom guesthouse on the other side of a four-car garage. The style was 1920s Hamptons Long Island Estate meets 1990s Internet Millionaire Monstrosity.

The original structure had an elegant wood facade, painted a dull white that had weathered into a lovely pinkish gray. The extensions were brash, futuristic abutments that seemed to be all tinted windows, harsh metallic angles, silver paint, and a few space-age air-conditioning ducts. A set of flagpoles dominated the driveway. In defiance of convention, the highest-flying flag was the Irish tricolor; slightly lower there was a "Harp on a Green Field"—an old flag of Irish republicanism—and lower still the Stars and Stripes. There was no garden, merely dunes and crabgrass on the ocean side and a sandy driveway at the back.

It was a house in poor taste and it made me wonder about Gerry's overall judgment and certainly his construction skills; but perhaps it looked better from the sea. Preferably out beyond the three-mile limit.

Gerry had seen the Mercedes arrive and came out to greet us. He was dressed in a white Lacoste polo shirt and enormous blue shorts. His feet were bare and his Red Sox hat was on backwards. He ignored me and approached Touched. I was ill at ease, but my doubts were dispelled when, after a brief conversation, he walked over to me and gave me a hug.

"I'm glad you're with us, Sean, Touched says you were great," he said, squeezing the life out of me in what, for a moment, I thought was the subtlest murder attempt I'd ever experienced in my life.

He released his grip and embraced Kit, too. He lifted her

up in the air. Kit so small and frail, Gerry a man mountain. For a moment it was like the footage of the little kid who falls into the gorilla cage.

"I heard you were great too, Kit," Gerry said.

"I was ok. Sean was the star," Kit said.

Touched slapped me on the back.

"Damn right he was. You know me, Gerry, I'm a bit liable to fly off the handle. Fucking Sean, cool as a cucumber. He was a bloody natural."

"Is that right, Sean?" Gerry asked happily.

"Nah, wee bit of exaggeration. Touched ran the show. I was just helping out."

Gerry patted me on the head with his meaty paw.

"He's modest, too, unlike some people I could mention," he said, looking inside the house. Hinting, perhaps, that Jackie was not flavor of the month.

Touched put his arm round me and led me to one side.

"Ok, mate, do you trust me to divvy up?" he asked, his cold, greedy eyes waiting for an answer.

What choice did I have?

"Of course, Touched."

"Good lad. One thing about me, I'm honest, never cheated a mate in me life. Pal of mine will buy the stash for eighty percent of cost. He'll wash it in one of the casinos in New Hampshire. We'll lose a fifth but still, it's going to be a good score," Touched said.

I knew what that meant. After the "washing" and the divvying up, Touched was going to steal about half the money for himself.

Gerry dragged me away from Touched's claws.

"Come on inside. We're sitting down to dinner and then we're all going to go to the beach. We've had the maid make up your room in the guesthouse, you'll be living here now, not in that shithole," Gerry said.

"Thank you very much, but my stuff is over at—"

"It's already been brought over. You're one of us now, Sean. Part of the family. Now come on in, Natalia has made the most amazing dinner for us and Kit has been working on a pie."

I walked inside the house.

"Kit, you give him a quick tour, but it has to be quick, we're sitting down to dinner in five minutes."

Kit breezed me through the house. All eleven bedrooms, six bathrooms, observation deck, TV room, lounge, and finally dining room. It was actually worse than I was expecting, the McCaghans combining their talents to create a bad-taste masterpiece. Sonia, who seemed to have an old-money sophistication about her, was either colorblind or had decided that decor was not a place to fight her battles.

The paint scheme was gold, green, and silver. The carpets three-inch-thick white shag on which zebra-patterned throw rugs had been placed for contrast. No window was free of lace curtains, taffeta bows, ivy, and other elaborate treatments. Entire rooms were filled with white leather furniture, pictures of dirty gamins, kittens, and puppies. They had delicate and unfunctional chairs that you wouldn't dare touch, never mind use, and the beds were huge puffy affairs on which stuffed animals slept in cozy proximity. It also wasn't unusual to find antique porcelain dolls sitting on chairs, gazing out to sea with creepy eyes. No books anywhere but the coffee tables displayed copies of *Architectural Digest*, *New England Home*, and *France Sud*. Gerry had also invested in a great store of contemporary Irish art. The usual tat: the stony fields of the Burren, rain in the Mourne Mountains, sheep in the Antrim Plateau, deserted beaches in Donegal, gap-toothed children sitting in rowboats. Dozens of these artworks, in lovely antique gilt frames and placed seemingly at random all over the house.

The whole thing would have turned the stomach of a weaker man, but fortunately I was made of sterner stuff.

Kit's room was the only sane one in the house and even that was a bit overboard. She had painted the walls black, hung a massive Indian shawl from her ceiling, and put up several askew posters proclaiming her loyalty to The Cure, Nick Cave, and, alas, Poison. There were statues of the Buddha, Ganesh, and that scary deity with swords and lots of legs.

"Nice," I said.

She brought me downstairs to the dining room, which was relatively subdued and dominated anyway by a spectacular view of the Atlantic coast: the curve of Plum Island and Cape Ann stretching to the south, New Hampshire and Maine to the north.

"Amazing view," I said to Gerry.

"Can you believe they only had a tiny window in this room before we bought it? I knocked out the wall and stuck in support columns. Best view in PI."

Sonia showed me to my place next to Kit and facing the ocean. The sun had set, so the sea had become a bewitching shade of lavender and it would have been perfect had I not been sitting opposite Jackie, who looked as if he'd fallen off a bus. Something that gave me a tremendous and childish feeling of satisfaction. Two black eyes, a cut chin, a cut lip, bruises on his cheeks.

"Goodness, Jackie, are you ok? Kit told me you're thinking of suing the End of the State, because something fell on you? Is that right?"

"Aye," he said sourly and sipped from a Waterford crystal glass that was filled with fizzy beer.

Touched sat next to Jackie. Gerry sat at one end of the table, Sonia at the other. Seamus, Touched explained, was not feeling well and had gone next door to the guesthouse for a wee lie down.

There were two Mexican servants who brought in several bottles of expensive white wine and a formal dinner of soup, lobster, another fish course, and finally lamb. Although it seemed that their command of English was not particularly impressive, I could see that we were not to allude to this afternoon's events except in the most oblique of terms.

Gerry, though, was in rare form and pontificated on international politics, domestic politics, and baseball. Touched contradicted him here and there and Sonia was the voice of reason. Or if not reason exactly, at least of more informed comment than either of the other two. Jackie remained sullen for most of the meal and before the dessert came, asked permission to excuse himself from the table.

"Gerry, do you mind if I leave? The tide marker is giving me the heave-ho," he said.

"No, of course not, we'll all be joining you later. Off you go, Jackie," Gerry said.

Jackie stood and it was then that I noticed he was wearing board shorts and wet-suit booties. He ran to the guesthouse next door and appeared on the dunes in front of the house wearing an ankle strap and black rash guard, and carrying a surfboard.

"What was he talking about? The tide marker?" I asked Kit.

"That thing on the wall," she said, pointing at a clock with LOW and HIGH where the twelve and six should be.

"So what does that mean?" I asked.

"Well, if you look, the arrow is almost into the low, so that means for the next few hours surfing conditions will be pretty close to perfect on the Plum Island beach break."

"Jackie surfs?"

"Yeah, he's very good. He had an amateur tryout at Montauk a few weeks ago. He was seventh out of about forty or fifty. We all surf, well, me and Jackie do. Jamie as well, before he ran away. But Daddy and Sonia both bodyboard."

"I love the ocean," Gerry said. "I love the feeling of being in the ocean."

Sonia nodded in agreement.

"It's really the best feature of living on Plum Island," Sonia said. "It can be such a hassle, sometimes the bridge is closed and I don't know if you've noticed this, Sean, but there can be a lot of insects. . . ."

"No."

"Well, that's the downside but the upside is a beautiful unspoiled beach, and you should see what it's like in the wildlife refuge, it's America before the white man came and wrecked the place," Sonia continued.

"I'll have to check it out," I said, trying to sound sincere.

"Oh, it's a family rule, if you live in this house, you have to do something in water," Gerry insisted.

"Even made me boogie board and I hate the fucking stuff,"

Touched said.

I turned to Kit.

"Where did Jackie learn to surf? He's a goddamn Mick. We don't surf. Charley don't surf. Micks don't surf. That's it."

"Oh no, he's from Sligo, that's a big undiscovered surfing mecca. Amazing breaks out there, completely unspoiled. He's very good," she said with admiration.

Many a good pejorative Yeats line about the eejits from Sligo but Sean wouldn't know them.

"So how come you're not going out there with him?" I said, trying to keep the sneer out of my voice.

"Oh, it's too gnarly at the moment, I need the really low tide. But Jackie's good enough to surf it right now."

Something remarkably like jealousy was growing in my breast and Gerry mercifully changed the subject to the island itself.

"It's all changed, Sean. Plum Island used to be very poor. Irish crab, lobster, and clam men eking out a desperate living on a bleak spit of sand south of the Merrimack River. Thoreau once called the dunes of PI the 'most desolate walk in New England.' And in the book *Albion's Seed* . . . well, anyway, I'm growing prolix, but things are quite different now. Boston spreads her influence north and more people have begun commuting into the city using the highway or Route 1."

"The real boom is going to start once the light rail hub's finished in Newburyport, the train taking you to North Station in downtown Boston in less than an hour," Sonia added.

"Oh yes, Sean, I could see all this a couple of years ago when we moved. What was once an unwholesome spot for poor crabbers and a couple of summer houses is now valuable real estate. Once we get water and sewage lines here it's going to be paradise itself."

When the meal was over, we were going to eat a rhubarb tart that Kit had made early this morning, refrigerated, and then immediately popped in the oven the moment we'd come back. Bank robber, wannabe revolutionary, goth girl, and rhubarb tart maker—obviously a Renaissance woman.

She went to get it and a brief moment later there was a

scream from the kitchen. She came back into the dining room with a furious expression on her face.

"Daddy, did you eat all the ice cream? You know we have to have it with vanilla ice cream because it's the perfect combination. You know I put that ice cream to one side, because I was saving it," she said furiously.

"I took it," Touched lied, saving Gerry's bacon. "Sorry about that, Kit."

"Well, we can't not have ice cream," she said, huffing.

"I'll go to White Farms and get some more," Touched said.

Kit shook her head.

"No, they don't do good vanilla. I'll have to go to Grandma's in Newburyport. Anyone come with me?"

"I'll go," I said, seizing the opportunity.

She ran upstairs to get her car keys and her sunglasses. Touched led me out the back onto the porch. He reached in his pocket and brought out a huge wad of twenty-dollar bills and gave it to me.

"Your cut. Five grand," Touched said.

"For me?" I asked.

"For you, me old mucker. A fifth to my laundryman, five percent to the general fund, and the rest between the four of us. Equal shares, too, you, me, Kit, and Seamus, no finder's fee for me or anything," Touched said without a trace of a lie in that cold, unemotional face.

"Cheers, mate," I said happily, knowing now that he must have pocketed at least twenty thousand for himself.

"Nay probs, Sean boy, now don't go crazy, flashing it about. Rainy day and all that," Touched said in what was about as close to a speech on fiscal prudence as I was likely to get.

"Anyway, that should keep you in eggs. Ok, I have things to do, wee thing to scout tonight, down at the National Guard, shit, shouldn't have said that. Wipe that from your mind. It's the next wee op we might be going on, don't worry about it. Anyway, I'll be gone when you get back. You just look after yourself, don't let that young lady talk you into risking your life on a bloody tree in the middle of the bloody ocean."

"I won't."

Kit appeared, grabbed me.

"We've got to get the ice cream before the pie cools," Kit said.

She led me to the four-car garage and got in a pink Volkswagen Bug that had Greenpeace and WWF stickers on the back windshield. Hardly the vehicle of a committed terrorist. Maybe the signs of complexity in her character.

We drove into Newburyport and I let Kit chat about surfing and music. She wanted to talk about anything, just not what had happened that day, which was fine by me. She blabbed away and I stole looks at her and was a good listener. As we pulled into State Street she scanned for parking and I spotted the All Things Brit store.

"Kit, have you ever tried clotted cream? It's fantastic, it would go really well on the rhubarb tart. It's an English thing. I'll bet we could get some at that British food store."

"But I was going to get ice cream."

"We can get both. It'll be a real treat. Your da will love it and if you want to be really decadent, you can even put it on the ice cream."

Kit nodded and luckily found a parking spot right in front of All Things Brit, which was only a block from the ice-cream store.

"I'll check out this cream of yours, and then we'll have to dash to Grandma's. I mean, look, the line is out into the street."

All Things Brit was just closing down for the night. The woman who ran it was wearing a frumpy orange and brown floral dress and a huge grin.

"I'm just closing up, can I help you darlings at all?" she asked happily.

"Yes, we'd like some clotted cream, please," Kit said.

"Certainly, my dear, and can I just say that you're the prettiest girl we've had in here all day," Samantha said.

I rolled my eyes behind Kit's head. Samantha's face was transparent with delight.

"We have a full selection in the refrigerator by the door," Samantha said.

Kit walked over to look.

"Oooh, this does look good, we'll get have to get some for everyone," Kit said.

"Kit, I know which ones to get, I'll pick them out, you run and get on line for the ice cream and I'll meet you up there," I said.

"You don't mind paying?"

"Not at all," I said. "I'm flush at the moment."

Kit smiled and dashed outside to join the line at Grandma's.

There were no other customers in the shop but someone could come in at any minute. I knew I would have to speak fast.

"I'm in," I said.

"To the cell?"

I nodded.

"Congratulations," she said with a condescending grin that I didn't like at all.

"It's as I've said, Samantha, it's a bit of a shambles. I think they're falling apart. They've had three defections altogether. That Mike guy, someone called O'Neill, and a kid called Jamie. They've been decimated by the assassination attempt on Gerry. Don't think the IRA isn't smart, because they are. The psychological effect of that hit has paid dividends. They're running. They're running scared and I don't think they're going to do anything major at all. They're all talk."

"So who's left in the group?"

"The total group is just Sonia and Gerry, Touched, Jackie, Kit, Seamus, and me. That's it. Sonia's no player, though, and Kit is just a wee girl and Seamus has been knocking back two bottles of vodka a day since the hit in Revere. So I think this whole goddamn mission has been a waste of time. Everyone has basically got the IRA's message and they're not going to do anything. I think you can let me go back to Chicago with a handshake for a job well done."

Samantha looked at me.

"What else?"

I sighed.

My hand was on the counter. She put hers on top.

"There's something you're not telling me," she said.

"It's really nothing."

"What is it?"

"Well, it's very stupid, you might have heard about it on the radio. That bank robbery in New Hampshire. That was us."

Samantha's eyebrows raised.

"It's not what you think. God knows, Gerry doesn't need the money, it was just a test, to see if I was up to it."

"Was Gerry involved?"

"No."

"Gerry's the one we want."

"I know."

Samantha smiled.

"I'll tell you what. Why don't we give it a couple of weeks. If it doesn't look like they're going to do anything—if, as you think, they are running scared—I'll pull you out. We'll see. Who was in on the robbery?"

"Touched, Kit, me, and Seamus."

"Hmmm. I'd take three convictions for armed robbery and consider this a successful operation. We might even agree to suspend Kit's sentence if Gerry would return to Northern Ireland to stand trial. He might do that to keep his daughter out of jail. What do you think?"

"No, Kit waited in the car. She wasn't involved at all. You can't arrest her for anything," I lied, firmly.

"Of course we can, she's an accessory. Anyway. You've done well. I'll check out the robbery to see if the police have any leads. We might have to get the locals to slow-play if you left any clues. And I hope you're right, I hope they're not trying anything. But you'll have to tell me the truth. If they are planning something big, we've got to know."

"But if not, I'm out. Right?"

"Right."

Kit came back in with the ice cream.

"What's keeping you?" she asked.

Samantha hurriedly removed her hand from mine.

I don't know if Kit saw but if she did, she didn't think

anything of it. We drove home, distributed the ice cream, and as she had predicted the combination of rhubarb and vanilla was close to perfect. . . .

An hour later.

Kit and me sitting on the dunes. Gerry and Sonia body boarding on the beach break. Sonia had changed into a neat one-piece swimsuit that showed off her lithe body and long legs. Gerry, unfortunately, was also showing off his body, in a pair of size 48 board shorts.

Touched was off doing something secretive that involved the Massachusetts National Guard and Seamus was sleeping away his hangover.

Kit had changed into a black Body Glove one-piece wet suit and was resting her feet on a surfboard that said "Hello Kitty" above an anime cat.

There were about a dozen surfers on the water and at least twenty or thirty kids and older people body or boogie boarding on the breakers. Amazingly, Gerry was one of them. Amazing and a bit terrifying. A wave could easily have swept him up and plonked him down on some poor unsuspecting five-year-old.

"How long has your dad been into that?" I asked Kit.

"Since we moved here from Boston."

"How long ago was that?"

"Since my mom died."

"It looks like fun."

"Family that surfs together stays together."

We sat and watched her da and Sonia and then she pointed out Jackie on the beach break. Of all the surfers there, he was catching the most waves. He really was very good.

"Jackie is definitely the best one there," I said generously.

She turned to me and I caught her looking at my prosthetic foot.

"Come on, let me show you some moves," she said.

"It looks easy in theory," I said.

"It's not that hard."

I lay back in the sand.

"Maybe another time. For now I just want to be mellow, sit

down, enjoy the evening."

Kit nodded. "We got the rest of the summer to learn to surf and at least into October. If you're wearing a wet suit nobody would even notice your, uh . . ."

"My foot. You can say it, I don't give a shit."

She smiled.

"Hey, I was thinking, you know what we're a bit like today?" she said after a moment's pause.

"What?"

"You ever see that movie *Point Break*?" she asked.

"No, I don't go to the movies much."

"You haven't seen it? I thought everybody had seen that movie."

"Is Lee Marvin in it?"

"Who's Lee Marvin?"

"Ok, I guess he's not in it. So, ok then, I haven't seen it."

"It's Keanu Reeves. Have you at least heard of him?"

"Of course."

"It's like us, it's about this gang of bank robbers who go surfing. And look at us, we robbed a bank today and now we're going surfing," Kit said with obvious pleasure at the intersection of celluloid and reality. I smiled.

"Listen, if you want to get into the water to complete the similarity, don't let me stop you, I'm fine here," I said.

"I'll go in a minute," Kit said. "I'll sit beside you for a little bit more. Maybe encourage you to body board at least."

I shook my head.

"Honestly, I'm not going in. I'm no Keanu Reeves."

She laughed.

"You wouldn't want to be anyway. He was the bad guy, well sort of, he played this undercover FBI agent who wants to stop them robbing all the banks. . . ."

Kit's talk continued for at least another two or three sentences, but I didn't hear a goddamn word. The blood had chilled in my veins and I was trying not to show it.

"Ok?" she asked finally.

"Yeah. Sure."

I had obviously agreed to her departure. She got up,

grabbed her board, said hi to Gerry and Sonia, and paddled out into the water.

FBI agent. Jesus. Out of the mouths of babes.

Kit sat in the water for a long time and finally took a wave. Jackie had also selected the same wave. He cut back and forth several times and even attempted a 360. Kit just rode it sedately into shore.

She ran back up the beach.

"See how easy it is?" she said, sheer joy making her look cool and confident and happy. Big contrast from earlier in the day.

I nodded. She sat down on the sand. The sun had long disappeared over the salt marsh and the sky behind us was a burnt *amarillo*. And in front, from Cape Ann all the way up to Canada, a pink haze dissolving into black.

Kit leaned back beside me and we sat together watching a fleet of fishing boats from Gloucester heading up to the Grand Banks.

Beautiful.

The still Atlantic. The endless shore. Golden light disappearing beyond the Earth's curve. The sea breeze tousled her hair and calmed me and I imagined us out in that blue swell. Dissolving, becoming part of all that space.

My fingers went down into the wet sand.

Kit's were there too. The darkening sky. Birds. The tide coming in.

Water lapping at our ankles.

Her fingers touching mine. She was beautiful and young and I liked her. She had a depth that she let no one see. Not Jackie, not her dad.

She was in that stage of transition from teenager to woman.

She was breaking out of the mold she'd been in for years and anything was possible. College, the pro surf world, or small-time terrorism.

She reminded me of Bridget. Bridget in the half minute after she found out I was alive and as she was deciding that she was going to have to kill me.

I looked at her.

Could Kit kill me?

Could I kill her?

Before the week was out, I'd know the answer to both those questions.

7: DEATH ON THE PARKER RIVER

Gray wind. Green water. A vesper of sound on the cadence of the bog. Rose petals, seraphim, Levantine cotton sheets. The ceiling, a facsimile of a busy part of the Sistine.

I slip outside.

Fog rolling in lazy tongues, the dead sound of a buoy bell, and the ocean hidden, silent, pretending to be benign.

I rub my face and look at the sky.

It unnerves me.

There's an ashen silver aftertaste on the horizon as if the morning has come reluctantly out of the east, hungover, snarled in a slabber of ugly clouds. There's hardly any sun. Only a smudge behind the clouds over Cape Ann. Chilly, ponderable, empty of life and color. A cicatrice covering old wounds.

Something bad is going to happen today.

Aye.

I lean on the balcony rail. My hand comes up coated with dew.

A night of no moon and no dreams. No saltwater kisses from cool lips. A fall into the black pit and out again.

I yawn and look down at the dunes. Dogs, speed walkers, joggers. And Jackie carrying his surfboard with grim determination. Carrying two surfboards.

And of course, a moment later, coming from the big house,

Kit in full wet suit and bare feet. They meet, kiss, and walk along the shore to the point where the waves are breaking over the reef.

I go back inside and grab a cup of coffee that has brewed itself in the automatic percolator. I walk out onto the balcony again. This is the only one of the guesthouse rooms that has a balcony. I suppose it's because I'm the flavor of the month, the beamish boy.

It's early. Six in the morning, but I have slept well. My first decent night's sleep in a fortnight, since before the riot began in Spain. The air-conditioning chilling the room down to a lovely fifty-eight degrees, the bed very comfortable, and for once, my blood not food for biting flies.

I sip the coffee and watch the clouds break up and the sun rise and creep over the vortex of wooden structures that make up the landscape here. A few big houses, a beachside café, a bait-and-tackle shop, a lobster bar.

I edge round the dewy wooden balcony, one hand on the guardrail and one hand holding my coffee. I take another sip of joe and almost wave to a woman in the mansion opposite who's got a glimpse of me through her upstairs bathroom window. She pulls down her blind before I can do anything, a violated look on her face. Impossible to tell through the dirty glass if she was in her nightclothes or not.

On the roof of the same house they have constructed a kind of shanty hut, which when I look closer is an observatory with a telescope peeking out of a metal dome. After a time a man comes out of the gap in the metal that serves as the observatory's door. He's so knackered from a night's stargazing that I'm convinced for a moment that he's going to plummet to his death right before my eyes. But gradually he gets his act together and finds the outside stairs to the floor below.

I finish the coffee and go to the en suite loo, pee, brush my teeth, and put a dressing gown over my shorts and T-shirt. The robe is a plush white terry-cloth job with a gold-leaf monogram that says "G.McC." And again it occurs to me that Gerry must be bloody loaded.

I'm about to wonder what I do next when I notice that a

note has been pushed under the door.

I pick it up, read it:

"*Dux femina facti*. Sonia requests our presence at breakfast at seven o'clock sharp. Be there, in casual attire. —Gerry."

I have no idea what the Latin means but I find it extremely irritating. Who is he trying to kid? He's not a Yankee shipping magnate brought up on Homer, Virgil, and Emerson, he's a fucking scumbag killer from Belfast who got kicked out and somehow lucked himself into becoming a bloody multimillionaire in America.

"Aye, well, watch out, mate, I'm the likely lad who'll bring you down. You and your playing-both-ends minx of a daughter," I mutter, angry at her, too.

A maid shows me the inside passage from the guesthouse to the main house and I quickly find the kitchen.

Seamus, Touched, Gerry, and Sonia are sitting at a large oak table eating sausages, waffles, and blueberry pancakes. Everyone is dressed. Seamus and Touched in T-shirts, Gerry in a huge white jacket, white shirt, and—God save us—white cravat.

It's hard to believe that these happy people are killers. Everything is soft. It's either a diversion or a reinvention. Whatever it is, it gives me the creeps.

Gerry in the middle of an explanation about something.

"Ok, now listen to this. Are you listening, gentlemen? If you bring your forefingers very close in front of your eyes, as close as you can without them touching, and you hold your hands close to a bulb or a lamp, you can actually see the light refract its way around your fingertips and interference patterns emerge. Try it. At dawn on the grassy steppes of Tuva they call this the 'Hun Huur Tu.'"

Everyone begins holding his fingers up to the sunlight streaming in through the window. Then Gerry notices me.

"Ah my boy, our new warrior, another one of the few, sit, sit, did you sleep well? Sit, have some coffee and pancakes, Sonia made them and they are the finest you will ever taste on this or any other world."

Oh Jesus, I think to myself, he's talking like a pompous ass again. Does he think he's Sydney fucking Greenstreet?

I sit down. Pour myself a glass of orange juice.

"You're right, I can see little black lines between my fingers. You are full of information, Gerry," Touched says, but there's no way I'm going to take the bait and ask what the hell they are talking about.

I fill my plate with Belgian waffles, deliberately ignoring the pancakes.

"Did you sleep well, Sean?" Sonia asks.

"Fantastic, thank you. Best sleep since coming to America," I tell her.

"I'm so pleased. We put you in Jamie's old room. It has the balcony," she says.

"Aye, thank you, it is a nice room. I saw the sunrise from the balcony. It was lovely," I say.

"No, not such a nice sunrise today, Sean, the fog ruined it a bit, but you'll see wonderful sunrises as the summer winds down and the autumn comes and the sun moves a little higher in latitude," Gerry says.

"I'll look forward to it," I tell him and take a bit of sausage and maple syrup. Touched and Seamus get into a conversation about car mechanics, and bored by this, Gerry picks up a stack of newspapers.

"Help yourself to a paper," he says to me. "We get the *Globe*, the *Times*, and the *Journal*."

"Uh, no thanks, I don't like to face bad news until I've got some food in me belly."

"Very wise," he says.

Sonia's been looking at me funny. I smile at her. Sip coffee and OJ and eat the fantastic grub. Catch her eye again.

"Sean," she begins with embarrassment, "I couldn't help but notice last night, on the beach and now this morning, um, I hope you don't think I'm being rude, but your left foot . . ."

"Oh yeah, that . . ."

"Did you lose that in the Troubles in Belfast?" she asks sincerely.

I flash up her bio in my head. Forty. Politics or history professor at UNH. One of those leftie it's-all-the-fault-of-dead-white-guy types. The sort that used to screw Black Panthers and have posters of Che. Have to check but I bet her father is a general or an admiral or the CEO of the Ford Motor Company. I don't know what she thinks life is like in Ulster, but she probably imagines it as something akin to apartheid South Africa or the Jim Crow South. It's tempting for me to say that I lost my foot to a British plastic bullet but I've already spun Kit the line about the motorbike accident.

"Bad motorcycle accident when I was a kid. My fault. Going too fast."

"I am so sorry to hear it," she replies sweetly, and her smile makes me soften to her immediately.

"I'm over it," I tell her.

"Good, and I am relieved it wasn't in the armed struggle, you would no doubt, by now, be consumed with hate," she says, her accent becoming a little more obvious as the passion rises in her voice. Patrician, boarding school, Seven Sisters, yachting in Newport, yet with a foreign tilt. Maybe a couple of years in the bloody Sorbonne. Although you'd think after a year living with Touched she'd be cursing like a trooper, smoking like a chimney, wearing green, dropping folksy remarks about the wee people, and swearing by Irish coffee as a nostrum against colds, stomach upset, and other ills.

"Nah, just me falling off me bike," I say. "Is that a bit of a foreign accent you have there?"

Sonia smiles, pleased, but before she can answer Touched cuts her off.

"Sean," he mutters, staring at me with interest.

"What?"

"Let's see your foot," he says.

Without self-consciousness I lift it onto the table.

"Does that mean you can't run or lift heavy things or anything like that?" Touched asks with a bit of concern.

"Nope," I say, and then ignoring Touched, "So, Sonia, have you been over to Ireland ever?"

"I have yet to visit, but I am passionately engaged in the struggle for you to free your homeland from the imperialists."

Oh boy, here it comes, I say to myself with some

prescience.

"Yes, Sean. It is a tragedy. The tragedy of the green. Since Elizabeth the Bloody sent the English into your country, it has been four hundred years of oppression and terror."

Gerry cannot let his wife fall into doctrinal error and he takes up the conversation:

"Sean, as you probably know, the English came over with Strongbow, so it's eight hundred years of oppression."

And now Touched, seeing this an opportunity to propagandize, throws in his two cents:

"Eight hundred years, Sean. That's why we have to fight the stubborn English-loving Protestants of Ulster who still won't permit their Catholic brothers in the Six Counties to join with their fellow Irishmen in the South. We have repeatedly told them we would make them welcome and we even put the Orange Order's color on our own national flag. But they're different from us, Sean. They have no real culture or sense of pride. They've had their chance to be convinced by reason, but neither they nor their masters in London will listen to reason. That's why it's the time for force, Sean. The time for force."

My smile fixes and I nod but actually I couldn't care less if Northern Ireland was part of the Republic of Ireland or Britain or the People's Republic of fucking China. I hadn't lived there for six years and every year that passed I found it harder and harder to give a shit. And Touched was wrong. I've met plenty of Protestants and Catholics and they're so alike that the differences between them have become ridiculously exaggerated. Freud, I think, calls it the narcissism of the small difference. Ethnically, culturally, and even spiritually, they're the same bloody people. Not that you could convince these eejits.

I've zoned out for a minute and when I zone back in I find that they're looking at me, waiting.

"Sorry, what was that?" I ask.

"Jesus, get some coffee in ya. Pay attention. I was just saying, Sean, that it's like history was put on hold for fifty years. Sonia here doesn't realize that in the 1970s a bunch of men arose in the North with the vision of Michael Collins. Us. Me and Gerry, a new generation. Our generation. The IRA. We decided to use force against the might of the British Empire. Have to. Brits don't understand anything else. People say, 'What about India?' Well, I say, 'What about Palestine in '47?' Eh?" Touched says, triumphantly.

"Didn't the IRA kill Michael Collins?" I ask naively.

Touched starts mumbling some lame reply while I take a good look at Sonia. Perhaps the smartest person in the room. Certainly if the bios were correct the only one of us who had been to university. How exactly had she ended up falling for this nonsense? How had she met Gerry in the first place?

"How did you meet Gerry?" I ask her.

She laughs.

"We met at an Ireland-Quebec friendship dinner in Boston," she says, a surprising and surprisingly boring answer.

"I never heard of such a thing."

"It is part of the small-nations commerce initiative that the Boston Chamber of Commerce ran last year. I am in the Chamber of Commerce and my mother was from Quebec," she says, except that she pronounces it *Kaybeck*.

"Are there a lot of similarities between Quebec and Ireland?" I ask and steel myself for the floodgates to open, which of course they do.

"Quebec, like Ireland, is oppressed by a tyrannous neighboring culture. Our voice has been drowned out. A free Quebec would be a bastion of socialism, liberty, and idealism in North America, just as a free socialist Ireland would be the ideal counterweight to imperialist England. This is something you don't know, Touched, but the Quebec people . . ."

I cease to listen. One of my attributes. In my book, Quebec's only interesting because it's a quirky, French, Catholic part of Canada. If Quebec were ever independent it would be a dreary, white, monoglot, Catholic country. Probably turn fascist in a decade. Still, it decides me. She's not the smartest person in the room. Not her, not Touched, not Gerry, certainly not Seamus. Dangerous, yes, but they weren't going to out-think me. Her lips stop moving, she has finished her lecture.

"Vive le Québec libre," I say. It makes her smile.

"One day, and I hope to see it, all small nations will be free. Ireland was the first of the twentieth century's great liberation movements to succeed, an inspiration for all of us," Sonia says. Her face is flushed and she's out of breath. Her chest heaving in and out. And suddenly she doesn't look at all unattractive. The top button of her sweater has come undone and you can see the outline of her very pale breasts. Her lips are glistening a little in the light and her . . . Jesus, get a grip, Michael, your life's too complicated by women already.

I take a large mug of coffee, and through the enormous kitchen window I see Kit and Jackie coming back, wet, sandy, happy, arm in arm.

They clean the sand off their feet, grab towels, and join us at breakfast.

"How was the surfing?" Gerry asks, giving Kit a hug.

"Well, at first I wasn't stoked at all because it was, like, a little gnarly out there. But Jackie, like, totally rocked, you should have seen him, and so I followed him and took a few and it was good," she says excitedly.

"It was good," Jackie says, stepping onto the deck to strip off his wet suit and pulling on a T-shirt over his boxers. His bruises are healing nicely, and wet, tanned, and sober, he almost looks quite the handsome little surfer boy. The newcomers sit.

"Have you seen much of America so far, Sean?" Sonia asks.

"No, not really, flew into New York, saw a bit of that and then I came up to Boston looking for work, hardly seen any of the country."

"And speaking of accents, sometimes it's almost as if you sound a bit American," Sonia says without suspicion. But still it sets the alarm bells ringing. It's something I'm aware of. I've been trying to fight against it but after five years living in America, of course I had lost some of my Irish accent and colloquialisms. Regardless, I'd have to damp that fire immediately.

"Yeah, I pick up accents very quickly, it's one of my failings. You should have heard me when I lived in London. I was talking like Mick Jagger after a few months. I suppose it's a symptom of a weak personality. I'm definitely a follower not a leader," I mutter with a touch of meekness and embarrassment.

Gerry nods wisely.

"Don't worry about that," he says. "Can't have too many leaders, Sean. Every group needs followers. Men who will obey and do their duty. In any case, it's nothing to be ashamed of—you, me, Touched, and Jackie all came from the Old Country originally and only Touched has preserved the exact timbre of his north Antrim dialect. He won't be swayed by anyone."

Gerry laughs. Sonia looks at him with frustration.

"I've forgotten what I was going to say. Oh yes, now I remember. All I wanted to say is that if he hasn't seen much of America we should show him some things. We'll have to drive out to the Cape, although I know you hate the Cape, but it doesn't matter and we'll have to go there and up to the cabin in Maine, or better yet, Nantucket."

"Count me out. I certainly do not fancy an autumnal ferry ride across the choppy water to Nantucket. But certainly next month, my dear, we will have to go to Salem," Gerry says.

"What's in Salem?" I ask innocently.

"It's where they live on *Days of Our Lives,*" Jackie contributes. "Everything happens there."

Gerry frowns at him and looks at me significantly as if to say "Can you believe he is seeing my daughter?"

"Think they mean Salem, the witch place," I say.

Gerry shows his gleaming teeth, as disarming as Mack the Knife's pearly whites.

"Salem has a wonderful Halloween parade. It's very scary. Kit used to be afraid to go, didn't you, Kit?" Gerry says, making a ghostly groan.

"I thought there were no witches; wasn't the whole thing a huge mistake?" I ask.

Sonia nods at me in agreement.

"It's in very poor taste. If you think about it, it's the site of an awful massacre of innocents. It would be like holding a jokey parade to remember Auschwitz. I, for one, certainly wouldn't go there," Sonia says, huffing at Gerry for pooh-poohing the Nantucket idea.

Gerry knows he has to make amends.

"The cabin then. It's lovely this time of year."

"Everything is nice about it, except the name," Sonia replies, not completely won over.

"How many times do I have to tell you? It wasn't my doing. That's the real name of the actual place," Gerry says defensively and looks at me with an impish grin.

"Oh, the fucking suspense," I almost say sarcastically but instead: "What is the name?"

"The Dead Yard," Gerry announces with fiendish satisfaction.

"Unusual," I add, playing along.

"It used to be railway land. On the old Maine-Boston Atlantic line. And at certain points along the tracks they needed a clearing to put damaged or unused rail cars, so they'd just fell a big chunk of forest and leave the cars there in what they called a 'dead yard.' Of course, the train tracks are long gone now. Sad. Passenger trains don't go to Maine at all now. You might have noticed the old ruined rail bridge over the Merrimack in downtown Newburyport."

"I hadn't noticed," I say quickly before Gerry can trot out *sic transit gloria mundi*. "But I have to agree with you, Mr. McCaghan, that it's a real shame to see railways disappearing."

Touched grunts, and I'm expecting an atypical contradiction of Gerry but instead he says: "If you knew your Civil War history, Sean, you'd know that the Dead Yard was also a nickname for an infamous Southern prison."

Gerry nods knowledgeably, but mercifully, before Touched can launch into a description of the horrors of Andersonville, the maid comes in to clear the table.

Touched checks his watch and gives Gerry a look.

Gerry stands, pats his ample belly.

"Well, folks, if you'll excuse me, I have a wee bit of business to attend to, *tempus fugit*. I have to travel up to Portsmouth."

He gives Sonia a kiss and goes upstairs.

"I'll take a shower," Jackie says.

"Jackie, upstairs, Gerry's den, ten minutes, ok?" Touched says.

Jackie nods and excuses himself from the table.

Touched looks at Kit.

"Kit, you're going to help your dad today? Is that right?" he says in a slightly clandestine tone. Whether he's unwilling to openly discuss things in front of me or the maid I'm not sure, but he's certainly holding back something.

"What are you saying, Touched? I should hurry up?"

"Love, I wouldn't presume to tell you what to do, but you don't want to keep your da waiting, do ya?"

Kit says nothing, walks slowly from the table and when she's round the corner, bolts up the stairs. Sonia goes into the kitchen and Touched looks at me with a conspiratorial smile.

"Listen, Sean, you came about the right time. Now you're here we can do a few more things of an operational nature. We can progress a wee bit faster."

"Why? Is there something on for today?"

"There is, as a matter of fact. Can't discuss it here. Now go back to the guesthouse, shower, shave, brush your teeth, and join me and Seamus in Gerry's den ASAP. Ok?"

"Ok."

"And next time you come for breakfast, change out of your jammies, it's bad fucking form, mate."

❖   ❖   ❖

The den was in a round tower constructed in a corner of the house facing the ocean. This was where Gerry kept his private papers and conducted his most secret meetings. This, apparently, was also where he kept his books. *Expand Your Word Power, Teach Yourself French, Teach Yourself Irish, 100 Latin Aphorisms Everyone Should Know.* Titles like these showed where Gerry's florid language came from and also revealed perhaps why he was doing it. He was trying to impress his half Quebecois new bride. Gerry was about fifteen years older than her and from a different class, but he needn't have bothered with any of this shite. I could tell that Sonia loved him and no matter what happened she wasn't going to be the weak link. Her attraction to Gerry was not physical nor intellectual, but rather, romantic. Gerry was a poet of violence, a crusader for his oppressed people, a bane for the wicked oppressor. Though if she was into Byronic freedom fighters surely my dodgy foot made me a better match.

The maid had brought up a pot of tea and chocolate biscuits and then discreetly disappeared down the stairs. In Gerry's home there seemed to be two maids and a cook, all Mexican, all quiet and unobtrusive. Exactly the type that might prove very fruitful and productive if it ever came down to prosecutions. Servants always know a hell of a lot more than people give them credit for and they'd either be loyal right to the bitter end or have a host of resentments that they'd like to pay back in kind, possibly in a court of law.

Touched noticed that I was looking at a little green toolbox on Gerry's desk.

"Is that your screwdriver set?" I asked.

Touched grinned as if I'd just made a faux pas.

"Something like that," he said, took the toolkit, and stuck it in a drawer.

He rummaged in the same drawer and found a couple of Gerry's cigars wrapped in silver tubes.

"Havana Churchills, very good," he said and offered us a smoke.

Each of us declined, so he lit one only for himself. Seamus, myself, Jackie relaxing in leather chairs while Touched puffed his cigar and explained the op.

As usual with this talky crew, he outlined his grander theory first. Real chatty bastards, the lot of them. Touched blew out a smoke ring and began his spiel:

"I suppose you all want to know where Gerry and me plan to go now we've had a bit of a setback. Well, while you lads have been relaxing, we've been out doing work. As you may have realized, the IRA cease-fire has sowed chaos not just for us but for the Ra, too, and its partnership organizations. Been a bad few weeks. Very bad. But the silver lining is that things are starting to turn round now. I've made a few contacts with a group calling itself Real IRA, which is based in Dundalk under the command of a good friend of ours, Ruari O'Lughdagh. And I've also had feelers from a group called Continuity IRA, which I don't know too much about, but I'll make it a priority to find out. We're not necessarily looking for an umbrella group but it would certainly help us out, especially in these times. Now to impress those boys, we'll have to get cracking, we'll have to do some jobs. Don't worry, Sean, I see your eyes widening. Gerry and I have about thirty years experience between us and although you boys have none, if you're willing to learn, we're willing to teach ya."

During this entire speech, Jackie had been giving me the evil eye. It annoyed me; I thought I'd already put that wee skitter in his place.

"Jackie, stop looking at me, you'll wear your fucking eyes out," I told him.

"Fuck you, Sean" was his witty comeback.

"Go to hell," I retorted.

Touched had been interrupted. Something that drove him apoplectic. He stood, pointed his finger at us.

"You two better cut it out, especially you, Sean, you're still on probation here and Jackie is your superior, and you'll do what he says. You're going on a fucking op tonight and if you can't handle taking orders you can go home right now," Touched shouted furiously.

"Sorry, Touched," I said, trying not to see Jackie's look of triumph.

"You will be bloody sorry. Getting too big for your boots and you're here one bloody day. Dial it back, mate, dial it back a lot."

"Won't happen again, Touched," I said.

To make himself more comfortable, Touched took the revolver out of his trouser pocket and placed it on the table. As an intimidation tactic it got my attention. Probably Jackie was armed too.

"I've lost my drift," Touched said, breathing deeply and

looking pissed.

"The Real IRA, Continuity IRA," Seamus told him.

"Oh aye. Ok," Touched said, sitting down again. "This is the picture. We're going to start small and smart. A bombing a week. British businesses, companies, status symbols, that sort of thing. No casualties in the first few months of the campaign. Very important. Get the public on our side and show the boys across the water that we are disciplined and controlled. Get them to sponsor us. After Christmas, when we have some depth and political clout, we intensify things. I know about a few soft targets we can hit. This is where we have to have moral courage. It's going to mean killing. Now, I know you had a problem with that, Sean. . . ."

"Not me," I assured him.

"It won't be civilians. Biggest fucking mistake we could make would be to kill American civilians. We were all very impressed with McVeigh and Nichols killing 160 with one truck bomb. But even if they'd gotten away with it, where would it have left them? Nowhere, because the public was against them. We have to keep the public on our side. Or at least, our public, Irish Americans, the *Boston Herald,* our section of society. I'm talking about targeted hits, British military officers living in America, British consular officials, CEOs. Hit the empire where it hurts."

"How would you do that? Shoot them?" Jackie asked.

"No, no, nothing so risky. We'll be long gone. Very simple. At night, plant a bomb under their car with a mercury tilt switch. It goes off as soon as they go up or down a hill. Three, four pounds under the driver's side. Very nice. Done it myself half a dozen times."

Jackie kicked his shoes off and put them on Gerry's desk, wiggling his ten toes in what was possibly an extremely childish attempt to bait me. Touched continued.

"Our problem today, lads, is explosives. For both campaigns we're going to need explosives. As you know, Gerry can get access to dynamite and other industrial explosives aplenty because he's in the construction business. But the difficulty is that those explosives could and would be traced back to him. And if, as we suspect, the FBI is keeping a wee eye on us from time to time, we have to be very careful about that."

"So how do we get explosives? Do we make them? McVeigh made his, right?" Jackie asked.

"McVeigh made a truck bomb. We are talking about finesse and you don't finesse with fertilizer and gasoline. Nah. I've got it sussed. I've been doing a wee bit of intelligence work," he said and then stopped talking to puff his cigar and keep us in suspense.

"Go on," Jackie said.

"I have a wee mate in the know," Touched said.

This time I took the bait.

"Aye?"

"Massachusetts National Guard base on Route 1A. The headquarters of the 101st Engineers. You've probably all seen it. According to my mate, the base is only used Friday nights, Saturdays, and Sundays. On weekdays it's completely empty."

He produced a plan of the base that someone had photocopied for him. It was small—half a dozen rooms, a gym, an indoor range, and, of course, next to the range an armory that Touched had marked with a red X.

"This is your objective. The base has a five-foot-high wire-mesh fence with a single line of barbed wire on top. The rear exit, here, is chained and padlocked. Seamus, with bolt cutters and your expertise, you should be able to get through the chain in about two seconds."

Seamus nodded.

"You'll go in the door, turn left, walk down the corridor, you'll see another door, also chained and padlocked. Again Seamus with the bolt cutters. That's the door to the range. Once you get in, the armory is the door off it to the left. On the door there's a sign that says 'No Admittance Without Officer' or something like that. This door you'll have to smash with a sledgehammer, because it's got an internal lock. The door's thick but it's wooden and apparently in not the best shape, so it should give in about a minute or two. The armory is Alice-in-fucking-Wonderland, but you are to ignore everything, all the guns, grenades, everything except for a stack of green boxes marked 'C4—Handle with

Care.' You are to take one box each and get out of there. Any questions?"

"How heavy are the boxes?" I asked.

"Good question, Sean, I'm not too sure. But I've been told one man, one box isn't unreasonable."

Touched took a big puff on his cigar and smiled at us, well pleased with himself.

"Any more questions?"

"You're not going to be there?" Jackie asked.

"No, I'm going up to Portsmouth to scout something else. This will be Seamus's op. You'll all do what he tells you," Touched said, looking at me.

"Ok," I said.

"Maybe he won't be able to carry a heavy box with his bad foot," Jackie said maliciously.

"Piss off. I'll have no problems at all, Touched, I guarantee you," I said, really starting to hate Jackie.

Touched nodded.

"Now, can I rely on the three of you to get this right?"

He stared at Seamus very seriously.

"Don't look at me like that," Seamus said. "In the side door. Along the corridor. First door on the left. Break the lock, go to the armory, sledgehammers, ignore the guns. Take the boxes marked 'C4—Handle with Fucking Care.'"

Touched looked at him with skepticism. He still wasn't too sure. "Gerry could probably go to Portsmouth by himself. Do you want me to come along?" he asked.

"Fuck off, Touched, I can handle it," Seamus said angrily.

"We'll be fine," I chipped in, and not to be outdone by the new guy, Jackie added:

"Be a piece of piss, Touched, leave it to me."

"Even though there's going to be no one there, I want you in and out in five minutes, is that understood?" Touched said, still clouded by a lingering doubt.

"Understood," we all said.

"All right. Now, standard operating procedure, I'll go to the bus station and steal you a car from the long-term parking. But the rest you'll all have to do by yourselves, ok?"

"O-fucking-k," Seamus said, wearied by Touched's lack of confidence in our abilities.

Touched stood up, walked around the room.

"I want you to spend the rest of the day thinking about the plans, getting the tools, and I'll want you to do a couple of drive-bys so you're familiar with the lay of the land. Then, Seamus, I want you to take the boys out for something to eat. No point doing a job on an empty stomach. And then as soon as it gets dark it's go time and I'll want you in and out. Gerry and I'll be back around nine tonight. I'll leave it up to you to decide your own arrangements, Seamus, but if you're back around that time, it would be pretty good."

"No problems," Seamus said.

Touched looked out the window. Saw something he didn't like.

"There's that fucking car again. All right, meeting's over."

Seamus motioned us to get up. I tried to see out the window to check on the mysterious car, but Touched hustled us from the room. When we finally got outside, the car was gone. I hoped to God that it wasn't a burgundy Jaguar Mark 2 but there was no way of asking Touched about it without tipping him the eye. In any case, I had more than enough to worry about without adding to the bloody ledger.

✿   ✿   ✿

We parked the stolen Jeep in a lay-by near the swamps of the Parker River, and then cut through the boggy undergrowth at the back of the base. The sun was down an hour and the insects were attacking us with gusto even though we were all drenched in Deep Woods Off!

Massachusetts obviously did not think much of its history as the vanguard of the American Revolution, because the Minutemen's current incarnation, the Massachusetts National Guard, couldn't have been housed in a more squalid-looking institution. The 101st Engineers' HQ was a sorry sight. A small, rundown building that resembled a money-deprived elementary school in an unfashionable southern state. Touched had been wrong about the barbed wire, too. The wire was barbed only along the side of the base facing Route 1A. At the back, all that protected the base from vandals and thieves was a five-foot-high wire-mesh fence. Even though I was carrying a sledgehammer and Seamus had bolt cutters and a gun, we were both over it in under thirty seconds. Jackie had a few problems because his baggy pants got caught on the top of the fence, but Seamus tugged him and he was over too.

I watched him come down, the barbs ripping his pants. He landed with a thud, cursing. It affected me strangely.

I froze.

The last time I was on a wire . . .

It came without warning. The flash again. Mexico. Scotchy, in slow motion, falling through a roll of loose-spun razor wire, screaming in pain and frustration. After all we'd been through. So close to getting out, so close to being free from that prison. And then, to die like this, like a punk, shot in the back and bleeding to death.

"Come on, Sean," Seamus said, and I let it go and followed him through the car park behind the base. There was a military Humvee just waiting to be nicked and, even better, an armored personnel carrier and a half-track bulldozer.

We walked to the back door, chained and padlocked but so old and weather-beaten that if you didn't have lock-cutting gear you could have just shoved a screwdriver under the hinges, tugged, and it would have fallen off. Seamus took the bolt cutters and I held the chain for him. He cracked it down, using his thigh as the lever, and the chain snapped on the first try.

"We're in," Jackie said with delight.

"Ok, lads, be careful," Seamus said.

I was glad this was finally coming to a head. It had been a tedious day with those two. Scouting the base, having dinner, making small talk. Putting up with Jackie's attempts at sarcasm and ignoring Seamus's repeated trips to the bathroom to drink from his whiskey flasks. Flasks plural.

And then bloody tourism. Sonia or someone had evidently asked Seamus to show me a bit of Newburyport so even though we were in a stolen car and on assignment, he parked right in the middle of downtown, took us to dinner at Angie's Diner, and then walked me round Newburyport's high-density collection of candle stores, ice-cream parlors, exotic-food delis, and souvenir shops. I pretended to be fascinated but I did take five minutes to take the boys inside the All Things Brit store and buy them some British chocolate bars. Along with the five-dollar bill, I'd passed Samantha a note that said: "Touched has noticed your Jaguar," in case I was right about my guess. I hadn't liked Touched's remark about spotting a car outside Gerry's house and the report I'd read on him was wrong in several aspects. He might be violent, he might be ruthless, but he wasn't crazy and he wasn't dumb. He was a very sleekit operator.

Gerry was comfortable and getting old, but Touched had lost little of his edge. Clever to keep himself out of this little mischief. Much more serious than a bank robbery. And he'd made sure Gerry wasn't even in on the discussions. Touched was smarter and more cunning than everyone gave him credit for. Yesterday's run had been presented to me as a fait accompli. I'd had no choice, either take it or leave it. The same today. And both times he had kept the big boss out of it. I hadn't witnessed anything yet that the feds could trace back to Gerry. However, if tonight's operation was successful and we got ourselves a handful of plastic explosives, then all I'd need to do would be to let Touched and Gerry make one bomb. They wouldn't even have to detonate it. As soon as they made that bomb, we could nab the whole lot of them. Get them on felony conspiracy charges and Touched on armed robbery and conspiracy to commit armed robbery on an army base. It would more or less be the end of Sons of Cuchulainn. Kit would have to be part of the deal. For although the wee girl had dubious musical preferences and her taste in boyfriends was shocking, you couldn't pick your parents and it wasn't her fault that Gerry had roped her into all of this. Have to see to it that her sentence got suspended or at the most a few months in minimum security.

Samantha read the note and reacted like a pro: she didn't react at all. But I could tell she understood. I would have liked to give her a fuller debriefing but Seamus took us out of there.

Now, thank God, we were doing something.

Jackie unthreaded the chain from the lock.

"Where's the flashlights?" Seamus asked.

Jackie fumbled in his backpack and gave us each a flashlight. It was his only real responsibility tonight but I was still surprised when the flashlight actually worked.

It was awkward carrying the big sledgehammer and the flashlight but I'd be damned if I was going to ask for help. In any case, I didn't want to speak to these two eejits any more than I had to. Gingerly, we walked inside the base. Seamus leading, Jackie second, me picking up the rear.

"Do we need to put our masks on, Seamus?" I asked.

"Place is deserted," Seamus said, dismissively. "Come on, down here to the left."

Jackie stifled a yawn. Up before dawn to surf. Price you paid, buddy.

The paint was flaking and there were posters on the walls discussing benefits, sex discrimination, the regular army, and the "Don't Ask, Don't Tell" policy.

At the end of the corridor there was a notice board with a single notice—a sign-up sheet for last year's Boston marathon.

"It looks abandoned. I hope Touched was right about his information," Jackie said.

"It's not abandoned, didn't you notice the tank outside?" Seamus said, scornfully.

We found the door at the end of the corridor. Seamus applied the bolt cutters, the chain snapped, we pushed it open and were immediately inside the indoor shooting range. Seamus shone his flashlight on the far wall and we saw the door to the armory. It wasn't marked "Armory" but there was that sign which said "No Admittance Without Duty Officer Sign In."

"That's it," Jackie whispered.

"I think it is," I concurred.

"Ok, let's go," Seamus said.

We began walking across the range. A room about fifty feet in length with targets running up and down wires that were hung from the ceiling. A lingering smell of cordite and gunpowder from plastic boxes filled with spent ammo.

I lifted the sledgehammer to my shoulder.

"When we get over, you want me to smack it?" I asked Seamus.

Seamus nodded.

"If you're up to it, that is," Jackie said.

I'd had just about enough of this wee skitter. I put my hand on his shoulder, grabbed him.

"What is that supposed to mean?" I asked.

"You being a cripple and all, you just might not be able to handle it," Jackie said, and I could sense him grinning in the blackness.

"Jackie, if you want another beating, you're going the right way about getting one. What will you say to Kit this time, you tripped over a paving stone and you're suing the town council?"

Jackie brushed my hand off him and squared himself for trouble.

"You had the advantage on me that time. This time I'm sober, so you just try it, pal," he said.

"I'll knock ya back to cow-fucking County Sligo," I said, holding the sledgehammer in both hands, ready to swing in case he was dumb enough to try anything.

"Go on then, give me your best shot," Jackie said.

Seamus reached into his inside pocket and pulled out a revolver. He pointed it at me and then at Jackie.

"If you two don't fucking cut it out, I'll shoot the pair of you right here," he said. It wasn't a serious threat, but the gun got our attention. This was escalating things. It took the wind out of the exchange. I eased my grip on the sledgehammer.

Jackie spat on the range floor.

"Tell him not to touch me," he muttered.

"Tell him to watch his mouth," I said.

"Enough. Let's go," Seamus ordered.

We walked over to the armory. Now that we were closer we could see a frail beam of light leaking under the door.

Unnerving. It looked as if there was a bulb on inside

the room.

"What do you make of that, Seamus?" I asked, pointing at the light and dropping my voice into a whisper.

"Somebody left the light on from the weekend?" Seamus suggested.

I nodded.

"I suppose," I said.

Seamus examined the door handle. It was, as Touched predicted, a metal handle connected to a wooden door. Three or four good smashes should do the trick. I lifted the sledge hammer and brought it crashing down on the handle. It gave first time.

A voice from inside the armory screamed and a split second later an alarm went off: flashing emergency lights and a loud continuous bell.

Jackie pulled the armory door open. A long, narrow room filled with boxes in metal cages and guns in racks. And a thirty-year-old soldier, bald, fat, frightened green eyes, wearing fatigues, sitting on a stool, holding a clipboard in one hand, the other having just pushed a big red button on the wall. He made a grab for a weapon next to him on the floor. I chucked the sledgehammer at him and it caught him on the chest, knocking him off his stool backwards into a box of stun grenades.

I lunged for and grabbed his Colt .45 sidearm, lying in a holster beside the chair. He tried to get at me but I elbowed him in the face, took the gun out of the holster, slammed home the dislodged clip, pointed it at his head. He put his hands up.

"I surrender," he said.

I turned to Seamus and we looked at each other, horrified, for a moment.

"What do we do now?" Jackie asked Seamus in a panic.

"He's seen us," Seamus said.

"I haven't seen anything," the guy replied, closing his eyes.

"He's bloody seen us," Jackie wailed.

Seamus reached into his pocket, brought out his hip flask, and took a drink. He wiped his mouth.

Just then, across the bog and the cottonwoods, and over

the shrill alarm bell, we heard the distinct wail of a police siren. It might be connected with us, it might not.

"That button you pressed, who does it alert?" I asked.

"I don't know," he said and he meant it.

"We got to get out of here," I said to Seamus. "Peelers are coming."

Seamus looked as if he were about to pass out. His skin was pale and he was sweating. The last few weeks had been too much for him. He couldn't take the bloody stress. At least not sober.

"Take him with us. Touched will know what to do," Seamus said.

"Slow us down," I said angrily.

"We'll take him with us. Do as you're told, this is my show," Seamus screamed.

"What about the explosives, Seamus?" Jackie asked.

"Why don't you tell him all our names?" I said to Jackie and motioned the soldier to follow us out of the armory.

"Forget them. Let's just get the hell out of here," Seamus said.

"Come on, you," I said to the soldier. "Keep your hands above your head."

We ran across the range and I put the gun in the soldier's back as we jogged down the corridor. He was definitely older than me. Overweight, shaking, terrified. Jackie going ape-shit at him didn't help matters:

"Jesus, what the fuck were you doing in there? This place is supposed to be empty," he said.

"I had to do the inventory," the soldier replied.

"You're only supposed to be here on the weekends," Jackie said furiously.

"The colonel's coming this weekend, we had to have it checked out and—" the guy began but Seamus interrupted the explanation:

"Shut up. It doesn't matter how it happened. It has happened," he said.

We sprinted down the corridor and ran outside just as a cop car pulled in on Route 1A in front of the base.

"Over the wire," Seamus said. "Come on."

We ran to the rear fence.

"You, over it," Seamus told the soldier. All four of us scaled the fence. The state troopers shone a powerful searchlight onto the base but we were well clear at the back. We crouched low.

"They won't see us," Jackie whispered.

We flattened ourselves into the reeds, Seamus pushing the soldier's head down to the ground. The spotlight passed us by and returned to the front of the base.

"Over here, over here," the soldier screamed, jumping up and waving his arms. The peelers shone the light at the back and spotted us.

"Halt, you there," one of the cops yelled.

"You bloody fool," I said as Jackie and I pulled the soldier to the dirt.

Seamus took out his gun and shoved it into the soldier's cheek.

"Try that again and you're going to die," Seamus said.

"For Christ's sake, come on. Let's go," I yelled at Seamus.

Seamus put his gun in the soldier's back, shoved him, and the four of us ran into the marsh that led down to the Parker River.

The cops fired a warning shot into the air and came tearing after us. They'd either have to run wide around the base or cut across the front fence, through the car park, and then climb the back fence. But even so, they'd be on our heels pretty goddamn quick.

"Gotta ditch the army boy," I said to Seamus as we waded through the boggy grass.

"He's seen our faces, you idiot. We take him to Touched," Seamus said furiously.

"We'll never get away, they'll have copters after us in a minute," Jackie said, sobbing a little.

"Get a grip, Jackie. Come on. It's totally dark. If we can make it to the Parker River, we can wade in, float downstream into the wildlife refuge at the bottom of Plum Island, we'll be ok," Seamus said.

It wasn't a bad plan at that. The water wasn't cold or fast moving. It might work.

"Better move fast then," I said.

Seamus nodded, encouraged by my approval.

"And you, no funny stuff, or I'll fucking shoot ya," he said to the soldier.

We waded through swamp, and then solid water and then swamp again.

After about ten minutes we could hear many more cops behind us. Three or four backup units had been called in, maybe a dozen cops altogether. Seamus, the soldier, and myself were still together but Jackie, the fittest and fastest of us, was a couple of hundred yards ahead now. He looked back to see if he should wait but Seamus waved him on. In another minute he was gone completely.

"I think I see the river," I said.

It was a bloody miracle that the mud hadn't sucked the shoes off my feet and it surely would have if I'd still been wearing Converse high-tops, not these big Stanley work boots. Shoeless, I would have been footless, and fucked.

As we got near the water the fat soldier slowed. He was out of shape and sweating but he wasn't exhausted just yet. He was planning something. I could sense it in his body language. I kept an eye on him, waiting for him to jump either of us. But he didn't. Instead, midrun he tripped on a vine and fell. He landed heavily on the ground and grabbed at his leg.

"Get up," Seamus yelled at him. "Get the fuck up or I'll shoot you."

"My leg, I've broken my leg," the man said, writhing in apparent agony.

"Get the fuck up, army boy," Seamus said.

"I can't, my leg's hurt," the soldier said.

I nodded at Seamus. There was no time to see if it was a lie or not. He had to make a decision.

"We got to leave him now," I said.

Seamus looked at him, looked at me, listened to the cops coming closer and closer, nodded to himself. He reached into his inside pocket, withdrew his flask, and took another drink. He screwed the top on and raised his gun.

"What are you doing, Seamus?" I asked. "He's lying, his leg's fine. Get up, mate. Come on. He's lying."

"I know," Seamus said coldly. "It doesn't matter, Sean, he's seen our faces, have to do it, Sean, no other way. I'm on fucking bail already. I can't go down for this and the shooting at Revere, I'd get twenty years."

"No, Seamus, wait a minute," I began, but he cut me off.

"I'm not going to die in prison, Sean. That's what it comes down to. Now, obey orders and get moving."

"It's murder, Seamus," I said, but he wasn't listening. He raised his .38 revolver and pointed it at the soldier's head.

"We have to kill him," he said but only to himself. His mind was made up.

"That's the murder of a federal employee in the commission of another crime. That's the fucking death penalty."

"Oh please, please, please don't do it," the soldier begged.

"Close your eyes, pal," Seamus said, his face in the moonlight, resigned, determined.

I lifted the soldier's .45.

"Put the gun down, Seamus," I said.

He turned to look at me.

"You wouldn't," he said.

"Put the gun down," I insisted.

"Fucking kill you, Sean. Kill ya both," he snarled and trained the gun on my chest.

The .45 banged.

A huge boom that stopped the cops in their tracks and set the birds a mile up and down the Parker River panicking into the air. Seamus collapsed to his knees, half his head blown apart, the skin on the other half hanging on to the skull by only a few blood vessels and nerve endings.

I wiped his brains off my arm and face.

He knelt there, little spurts of blood gurgling from his mouth.

"Sorry, Seamus," I found myself saying.

His left eye blinked, he hovered on his knees for a second, and then slumped forward, stone dead, into the boggy waters of the swamp.

8: MURDER IN NEWBURY

Flints in the night sky. Oxidizing blood. Mosquitoes by the swarm and double swarm. A burning smell on the warm, wet trade wind. And, as I stood there, holding the distinctive grip of a smoking Colt .45, covered in filth, bleeding, soaked, a dead man at my feet, another man on his knees in front of me begging for his life, I thought to myself: What else is new?

I sighed.

This is exactly what I was talking about when I said that trouble followed me like sharks trailing a slave ship.

I spat, clearing the bitter taste in my throat.

"Please, sir, don't kill me," the soldier said as the echo from the .45 rolled down the river.

I thumbed the safety on the army-issue Colt and squatted down onto one knee.

"Listen," I began but stopped as a light plane flew above us and somewhere in the distance a freaked-out cop unloaded his Glock into a harmless wading bird.

The soldier put his hands way up.

"I'm sorry about the fall. Please don't shoot me, please, I'm getting married at Christmas. I have, a, uh, a kid from my first marriage, please, oh God, please."

"Take it easy, you eejit, I'm an undercover FBI agent. Everything's going to be all right," I said.

His mouth opened in disbelief as he looked at me and then

at Seamus's blood oozing into the Parker River.

"I don't believe you, let me see your badge, let me—"

"Shut up. Now listen to me, we've got to buy some time. Help me drag Seamus into the water."

The soldier balked and stared at me, petrified.

"You gotta work with me, mate, come on, I'm not going to kill you, look, I'm putting the gun away," I said, taking the .45 and slipping it into my trouser pocket. I picked up Seamus by the left leg and nodded for the soldier boy to lift the right. Dazed, confused, now he wanted to be told what to do. He grabbed the leg and we dragged Seamus to the river's edge. I floated him in and watched him drift down towards the bottom of PI, Ipswich, and the ocean.

I climbed back up the bank.

"Please don't kill me now," the soldier said.

"How old are you?"

"Thirty-one," he said hesitantly.

"Thirty-one. Old enough to know better. Fucking pull it together, mate."

"Ok, I'll—"

"Be quiet. Follow me, we're going into the water, quiet now, crouch low. Hurry up, this way."

I got the soldier to bend down and I led him upstream for about a quarter of a mile. The peelers obviously had a canine unit because after about ten minutes the dog set up a terrible howling, which could only mean that they'd found what was left of the other half of Seamus's head. Hopefully the dog would pick up the rest of the dead man's scent and lead them to the river and then downstream. The wind was blowing off the sea so that would help a little too.

"What was that?" the soldier asked, spooked.

"That was a dog, they probably just found Seamus, come on now."

We kept going and paused while I adjusted my prosthesis.

As we got farther upstream the Parker River narrowed, but I kept us going until it was shallow enough so we could easily cross to the other bank.

"Follow me to the other side, be sharp about it," I told him.

He nodded glumly. Seeing Seamus topped like that had certainly gotten his attention and now he was Mister Cooperation. No more slow play, broken legs, or crying out.

I helped him up the slippery embankment and led him under a tree. It was a pretty good move to lose our scent in the water, but it wouldn't fool Fido for long and Jackie was right about one thing, sooner or later they would have a chopper. I had to think fast. I sat the character on a big root. He was hyperventilating and afeared. He had to calm down and he had to believe me.

"First thing, take a big breath," I told him.

He breathed deep and exhaled.

"Second thing. What's your name and rank?" I asked.

"My name and rank?"

"Yeah, you have to tell me. Even if I was the enemy you'd have to tell me."

"Specialist David Ryan," he said, confused but maybe a little less frightened.

"Ok, David, listen, it's gonna be ok. I'm going to let you go, but you gotta be cool and do what I tell you. Ok?"

He nodded.

"Good," I said.

"He was going to kill me. He, he was going to kill you, too," he muttered, recalling the grisly incident. He began to shiver. I couldn't afford for him to lose it now.

"Take it easy, mate. You were never in any danger. Not for a second. Neither was I. He had a gun but you'd need fucking kryptonite to take care of me. Now be cool and shut up a minute while I sort this out."

I rummaged in my cargo pants pocket and took out the mobile phone that Samantha insisted I always carry for a situation such as this. The question was whether it would work when I needed it. The pocket was soaked and the phone was slathered in wet reeds, petals, and pollen.

"Just fucking work," I ordered it and turned it on. It lit up by force of will and I got a dial tone. Thank God.

I rang Samantha's number.

She picked up.

"Hello?"

"It's me," I said.

"Mi—? Where are you? Are you on a portable phone?"

"Yes."

"Hang up now and call me from a landline."

"It's an emergency."

"Ok, well then, um, be very careful what you say."

"I don't have time for that shit. Seamus is dead. You're going to have to send a team of FBI agents to the Massachusetts National Guard base near Rowley on Route 1A. Right now. We broke in, it went wrong, and Seamus is dead. And there's a witness. They're going to pick up a soldier, Specialist David Ryan. If you want this operation to succeed you can't allow him to talk to the cops. The FBI are going to have to convince them this is a federal matter. We can't trust the cops not to blab. He'll be waiting there for them. He'll be prepped."

"What on earth is going on? Are you hurt?" she asked.

"I'll tell you later. It's a fuckup. It's going to be your call on whether it's a fatal fuckup or not. If you ask me, I think we should abort the whole thing. But like the good trooper that I am, I'm going to square it so we have all the options. Ok?"

"You have to tell me exactly what's happened," she said, an imperative tone overcoming her concern.

"No time. Listen to me. Write this down. Get the FBI to the National Guard Base on Route 1A, the 101st Engineers. It's near Rowley and the Parker River. Pick up Specialist David Ryan. You better bloody move it too. I've got to go to PI and make this right. You owe me big time for this. Big time," I said.

I turned off the phone and looked at Ryan.

"Ok, pal, now listen to me, the cops are going to be over here in a few minutes. I'm an undercover FBI agent, I've infiltrated a very dangerous cell of terrorists. They are on the verge of blowing tons of shit up. Remember Oklahoma City? Stuff like that. The lives of hundreds of people are at stake. If you tell those cops that I shot Seamus, my cover will be blown and months of preparation are going to go up the fucking spout and I'll be executed and the terrorists are going to get away. This is bandit country, the cops can't be trusted. Only the feds. Ok?"

"I can't lie to them, I—"

"Take it easy, mate, you don't have to lie, not exactly, what you'll say to the cops is pretty much what happened: three guys broke into the base, they took you with them, you got away, and you heard a shot. That's it. They'll take you back to the police station for medical treatment, maybe to a hospital, doesn't matter. You tell the cops that you got away from us and you ran and you don't know what happened to us. Ok?"

He nodded, but he still wasn't convinced.

"Don't feel bad about it. The FBI is going to be talking to you in an hour or so, you can tell them the truth. There's probably going to be an agent called Harrington. You can tell him everything. But if you tell your buddies or your fiancée or the cops or anyone else that I shot Seamus, I'm fucked. The terrorists will find out what really happened tonight and they'll kill me. Do you understand?"

"Why should I believe you?"

"Because it happens to be true."

He blinked rapidly, his eyes wide and inexperienced. The fear was dissipating.

"Ok, I think, I—"

"No, no thinking. You'll either do it or you won't, tell me which it's going to be. Hurry up," I said.

He thought for a moment, struggled with it, but obviously he wanted to buy the story, either that or he was a hell of an actor.

"Ok, I'll do it," he said.

"You better not be lying. My life's at stake. Dozens of lives."

"I'm not lying."

He looked at the gun butt peeking out of my pocket. I clicked my fingers in front of his face. I needed the locus of his attention on me.

"Tell me what you have to do. Repeat it back," I said.

"I don't tell the cops shit, but I do tell the FBI."

"Very good."

I had him, but I had to be a hundred percent certain. I

crouched beside him, looked into his eyes.

"Now listen, Ryan, I'm trusting you with my goddamn life, so you better not fuck up."

"I won't man, I owe you."

"One last time. Don't tell the cops, but tell the FBI."

"I understand," he said seriously. "It's like when you have to do deep recon."

"That's exactly what it's like. Good. I like that. Ok, I have to go, give me ten minutes and then you can start screaming for the police. Got it?"

"Yes."

I stood.

The soldier looked at me. He wanted to say something. I waited.

"Thank you for saving me," he said. "And good luck."

"I'll need it," I said.

I took the .45 out of my pocket, threw it into the Parker River, and ran as fast as I could into the swampy undergrowth.

I headed north for fifteen minutes until I came to a wood. Here I adjusted the straps on my prosthesis again, caught my breath, got my shit together.

What now?

Go back to Gerry's?

How?

Hoof it.

Plum Island is a long sandy outcrop that runs parallel to the coast of northern Massachusetts. On the maps it's an island but in fact at low tide the island is effectively joined to the mainland by a marshy spit of land. From where I was, north of the Parker River, it wouldn't be a difficult trek east across the marsh and up onto the west shore. I could easily make landfall in the Plum Island wildlife reserve, cut across the quarter-mile-wide island to the Atlantic side, and walk up the beach to McCaghan's house.

That would take about an hour.

I thought about it and it seemed feasible, and I was about to get going but then, like the sleekit wee character I was, a new plan began to grow in my mind.

A better one.

A much fucking better one.

What was it that I'd said to her? I saved your operation tonight. That I bloody had and they owed me.

I stood and instead of going east to Plum Island I went west out of the woods and towards the highway.

Brambles, an old graveyard, and eventually the trees intersecting with Route 1A again. Perfect. Not far now. I turned north, keeping to the undergrowth by the side of the road. Just before the town of Newbury I stopped at a gas station that I'd noticed several times before.

It was after nine o'clock, so the gas station was closed for the night. Still, I staked it out in the forest until I was damn sure it was unoccupied. At a break in the traffic I ran across the road.

The gas station *was* deserted and the object of my mission, the pay phone outside, was in full working order. I could call Samantha now without a danger of our call being intercepted. I picked up a rock and after a couple of tries I smashed the big light illuminating the gas station's forecourt.

I popped in a quarter and dialed Samantha's number.

"Hello?"

"Samantha, it's me. I want you to pick me up at the gas station south of Newbury on Route 1A. I'll wait here for fifteen minutes."

I hung up before she had a chance to say anything and then retreated into the shadows. Her burgundy Jag appeared a little over ten minutes later. She had pulled a coat on over her nightgown. Her eyes suspicious, her lips thin and furious. She opened the car door.

"North on 1A," I said.

I got in, she turned the car, and we drove for Newburyport.

"Michael, what do you think you're—" she began, but I put my hand on her thigh and cut her off.

"Just listen . . . listen first. This is the whole story. We broke into the National Guard base to steal explosives, there was a soldier on guard duty, Seamus grabbed him, and he alerted the peelers. We ran out into the swamps, Jackie got away, but the soldier fell down and Seamus decided to kill him. . . . I had to shoot Seamus to save the soldier. I told the soldier not to say anything to the cops and to save it for the FBI. I think he'll do what he's told."

Samantha redigested the information.

"Who was with you?"

"Seamus, me, Jackie."

She thought for a moment.

"Are you sure the soldier won't speak to the local police?" she asked.

"No, he won't. I told him to tell the FBI what happened but not the local police. If I were you, I'd get on the blower straight away."

"Good. Hold on a minute, darling. This line is secure. Let me take care of it."

She picked up her car phone and called someone who told her that the FBI were on their way to Rowley. She asked to be transferred to Stephen Harrington. She filled in Harrington and told him to get Specialist Ryan away from the cops as soon as possible by telling them this was an FBI and ATF matter. When she was done, she hung up and blew me a kiss.

"You did well, Michael, you saved the day," she said with a grin; but I wasn't having any of it. She wasn't going to butter me up.

"Damn right I did. In more ways than one. Not just telling the soldier boy what to say. I could have given myself up to the cops and my cover would have been blown and you'd have had to pull me out. Operation over. And the best you could have gotten from the whole thing would be Jackie for an attempted burglary. That would be it. Gerry, Touched, everyone else scot-free and a million times more suspicious. A million times more careful. Oh, and one more time, keep your bloody car away from Gerry's house."

Samantha nodded.

"I'm sorry, I just drove over there today to make sure that you were installed safely, get the lay of the land around the house. Did someone comment on it?"

"No one commented on it, but don't do it again, Touched

notices things. And you don't need to walk up the beach to give me warnings either. I may be a novice at this but I can handle myself. Just stay off Plum Island completely. With me you have to lay back. Give me room to breathe."

She nodded. She had been overprotective and she had made a mistake. I was right to put her in her place.

We reached Newburyport. She drove up State and down Pleasant and pulled round the back of All Things Brit. She parked the car and turned off the lights. I looked at her. She knew I was gunning for something.

"What?" she asked.

"You want to talk here or in your flat?"

"We don't have to talk."

"Oh, I think we do," I insisted.

"What do you want me to say, darling? Don't make me cross. I've already told you that you did a jolly good job," she said.

"No, no, it's gone beyond the pat on the back. I saved the operation tonight."

She opened her handbag and pulled out a pack of cigarettes, offered me one. I declined; she lit one for herself.

"What do you want?" she asked.

"I want a million dollars. Half a million each for the convictions of Touched and Gerry."

"You want money?" she asked incredulously.

"Aye, I want money. The FBI gives me a stipend of about five hundred a week. It's nothing. I want to be set for life. This is my opportunity."

"A million dollars. Don't be silly, there's no way Six would ever approve—"

"Oh, they'll approve. You were right, Samantha, it's not just a bunch of dreamers. These guys are serious. Have you heard of a group called the Real IRA?"

"Yes, dissident republicans, very small, nothing much to worry about—"

"You think not? Well, I beg to differ. Gerry and Touched are planning to go under their umbrella in the next few months. Their plan is to set up cells and start a bombing campaign as soon as possible. By Christmas, they'll have bombed a lot of commercial targets, got the nod from the Real IRA, and then they're going to go for targeted assassinations. They are going to be killing people. Ambassadors, businessmen, retired army officers. These boys are bloody serious. And they're careful and they're good. And I'm the best chance you've got of bringing them down before they get started. We'll save lives, save treasure, nab the fuckers. It's the only way. You won't discourage them by harassment. They're hard-core. They're pissed off at the IRA, at the American government, at the Brits, at anyone in their way. Very, very dangerous."

Samantha looked at me with contempt.

"If that's true, then it's your duty to help bring—"

"Duty nothing. I had a way out tonight. You know it, I know it, and there's bugger-all you could have done about it. I could have turned myself in to the peelers and blown my cover. But I didn't. I had to kill a man tonight. Let's not forget I saved that soldier boy's life and topped a pal of mine."

"Seamus wasn't your—"

"It doesn't matter if he was or he wasn't. It's still not easy. Ok? So as I see it, I've made plenty of sacrifices for you already and if this operation is to continue I want the fucking money. What's a million to the civil service? To MI6? I don't know, what would it be, less than a tenth of one percent of your annual budget? It's nothing. And this will be a major coup. Kudos from the Yanks, *muy* prestige, promotions all round."

Samantha thought for a moment.

"I suppose I could ask. It really wouldn't do any harm to ask."

"Damn right you'll ask and you'll get it."

"I can't guarantee anything. But certainly, darling, I'll see what I can do," she said.

I shook my head.

"No, that's not good enough. You won't see what you can bloody do. You'll make an oral agreement with me right now, and you'll have it drawn up by tomorrow. I want a pardon from Mexico and from Spain and I want my record wiped and I want a million bucks for information leading to the convictions of Touched and Gerry."

She puffed on her fag, stubbed it into the ashtray. Opened the box, took out another.

"Well?" I persisted.

She nodded, looked at me.

"Ok, Michael," she said softly.

"You'll get it done?"

"I'll get it done."

"Good. Now, you got any water? I am dying of thirst."

She reached behind her seat and handed me a bottle of water. I drank the entire thing in one big gulp.

"You want to take a shower at my place?" she asked.

"No, I can't."

"What are you going to do now?" she asked, concern drifting back into her voice.

"I'm going to go back to PI and square it with Touched. I'll say I got separated from Seamus and the soldier and I don't know what happened next."

She thought for a moment.

"I'll get the ATF to take over the investigation tonight. And we'll do a press release tomorrow. We'll say that it was a burglary gone wrong and the burglars took the soldier hostage and he escaped."

"Seamus worked for Gerry, so when you find his body you'll have to send a couple of FBI agents round to the construction firm. It'll be too suspicious if you don't," I said.

"Of course. And we'll bring Gerry in for questioning, too. It's the least he'll be expecting. And this might be enough to get a judge to order a tap on his phones, although I believe they're awfully strict in this country," she said.

"Tap all you want, but I'm not wearing anything," I said.

"I wouldn't ask you to, you're doing enough as it is, darling," she said sweetly, her smile coming back again.

"Damn right."

She blinked, hesitated. I wound down the window to get rid of the smoke smell.

"Michael, I have to ask this. Was there any other way with Seamus?"

"Talk to the soldier. He'll tell you. It was him or us."

"Ok," she said quietly.

"I can't bloody dillydally. Drive me close to the Plum Island turnpike and I'll make my own way to Gerry's."

She nodded, stubbed out her cigarette, started the car, drove in silence to Plum Island, and dropped me at the deserted entrance to the wildlife refuge, where there would be no witnesses to see me get out of the vehicle.

"So you'll have my contract and my pardons by tomorrow?" I asked again.

"Yes, Michael," she said, biting her lip.

"Good."

I clicked my seat belt off and went to get out of the car. Samantha stopped me.

"Wait."

"What?"

"Uh . . . I don't know if it'll be useful, but I found out about Kit's real mother and father, they're from New York. Hector and Lilly Orlandez, so she's really a Latina, surprising with her complexion, you wouldn't have thought—"

I cut her off with a shake of my head.

"That's not what you wanted to tell me," I said.

"No," she agreed.

"What then?"

She hesitated.

"Just this," she said.

She leaned across the car and she kissed me. She'd been drinking and her lips and tongue tasted of red wine. I kissed her and I ran my dirty hand up her thigh and I felt between her legs. She moaned and pulled me close.

"Michael, you will be careful, won't you?" she asked.

"Are you kidding? I'm one step ahead of everyone," I said.

I pushed back her seat and took off her panties. I pulled down my filthy trousers and we had frantic, fugitive gunman sex.

Twenty minutes later, I was walking alongside the black ocean towards the big house on the dunes, where every light was on, and inside, no doubt, chaos reigned.

I scooped some seawater and washed off any residual dregs of Seamus's blood and brains.

I went to the kitchen's patio doors and knocked on the glass.

Touched appeared with a revolver tucked down the front of his pants. A grin on his face. He, at least, was pleased to see me. He pulled me in and hugged me.

"Jesus, Sean, thank God you made it," he said.

Everyone was up. Everyone but Seamus, who had not yet returned. Sonia in a man's shirt and white sweatpants. Touched and Gerry in their street clothes. Jackie showered and in a robe, trembling from head to toe, holding a hot whiskey. Kit, in her tight Body Glove T-shirt, stroking his hair.

I would have had Jackie packed off to Boston or Timbuktu on an alibi or in case the peelers showed, but not these guys. Loyal to their crew, looking after him like mother hens.

"What happened, Sean?" Touched asked.

"It was terrible, Touched, it all went wrong. Terrible," I began, but Sonia interrupted me.

"Unless it's life and death, I insist you get out of those wet clothes and go and take a shower first," she said. Gerry shook his head and that was enough to assert his authority.

"Where's Seamus?" I asked. "Nabbed?"

"We were hoping you could tell us," Gerry said, his eyes bleary with worry.

I sat down at the kitchen table. Kit was holding Jackie's arm and stroking his back. Jackie looked as if he was well medicated. Touched pulled up a chair and sat beside me.

"Better spill it from the beginning," he said. "Don't worry about repeating what Jackie said, I want to hear your version."

I told it like it was, except for the very end. Jackie got separated from Seamus and the soldier and then I got cut off from them when I swam across the river. I made it to the woods. I thought I heard a gunshot but I wasn't sure. I followed the coast and waded over the Plum Island River to the wildlife refuge, to here. But the whole thing was a disaster, a debacle of the first order.

Gerry nodded and patted me on the shoulder. Touched

leaned in close and rubbed the stubble on his chin. His eyes were wary and cold. It made me nervous. His breath stank of cigarettes.

"This is very important, Sean. Were we set up? Was it a police setup?" Touched asked.

I shook my head.

"No, I don't think so. Just a fuckup. The soldier was as surprised as we were. The cops came because of the alarm."

Touched looked at Gerry. His face was a mask. It either confirmed or shot down what they were thinking.

"What was the last you saw of Seamus?" Gerry asked.

"I don't know, he was pretty slow, he looked beat, he told me to keep going. I ran ahead of him and when I looked back he and the soldier were way behind me. Then I waded over the river and I thought they were behind me but they were gone."

"And did the police see where you went?"

"Nah, I lost the pigs. I hope Seamus did as well, but he seemed a bit . . ." My voice trailed off.

"He'd been drinking?" Touched asked, his eyes narrowing.

I hesitated. I wanted to appear loyal and as if what I could say would be telling tales out of school. I looked at Jackie and then at Touched.

"I don't know," I said.

Touched nodded grimly.

"How bad was he? I want the truth," Touched said.

"I don't know, Touched. He was ok," I said, appearing to be in the throes of an internal struggle.

Touched shook his head but he seemed satisfied. It was neither my nor Jackie's fault and we'd done ok by getting away.

Sonia came downstairs.

"I'm running the bath in the guesthouse. I absolutely insist that he use it," she said.

Gerry nodded.

"I'm done, what about you, Touched?"

"Me, too."

"Ok then," Gerry muttered. "Come with me, Touched."

THE DEAD YARD / 185

Touched and Gerry went to the upstairs den to confer and probably have a blazing argument. Jackie sat next to me at the kitchen table.

"Are you ok, mate?" he asked, trying to be conciliatory.

"Thanks for asking, Jackie; to tell you the truth, I'm bloody wrecked. Wrecked but basically in one piece. What about you?"

"I did something to my ankle, and there's a cut on my thigh from the barbed wire, but I'll be fine in a day or two," he said.

"You see, Jackie boy, that's the advantage of having the old bionic ankle," I said and lifted up my prosthesis.

Jackie smiled, patted me on the back.

"You did well, Sean, as well as could be expected under the fucking circumstances."

"How did you get away?" I asked.

"I just ran; I got to the river and kept going. I hope you don't think I left you in the lurch or—"

"No, Jack, you did your best," I interrupted.

Kit smiled and held my hand. Jackie, God bless him, didn't seem to mind.

Gerry and Touched came back into the room.

"Listen, folks, we may as well go to bed. Seamus either made it or he didn't. We'll know in the morning," Gerry said.

I didn't need to be told twice. I said my good nights, walked across to the guesthouse, had a quick bath, found my room, and lay down on the big bed.

"We'll know in the morning," I whispered to myself. Then I closed my eyes and slept.

❄ ❄ ❄

A tangle rain. A thick sea mizzle that came from the east, cold and sleekit, with a hint of knife that might freshen into gale. The kind of damp that penetrated everything. I shivered in my robe and bare feet. Up here on the balcony with its enormous field of view you were really aware of the weather. Normally, September in America still has a summer feel but September in Ireland is definitely the autumn. This felt like an Irish day.

Condensation blocked the window and the view of the woman next door, but I saw her husband in an overcoat climbing down from his observatory. No stars last night, so he probably kept his porn collection up there. He nodded to me and I nodded back. Secret sharers, the pair of us. I sipped the coffee and bit into the croissant that had been placed outside my door on a silver tray.

The cops had not come yet.

The news on the local radio said that a body part had been found at the scene of the robbery. The all-news station wouldn't say what part had been found. But I knew. Half a bloody head.

Still, it had been an ebb tide and the current was the Gulf Stream, so maybe they'd never find Seamus.

The radio also said that a soldier had initially been taken hostage by the burglars but had escaped. There were three burglars. White males, twenty to forty. The reporter said the whole scene was still one of confusion. Some people were speculating that it could only have been an inside job, others that the whole thing was a practical joke gone wrong.

Confusion was good; the FBI would help muddy those waters.

I finished my coffee, showered, changed into a sweater and blue jeans, went to the big house.

The servants had been given the day off. Sonia was making breakfast. Touched saw me and shook me firmly by the hand.

"What news?" I asked.

"Nothing definite. But I've talked to a couple of sources in the cops. There were no arrests but they found an ugly mess that they think was bits of somebody's head."

"Seamus?"

"I don't know, Sean. They haven't found a body, so no one knows."

"The radio said a cop fired his gun. Could he have hit Seamus?"

"I don't know, Sean. Seamus hasn't been arrested and he hasn't showed up here, so either he's scarpered or he's dead."

"Christ. What a fuckup," I said.

Touched nodded.

"I take full responsibility," he said. "I should have run the show. Seamus was hit pretty hard by what happened in Revere; I thought showing him that I believed in him would help snap him out of the funk he'd fallen into. Clearly a big mistake. I've told Gerry. My fault. I apologized to him, and I apologize to you, too, Sean. You're only new, shouldn't have let you go there under Seamus's command. I should have known better and I'm sorry."

"It's ok, Touched. We're out in one piece and the descriptions they've put out are pretty vague."

"Aye, well, we'll see about that. If Seamus was hit and managed to crawl a couple of hundred yards, they'll eventually find the body and they will ID him. And of course they'll come to Gerry and ask him questions. Gerry was his employer and he lived next door. They might bring that soldier boy to do a lineup on all of us. We are not out of the woods by a long way."

"And if Seamus is wounded? But on the run?"

"He better keep running," Touched said sourly.

We sat in silence while Sonia brought a plate of pancakes and more coffee.

"Are you hurt at all?" she asked me.

"No, I'm fine. Everything aches, but I'm fine."

"Kit took Jackie to the hospital this morning. He needs to get stitches on his leg. I looked at it myself, nasty cut on his thigh. While he's there, he's also getting an MRI on his ankle, he was in pain all night," Touched said sadly.

"He's going to a local hospital?" I asked, surprised.

"No, we haven't fallen that far from the straight and narrow. Kit drove him all the way to Mass General in Boston."

He put his head in his hands.

"I can't fucking believe this. And things were starting to come around," he muttered to himself.

I said nothing and scanned the sports section of the *Times*. Gerry appeared and put his big paws on my shoulders.

"Are you ok, Sean? Did you hear about Jackie?"

"I heard. I'm fine," I said.

Gerry looked at his comrade-in-arms and his face contorted as he dredged up a just-memorized quote from Virgil or somebody.

"Cheer up, Touched. *Forsan et haec olim meminisse iuvabit*. This is not the end of the world," Gerry said, terribly pleased with himself.

"It's bloody close, Gerry. Even if the cops don't get us, the FBI will have to take an interest now. An even bigger interest. And as for our plans to get the Real IRA to sponsor us, we can forget that, we're a fucking laughingstock. Can't even do a bloody burglary. Jesus Christ, Gerry, what a bloody joke. I don't know. Maybe we're getting too old for this. Maybe we should pack it in," Touched said.

Gerry shook his head and sat down.

"Come on, lads. You can't pack it in after one stupid setback," I said, thinking of my pardon and my million.

Gerry nodded at me.

"Yes, listen to the youngster. And he went through it, Touched, the new generation sparks the old, remember that. What was it Jefferson said about the tree of liberty and the blood of the young or something . . ." Gerry said.

Touched tapped the table, forced a smile onto his depressed face, and ran his fingers through his long, graying black hair.

"No, I suppose you're right, Sean," he said after a while.

"I know I am," I said. "You have to bounce right back up. Start organizing, be one step ahead of the peelers."

Aye, start organizing right now, boys, a nice big conspiracy that'll net the pair of you and lead to bloody easy street for me.

Touched grinned at Gerry, that big charming grin that gave me the willies.

"There's always Portsmouth. Our little plan B," Touched said.

"I don't know," Gerry muttered.

"It's your call. It's a target of opportunity and the window is slipping away. Although pull that one off and it's instant respect from across the water," Touched said knowingly.

Gerry nodded.

"I'll think about it," he said.

"Though I'll need to do a lot of work on that still, Gerry," Touched said.

"Well, what are you waiting around for?" Gerry asked.

"I'm waiting for the cops to show up and ask about Seamus," Touched said angrily.

"What exactly is the point of that? If you make yourself busy, things will seem a lot better. Come on, Touched. I have houses to build, people to hire, people to fire. Stop your fucking moping. If the police come, we'll deal with it. If they don't, we'll deal with that, too."

"And what about the FBI?" Touched asked, his mood darkening and his mysterious little Portsmouth op getting pushed to the back of his mind again.

"Are you afeard of the FBI, Touched McGuigan? Show some initiative, man; where is the bold wild colonial that I met twenty years ago, full of fire? Come on. Seize the day. Get out of here. Go and do something. I've got a spade and a shovel waiting for you, if you cannot think of anything else."

Touched stood, laughed.

"You're right, Gerry. As always."

Gerry hugged him.

"Now get out of here."

Touched nodded to me and went outside. Gerry punched me on the shoulder.

"You too, Sean. Outside."

"It's raining."

"So what? Have you forgotten rain in your fortnight in America? Get my daughter and the pair of you go for a walk. That young lady has been mooching around ever since she left Jackie at the hospital. You'd think he was going to have open-heart surgery, not a couple of stitches and an MRI. Come on, out of my house."

I got to my feet.

"Kit, get down here," Gerry bellowed up the stairs.

"What is it?" Kit screamed from her bedroom.

"You're taking Sean for a walk," Gerry said.

"It's pouring," Kit protested.

"Get down here," Gerry yelled again and gave me yet another conspiratorial wink. I might be wrong but it seemed that Gerry had taken a bit of a shine to me, and that Jackie rubbed him the wrong way. I got the feeling that he wouldn't have minded if I replaced Jackie in his daughter's affections. I wouldn't have minded that myself.

Kit appeared. Beautiful and sullen in a black tank top, black jeans, and combat boots.

"What now?" she said.

"Go for a walk with Sean, you both need some air," he said.

"I gotta wait for Jackie's phone call," she said.

"Oh, for goodness sake, he'll be fine. And I'll pick him up if necessary. Now get out of here, the two of you."

Kit looked at me with resentment but she wasn't going to disobey her father.

"Come on then, let's get our coats," she said with all the enthusiasm of a trip to the oral surgeon.

✿   ✿   ✿

Drizzle. A path without a footprint. Shells crunching under our feet. Her big coat a sail that wraps me in the lee.

"Where are we going?" I ask her.

"Well, we live on an island, so there's not many places we can go," she says.

"Don't tell me then," I say.

And she doesn't.

The beach is deserted except for a few hardy dog walkers and lunatic beachcombers and we walk in silence until we come to the very top of Plum Island.

A lighthouse, a Coast Guard station, and a long stone pier that protects the entrance to Newburyport's natural harbor.

"Are you up for something?" she says with a conspiratorial grin.

"What sort of something?"

"Come on," she says.

Threat and mischief spill from her face. She walks to the sandy tip of the island, finds a rowboat, takes off her shoes, and launches the boat into the water.

"What are you doing?"

"Come on," she says, "get in, I'll row. You just have to sit there as ballast."

"Is this your boat?"

"No."

I get in and she puts the oars in the oarlocks and rows me out into the channel where the Merrimack River, the Plum Island basin, and the Atlantic meet. It's not rough today but the drizzly rain has kept water-borne traffic to a minimum and it looks as if a squall could come up at any minute.

"Where are we going?" I ask her.

"Over there," she says, pointing to a spit of land on the other side of the Merrimack River.

"Is that New Hampshire?" I ask.

"No, silly, it's still Massachusetts."

"You know I'm not the best swimmer in the world," I say, a grin trying to hide my concern.

"We'll be fine."

She rows against the tide and the river but it's hard going to prevent us being taken out to sea.

"I'll have a go," I suggest.

"Ok," she agrees, and after a precarious exchange of positions I take over. Kit sitting in the stern, soaked, smiling, her hair plastered over her forehead. A canny wee nature girl and no mistake. The waves chop water over the gunwales, and a passing Coast Guard cutter rocks us, but finally we're in the middle of the channel. It's as sensible to go on as it is to turn back. I row and the tide tries to suck us out and I adjust for it, pulling harder on the left-hand oar.

"You're doing very well," she says, her cheeks carnation-colored, her eyes today almost a sea green. In ten minutes, I feel sand under the bottom of the boat and I row us onto the north shore of the Merrimack. We pull the boat up onto a gravelly spit of land, with high dunes, marram grass, and scrubby bushes.

"What is this place?" I ask her.

"It's a state park. It's totally isolated, you can get here by road but hardly anyone comes. I used to row over here to smoke pot. It's a great view."

I can see most of Plum Island and Newburyport and a great swath of the Atlantic that's more familiar now that it's gray and threatening rather than blue and warm.

"I think you can actually see your house," I say.

"You can," she agrees. "It's that huge one halfway up with all the flags."

"You know, the Stars and Stripes should really be above the others."

"What are you, mister patriot?"

The wind freshens and we huddle together in the dunes, Kit putting her arms together and moving close to me. White-caps on the Merrimack and a swell on the ocean. The breeze bucking over the sand and making a little seif dune parallel to the wind.

"Do you think we'll be able to get back?" she asks.

"Who cares if we get back?"

The wind really howling, folding space about us in sandy logarithms, her hair dislodged and messed and blowing in her eyes. She looks at me and sneaks under my shoulder. I put my arm around her.

She doesn't know what to make of me. What to do, or say. The wheel of her hand is flat on the arm of my leather jacket and tapping it. I take off the jacket and put it over us.

Suddenly, from nowhere, she's about to cry. She fights it.

"Do you think everything's going to be ok?" she asks.

"What are you talking about?"

"With my dad and with Jackie and everything?" she says, tears running down her face.

It's only a couple of frigging stitches, love, I just about resist saying.

"Everything's going to be ok. Do you mean last night? That was nothing. It's all gonna be fine. I promise."

"I hope so," she says and a grimace comes over her face. She wanted to be stronger and now she's blown it. She sobs a little.

"Are you ok? What are you worried about?" I ask her.

"I'm not worried, honest, I, I just want to get it over with. We've been happy here, I've been happy here, and, you know, I understand that Dad has a bigger duty, something he has to do, but, well, I don't want to lose him," she says.

"You won't."

"How do you know?"

"I know things," I tell her reassuringly.

She smiles and holds me. We listen to the wind cutting the water and blowing over the dunes. It's wild and lovely and she starts doing a little better.

"It's Touched, you know, it's all because of him," she says angrily.

"Aye, he's a bad one," I tell her, sensing an angle.

She looks at me. She wants to open up further, but she doesn't.

"My mom would have been happy here, up by the ocean, she was crazy about the sea, would have loved it," she says.

"Where was she from?"

"She was from Long Island originally. Near the sound, I think. Then Boston."

"Where you grew up."

"Yeah, we lived in the city. Dad said he was always going to move up here to be near the sea. Not the Cape, Dad hates the Cape, but up here on the North Shore, where it's more down-to-earth. And we were planning it, but she got this degenerative lymphoma, and, and we had to be near the hospital. We didn't move here until after she . . ."

I know, Kit, I know.

I pull her close as a huge black cloud erases the view of her house and soon the other side of the Merrimack.

She shivers.

Bodies are dialogues and we tell each other things without a word. Her look into my eyes is trust and, perhaps, a seed of something else.

"I suppose that's why she didn't want any kids of her own, it was a genetic disorder. That's why they adopted me. I guess I should be thankful in a weird way."

I don't say anything.

"Your parents are dead, aren't they?" she asks.

"Yeah, my mom when I was little and my dad a few years ago," I say automatically from Sean's biography. "It sounds terrible, Kit, but I wasn't really close to them," I add from mine.

"It's not terrible, it happens like that sometimes," she says.

"Aye," I reply gloomily. Gloomy because she is opening up to me and I'm giving back nothing but lies.

"He's a loafer. He doesn't do any work. Jackie worked hard for my dad and he goes in whenever Dad needs an extra body, and he's got interests, he surfs and everything, he's cool, but Touched doesn't do anything," Kit says, harping back.

"Well, I don't like to cast a stone, but I've heard some ugly rumors about him," I tell her.

"What rumors?"

Before I can respond, the wind wafts up the arm on my T-shirt and Kit pulls it down again.

"Was that from your motorcycle accident as well?" she asks.

"What?"

"You have a little scar on your shoulder. I noticed it when you were dressed as a gladiator, too."

And I look at her to see how far I can go. This is a real opportunity. The professional, cool, clear-thinking Michael Forsythe would say "Yeah, from the motorbike accident," but I know I'm not going to. I'm going to jump across that river and give her a piece of the truth. I'm going to give her a wee bit of the real me and see what she does with it. Will it be reciprocated with trust and silence?

"I had a tattoo removed," I say.

"What was it?"

"Can you keep a secret?"

"Sure," she says, much too breezily for my liking.

"You can't tell Touched. You can't tell anybody. They'll get the wrong idea."

"I promise," she says, getting serious now.

"It was a winged harp, which was my old regimental

insignia. I was in the British Army for about eleven months. The Royal Irish Rangers. They don't exist anymore, they got merged into another regiment."

"You were in the British Army?" Kit asks, to confirm it.

"That's right. I was unemployed, had nothing else going for me. It seemed the right idea at the time, but we didn't gel, the army and me, they kicked me out with a dishonorable discharge."

"I can see why you don't want Touched to know," Kit says without inflection.

"You'll keep it a secret?"

"Of course," she says indignantly. "It doesn't bother me in the least."

"Thanks. It's the only secret I've got, I promise," I tell her.

"Well, I can think of a million worse ones than joining the army when you were young and dumb," she says, pleasing me with the answer.

"Me, too."

She manages a little grin and then I grab the moment and kiss her lightly on the forehead.

"Do that again," she says, those big azure eyes closing in anticipation.

I kiss her on the mouth.

"I liked that," she says. "I shouldn't, but I do."

"I liked it too," I tell her and I'm glad now that I told her that little piece of truth. For although I'm a liar, this, between her and me, isn't part of the lie. I'm not using her to get that million dollars. She's a different part of this completely.

And what is it about her exactly?

She's beautiful. But that's not it. And she's mixed up, but that's not it either.

There's something else.

It's that feeling of regret I get when I look at her. It's that ache of memory.

Again she reminds me of Bridget, that other lost girl, in a place and time that seem centuries ago.

I couldn't save Bridget. I couldn't stop her following my path, the road to horror and war and vengeance. I couldn't stop Bridget forgetting her old self and becoming this cold and terrible machine of death. I couldn't stop her because it was me that pushed her down that road in the first place. It was me that killed her fiancé. And if Dan Connolly is right, that story isn't finished yet.

But there's nothing I can do about that now. History can't be unwritten.

Kit, though. I can save Kit.

I can stop her descent into hell.

I can eliminate the influence of those two evil stars.

And when it's their time, I'll figure out a way to get her out. Away from these people and this situation. When it goes down, I'll fix it, so she won't go sink too.

"Kit, I . . ." I try, but I don't know what to say.

She finds the words.

"Sean, I know it's wrong, but I want you to touch me," she says in a whisper.

I slip my hand under her sweater and I touch the cool skin of her belly and her small breasts and I hold her back and I pull her close and kiss her.

"Slowly," she says.

And I kiss and I hold her, and run my hands down her spine and up her thighs and between her legs. And she tenses and I ease her away and let her go and it is so painful that in a moment of candor I can no longer deny what I've been fighting against.

"I need you," I tell her.

She shakes her head.

"You don't," she says.

I kiss her and, my God, I want her. Here on this beach under this dark sky. It will do everything for me. It will heal me. It will make me whole. It will unmake from me the murder in my blood and fingertips. I need to give myself completely to her. I need to hold and be inside her and be one with her. And I know she needs me, too.

I lift her shirt and kiss her belly.

"Yes," she says.

She pulls me on top of her and her hands run over my back

and they're so cold. I kiss her and lift up her shirt and kiss her underneath her breasts and her nipples and gently I begin to undo the buttons on her jeans.

"Stop," she whispers.

I kiss her belly button and her shoulder tattoo and undo the last button and begin to pull down her trousers.

"No," she says. "Stop."

And I shake my head and moisten her lips and kiss her freezing arms and—

"I said stop," she says angrily and pushes me off.

"Ok, I'll stop," I tell her, hurt.

"You're all the fucking same, aren't you? Fucking all alike. And I thought you were different," she says, crying.

"Kit, what are you talking about?"

But she's standing now, buttoning up her jeans. Furious; at me, but mostly at herself. She's confused, guilty, unsure. Her hands form themselves into fists.

"I'm not going to have sex with you," she says.

"What?"

She starts marching away from me down the dune.

"I don't have to have sex with you. I just want to be with you. Come back here, please. Kit, please, we don't have to do anything. We'll talk or not talk, anything. Just stay here."

"Fuck you. And I told you, I already have a boyfriend," she screams and runs to the rowboat.

"What are you doing?"

"I'm going back to Plum Island," she shouts, launching the boat into the surf.

"Wait a minute," I yell, struggling to my feet and running after her. She jumps aboard and rows away from the beach. The wind has dropped but it's raining again.

"Come back. It's not safe."

"Fuck you. I can do this in my sleep. Go to hell," she yells, pulling away from the shore in broad, confident strokes.

I try a different approach.

"But how am I going to get back?"

"Walk back."

"How?"

"Follow the Merrimack and you'll eventually come to Newburyport and then . . ." but I can't hear her anymore. I wave to her and wait to see if she'll come back, but she doesn't and soon she's way out in the channel, a disappearing speck in the gray waves.

Shit.

I watch until I'm sure she's safe, and when she lands the boat on the Plum Island shore I pull my hood up and begin the long walk back to town.

Four or five bloody miles by the looks of it.

"Women. Jesus," I mutter to myself.

No, not women, girls. That was the bloody problem. Stupid teenage, know-nothing wee girl.

Fuming, I walk over the dunes and out of the state park.

Back on Route 1 again. This awful bloody road. This bloody state, these bloody people. Should have asked her about her real ma again; that always sets her off. Give her something to be really pissed about.

'Course it's raining, too. Typical.

I stick my thumb out but not a single person gives me a lift.

I finally reach the bridge over the Merrimack and trudge across it into Newburyport. When I get into the center of town, I'm still fuming. A bloody cocktease, that girl, she knows what she's doing. Wee hoor. Beeatch, with a capital *B*. Have to wonder about anyone with the taste to go out with Jackie in the first place. No sense at all.

I walk past the police station, the ice-cream shops, and the theater showing *Cats*.

The Firehouse, Water Street, State Street. I stop outside All Things Brit.

The Closed sign is in the window but it's only seven o'clock. It usually stays open till eight or nine. I try the handle. It doesn't turn. Maybe she went down to Boston to get my pardons and the forms for my money. Come on, Samantha, I could do with a cup of hot tea.

I open the letter box and shout through it:

"Hello, is there anyone home? Hello?"

No answer.

Aye, she's gone. Probably bloody bird-watching in Maine. That's exactly the kind of support you need when you're an undercover on a dangerous assignment.

Another silly woman.

"Hello, is there anyone home?" I try for the final time.

I'm about to go when I see a shadow appear at the bottom of the stairs.

"Hello? Who is that?" I shout again.

The shadow walks towards me.

It's Touched.

"What are you doing here?" I ask.

He opens the door.

"No, the more pertinent and important question is what are *you* doing here?" he asks, pointing a silenced 9mm at me.

"I came to get some chocolate for Kit," I tell him.

"Is that so?" he says suspiciously, closing the door behind me.

"Uh-huh. We had a bit of a fight."

"You often shout into the letter box of closed stores? Eh?"

"The wee lady who runs the place told me she's open till nine every day," I say.

His face is cold. His eyes are the color of granite slabs cut for tombstones.

"How well do you know this wee lady?" he asks in a voice with no emotion.

"Seamus, Jackie, and I were in here yesterday and Kit took me in here once to get clotted cream," I say as calmly as I can, for I realize now that he's killed her. That somehow he's found her out. But she didn't tell him anything. I know that because I'd be dead too by now, or if not dead, shot in both kneecaps and being dragged screaming to the back room to be tortured lovingly and long.

"Aye, I remember that. Well, you better come see this," Touched says.

"What's the gun for?" I ask him.

"Excuse me, Sean, but I'm going to have to watch you very closely for the next couple of days. Too many wee things happening at once. Suspicious, so it is, very fucking suspicious.

Last night going wrong like that and now this."

"What are you talking about?"

"Something has come up, Sean," he says soberly.

"Like what?"

"Upstairs with me and you'll see. You first, mate," he says.

I walk up the stairs.

I can smell the blood from the second step.

On the landing, at the top, I turn right and walk into her bedroom. She has been gagged and tied naked to the bed. Her eyes have been cut out of their sockets and she has been slit open from her vagina to her throat.

But not deeply, not enough to kill her straightaway.

Blood is everywhere. On the sheets, on the walls, even on the skylight. There is still a scalpel blade embedded in her thigh and Touched's little green toolbox is open between her legs. It's not a toolbox at all, but is in fact a dissection kit. His instruments: knives, scalpels, retractors, covered with skin and gore—well used.

My knees buckle and I throw up in my mouth.

"Oh God," I say.

"She was smart," Touched says. "She had no paperwork of any kind. And she denied everything, right to the end."

"What the fuck have you done? Who is she?" I manage.

"She's been spying on us. I'd seen her twice. I'm always watching for new people. I wasn't sure, though. Even tonight. I just wasn't sure and for a while I thought I'd made a mistake."

He laughs.

"Jesus, yeah, thought I'd really fucked up and she was just a dumb tourist, nosing around the biggest house on the island. I really thought that."

"What are you talking about?"

"I was on my way to Portsmouth and I saw that big Jag parked outside the shop here, and when I came in to see who owned it I saw her. First thing that bothered me was that I was smoking a cigarette and she didn't ask me to put it out. No Smoking signs everywhere and she didn't ask me to put out me fag. Why?"

He looked at me. It wasn't a rhetorical question. He wanted me to think about it.

"I don't know, Touched."

"Why? I'll tell you fucking why. Because I'd put the wind up her, thrown her, she was afraid of me. Why would she be afraid of me when she doesn't even know me? Aye, Sean, I can smell it, you know. Fear. I can fucking taste it."

"I'm sure."

"Aye. So that was the first thing. And so then I asked her about herself. And it turns out she's only been here a week or two and she's British. Ask her all these questions and she doesn't say 'Stop wasting my time' or 'Are you going to buy something?' Ever see a shopkeeper who just wants to chat? She gave herself away, mate. She was too friendly. Overcompensating. And I realized I'd have to probe this further."

"Christ. You killed her because she was polite to you?"

Touched smiles sadly and pats me on the back, all the while keeping the gun pointing at my belly. He runs a gloved hand through his hair and grins, licks the blood from his lips.

"Aye, Sean, for a while there this evening I thought I'd made a mistake. Tied her up, gagged her, had my way with her, searched the place. Nothing, fucking nothing. And really that was another mistake. I mean, everybody has to have some personal stuff. Driver's license, passport, library card, letters, anything. And she had nothing."

I shake my head.

"But fortunately, Sean, my instincts were right. At the very end, at the very fucking end, I take the gag off her, and she's hurting, oh yeah, she's hurting and she begs me to finish it, begs me. She says, and this is the kicker, Sean, 'Please, Touched, kill me, just kill me,'" Touched repeats, his eyebrows raising in a look of triumph.

"I don't get it," I tell him.

"No one calls me Touched. Except Gerry and the Sons of Cuchulainn and the lads back home. She was FBI, Sean, or a British agent working for the FBI."

"You sure?"

"I'm sure. And that's why I don't like to see you shouting through the letter box as if you and her are best pals. And that's why we're all going to have to split town for a while. Get rid of this bitch. Switch to plan B like Gerry says. This is when they'll be least expecting it. What do you think?"

"I don't know," I say, reeling.

"Yeah, well, whatever we do I'm going to have to keep an eye on you, mate. Very close eye," he says with a grim face.

"I met this woman twice in my whole fucking life," I protest.

Touched nods sympathetically.

"Sean, put yourself in my shoes. You just can't be too careful."

"I know her about as well as Kit and Jackie know her," I say.

"Aye, but they have several years of trust in the bank with me. You have less than a week. And a bad week at that."

I catch his eye and nod.

"You're right. I'd do the same thing myself."

He grins.

"You're a good lad. At least I hope for your sake you are."

And we stand for a moment and stare at the bed. And suddenly I notice her chest moving up and down.

"She's still alive," I gasp in horror.

"Aye, but not for long now," Touched says clinically.

He's right.

She has bled all over the floor.

Her cheeks dead white, her teeth smashed in, the breath exhaling from her body in frothy bubbles of crimson blood.

There's nothing I can do and anyway he has the gun.

But if you can hear me, Samantha, if you can hear me, hear me.

"If you're wrong about this, Touched, I wouldn't like to be in your shoes."

He looks at me to see if I'm threatening him, but my face is expressionless, blank. He lets it go and I watch her breaths grow fainter and fainter until they finally stop.

Death has ten thousand ways.

And in the minute it takes Samantha to pass, I imagine that, on Earth, about a thousand other human beings are making that mysterious transition from life to lifelessness. Still, Touched is a master of this art. Touched is Death's apprentice. True, there are old people in Buenos Aires who for a time in the 1940s were killing tens of thousands every day; and there are men in Cambodia and Rwanda who have personally slaughtered hundreds with their own hands. He will never match those individuals in terms of body counts. He doesn't need to. He's a specialist. Quick and lethal or slow, dreadful, and terrifying. With Samantha he took his time. An hour or two, perhaps longer. He tortured her, horribly, and there can be few alive who take such pride in the pain they inflict in the commission of their work.

And a coup for him. A British agent. A woman agent.

Sweet.

I lean on the wall to steady myself.

Breathe in, exhale. Breathe in, let it all go.

And then the fear begins to leave me and I open my eyes to memorize the scene. The tiny precise cuts all over her body. The eyes. The smell.

Aye. One thing, Touched. You can't know that I also am a favored son. That I, too, have welcomed many into the arms of Death.

Oh yes.

Let me look at you. You're calm, relaxed, confident.

It'll be a match, you and me, we brothers of the sword.

On that day of reckoning.

Put down that gun and you'll have it now.

He doesn't move.

But that's fine, Touched.

You're already dead. Here, in this room, as we live and breathe, and as you stare at me with distrust in those granite eyes, and I look back to you, a cipher, I vow to meet you in an unfair fight and spare no quarter and butcher you and cut you down.

Aye, my friend.

Joyfully, with mine own hand, will I despoil your corpse

and throw your tattered carcass onto that black barge that Death steers into the silent sea, from which none return. The day *will* come.

And it can't come soon enough.

9: A BURIAL ON PI

Touched pulled down the blinds and dimmed the lights, all the while, casually, keeping me in eyeline, his itchy trigger finger pointing the 9mm at my chest.

Big-eyed, bloody, his face a sunburned brown, his disordered graying hair a grisly crown of pride. He was pleased with himself. Happy.

He looked at the body.

"Aye, she's dead now, Sean. You ever seen someone die before?"

I shook my head.

"No, I suppose not. Ok. Well, it's only a first step. The night's not over yet. You're about to get a valuable learning experience," he said.

"What do you mean?" I asked, keeping the lid on the pressure cooker.

"Clean up. Have you touched anything since you came upstairs?"

"You know I haven't, I've just been standing here," I said.

"And I was wearing these for most of the evening," Touched said, showing me his black silk gloves.

"I see," I said.

"Sit down on that stool and don't do anything for a minute," Touched ordered.

I sat down. Touched pulled out his mobile phone and

speed-dialed a number.

"Aye, Gerry, it's me. . . . Yeah, I took care of it. I'll want you to come by with Jackie, and we'll get rid of her. Bring plastic sheets, that big sail bag, cleaning supplies, and overalls. . . . Nah, no problems. . . . Listen, mate, interesting sidelight, young Sean showed up looking to buy chocolate biscuits. He was shouting through her letter box. I'm not sure if I like it. There's a chance that she was the FBI agent on the outside and he's the inside man, so we're going to have to watch him, interrogate him. I think he's kosher, he's a good lad, but you know me, Gerry, fucking caution is my middle name. . . . Aye. Listen, the sooner the two of you get over here the better. You best tell the family we're going to have to go up to the cabin, especially if you still want to do plan B. . . . Aye, until all of this cools down. . . . Ok, see you, mate."

He clicked off the phone and looked at me.

"You don't have to worry about me, pal," I said.

He smiled, rubbed his chin.

"Listen, Sean, I think you're ok, but Jesus, we have to be careful. We don't really know you from Adam. So after we get rid of this bitch we're going to have to give you a bit of the old fucking third degree, ok?"

I said nothing.

Touched leaned against the wall, shook his head, got a glimpse of Samantha out of the corner of his eye, grinned.

"Yeah, Sean, it's like this. Gerry and me have already decided we're going to split town for a few days. We can't do anything with the FBI breathing down our necks and they're going to get nervous when their agent disappears. We'll dump her body and we'll clean this place so it's spic-and-span even under the UV lights but, still, they'll definitely increase sur-veillance on us when they realize that she's missing. But we'll have the drop on them. We'll be up in Maine at Gerry's cabin, which he has kept off the books and no one even knows about. It's a fantastic spot. Aye, remember we talked about it? He calls it the Dead Yard because of the trains. Even if they are looking, the FBI wouldn't find us in a million years. "

"What's up there?"

"Nothing's up there. Except us. We'll be up there and hopefully with a wee surprise, too."

Touched looked at his black T-shirt, speckled with blood and saliva and God knows what else.

"This T-shirt's ruined," he said, leering, itching to tell me details. How she was an uncooperative cow, how she bled so easy, how she screamed under the gag . . .

He coughed, blinked. Motioned me to get up and go downstairs. I went ahead of him down the steps and into the shop. He went to the door, checked the street, pulled the blinds, grabbed a Flake bar, threw it to me. I shook my head and forced a hurt and disappointed look onto my face.

"Eat your chocolate," he said. "That's why you came in."

"I came in to get some for Kit, we had a bit of a fight."

"Eat it, you'll need energy for later."

I shook my head.

"What's the matter with you? Are you upset about her upstairs?"

"If she was a British agent, she got what was coming to her," I said.

"Are you pissed off at me for doubting you?" he asked.

"No, it's not that either. It's just, you know, things look like they're getting a bit out of control," I said, to show him that I was a naive immigrant who knew nothing of this violent world he inhabited.

Touched was sympathetic.

"I know, Sean. I know. From your perspective things probably look really fucked up about now. But you gotta believe me, mate, these are just setbacks but they're not fatal setbacks. Ok, so we don't know what the hell happened to Seamus. If you ask me, he's either dead or he's on his way to fucking Australia by now. Doesn't matter, unless that soldier boy IDs you and Jackie, and the news says he can't do any descriptions, then we can draw a line through that episode and forget the whole thing. And this, well, you could almost see this as a good thing. Now we know the feds are keeping tabs on us, so we'll all have to be more careful," he said.

I nodded, unconvinced.

"Come on, mate, cheer up, you don't want to look this blue when the lads show up," he said, giving me a wink.

Touched seemed a different man than the morose and depressed character of this morning. A couple of hours of rape and torture had clearly invigorated him.

"But you've murdered one of their agents now. Won't that make things worse?" I asked, making sure I said the word *murdered*, not *killed*.

"No, they'll never find her. Not where we're going to put her. They won't know what happened to her. It'll fuck them up for weeks. And let's say the feds *are* watching us, the last thing they'll expect us to do is what we're going to do next. They'll figure we'll be running scared. They'll think that. Not us, mate. You'll see, Sean, we'll impress you yet. And if you go back to Ireland someday, you'll say that the Sons of Cuchulainn were the baddest, smartest, coolest lads you ever worked with. You'll see."

Touched laughed. He was so excited and relaxed that it was making me physically ill.

"So what happens next, tonight?" I asked.

"Gerry, me, you, and Jackie are going to dig a hole in the salt marsh on Plum Island and dispose of that lass. Then me and you are going back to Gerry's house and I'm going to have to question you like you've never been questioned before. And then, after that, as much as you were on probation before, you'll be in purgatory now," he said dispassionately.

"What about the mess upstairs?"

"I'm going to be busy with you. Gerry is not in the best physical shape, so I suppose young Jackie will have to spend most of the night doing that. I'll swing by in the morning with my UV scanner to check it out. Be a job, but don't worry about that, the hard work will be good for him."

There was a knock at the back door.

"There's the boys," Touched said.

Touched kept me in pistol shot and opened the back door. Gerry and Jackie were dressed in old clothes, carrying a holdall and a huge plastic sail cover that presumably was to be the improvised body bag. Jackie limped over and shook my hand. Gerry, too, greeted me warmly.

"Sean," Gerry said loudly. "I believe the shadow of suspicion has been draped over you. Not to worry. *Macte nova virtute puer.* You were in the wrong place at the wrong time. Kit told me about the little trick she pulled, no wonder you needed some refreshment after your long walk."

"What are you going to do to him?" Jackie asked.

"We're going to have to quarantine Sean a wee bit," Touched said. "And check him out."

Jackie looked upset.

"I don't mind it, Jackie, really, better safe than sorry. I mean, I can totally see Touched's point of view," I said.

"Anyway, don't worry. We're going to have a grand few days. We're going to switch to plan B and we're going to go to the cabin," Gerry said.

"I've filled him in already, Gerry, can't let him know too much, though; I told him he's going to be in purgatory for a wee bit," Touched announced.

"Of course. We'll have to keep an eye on you," Gerry said, slapping me on the back a little too hard.

"Ok," I said.

"These are difficult times," Gerry said, his eyes tight and betraying nothing.

I nodded and Jackie came over and patted me on the back too. Not like Gerry. Gentle, affectionately.

"I believe in you. You were cool under pressure last night and as far as I'm concerned you're a mate for life. And, for, for, for my part that shit between us is all in the past," Jackie said, his cheeks reddening.

I give him a Gleason tap under the chin.

"Thanks, Jackie," I said, trying to sound moved.

"Well, if the fucking lovefest is over, we have work to do," Touched declared. "Gerry, since you are not the most physically able of the four of us, I'm going to have to ask you to keep Sean covered with the gun. I know it's bloody distasteful but you'll have to do it."

Gerry nodded and gave me a sympathetic look. Touched opened Gerry's holdall, removed overalls and gloves. We put them on. Touched grabbed the sail bag and led us upstairs.

We went into the Mediterranean blue bedroom, with the lovely pictures and new drapes. Jackie took one look at the bed and had to leave. We heard him retch into the toilet bowl.

"Make sure you bloody flush," Touched said.

I looked at her again. Samantha was naked, cold, but she didn't look dead. Even disfigured, there was, even now, a hint of the woman. That big personality who, if she could, would be telling me to keep a cool head and be careful.

There she was, still and lifeless, three men in her web, looking at her.

"Better get started," Touched said.

Gerry didn't say anything, which in itself was remarkable. No "Oh my God, Touched, what the fuck have you done?" or "You're a fucking animal, we need to get you help" or "This time you've gone too far," nothing like that. Just a shrug and on with the bloody task at hand.

I untied her wrists and lifted her by the head, secretly caressing her frigid cheek.

"That's the ticket, Sean. Hold her up. Get in here, Jackie," Touched said, lifting her legs. We eased her into the sail bag and Gerry zipped it up.

"I don't recognize her at all, are you sure about this, Touched? I mean, just because she drove past our house a couple of times," Gerry wondered.

"No mistake, Gerry, I'm telling you she was FBI. I promise. I'm ninety-nine percent sure."

Gerry nodded. That was good enough for him. It had to be good enough for him.

We carried Samantha to the stairs and as far as I could I made sure the passage down was gently done. Gerry checked that the coast was clear and we heaved the body outside to one of his big white vans. We shut the van and closed, but didn't lock, the back door of All Things Brit. Touched drove us away from the scene of butchery, Gerry pointing the gun from the front, Jackie and me in the back with Samantha.

We hit the Plum Island turnpike, went over the bridge, and turned right towards the wildlife sanctuary. This was almost the very spot Samantha and I had been at last night. And here she was again in different circumstances entirely.

We easily skirted the barrier the Department of Fish and Wildlife had put up to stop people going into the reserve after dark and drove about a mile down the single-lane road, finally coming to a halt at a sign marked "Salt Pan."

All four of us got out. A desolate part of the island, between barren sand dunes and the tidal marsh with no trace of people, birds, anything.

Gerry distributed shovels and Jackie, Touched, and myself began digging a hole in the weird, sucking, salty earth.

I began to get nervous.

Of course, they could just as easily shoot me and throw me down this hole too.

I could, at any moment, make a break for it, run off into the darkness. But Touched and Jackie were very fit. They'd track me and kill me for sure. And from what I'd read, Touched was a marksman.

I looked up at the waxing moon and the surroundings.

Not much cover in these dunes.

I decided to play it cool, for now. Though I'd have to give it a go if I twigged that they were going to execute me.

"Why bury her here, Touched?" I asked.

"It's a good spot," Touched replied. "The ground is so salty no big animals can stand it, so nothing's going to dig her up. She'll stay here undiscovered, pretty much until the end of bloody time. I found out about this place, when, uh, when, well, let's just say, I had a similar problem about a year ago. Woman trouble. You know what's it's like. 'Course I had to do the digging all by myself. Gerry would not help me."

"Damn right, Touched, you got yourself into that mess and no bloody mistake," Gerry said and chuckled as if Touched had failed to pay his parking tickets or been caught sneaking into the cinema.

Touched wiped the sweat from his brow and took a breather. It was now a hot, sweaty night and naturally the flies were murderous. Gerry, keeping the gun on me and excused from digging, passed us a water bottle. We all took a swig.

"Have you been to Maine before, Sean?" he asked when I gave him the water back.

"Nope," I said, grunting between shovels.

"You'll like it. Fall in the Maine woods is a truly beautiful experience. And I think the leaves just might be starting to turn when we get up there, although it'll probably still be too early. We'll see."

We dug for another fifteen minutes. When Touched called a halt, I was relieved to see that there was room enough for only one body. We laid Samantha in her final resting place and threw in our overalls and Touched's bloody clothes. When no one was looking, I put my cell phone in one of my gloves and dropped it in too, just in case they had the wit to check the call log. Now there was no link between me and her.

I made sure my shovel was the first to throw the dirt on her. It's not an insult, it's a blessing, I said to myself.

We filled in the hole quicker than we dug it. Touched stamped down the sand and put his hands on his hips, admiring a job well done.

He looked at Gerry.

"The old ways?" Touched asked.

"We got time?" Gerry replied.

"Aye," Touched said. "Come on, lads."

Touched unzipped his jeans, took out his penis, and began urinating on the grave. Gerry began unbuttoning his fly and I saw that this was an opportunity not to be missed. I unzipped my pants and unleashed a strong stream of urine onto the grave.

"Fucking bitch," I muttered under my breath but loud enough for the boys to hear.

Gerry laughed and Touched nodded with satisfaction.

"Come on, Jack, you too," Touched said.

Jackie took out his prick but he couldn't pee. He wasn't a bad sort, Jackie, and this was all just too much for him.

"I can't go," he said when the three of us were finishing up.

"Forget it, Jackie. It's enough. We better get cracking," Gerry said.

Touched grunted and took something out of his pocket.

"I'd be much obliged if you put these on, Sean," Touched said, passing me a pair of handcuffs.

Jackie was incensed.

"Is that really necessary? For fucksake, he's one of us," he said.

"Jackie, you shut the fuck up now. I'm head of security here and I've already explained to Sean why I'm suspicious and he understands it."

"I don't mind, Jack," I told him.

I zipped my pants and cuffed my hands in front of me. Touched checked that they were tight with a tug on both wrists that made me flinch with a momentary flash of terror, for now that I was safely restrained this was another occasion for an abrupt change of mood: screaming, yelling, kicking me to the ground. . . .

But it didn't happen.

"All right, job well done," Gerry said.

We walked back to the van.

Gerry drove. He dropped Touched and me back at the house on PI and gave Jackie a lift back into town for his long hours ahead. Jackie would have to scour the place of blood and any clues that she'd met a violent end. Definitely an all-nighter. But at least he wouldn't find a fax from the FBI or MI6 confirming Samantha's request for a million dollars and a pardon from Spain and Mexico. She either hadn't gotten round to asking for that yet, or, like the professional agent she was, she'd destroyed the note as soon as she'd gotten it.

"This way," Touched said, leading me not to the guest-house but instead to a basement room in the main house.

I was relieved. If I didn't sufficiently convince Touched and this was to be my prison cell it would be ok. Eventually the FBI backups were bound to notice that Samantha was missing and they'd come looking for me; and if I was still alive they'd find me down here. Hopefully, before Touched had a chance to work his magic.

※　※　※

The dead channel of the TV casting a dismal glow out into the thick air of the musky room. The blinds drawn but sunlight filtering through the gaps, illuminating the dust spirals rising from the heat of the floor. Outside crickets and grasshoppers beginning their summer song and greenheads and biting flies waking from their nighttime slumber, ready for another day of greedy torment on the human population of the island.

Morning.

I was knackered, but Touched was exhausted too. He wasn't up for this. Asking questions without torture, where was the fun in that? Harder than it looked.

He had sat me in a comfortable old leather reclining chair, but five hours with my right hand cuffed to the radiator and the worry that one slip would mean certain death was still a dark night of the bloody soul.

Touched yawned.

"Let's go through this one more time," he said, rubbing at the blear in his eyes.

He'd asked about random times in my life, what school I'd gone to, my teachers, where I'd shopped in Belfast, the names of various pubs. And of course he realized that if I was an Englishman or an American pretending to be an Irishman I was impossibly good. Still, that didn't prove I wasn't working for the FBI. He'd asked about every year of Sean's life, asked names, contacts, addresses. But I'd broken the back of him in the wee smalls and after that his heart wasn't in it.

Or at least so it appeared.

One thing you couldn't do with Touched was underestimate him.

That was ok too. I was patient and I'd wait him out. I wanted to wait him out. I was in a dangerous place, but the moment I'd seen Samantha I'd made a decision. The mission had changed. It was no longer about money or the Sons of Cuchulainn. Touched had taken it into the realm of the personal, and I'd decided that whatever else happened I wasn't running now. I was in it for the long haul. Now it was between him and me. Let the Sons of Cuchulainn carry out their little fantasies, let them have their delusions of grandeur. Let them do what they wanted. But give me time alone with him. Before I escaped to the feds, before I got away from these people, I'd make bloody sure that he got what was coming to him. No trial for you, Touched. Gerry and the rest, yes, but I'm taking care of you myself.

Touched yawned loudly and I could see he was hamming it.

He was about to roll his final play.

"So between March 1992 and November 1992 you don't remember where you were working at all?" he asked quietly.

I shook my head.

"It was either in London or it was Spain, I don't fucking remember, Touched, I really don't. I'm beat," I said.

He stood up and got himself a drink of water from a tap in the corner. He hit the TV set to switch it off.

He turned and looked at me.

Carefully, he took his little green toolbox from an inside jacket pocket. He opened it and removed a blood-encrusted scalpel.

His eyes narrowed.

"You think you're so fucking smart. Well, you're not. You're as smart as her and that's not smart enough," he said coldly.

He walked over, threw his arm round my neck, pulled my head back, and brought the bloody scalpel up to my eyeball.

"Tell me the fucking truth," he said. "Tell me the truth or I'll fucking cut you right now."

The bloody blade touched my eyelid. It made me wince. Fear rushed through me.

But I wasn't going to lose it now.

"I don't fucking remember, Touched," I insisted.

He pushed on the blade for a horrible ten seconds but then he let go the grip around my neck, removed the scalpel, and shook his head.

He yawned.

"Ugh, it doesn't matter, Sean, I don't remember anything of the 80s and not much of the early 90s either," he said with a half-laugh.

I nodded.

"So you finally believe me?"

"Aye, I think you're ok. I have a sixth sense for these things. You're one of us. I've thought so all along. . . . There's just that one wee thing."

"What one wee thing."

"Well, ach, it's nothing, it's just that you're a bit too good to be true, you know? You're cool and you're clever and you're young. And you fell in our lap at just the right time. Do you see what I mean?"

"Not really."

"No. Well, it doesn't matter. The thing is, I want to believe you and it's easy to believe you."

"You should believe me 'cos I'm telling the truth."

"Aye, so you say. You probably are. It's nothing to do with you and I'm going to tell Gerry that. It's my fault, I'm just a suspicious old dog," he said with a mechanical wink.

He gave me a cup full of water. I drank it and leaned back in the reclining chair. Touched rubbed his face.

"It's morning," I said, looking out the basement window.

"Aye, we've been at this all night, and I still have to go and check up on Jackie and ring my wee pal in Portsmouth Harbor. Fuck it. Ok. Ok. I think we'll call it right here," Touched said with weary eyes.

"Fine by me," I said. "You wanna undo the cuff?"

With him tired and the cuff off and the gun in the other corner of the room I could fucking kill him right now. But Touched was an old pro.

He backed away, got his gun, and took another drink of water.

He shook his head.

"Like I say, I'm a sussy oul dog. But still, we're on the job today and I'm going to have to keep you under close observation until then. Do you mind?" he said, sounding a bit ashamed of himself.

"You got to do what you think is right," I said like a good little disciple.

Touched stood, threw me another set of cuffs, and motioned me to fasten my wrists together. Only then would he undo the chain to the radiator.

"Ok, what time is it? Let me see, six, ok, I can hear them moving around upstairs. Well, what I suggest is this. You and me go upstairs and get some breakfast and I'll buzz Jackie and we both have a big bloody sleep for four or five hours. Let them do all the packing and hard work. We'll kip, have some lunch. Go to Portsmouth, get our man, and head to the cabin. What do you say?"

"Sounds good to me," I muttered.

"It wasn't too bad, was it?"

"I'm wrecked, Touched, totally wrecked. I hope you did all this with Jackie and Seamus, too, and all the others," I said.

He put his arm round my shoulder.

"Come up for breakfast. Got to keep those cuffs on ya until after the op or at least until I'm sure. Do you think you can sleep with them on?"

"I doubt it," I said.

"Cuff your good ankle to the bed. What about that?" Touched said in an attempt to be tender.

It made me hate him all the more.

"Whatever you say, mate," I told him.

He led me upstairs. He threw me the key so I could eat breakfast, but he was sitting at the other end of the table and he had the gun in his pocket now.

After I'd forced myself to swallow some toast and eggs, he made me cuff myself again, took me to my old room upstairs, and handcuffed my ankle to the iron bedstead, only then undoing the wrists. Suspicious old dog was right. And from his extreme caution, it was not impossible that he'd seen through my act and actually he was the one fooling me, not vice versa. Not impossible, but not likely.

Touched waved goodbye, shut the door, and I lay back on the bed.

I closed my eyes. But I couldn't sleep. I couldn't come down from the high plateau of concentration. One wee slipup and I'd be joining Samantha in a hole in the salt pan.

Samantha.

Oh my God, Samantha.

What a hero she'd been. Saying nothing, when it would have been so easy to give me up to end her pain. If I got out of this alive I'd make sure the Brits knew about her courage.

I stared at the cloud patterns through the window and watched the tide come in, and then, despite everything, I did manage to doze for a while. . . .

Two, three hours later?

The door opened.

Gerry was standing there.

He walked to the bed and undid the handcuff at my foot.

"We won't be needing that anymore," he said.

I was free.

I sat up, rubbing my ankle to get the circulation back.

Gerry was easy, even if he was armed. A dropkick to the sternum. Get him on the floor, rip that revolver from him, grab a pillow to act as silencer, shoot the fucker twice, one in the gut, one in the head, run down through the house looking for Touched. But where was Touched and the rest of them?

"Where is Touched? I should really tell him that there's no hard feelings."

"Oh, he's gone already, and listen, I want to talk to you about that, better that he's not here."

"Go ahead."

His big frame lumbered up beside me and his sad eyes blinked slowly.

"Sean, I just want to let you know that I'm very sorry about all of this. This is not how I customarily treat my guests," he said.

I don't know what was worse, Touched's suspicions or Gerry's constant fucking apologies.

"It doesn't matter," I said.

"I had no idea he had shackled you and it will not happen again. . . . I want to let you know that I for one never doubted you."

"It's ok," I said, standing up and balancing myself.

"No, it's not ok. Goddamnit, you saved my daughter's life. And I was moved by that more than you can ever know, Sean," Gerry said, his eyes getting all watery. "Touched doesn't want me to tell you this, but I feel so terrible about the way he's been abusing you in the hospitality of my house. And he even wants to . . ." Gerry's voice trailed off.

He'd certainly piqued my bloody interest, though, and I couldn't let it stop there.

"What?"

Gerry sighed. "Oh, I suppose it's nothing really. But I wanted to let you know that he's asked our friends in Belfast to check you out too. We should have word back in a couple of days and then the cloud will be gone permanently. We'll do a proper induction ceremony into the Sons of Cuchulainn and after that, my boy, you'll start to see how we really work. What the FBI don't realize is that we're not lunatics or chaos merchants, we're smart, and we're long-term thinkers, and we'll get it right, you'll see."

I hoped I wasn't showing any emotion. There were two ways they could check me out back home. They could look into the police computer files, school records, that kind of thing and Sean McKenna would be fine. Six had sorted all that out for him. But the other way might be more tricky. If these "friends" actually went to the trouble of asking questions in the alleged neighborhoods where I used to live, went to the schools I used to attend, talked to the men I supposedly knew, well, then things could be quite a bit hairier.

I shrugged and smiled.

It didn't matter to me anyway. I had already made up my mind. I was staying in until I butchered him and if it meant I had only a couple of days of safety, well, then that rapist-murderer had only a couple of days too.

✿   ✿   ✿

We stood in the driveway while Gerry lowered the flags. The van was loaded up, and the two vehicles were ready. Kit was wearing a black trench coat that didn't suit her, a wool sweater, and a Boston Red Sox wool hat.

"How far up is this cabin? You look as if we're going to the North Pole," I asked her.

Kit looked at me and smiled. She was goofy but she could get me killed, that girl. One blab to Touched about the army and I'd be dead meat.

"You'd be surprised how cold it can get. You ever look at the weather reports in the papers? On days when it's ninety degrees in Boston, a hundred degrees in New York, check out Mount Washington and it's like forty."

Sonia laughed.

"She's exaggerating, Sean. It won't be that cold. And the cabin isn't even in the mountains. We won't be anywhere near Mount Washington," she said.

Kit's nose wrinkled up in a way that would have made the Ottoman eunuchs weep into their sherbet.

And because she looked so beautiful I had to insult her.

"That coat doesn't really work on you, it's trailing along the ground," I said.

"That's what I told her," Jackie said.

"You two know nothing. It's called a trail-duster frock coat. They're, like, making this film next summer called *The Matrix,* Keanu is in it and that's the whole look," she said.

"Again with Keanu," Jackie groaned.

I turned my attention to Sonia, who also looked radiant in a summer dress that shimmered brilliantly with the light behind her.

"It's in the woods though, right?" I asked.

"It is in the woods, a very beautiful part of the state, I think you're going to like it very much. We'll have so much fun," Sonia said happily.

Sonia, it seemed, was unaware of the "surprise" that was going to happen to us when we got up there. The mysterious plan B.

"Gerry said something about the fall colors."

"Oh, we're far too early for that, but you never know. Anyway, since I'm the pathfinder I'd better go," she said. She kissed Gerry and Kit, waved, and drove off in the Mercedes.

"She's not going with the rest of us?" I asked Kit.

"Nah, she's going first to get the cabin ready. I was supposed to go too, but there was no way," she said.

"She's totally incorrigible," Jackie said. He considered me a mate now to whom he could lightheartedly bitch about his crazy girlfriend.

"Was it really bad last night, back at the flat?" I asked him.

"I do not even want to talk about it," he said.

"What happened last night?" Kit asked. "Was it that woman you chased out of town?"

My mouth opened and closed. Chased out of town? Who had told her that bald-faced lie? And what other unpleasant episodes had they kept from her?

Hmmm. Exactly how sure were they of her and Sonia? And if her own father was ashamed to tell her about the horrors Touched had perpetrated, it might mean that she was pliable and not as committed as the three men. Good. I would choose to believe it that way. Maybe I could even like her without the guilty conscience.

Kit tapped her foot. She was waiting for an answer. I looked at Jackie but he wasn't ready for an off-the-cuff remark and I wasn't going to help him out.

"Nothing," he said finally. "I had to clean up a big mess."

Kit looked at him suspiciously and let the matter drop.

Jackie smiled at me and fidgeted with a gun in his pocket. A small-caliber revolver. So both he and Gerry were packing heat. But that was ok too, I wasn't worried.

Having lowered his flags and put them away, Gerry walked over.

"Ok, lads and lasses, we better go. I told Touched I'd pick him up by six and the afternoon is wearing on."

"Where is Touched?" I asked him.

"Oh, he went up to Portsmouth already, Kittery actually, Kittery, Maine," Jackie said.

"We're meeting him there?" I asked.

"Yes, well, we are. We have a slightly tricky but ultimately rewarding task to accomplish. Important for you, Sean, in particular. I think this will be an opportunity for you to show Touched that paranoia is perhaps not the most agreeable of notions."

Gerry locked the house and we piled into another big

McCaghan Construction van. Jackie driving, Kit and Gerry squeezed into the other seats of the front cabin. Only a half-partition between them and me in the back. Gerry had locked me in, I'd noticed, but it didn't faze me. If I wanted to escape I could easily cry for help any number of times in the slow drive through Newburyport before we got to the highway. True, Gerry could have shot me with his silenced 9mm, but it was moot, I wasn't looking to escape, I was looking to bide my bloody time. . . .

It was nearly dark when we arrived in Kittery—a small town just across the water from Portsmouth, New Hampshire.

We drove into a landing place for boats and, sure enough, there was Touched, large as life, twice as nasty, looking sinister in leather jacket, boots, and a brown shirt.

"There he is," Kit said happily.

Yeah, good old Uncle Touched.

He slammed the side of the van and, using his own key, opened it and got in the back next to me. He nodded a hello and I nodded back, but when he noticed Kit his good humor departed.

"Gerry, what the fuck is she doing here?" he asked.

Gerry looked shamefaced.

"I couldn't keep her away," he said.

"Jesus Christ, Gerry, I thought we discussed this," Touched said. "She was supposed to go with Sonia and get the cabin ready."

"We did discuss it—" Gerry began but Kit cut him off.

"First of all, Touched, it's not 'she,' my name is Kit. And second of all, you are not the boss of me, and third of all, how come you're bringing along Sean, who's been with us for less than a week, and not me? How come? I'll tell you how come. Because I'm a girl and you're a fucking sexist pig," Kit said loudly.

"Keep your voice down for one thing. And for two, just because you're Gerry's daughter doesn't mean I can't give you orders. I *am* the boss of you and you'll do as you're fucking told," Touched said.

Kit stared at him, then at her da. Touched clenched his fist.

Another time, another crowd and he would have belted her. But Kit slipped in one of her devastating apology/seductress smiles. Touched quivered, cracked, relented.

"Well, anyway, I guess now that you're here," he said, "I suppose I have no bloody choice."

"No choice," Kit said triumphantly.

Touched looked at Gerry. "Did you tell Kit and Sonia about Sean's wee dose of house arrest?" he asked.

Gerry coughed. "Er, no, I'm afraid I did not have an occasion for that, we were all so busy and what with the packing and everything," he said.

Touched sighed. "Kit, it's like this, we had a bit of a close call yesterday and now Sean is under close watch. He knows it and he approves of it, so he doesn't get access to firearms and you're not to be alone with him. Understood?"

Kit looked at me strangely, a little intrigued by my new status, but she obediently nodded.

"Better brief them, Touched," Gerry said.

Touched cleared his throat and grinned excitedly.

"Ok, folks. This is what we call a target of opportunity. I know what you're thinking, we should lie low for a few weeks after all that's happened in the last couple of days. But it's exactly the opposite. We have to prove to the real Provos in Ireland that even in the face of a couple of setbacks, we can hit fast and hard and effectively," Touched said, explaining nothing at all.

"Yeah, but what's the mission?" Kit asked.

"The mission for you is to do nothing, Kit. I'm handling it. Me and Gerry will do all the work, the three of you do what we say and stay out of it. Me and Gerry are old hands, we know what we're doing."

Touched reached into his jacket and gave Kit and myself each an old Webley revolver.

"These are just for show, they're not loaded. Gerry and me will do any shooting that's necessary," Touched said, but I checked the gun anyway in case there was one in the chamber.

"What about me? I can help. I got mine," Jackie said.

"Jackie. Don't you do a goddamn thing without my say-so.

Understood?" Touched said.

Jackie nodded.

"The mission, explain the mission," Gerry said.

"Ok then. I've got a motorboat and we're going to that yacht over there in the harbor with the two masts and the yellow paint. It's called the *Elizabeth Regina*. We're going to go on and get someone and get off it again. Simple as pie," Touched said.

"Who are we getting?" Kit asked.

"The *Elizabeth Regina* is owned by Peter Blackwell," Touched said significantly.

Kit, Jackie, and I looked stupidly at one another.

"Surely you know who he is, Sean?" Touched said.

"Sorry, Touched, no clue," I admitted.

"Peter fucking Blackwell is a full general in the British Army. He was commander in chief of the British Army in Northern Ireland for full four years. Four years. Two tours. Target number one for the Provos for four years and they never got him. He's on leave from Germany now, but still, he has to be very high on everyone's list back home. As high as Thatcher, some people might say," Touched said triumphantly.

I couldn't help looking at Kit for a moment. She knew that I'd been in that army too. But Kit didn't bat an eye. Good for her.

"What's he doing over here?" I asked Touched.

"Intelligence wins the day, Sean. I found out that his boat the *Elizabeth Regina* was entered in the Kittery Twenty-Four-Hour Race that begins the day after tomorrow. He flew in yesterday, he's spending the night on the boat, his crew joins him in the morning, and then he goes off racing. Except that he doesn't. We get him first."

"What do you mean, get him?" Kit asked.

"We lift him. We kidnap him," Touched said.

"You should tell them why," Gerry whispered.

"We grab him and on a stolen cell phone we call the State Department and tell him that unless Hannity, Buchanan, and O'Reilly are allowed to go to a third country unhindered then we'll kill Blackwell. If they release the Newark Three, then we let him go and it's kudos for us, if they don't release them we kill Blackwell and again it's kudos for us."

I looked at Kit, but her face was turned away. Was she upset? What was she thinking?

The plan was ok but no Manhattan Project. Hannity, Buchanan, and O'Reilly, the Newark Three, were a trio of IRA hoods who had been in an INS detention facility in New Jersey awaiting extradition back to Ulster. They were small-time gunrunners, so I suppose Touched and Gerry thought it was just about possible that the British government would pressure the State Department into letting them go in return for General Blackwell's safe release. Possible, but not proba-ble. The Brits had a long-standing policy of not negotiating with terrorists.

Still, the underlying assumption was correct. It would be a win-win for Touched. If they didn't release the three, he killed the general and got big respect from every dissident republi-can in Ireland. If they did let the three out, again big fucking respect.

But even so, a high-profile kidnapping that could go horri-bly wrong in many ways was more a sign of weakness than one of strength for the Sons of Cuchulainn.

"Won't they trace your call?" I asked.

"No, they won't. Thought of that. I got a couple of nicked phones from my mate in the Hampton Beach casino. I'm only making one call and then I'm throwing the phone away. If they release the Newark Three, we'll hear on the radio, and if they don't we'll hear that, too."

"We wouldn't really kill the general in cold blood, would we?" Kit asked, her face controlled, calm.

"Damn right we would. He's a war criminal. A British occupier. We'd have to, Kit. It wouldn't be a murder, it would be a sanctioned execution," Touched said.

"So far it's been all hits against us. Revere and Seamus and the FBI snooping on us, but now we're striking back, we're taking the war to the enemy," Gerry added.

"Would you kill him, Dad?" Kit asked.

"Time is pressing," Touched said before Gerry could

answer.

We got out of the van and went down to the boat Touched had rustled up from somewhere. A large, long boat that in Ireland we called a dory. Tied to a wharf, it was still a little tricky to get in it, especially for Gerry. But eventually, when we were all nervously aboard, Touched pulled the outboard and it whirred into life.

Portsmouth Harbor was packed full of ships and boats. To the right was the Piscataqua River and to the left was the Atlantic. The *Elizabeth Regina* was not the biggest boat in the harbor, but it was still large. A two-masted schooner, about sixty-five feet long.

Not the sort of thing you could afford on army pay. The general obviously had money.

Touched steered us closer, the dory struggling against the current and Gerry's weight. Kit was next to me, shivering. She had removed her trench coat and was dressed in only a thin black silk sweater. I put my arm round her and she didn't refuse it and Jackie, bless him, didn't mind.

Since I was near the back, Touched handed me a pair of binoculars.

"Is he still moving about, Sean?" he asked me.

I looked through the binocs and, sure enough, I could see a figure belowdecks futtering around.

"Aye."

"And there's only one person, Sean?" Gerry asked.

"Yup. I think it's just one guy, but I don't know how on earth you could know that for sure," I said.

"Don't get smart, Sean, I've been watching the bloody boat for the last four hours. It's one guy," Touched said.

"One old guy. One unarmed old guy," Gerry said.

"How do you know he's unarmed?" Jackie asked.

"There's no way he would have been allowed to enter U.S. territory with a gun on his boat," Gerry said, discounting the possibility of a flare gun, boat hook, ice axe.

"Which is not to say that he is not armed and not dangerous. He will definitely be the latter and maybe the former. So if it comes to trouble, Kit, you hang back, looking menacing;

Sean, your job is to look after Kit; me, Gerry, and Jackie will handle the old man," Touched said.

Closer. There was music coming from the boat.

"Hey, that's Radiohead," Kit said to me.

"Sounds like the general's up with the kids," I said skeptically.

Whether he was into Radiohead or not, he had very helpfully placed half a dozen fenders along the port hull of the *Elizabeth* so that other boats could easily moor alongside.

"Masks on," Touched whispered. We pulled on black ski masks and gloves. It wasn't completely dark yet, so if anyone was passing in a fishing boat or a dinghy they'd certainly notice us.

Unfortunately, no one was passing.

Touched cut the dory's motor and we drifted for about twenty feet until we were against the *Elizabeth*'s hull.

"Fend off," Touched whispered to Jackie. Jackie had no idea what Touched meant but he put up his arm anyway to stop us crashing into the side of the boat. We were near the ladder at the stern and Jackie had the presence of mind to nudge us along so that we could climb it rather than having to haul ourselves up over the rail. Gerry probably couldn't have managed that in any case.

"Up you go, Jackie boy," Touched said.

Jackie climbed the ladder and pulled out his gun. There was no sound from the subdecks. I went next, then Gerry. The whole stern of the boat bobbed in the water when he came onboard; but again nothing from belowdecks. Kit next. Touched last.

Touched led us to the cabin entrance and he opened the sliding hatchway that led down below. I followed him into the forecabin. A large luxury yacht, fitted out for at least a dozen crew, not really a racer, more of a cruiser because it had a big heavy cooking stove, a drinks cabinet, even a library up against one wall. Radiohead coming from a CD player.

A door opened at the rear of the boat. A young man in a bathrobe humming to the music. Curly-haired, blond, early twenties, maybe even younger, an Eton pugilist's nose, a handsome face with deep green eyes.

He froze when he saw us.

"What the fuuu . . ." he said in complete terror.

"Put your hands up," Touched whispered.

The kid began to tremble.

"What do you want?" he asked in a frightened British accent.

Touched put his fingers to his lips.

"Put your fucking hands up. Where's General Blackwell? Is he sleeping?" Touched whispered.

"Are you the IRA?" the kid asked.

"Where the fuck is he?" Touched asked, louder this time.

"He w-went to Boston," the kid said.

"What?"

"Boston, he's in Boston."

"Fuck," Touched muttered to himself and then turned to me.

"You and J., make sure he's not lying."

Jackie and I searched the boat, but the kid was alone. Jackie didn't see me pick up a pen and slip it into my pocket. My own wee plan B.

"Nobody here," Jackie said.

"What's your name, boy?" Touched asked the kid.

"Peter."

"Peter Blackwell?" Touched asked. "You're his son?"

"Yes. I'm the youngest," he said, too frightened even to lie.

"Keep those hands up," Touched said, and he turned to Gerry. "What do you want me to do?"

Gerry shook his head.

"When does your father get back?" Gerry asked.

"I don't know, I think tomorrow, he's meeting the crew and they're all supposed to come up tomorrow."

"We could wait overnight, get the jump on him tomorrow," Touched whispered to Gerry.

Gerry looked doubtful.

"How many crew?" he asked Peter.

"I don't know, I think five or six," Peter said honestly. If it had been me, I would have said a dozen.

Gerry sat down on the edge of a foldout bed.

"I think we'll have to abort, the better part of valor and all that, six men plus Blackwell, it's got all the makings of a disaster. We'll have to shut this one down," he said.

Touched was furious, his face contorting with rage and frustration.

"No way, no way. I planned this out meticulously. We cannot afford another defeat. The way things have been going, this will be the end of us," Touched said.

"What do you suggest?" Gerry asked.

"Kill him as a message. Or the original fucking plan, take him instead. Even better this way, exert real moral pressure on the Brits. They'll cave, fucking Blair will cave."

Gerry considered it.

"We would ask for the same prisoners?"

"Absolutely. Same deal. Give them forty-eight hours and we let the kid go," Touched said.

"I don't have anything to do with Northern Ireland, I've never been there or anything," Peter pleaded.

"Shut up. You're coming with us," Touched said.

If he came with us, he was dead. I knew it and Peter knew it. It was not likely that the Brits would give in to this kind of intimidation, especially not a new prime minister who was perceived as weak on foreign policy.

"Fuck it, there's no point bringing him. This wasn't the plan. He's no good to us at all. Look at him. He's barely out of his teens," I said.

I could feel Touched's look. I turned and sure enough those cold gray eyes were boring into me. After all the good credibility I had built up overnight, I had made him suspicious yet again. Goddamnit, Michael, that mouth of yours is going to get you killed one day.

"Yeah, please, you can't take me. No one gives a shit about me, just leave me and I won't say anything, I promise, just let me go please," Peter begged.

"Shut up, Englishman. We decide, and you shut the fuck up," I yelled and smacked him hard on the skull with the butt of the revolver.

He crumpled to the deck like a Chinese lantern folding up.

"I think you killed him," Jackie said in horror.

Touched leaned down and checked the pulse at his throat. "Nah, he's alive."

"Well, what do you think, take him or leave him?" I asked Touched cheerfully.

He didn't answer me. He stood, nodded to Gerry.

"Let's get this bloody show on the road," he said and nodded at Jackie and me to pick him up. We lifted him. The second person I'd had to carry like this in twenty-four hours.

"What do you think?" Gerry asked sotto voce.

"Gerry, you take a situation. You roll with the punch. I think it's ok. I think we're finally doing things right," Touched said.

Jackie and I carried him out onto the deck.

"You think we should get some of his clothes? We can't really keep him in his robe?" I asked Touched.

Gerry shrugged, looked at Kit, then back at me.

"You might as well grab a pair of trousers or something," Gerry said.

I ran to the rear cabin, closed the door, wrote "FBI Michael Forsythe Gerry McCaghan's cabin Maine" prominently on one of the walls, grabbed a pair of jeans and a T-shirt, and ran out.

They had Peter in the dory now. I handed Gerry the jeans and helped him into the motorboat.

A tight squeeze but we got to shore without incident. We lifted Peter out of the dory, dressed him, tied him up, gagged him, and chucked him in the back of the van.

Touched watching me every step of the way, very wary of me again.

Touched locked the van's doors from the outside and made me sit in the back with Jackie and Peter.

Gerry drove so that Touched could keep an eye on me.

But I chilled and didn't do anything else stupid to raise his suspicions. Instead, I lay down on the floor, put my rolled-up jacket under my head, and pretended to sleep for the four or five hours it took us to get up to Gerry's cabin in the woods of Maine.

We finally stopped.

The van doors opened.

An exhausted stumble-around in the darkness, a big house somewhere deep in the forest. I could tell we were miles from the nearest town because the stars were brilliant and unobscured.

Touched took care of me first. He led me upstairs to a bedroom and handcuffed my foot to a cast-iron bed.

"Piss pot under the bed if you need it, see you in the morning," he said brusquely and left.

*　　*　　*

Later. Noiseless outside. Then a door banging at an outhouse or a barn. Men speaking.

". . . do for him" is all I can catch.

Inside, the rest of them, excited, nervous.

Talking, laughing, timber chairs scraping on the timber floor.

The voices in murmurs. A few loud good nights then footsteps on the stairs. A tiny voice singing to herself in French. Sonia going to bed.

A door closing. Movement, and then one by one everyone else comes upstairs.

Jackie first, muttering to himself. Then Kit, almost making no sound at all. Finally Gerry, wheezing as he goes.

And the last man up. Touched. I flinch as he stops outside my door but he doesn't come in.

A few more timber creaks and groans but in an hour the house is quiet. Fantastically silent. A deep nothingness.

Just the room, the bed, the window, me.

Starlight.

A hill cutting off the bottom of the constellation Pegasus. The smell of wood, resin, old sheets, rusting iron, mold spores, damp.

Peace distills into my soul.

And I know that this is the place for the final chapter.

This is the place where it will end. Where Samantha will be

avenged or I will die.

Here in the woods. In blades and bullets, with the seasons poised as they approach the equinox. I can see it, because I will make it.

I'll be there, outside in the cold air. Under the trees.

Birds wheeling diagonals. An iodine sky. Chevroned pines. Oaks as old as the republic itself. Corpses sprawled on the cold earth.

It will be done. The diorama of death around me.

I don't know how. But I will make it happen. And though I'm bound and watched and unarmed, I wouldn't be in their shoes.

No. Only her will I spare the slaughterhouse. The screams, the blood. The salt tears dripping into the wet earth.

Only her.

It will be terrible. I promise. The owl of Minerva will fly afraid. And miles from here a black bear will stand on her back legs and sniff the air, alarmed, smelling the carnage coming to her on the soft south wind. Yes.

And I smile in my sleep and dream it close.

10: BETRAYAL IN BELFAST

Haze smothers a distant mountain. The sun excites a million trees. Butterflies and blue jays fluttering above the window ledge and more birds in the discased vacuum around the house. Cirrus clouds, vapor trails, the sky the blue of a hangman's suit.

I flex my fingers. Sit up, rub at the handcuff around my right ankle.

I'm a city boy. I don't know the names of trees, but there are several different types, from the valley bottoms to the hilltops, absorbing the topography in a blanket of green, brown, and black. An occasional firebreak or clearing or winding trail.

The air is filled with oxygen. We are not in the high country or I would feel it. We're in the forest and in fact we are near water. Saltwater. We're close to the coast or a broad bay or an inlet. I can smell the Atlantic. Something that gives me comfort when every morning I wake in a different room and I'm a different person in a different type of jeopardy.

I haven't been plain, uncomplicated Michael Forsythe for five years—back in the good old days. Not that they were ever any bloody good.

I check the handcuff and the cast-iron bed for a weak link. Nothing.

But knowing that we're near the sea helps. That, and the message I left in the *Elizabeth Regina*. And, above all, the feeling that this is going to be the day.

Aye.

Today, I wake under discipline of war. Today, I will take the fight to the enemy. Peter Blackwell has forty-eight hours before Touched will murder him and I have only the same time before doubts concerning my identity arrive from Belfast.

So now is the time to act.

Bearings are the first key. From the bed, a limited view of woods and hills and an old disused railroad line almost completely recolonized by nature, and indeed, in the trees behind an outhouse there's an old railway car minus its bogies and roof. But the cabin itself is not the humble dwelling one associates with the presidents on our low-denomination bills. This place is enormous. It bends round in an L shape and there are two floors and at least three different outbuildings. I wouldn't call it a cabin, it's more a log-hewn summerhouse. I don't know how many acres of woods go with the place, but I'm sure we're talking many millions of dollars for the entire estate.

That also gives me hope.

If the feds had been looking for a humble little Unabomber hut that was off the books, we'd be fucked; but this monstrosity couldn't have escaped the notice of a tax-hungry local authority. It might take them a while to get here, but eventually they would, hopefully not to find the two rotting corpses of the kid and me.

In the kitchen below me a cheerful voice begins singing in Quebecois French.

"Sur le pont d'Avignon, l'on y danse, l'on y danse. Sur le pont d'Avignon, l'on y danse tout en rond."

She hasn't a care in the world.

Doesn't Sonia know that Touched will kill that boy as easily as chopping wood? Are they all in goddamn denial about what they've done?

A knock at the door.

"Come in," I say.

Kit enters wearing a black dress and DM boots. She hasn't slept well, and her eyelids are heavy and dark. It only accentuates her loveliness. She's carrying a tray with breakfast. Fresh croissants and coffee.

She closes the door and sits on the edge of the mattress. She puts the tray on a little table next to the bed.

"Touched told me that we were going to have to keep you under restraint for a day or two. Apparently you said something on the boat that made him suspicious. I didn't hear you say anything, but he's always . . . Anyway. I'm really really sorry, Sean," she says and takes my hand in hers, squeezes it.

"Touched is crazy, he's completely crazy," I tell her.

"Jackie and Dad both pleaded your case, but he didn't listen to them," Kit says, and her fingers are cold and soft in my rough, scarred palm.

"Is this breakfast?" I ask.

"Oh yeah, of course, Sonia made these croissants from scratch, they're delicious, and there's maple syrup if you want to dip them. It's local. And then there's coffee."

"Thanks, I'm quite hungry," I say.

I take a sip of coffee. It's hot and good.

"Nice."

"I made it," she says, pleased.

"So, uh, where's the boy?" I ask her.

"He's out in the smokehouse. He's ok. He's, like, frightened, as you would expect him to be, but Sonia and I brought him breakfast and we told him that it was only going to be for a day or two and then we'd let him go."

I shake my head from side to side.

"Touched is going to kill him. I guarantee you that," I tell her.

"No. He wouldn't do that. Even if he wanted to, which he doesn't, Dad wouldn't let him. And Dad's in charge," Kit says, but she bites her lip a little nervously.

"Kit, Gerry knows and Touched knows that he's going to have to die. The State Department and Her Majesty's fucking Foreign Office will not humiliate themselves by doing a deal with terrorists just to save a general's son. And when the deadline passes, Touched will not let him go. He'll kill him or he knows the Sons of Cuchulainn will be finished."

Kit's brow furrows and I can see she's digesting what I've told her. But now is not the time to push it. Plant the seed now, fertilize it later.

"Where is here by the way? Where are we?" I ask.

"The cabin, silly."

"Honey, I know, but where's the cabin?"

"We're about ten miles from Belfast, Maine. Of course, when he was looking to build somewhere, Dad had to buy land up here because of the local connection. We should take you into town, show you this Belfast, and you can compare it to yours. There couldn't be two more different places on the planet Earth."

"I'm sure. That sounds like fun, I'd love to go into town. Could we go today?" I ask eagerly.

Kit shakes her head sadly. She takes a knot out of her bob and hunts for a hair clip to keep the fringe out of her eyes.

"Nah, I don't think so, I don't think Touched would let me take you," she says.

"Oh, that's a shame, well, you could always ask anyway, he can only say no," I suggest.

"Maybe," she says.

"So how often do you guys come up here?"

"Two, three times a year."

I fake a groan and take a sip of the coffee.

"What's the matter?" Kit asks.

"It's nothing. My leg hurts a little bit."

"Your good leg or your . . ." she asks delicately.

"The handcuff around my ankle's been cutting off the circulation and the cramp has been killing me. You couldn't do me a favor, could you, Kit?"

"What? Anything."

I touch her wrist. She shivers.

"Well, I know Touched doesn't want me going into town for obvious reasons, but you could just ask him if I could go for a walk, you could come with me and if he wanted to, he could have my wrists handcuffed for extra security. I'm really sore, I really need a walk to stretch my legs. It's pretty painful."

I bite into the croissant, dip it into the maple syrup, and take another mouthful.

"This is very good."

"I'll tell Sonia you like them."

"And will you ask Touched if I can go for a walk? I'm in total agony."

"When do you want to go?"

"After breakfast."

Kit gets to her feet.

"I'll see what I can do, we'll apply moral pressure. All of us think it's disgraceful the way he's treating you."

She leans in and kisses me on the cheek.

"Back in five minutes," she says.

She leaves the room and I hear her go downstairs. There's a conversation and then she comes back with Touched. His hair is wet, he's wrapped in a towel and dressing gown and wearing flip-flops.

"What's the matter, Sean? I thought you were ok with me keeping an eye on you for a day or two," he says.

"I am. I just need a wee walk, you can handcuff me if you want. But I'm dying of cramps here, I only have one good leg anyway and the circulation is being cut off in the other. Half an hour, forty-five minutes, just a wee stretch."

Touched shrugs. "Ugh, I don't see why not. Kit, go get my trousers from downstairs, will ya?"

Kit leaves.

"So, how's everything going?" I ask him.

"It's going well."

"Did you make your call?"

"I did. I told them they had forty-eight hours to release the Newark Three, or the kid dies."

"What do you think they'll do?"

"I think they'll release them. Those boys are not important and the Irish community has been lobbying Clinton to let them go. Win for everybody. Clinton looks compassionate, the Newark Three get out, and we establish ourselves overnight as players."

Kit comes back with Touched's pants. He takes out a set of

keys and hands them to her.

"Ok, Kit. Take that cuff off his ankle, let him stretch, pull his pants up, put his shoes on, and then cuff his hands in front of him. You can take him for a walk. Don't get out of sight of the house, and remember he's under observation, so if he does any funny stuff you give a holler and we'll come running."

Touched takes the 9mm from his dressing gown pocket and holds it while Kit uncuffs me and lets me put my shoes on.

Touched examines the gun for a moment and then begins to unscrew the silencer. I can tell what he's thinking. There's no one for miles. If he has to kill me or Peter, he can do it without fear of being overheard.

When she's cuffed me, he checks to see that she's done a good job.

He gives me a wink.

"You know how it is, mate. When this wee task is over and we get the all clear from over the water, it'll be different. We'll forget the fuckups. I'll take you for a big session as an apology. I can tell, Sean, that you are going to be our right-hand man."

He gives me a friendly dig on the shoulder.

"I hope so."

Kit leads me out of the room and helps me downstairs.

The "cabin" is even bigger than I'd thought. It's a huge edifice, with a large central room, almost an interior court-yard, and six or seven bedrooms arranged around the inner space on the second floor. The style is that of a Swiss chalet rather than that of an old Kentucky home. A large stone fire-place made from irregular local rocks, a kitchen, and the big open-plan living area and dining room. You'd need to burn half the surrounding forest to heat this place in winter, but in summer, with the windows open and the breezes off the mountain, it would be quite temperate.

And they're not living the simple life either.

A big-screen television, a stereo, and a speaker system that would give Aerosmith's roadies a hard time.

Jackie and Sonia are tucking into breakfast at an enormous pine table. Jackie's hair is also wet and he's wearing swim trunks. Maybe they have a pool or there's a lake nearby.

"Morning, all," I say.

Jackie nods. "You sleep ok, mate?" he asks, noticing me and trying to ignore the handcuffs on my wrists.

"Slept fine."

"Did Kit bring you breakfast?" Sonia asks.

"Yeah, it was delicious, thanks," I tell her.

"The maple syrup is from here," Sonia adds.

"Yeah, Kit told me, it was fantastic. . . . Where's the big guy?"

"He's still sleeping. He sleeps so well up here," Sonia says and gives me a little grin of domestic bliss.

Keep that smile, love, it's going to be a happy fucking tapestry when that poor kid, Peter, is screaming for his life.

"Gerry design this place himself?" I ask.

"Oh yes, this has been his labor of love," Sonia says.

"And do you own part of the forest, too?" I inquire.

"Twelve acres," she says.

"Must be a big tax bill on that?" I ask.

"I have no idea," Sonia says.

Kit looks at me.

"Well, do you want to gab away, or do you want me to show you outside?" she asks.

"Don't get out of sight of the house," Touched says, putting his 9mm on the table and tucking into the rest of his breakfast.

"I know," Kit assures him.

I can see that Jackie has only started his food, so it will be ok to ask him.

"Jack, you wanna come along for a wee walk in the woods?"

"Nah, I've just started breaky," he says.

Good.

We walk outside.

The Mercedes, the van, a few outbuildings. The woods beginning thirty feet from the house.

The sky is grayer and it's a little colder than I'm expecting.

"It's getting chilly," I say to Kit.

"Yeah, Sonia heard on the radio that there's a storm front coming down from Canada."

"Funny, I was just thinking it would be tricky heating this place in cold weather," I say.

"Yeah, despite what Sonia said on PI, it could even dip into the forties tonight. Touched said we might have to chop some wood and get the fire going. But don't worry. It'll be fun."

"Will Peter be warm enough?" I ask.

Kit sighs, as if I've spoiled a nice conversation by bringing up an awkward subject.

"He's in the smokehouse, it's pretty warm there."

I look at the three single-story log structures scattered around the clearing. They are all inverted V shapes. A steep slope from the ground to the top of the roof. One of these must be the smokehouse.

"Can we see him?"

"See who?"

"Peter."

Kit shakes her head.

"Touched would definitely not allow that."

"Ok," I say, not wanting to make a big deal out of it.

"So, Sean, what do you want to see first? Do you want to go to the back of the cabin or do you want to go on the little trail to the pond?"

"The pond sounds fun."

"It's not really in sight of the house, but, like, what exactly are you supposed to do to me with handcuffs on?" she says, laughing.

Oh, I'll do plenty, love.

"I'll be helpless," I agree.

We walk into the trees and follow a lightly worn trail as it curves downhill away from the house.

"It's so peaceful here. Are there any neighbors nearby?" I ask.

"Nah, the nearest is in the next valley and he's a German and I don't think he comes here much," Kit says.

"And Belfast town is ten miles away?"

"As the crow flies, but it's a little longer by road."

"Fifteen minutes, twenty minutes in the car?"

"Yeah. Something like that. But it is so quiet here, such a

contrast to Plum Island on a weekend when all the dregs of—
Ah, here we are at the pond."

The trail stops at a small lake about a hundred yards across
that is choked with pond scum, leaves, tree branches, probably hundreds of drowned animals, and maybe the odd former
associate who got on Touched's bad side.

"Yeah, I know, it's not very nice, but Daddy's going to get it
cleaned out and someday we can go swimming or even kayak-
ing," Kit says.

"I think Jackie already took a dip."

"Did he? Well, he's braver than me."

"Let's go over here," I say. I walk to a little rise away from
the trail and sit down on a fallen tree. It's a good spot. That
way I can hear and see anyone coming from the house.

"Sit next to me," I tell her.

There's only going to be one chance at this and I can't blow
it. She sits, her dress bunching up over her knees. She mois-
tens her full raspberry lips in anticipation of something excit-
ing.

"Kit, I want to tell you something and I didn't want anyone
around to hear," I explain quietly and take her hand.

"What?" she asks a little too eagerly.

"I think you know what I'm going to say."

"No?" she says, a touch of fear in her eyes.

"You do," I insist. "It's about you; me and you."

Kit's smile evaporates. Her eyes narrow. She *does* know
what I'm going to say. Women always do when you're in this
subject area.

"I hope you're not fucking with me," she says, even her
surfer/stoner accent disappearing in the gravity of the moment.

"I am perfectly serious, Kit. I think there's something
between us. Something important. Something real. I've been
in love with one person in my life but she was in love with
someone else, so that didn't work out too well. But I know
how I felt then and I know how I feel when I'm with you
now," I begin slowly.

I look at her.

I'm trying to keep the conflict out of my face. The

confusion of thoughts and emotions.

It's an odd sensation. I don't know if I'm playing her or not. If this is a lie or whether it's some part of the truth.

But I've begun and the only choice is to continue.

"I'm falling in love with you," I say and pause for a full beat.

"You shouldn't say that if you don't mean it," she whispers.

Her eyes close and she holds me tighter.

"I do mean it. And it's not that we've got a lot in common: you surf, I don't; you're rich, I'm not; you're American, I'm Irish. But none of that matters. It wouldn't matter what you did, or where you were from, or what you were like. I think I've loved you from the moment I set eyes on you. In the bar at Revere, when you were waiting tables and wearing your Marine Corps shirt. It was as if the lightbulb flashed above my head and a voice said, she's the one, Sean, you had one false start, but she's the one. And it wouldn't have mattered if you'd hadn't been nice, and sweet and funny. If you were a bad person or stupid or mean, I still would have fallen for you. But luckily for me, as I got to know to you, I saw that you were perfect. You are perfect."

She blinks and stares at me in amazement, and when she sees that I've finished speaking, she turns away. She's been robbed of her voice and she may even be tearing up. We sit in silence for two minutes, the only sounds the birds on the water, the breeze in the trees.

I'm waiting for her.

It's her move.

I'm feeling . . . what exactly?

Yes, that's it: guilt. Above all, guilt. At the lies within the lies within the lies. And I still don't know if that speech was part of them too.

"I'm not sure what to say, Sean," she mutters at last.

"You don't have to say anything. I just wanted to get that off my chest. To let you know how I feel. I don't even need reciprocation. I don't need you to say that you love me. I don't need you to say anything. Now that I've told you and you believe me, that's enough. That's enough for the present."

She takes my hand in hers and holds it. And then she kisses it.

"Talk about something else for a while. Let me think," she says.

"We don't have to talk."

"No, I want you to talk, I like to hear your voice," she insists.

"What about?"

"Anything. You talk and I'll listen and think. Tell me something I don't know."

"Ok. Um. Let me see. We're in Maine. Oh, I know. You probably don't know this story. But some people think the Irish were here first, in Maine or Nova Scotia or somewhere around here. Did you ever hear that? You ever hear the story of Saint Brendan?"

"No. Tell me."

"It's a bit of a fairy story, but the theory is that Saint Brendan and a bunch of monks sailed a coracle from Ireland to America. They sailed right across from Ireland and landed somewhere around these parts. And of course Brendan met the Indians and he proselytized to them and tried to convert them from their heathen ways. And then the monks traveled around and saw great wonders and built a church and had lots of adventures, then they came home again. A mad Englishman sailed a replica of Brendan's coracle over here sometime in the 1970s."

"What's a coracle?" she asks.

"I don't really know, it's some kind of leather boat, I think."

"When was this?"

"A thousand years before Columbus."

"Do you know the entire story?"

"Bits and pieces," I say.

"Tell me the whole thing."

And I do tell her. Everything I know of Saint Brendan and Saint Patrick and Saint Columba and all the Irish missionary navigators, and she listens to me and relaxes and laughs and holds my hand tighter and before I'm done, she turns to face me. She's nervous. Terrified.

"I want you," she whispers in a tiny, shy, almost nonexistent voice. And she lets go of my hand, takes off her shoes and her dress, and stands there naked. Her pale body and small breasts, her long legs and dark eyes and hair. She is so beautiful that she robs me of my breath. My pulse pounding in my ears.

She helps me take off my trousers and my boots. And she hooks herself under my outstretched, handcuffed arms, and she pulls me close and kisses me.

We lie on the forest floor and she arcs her torso over mine, my arms round her back and leading her. Touching her spine and buttocks and the back of her hair. Clement and meek, the both of us. Like it's our first time. She gives herself and I ease her to the leafy ground and grasp her tighter, touching her with my lips. I kiss her on the shoulders and the faint, scared smile on her face. And she rolls me back to the forest floor and stretches out her body on me, kissing me, breathing words that are careful and true.

"I feel the same way, Sean, from that night, from the journey in the car, I couldn't help it, I can't help it. . . ."

And she tells me more. "This, this is my first, my first time."

It shocks me. Incredible, in this day and age, that she has waited, saved herself, for the right moment and the right man. And it proves that a lot of her character was bravado and an act and it shows me that she thinks she's found that man at last.

And gently, very gently, I climb on top of her and I can see that this is the way it's supposed to be. That this is what it's been like for everyone else. Not hard or frantic or desperate. But like this. Geometries of movement and belonging, a giving of each other for each other. We maneuver our limbs and she puts me inside her and I can feel her pulse, a hasp of beating.

"Sean, I know it's strange, but I—"

"Ssshhhhh . . ."

I push, and for her it's an awakening. A revelation. And no less for me, too. And I fall in those blue eyes and the shadows of thoughts on her face. Things that I couldn't read but now I can.

"Hold me. Hold me tighter," she says.

"I am."

"Hold me. Hold me and never let me—"

"I won't," I say and hook my handcuffed arms about her back.

We make love under the trees like a human and his elven enchantress. Or is it the other way around, that I am the woodland spirit and she is the lost mortal girl entering the dark part of the fairy tale?

We make love and she cries and I talk to her and hug her.

And the moment is beautiful and complete and in the present tense there is no future, there is only her pulsing heart and her skin and the look of completeness on her soft lips and sylvan eyes.

It's perfect. But I've seen this movie before. It's the scene in the book of Genesis before the storm.

I hold her and we make love again, in the near absolute dark of the forest, without a noise or an interruption. A fragile promise of me and her. The calm before the hurricane.

      ✿   ✿   ✿

The woods were wild and thick and the regions between the trees were pierced by sunlight through the canopy.

The red men had taught them to tap the bark for syrup and showed them berries and the nests of bees. Drunk on sweetness, they forged between huge firs and giant elms and trees of no description yet known to civilized man.

They had seen nothing but forest since coming off the fish-swarmed shore and it was to the forest gods that the local people prayed. Fintan was here and Daana, too, and in the glades they felt the heathen presence of age-old Pan. They came sometimes upon an altar or mound or other pagan edifice, yet they were not afraid, for the knowledge of the One God sustained them.

They crossed a river of leaping salmon. They listened to

wolves and spotted eagles and even vultures—a bird no monk but one from Italy had seen before.

They rang the angelus for the first time in the breadth of river valleys and laid a monument to Patrick of humble stone, humbled yet under a huge mountain. Life was so much here. Beautiful and abundant and brimming over. Sprouting forth upon all dimensions and angles. The priest from Alba mentioned the Gnostic heresy and ventured that here the world was untouched by evil or the Fall. But Brendan was quick with him and made him do penance of sacking and chastisement. He knew in his heart that beauty was a corrupter, that the monks were being seduced by the very earth itself. . . .

I woke.

Kit was looking at me. She was fully dressed.

"You were dreaming," she whispered.

"How could you tell?"

"Rapid eye movement," she said, smiling.

"What time is it?" I asked, wiping the leaves off my back, shivering.

"It's nearly twelve o'clock, lunchtime."

"Won't Touched be going crazy?"

"No. I walked back to where I could see the house and waved to him. And he said: 'Where the fuck is Sean?'"

"And what did you say?"

"I shouted to him that you had a toilet emergency and were going to the bathroom," she replied with a wee laugh.

"What did he say to that?"

"He didn't seem that fussed; Dad and him were having a discussion about something but he told me to hurry you up."

"Yeah, but even so, Kit, you should have woken me," I said.

"You never wake a sleeping baby. And besides I had to do what I always do with Touched."

"And what's that?"

"Ignore him."

I rubbed my eyes, sat on the log, and pulled on my boxers and trousers. I fitted my prosthesis and with some difficulty tied my boots while she watched with fascination. If she was still in the business of comparing me with Jackie, this was a mark for him.

I caught her looking at me. She blushed and turned away. But then again maybe the time for comparisons was over. Jackie was an irrelevancy now. Things had progressed from that pissing contest to a matter of life and death.

I brushed the leaves and pine needles off my T-shirt and sat on the fallen tree and stared at her until her smile fixed and she saw that I wanted to say something.

"What?" she asked.

"Kit. I didn't mean to fall asleep. We don't have much time. And we might not get another chance to talk. I want you to sit down on the tree next to me and listen to what I have to say. You've got to listen to me very carefully," I said.

"You suddenly got very serious. While I am walking on air," she said, mocking herself in a silly, preppy accent.

"I'm not joking. Take a seat."

She frowned, but sat.

"Ok, say your speech," she demanded.

"They're going to have to kill Peter tomorrow. The Brits will not cave to Touched's demands. There is a long-standing policy about negotiating with terrorists. Neither the Brits nor the Americans are allowed to do it. They never give in to kidnappers, ever. It's a standing order," I said slowly and carefully.

"Reagan did it," Kit said.

I shook my head.

"That was a crazy one-off illegal scheme conducted by a rogue colonel. The British and American governments never make deals for hostages. Peter is not going to be exchanged for anyone. It's not going to happen, they're not going to release the Newark Three. I promise you that. What do you think is going to happen after that? I'll tell you. With his credibility on the line, Touched is going to have to kill Peter and you are going to be complicit in that boy's murder."

"You, too," she said.

"Me, too. All of us. For as sure as I am standing here, Touched is going to murder him."

Kit shuddered. "I don't think he'd really go through with it, it's more a sort of a bluff, like in poker."

"Touched has killed many people. Murdered many people. You know that woman who ran the All Things Brit shop? Touched killed her the night before we came up here. That's the cleanup Jackie was talking about. Touched raped her, tortured her, and then he slit her open from her vagina to her throat and he watched while she gasped for breath and bled to death."

All the levity had vanished from her expression now. I had gotten her attention.

I let it sink in and then continued.

"Touched is a sociopath. He'd kill you, me, anyone who gets in his way. He's a lunatic. If you don't believe me about the woman, ask Jackie. He was there, he saw what Touched did. He threw up when he saw it. Touched tortured her and it took her hours to die. And that kid is going to get the same fate. How old do you think he is, twenty, nineteen? And what was his crime? Nothing."

"They said they chased her out of town," Kit muttered, the words sounding ridiculous even to her.

"Chased her out of town? Are you joking? You don't believe that. You're cleverer than that. Chased her out of town? Is this a Western? You didn't believe it when they said that and you don't believe it now. Touched killed her. And Gerry and Jackie and I threw her body in the back of the van, dug a hole in the salt pan on Plum Island, and buried her. Buried what was left of her."

Kit looked stunned. She must have known some of this, perhaps most of it, but she'd been hiding it from herself. In denial about her father's business, about its ugly side. All she wanted to do was live in that big house and surf and spin romantic yarns about Ireland. Wear the green and sing rebel songs and hero-worship her freedom fighter and his old comrade-in-arms Touched McGuigan. But she knew. She wasn't stupid. She was wavering, there were tears in her eyes again, this time certainly not tears of joy.

"The British woman wasn't the first, not by a long shot; Touched told us that he killed a woman last year that he'd been having problems with. He said that in front of Jackie and your da, if you want to check that out too. Believe me, Kit, when this goes wrong, which it will, Touched is going to torture and kill Peter, who looks as if he's a goddamn hippie who never did any sentient creature any harm in his whole bloody life."

Kit wiped away her tears and looked at me imperiously.

"My dad won't let him kill that boy," she said.

"He let him kill that woman."

"She was an FBI agent."

"That's what Touched says. You talked to her. Did she seem like an agent to you? And so what the fuck if she was? Did she deserve that? Rape and torture and death?"

She shook her head.

"What are you saying, exactly, Sean?" Kit asked warily.

I took her hand and looked her right in the watery baby blues.

"We can stop this, Kit, you and me, we can stop it," I said.

"How?"

"You've got to make some excuse and drive into Belfast and call the FBI. They'll come and they'll arrest all of us and, Jesus, we'll do time for kidnap, but at least it won't be murder, and that poor lad will go free," I said.

"Why do I have to do it? Why do I have to betray everybody?" she asked. Indignant that the act would fall to her, but not, it seemed, outraged by the act itself.

"I can't do it, how could I, like this," I explained.

"Yes, you could, you could run away right now. I could say you hit me and knocked me down and you could run. You could get to the outskirts of Belfast in a couple of hours and I wouldn't have to tell on anyone."

"Kit. Look at me. Don't be ridiculous, with these bloody cuffs on and a prosthetic foot I wouldn't get a quarter of a mile, Touched and Jackie would find me and kill me."

Kit let go of my hand and stood up.

"We better be getting back now," she said coolly.

In that coolness was ambivalence and ultimately death. I hadn't closed yet and I was running out of time.

"Haven't you been listening? Only you can save his life.

Tell them you want to get supplies, take Sonia's car and drive into Belfast, go to the police station and tell them to contact the FBI."

She turned her back to me so I couldn't see her face and her emotions. Her shoulders were shaking in big sobs. I remained quiet. Letting it all sink in.

She wiped her face, looked at me.

"Even if I wanted to do that, I wouldn't; the FBI would come here and they'd kill us all like they did with Waco. I wouldn't be saving anybody's life. We'd all fucking die," Kit said.

"No, you wouldn't, you'd be ok, we'd all be ok."

"My dad would go to prison and I'd go to prison," she said, tears rolling down those white rose-hip cheeks.

"You wouldn't go to prison. You wouldn't serve a day. I promise you that, Kit. And your dad would get a deal too. Touched is the one they want," I insisted.

"How do you know? How can you promise anything?"

I stood up and put my arms around her.

It had to be the truth.

The truth would show her that it wasn't bullshit. That although I had deceived them all, I wasn't lying about my feelings for her. The truth would be a clear light illuminating the way out of this quagmire, this goddamn nightmare.

The truth would free me and her from the history that was weighing us down, breaking us, sinking us.

And besides, she'd already proven to me that she could keep a secret. She hadn't told them that I'd been in the British Army, not even when Touched said I was on probation or when we'd gone to the *Elizabeth* to get a general from that army. She'd already joined me in the conspiracy against him. She was flaky, she was young, but she was loyal to her own system of morality. I was asking her to do a betrayal but it was for the right reasons and with the best of intentions. And I could tell she hated Touched. If I handled this right, it wouldn't be me versus Gerry. It would be me versus Touched, and that contest I could easily win.

Especially this way. This would be the trump card, me putting my life in her lap. This would push her over the abyss.

I backed away, put my hand under her chin, and tilted it up to face me.

"Kit, I promise you, the authorities will be lenient with you and your dad. I personally will see to it."

"What are you talking about?" she asked, puzzled.

"The woman Touched murdered *was* working for British Intelligence and the FBI," I said.

"How—"

"Because I am too. They put me in that bar in Revere in the hope that I would run into you and win your trust. They got me that crappy job in Salisbury working with another British agent. I was brought here specifically to infiltrate your group, to stop you carrying out atrocities, to prevent a further escalation of violence in Ulster, and to help save the peace process. Everything I've done is for Ireland and for a peaceful future."

Her lip quivered, her mouth opened, but she said nothing.

"It's true, Kit. I've been associated with the FBI in one form or another for the last five years. My name's Michael, not Sean. Everything I've told you about myself is made up. But everything I've told you about me and you is true. I love you and it happened the way I said it happened. That night in Revere when they tried to kill your dad. I care about you, Kit. I want you to do the right thing. If you let Touched kill Peter, it'll destroy you. It will ruin your life before it's even begun. You'd be killing yourself and your father and Sonia and Jackie. All of us will die because of Touched's insanity. He's a fucking twist, Kit. He *is* touched. He was so crazy that they exiled him. You know what he would do to me if he found out I was an inside man for the Brits? That woman in Newburyport would consider herself lucky she wasn't me."

Kit walked backwards away from me, as if I'd punched her in the stomach. All the color out of her face.

"You, you, you're a liar," she said in such a quiet voice that I wasn't sure she was speaking at all.

"I did lie, Kit, I had to. But you yourself said the ends justify the means. Remember that? We can save Peter, we can save your father and all of us," I said.

"You lied to me."

"I had to. If I hadn't, there would be no one here to stop this madness. Kit, come on. You know it's the right thing to do."

"What?" she muttered.

"Listen to me. Pay attention. Say you're having your period and you need tampons, Touched won't question that; get the car, drive into Belfast, and call the police. Tell them to come after midnight when everyone's asleep. There won't be any gunplay. We'll all get arrested and—"

"You won't get arrested," she interrupted.

"No, I won't. But Touched will and he'll go to jail for life for his many fucking crimes and the rest of you will get a few years and be out again. Think of the alternative. Peter dead and the rest of you, haunted forever by a senseless killing, on the run from the police. And it won't stop there. Touched will kill and kill again until he's caught. He's like a virus. That twisted brain will keep on killing and infecting other brains with his evil. It'll be too late for your father then, he'll be an accomplice and he'll get locked up forever, or worse."

"We'll all be locked up now under your plan," she said softly.

She was forcing herself to be controlled, her eyes big and broken and on the edge of an emotional abyss. How could I do this to her? How could I? Easy. I'd really no other choice.

"No. Only for kidnap. Nothing else," I said quickly. "I'll testify that it was Touched's plan and everyone else went along under duress. A few years, Kit. That's all. Believe me."

"Believe you?" she said, her voice breaking.

"Yes. Believe me, you have to do it. It's the right thing to do. The way of life is better than the way of death," I said, but she still couldn't take it in.

"Your real name is Michael?"

"It is. I am from Belfast, but I've been living in America since 1992."

"Working as a policeman?"

"No. It's complicated. It's a complicated situation. Can't

you see? I'm risking everything by telling you this. You get that, don't you? I've taken my life and put it in your hands like a fallen bird. You can save it or you can squeeze it out. My life is the bird in your hands."

"I don't know, Se—Michael," she said, wavering.

"I need you, Kit. I need you to do this for me. And I need you because I love you and I want to spend my life with you. I want to make you happy."

She laughed bitterly and wiped streams of tears away from her cheeks.

"You're not making me happy now," she sobbed.

"No, I know. But it's only a little bit of pain and it'll all be over. You'll have to be brave. You'll have to be smart. You can't overact. You can't make them suspicious."

"What do you want me to do?" she asked in a monotone.

"Come back with me and tell Sonia you're having your period. And then tell your da that you'll need the car. Tell them in a couple of hours, a long time after you've talked to me, so they don't even associate the idea with me."

She stood.

"It's too much. All of this. It's too much. My head hurts," she said.

"No. You're doing great. You're doing so well, Kit. So well," I said.

She stepped backwards over the fallen tree, away from me.

"I need time to think," she said.

"Take all the time you need."

I leaned over to hold her hand. She flinched and backed farther away.

"Don't touch me," she seethed.

"Sorry," I said.

"I fucking need time to think about all this, for Christ's sake. Why did you have to tell me today? This was supposed to be the greatest day of my life. This is the thing I've been looking forward to for years, when I would do *it*, with the right man. And now this is the fucking worst day of my life. My head feels like it's going to explode."

"Take your time, Kit, take your time. I'll sit here."

Kit nodded and stormed off into the trees without looking back. I waited a minute, then five minutes. I sat down on the big fallen tree trunk. Would she come round? I didn't know.

It was my only play. I had no regrets. I had to do it.

I lay down on the mossy bark and waited; waiting still as the wind picked up and it grew colder and I watched the cirrus clouds and cerulean sky give way to the first black line of the storm front that was marching ominously south from Canada.

✿   ✿   ✿

A twig snapped farther down the trail in the direction of the pond. And of course I knew what it meant. Goddamnit. It meant I was going to die.

The birds were quiet.

I pulled up my trousers, tightened my belt, and got into a crouch.

Another twig snapped in the same place.

Now I was certain of it.

She'd told them what I'd told her. And they were coming to kill me. The twig snapping was the person Touched had sent to circle around me and lie in wait ahead of me on the path leading to the pond. They would come from behind. Maybe they'd even goose me out, like beaters after pheasants—they'd barrel down from the house with their guns drawn, screaming profanities and yelling blue murder, I'd run for the trail, and there he'd be, pointing a big hand cannon at my face. Jackie, more than likely, since he was the nimblest on his feet.

Gerry and Touched from the back. Jackie ahead.

No Kit, though. Touched would make Kit stay at the cabin with Sonia. There would be no arguing this one.

I listened but the woods were quiet.

It didn't matter. I was certain.

Yeah, Jack up front, the big lads at my back, probably coming ninety degrees apart from the northwest and northeast.

I slid off the branch, crawled into the leaves of the forest floor, and scanned the trees.

Waited.

Nothing.

Of course, that crack could have been a deer standing on a sapling, a squirrel doing a suicide leap from a tree, a dry branch expanding with the heat of the day.

But it wasn't.

It was goddamn Jackie or I'm a Dutchman.

I shrugged off my leather jacket, which Kit had draped over my shoulders, stripping to the dirty matte black T-shirt underneath. I slithered away from a log and towards the trail, mucking myself up as much as possible. Any camouflage would do. Even half-assed last-minute stuff.

Kit, oh God, Kit. You've signed my death warrant. It was hard. You had to choose between me and duty and you picked the noble cause over me.

Still, you don't kill Michael Forsythe that easy.

And I had several things in my favor. The forest was dark, I was on to their game, and they were a hodgepodge bunch of hoods. An inexperienced one, an obese one, and an overconfident crazy one. Whereas I was a Grade A survivor. The bad penny that always turns up. The cockroach that will not die. The man who took down the empire of Darkey White and cleaned the clock of his goons and lackeys.

I slid through the leaves and the dirt, down an incline.

Keep your head down and don't look up. Slide, don't crawl. I slithered over roots and through a bramble bush and a mulchy pile of rotting leaves.

Gunning for you, Jack.

The weak link.

The woods were as still as woods get and the silence was an alarm. They were close and closing. If it had been night, I could have hid and waited them out, but it was day and I had to move. Follow the slope downhill to the path to the pond.

Oh, Kit.

Put you in the God's-eye view. What do you hope will happen? They capture me? Or I get away?

I slid over a rock and down a gravel embankment that was

steeper than it looked. There'd been a fire or flood or tree fall because the earth was frictionless and scoured of bushes and roots. I slipped faster and faster and finally fell, tumbling over my feet until I reached the bottom of the slope at a small clearing.

I'd made a lot of noise. I tensed.

But they hadn't seen me.

I got to a crouch and listened for them. Again, nothing. I was now about a hundred feet from where I'd started, from where Kit said that I'd be. I was cuffed and alone and there were three of them with guns, but I might just . . .

If I kept going in the same direction eventually I'd come to a road. Maybe flag a car. Of course, if they lost me, they'd have to clear out of the cabin. Flee to some other bolt-hole Gerry had stashed away. They'd be in disarray. They'd know that they were fugitives, that Gerry couldn't return to his cozy life and his big beach house. Would they kill the general's son and then go? Would they take him with them? Would the dissent be strong enough for Gerry to decide that the game was over? Would he surrender?

I had to put the pressure on. I had to get away.

Not just for me, but for that eejit Peter, too, and for her. For all of them, come to that. Touched was as much a danger to them as he was to me.

He was a real dead-ender. He'd bring them all down in flames. He'd make them drink the Kool-Aid.

A white shirt in the trees fifty feet to my left. Gerry, carrying a massive double-barreled shotgun, wading through the woods, breathing hard, as determined as a big bear. He hadn't seen me. He wiped his brow on his shirtsleeve.

I slid backwards into the undergrowth.

Checked the sun, got my bearings.

The pond was about a hundred yards behind me. But the path that skirted the bank was not thickly forested. Still, if I could get there, I'd leg it. Sprint to the far shore and then just go like mad to the top of the next hill. Keep going over it, into the next valley and then east to a road or a farmhouse or anywhere.

I was almost at the pond path, but where was Jack?

He should be right here.

I moved slower.

Got ready.

The air freshened and a wind blew thick with moisture. It was going to rain at any minute. That would help me too.

Another downslope. Face first, eating dirt and all the bases.

Static from a walkie-talkie.

"Any sign of him?" Touched's nervous voice asked.

"Nope," Jackie said, a few feet from me on the top of a rise. "Not yet."

I stole a peek over a thornbush. There he was. Radio in left hand, pistol in right, back to me, head bent down out of the wind.

If I could take him out, and get a gun into the bargain, that would certainly level the goddamn odds.

Gerry couldn't follow me up the hill, so we'd be talking one against one.

Nice.

Jackie was walking away from me, up towards a rocky outcrop from where he could survey the terrain. I crouched on all fours and made my way behind him. Six feet away, five feet, four feet.

I'd jump him. I'd land on his back, left arm round his throat, pull hard. Snap his neck, soundlessly, take his walkie-talkie, his jacket, his gun, shoot the cuffs, run for the far side of the pond.

I loosened my fingers.

Tensed.

Stood.

A huge crashing noise.

A sharp hammer blow in the back of my shoulder. I was spinning through the air. I thumped into a tree and came down heavily on a rocky outcrop, cracking half a dozen ribs.

Jackie turned. He was right above me. I'd landed at his feet. I reached out to grab his shoe and pull him off balance but I was moving in slow motion and he easily stepped away.

Lightning triage. Ribs, broken nose. I'd been shot in the shoulder and the bullet had ricocheted off my head. Flesh wounds, but it wouldn't matter now.

"Don't move," Jackie said, nervously pointing a .22 pistol at me.

"I got him," Touched shouted. "I fucking nailed him."

"Get over here," Jackie called out.

Touched ran over, breathless, his .38 smoking, his grin as wide as ever.

"Is he dead?" Jackie wondered.

"No way, he's not dead. Don't think he'll die from that. Will you, Sean? Or whatever your name is. Just winged him, Jack."

"Hell of a shot."

"Aye, glad I didn't top him. For him it has to be slow. He's going to think that the unluckiest thing that ever happened to him in his miserable life was my bullet missing his traitor brain."

"Fucking liar, too," Jackie snarled.

"We may as well get started," Touched said, and I made an effort to turn my head and stare at him. Delight on his upcurved mouth and a frenzied look in his eyes.

You may as well, I tried to say, but there was blood on my tongue. Blood everywhere: in my nose, mouth, and ears and running underneath my T-shirt.

My limbs were heavy. My eyelids drooped. Closed.

Heartbeats. Voices.

Gerry: "You got him, Touched?"

"Aye, I got him."

"Dead?"

"No, Gerry, not dead. Not by a long way."

"What now? Dig a hole?"

"Aye. But we'll have to interrogate him first. We'll take him to the smokehouse with the general's son."

"We could use him as a bargaining chip too."

"Nah, we won't be doing that, Jack. We'll use him as a lesson. When they find him the feds will know they made a mistake. They'll know how serious we are."

Just leave me here, Touched, for old time's sake, I'll die

soon enough, I promise. Leave me.

"You want me to drag him?"

"Aye, have you got that rope?"

The birds, spooked by the gunshot, began chirping again. A rope uncoiled on my thigh. Water on my face. It was that rain at last. Icy cold rain from Quebec or the Hudson Bay or Newfoundland.

"No, Jack, a slipknot is what you need. Let me have a go."

"I've got the rope, I'll tie it round him. Lift up his legs."

"Tie it round his fucking throat, not his legs."

"Do what he says. Round his throat."

No, no rope. Just leave me, Touched. Out here in the woods. Leave me. I'll die and the rain will turn to snow and cover me up and no one will find my body until the spring, when they'll see me thawed—a vernal votive offering. Maybe they wouldn't find me for years, just a pair of boots, a skeleton, and the well-preserved carbon fibers of an artificial foot.

"Look, he's moving, he's crawling, he's trying to get away."

"Get that fucking rope."

Crawling. Who knew where? It didn't matter. North. Under cover of the front. Over the Saint Lawrence and the Ottawa and the Kapiskau rivers.

"Here you go, Touched."

A rope around my neck.

Crawling, perhaps I'd go on forever until I was in the kingdom of the bears. There was nothing between here and the pole and I could slip through unseen because I was invisible now.

Rope tightening. My breathing stopped.

"Drag him now?"

"No, Jack, we have to soften him up first."

And the kicks came.

From three pairs of booted feet. Angry, furious, violated, betrayed. In my side, in my legs, in my back, in my testicles, in my head. I tolerated them for a minute and then I took myself to another place.

11: THE SMOKEHOUSE

The bottle is the most important thing in the world. The dirty Coke bottle on the floor. That no one notices.

Fear is my enemy.

Pain is my friend.

An image. The remains of a man, naked, his skin bruised black and verdant green and lying facedown dead in a sheugh on a one-lane road in the bog country. The rain falling and there's a breath of wind from out of the Sperrins, a hackle of dogs howling, and the warped glass of a camera lens taking pictures. The body is not the body of a man. His genitals have been torn off, his eyes gouged out with a screwdriver, and his fingernails burned off one by one with arc-welding gear. His kneecaps have been smashed in with a sledgehammer and the synovial fluid lies caked on his shins like dry white spittle. He has been scalped and his feet wrapped in barbed wire. Electrodes have been attached under his arms, where they have burned him and cauterized him hairless. A helicopter is hovering grimly above him with the swamp grass rising to meet it as if it were some monstrous god—the hushed void of peat, vaporous and awed in its considerable presence.

I have seen this picture.

An informer shot in the temple. I have seen this picture more than once. From Samantha's files. Touched's handiwork in the flesh. In the washed-out black-and-white tones of the bogland.

With Samantha he exercised what, for him, was a chival-
rous restraint.

I know what he is capable of doing.

Someone is shaking me.

Fear is my enemy.

Pain is my friend.

The Coke bottle. Focus on that.

A shake.

"Are you with us, brother Sean?"

A cough. I squint into the dark. I'm tied, naked against a
wall. My arms stretched out and my wrists bound about the
wooden support beams of the smokehouse. The cuffs
wouldn't stretch round the big beam, but this is better in any
case. Tying me out like this is a stress position that's like a slow
form of crucifixion. My lungs are filling with fluid. I'm gradually drowning.

A man has a chair turned round and is sitting in front of
me.

"I can see that your eyes are open and I would assume,
having some considerable experience in this field, that you are
unconcussed."

"I'm suffocating."

"So I see."

"You're killing me."

"That's the idea, my boy."

"Go to hell."

"Ha, ha. I admire your pluck, but that is hardly the tone to
take with me, considering your position and my position."

"Fuck off."

I open my eyes to look at him. It's Gerry, of course, saying
this. He's wearing a wool cap and sipping from a big plastic
drinking cup.

He's pulled a light on above his head and I notice Peter in
the far corner. Also tied to a crossbeam, but his hands are
behind his back. He won't suffocate, he'll live until the final
bullet. They've kept him blindfolded, Touched sustaining the
pretense of being able to let him go someday.

"I see you have no trouble speaking," Gerry says.

"Not yet."

"That's good, we want you to talk. Come on. Look, let's make it easy on ourselves, shall we? Just tell me your name," Gerry says cajolingly.

"Sean."

"Your real name."

"That is my bloody real name."

"You told Kit your name was Michael."

"I lied. I was trying to impress her. It was all a lie. I'm Sean McKenna."

"Why would you say your name was Michael? I know you want to talk. You're itching to. All those pent-up feelings, emotions. We want to know your real name, and your contacts and what you've told them about us. We do know one very important thing, though. You haven't been out of our sight for two days, so obviously they don't know about this place. No one is going to rescue you. You're going to die here unless you cooperate."

"You've got it all wrong, Gerry. I was just trying to impress her. I think Touched made a big mistake with that woman in Newburyport and I think you saw that too. This is a big mistake too, Gerry. I was bullshitting Kit. I was trying to scare her a little bit, that's all, and I—"

"Enough."

He pushes me back against the wall, a simple push, but there's a sharp stab of pain from the ricochet wound in my shoulder and head. I suppose I'd been lucky that it hadn't embedded itself in me, festering, breeding bacteria. Adding yet more pain. But as Touched said, probably in a while I'd be praying that it had killed me.

Gerry tugs my hair, looks at me, disappointed.

He must have told Touched that he could get more out of me with the gentle approach. Softly, softly, catchee monkey, and all that malarkey.

Well, perhaps it's an opportunity.

If I can drive a wedge between Gerry and Touched, the rest will go with Gerry. Sonia and Kit must be appalled by what's been happening and Jackie didn't look too impressed with what Touched did to Samantha. It's a thought. A possibility.

"Gerry, I want you to believe me. I made that all up for Kit, I'm not what you think I am. But it doesn't matter, I know you'll kill me no matter what; Touched killed that woman he thought was an agent. He'll do the same to me. But I'm no agent. I'm a builder. A navvy. I'm on your side, Gerry. It's the truth, I'm telling you the truth," I say as convincingly as I can.

"So you're not going to open up to me?"

"I am, I have been," I insist.

"Sean, you don't want me to let the boys play with you anymore. You already look like yesterday's dog's dinner. Tell me your name and we'll go easy on you," he says.

"It's Sean."

"Do you want a drink of something? Tell me and I'll give you a drink. Help me here, Sean, work with me, come on," he says, holding out the plastic cup.

"How can I help you when I keep telling you the truth and you won't fucking believe me?"

Gerry leans forward with the cup, which seems to contain iced tea. I'd sell my soul for one sip.

"Come on, you want a drink."

"Yeah."

"Well then, tell me your name," he says softly.

"I've told you, Gerry. I've told you the truth."

His patience slips away. He puts the cup down, gets laboriously to his feet.

"Listen to me, you wee fuck. How stupid do you think we are? We know everything. We know you are called Michael, we know you were working for the FBI. We know that woman Touched killed was working with you. You are fucked, mate. What can you possibly hope to get out of this?"

He slaps me across the face. I recoil from the blow and the waves of pain. It throbs through me for a minute or more.

"To stay alive as long as possible," I say in answer to his question.

"And you think the longer you hold out, the longer—"

"Yes," I say, interrupting him.

"We'll make you talk in the end."

"Probably in the end I'll say anything Touched wants me to say. I'll confess to fucking anything to stop the torture. You know that, Gerry. I'll say I'm a British agent. I'll say I shot JFK. I'll say I faked the moon landings. I'll tell him anything."

"So why not make it easier on yourself? Tell me, tell me the truth, let's keep him out of it," Gerry says.

"I've told you the goddamn truth."

"We're deadlocked then."

"Yes."

"You're not convincing me."

"Or you convincing me."

"No," he says and almost laughs.

Instead he sighs, looks around the smokehouse, shakes his head. He kicks away the chair and leans in. His breath bad, smelling of onions and some kind of spirit.

"Ok, goodbye now, Sean. I've given you a fair chance for a quick death. It's all been me. I took you into my home, I gave you a job, and this is what you do to abuse my trust."

"I didn't abuse it—"

Gerry puts a meaty paw around my throat and squeezes hard to cut me off.

"Abused my trust, fucker. And a worse piece of shit I have never seen in my life. And when I do blow your fucking head off, Michael, I'm going to go back to Ireland and find your ma and cut her throat too. Your ma and da and brothers and sisters. I'm going to top them and burn their houses down and make them wish they'd never heard of you. Do you hear me? Do you fucking hear me?"

He releases the grip on my throat so I can answer him.

"You won't be going back to Ireland, Gerry. You won't be going anywhere but a fucking federal prison," I say as smugly as I can.

"What does that mean? Open those eyes. Look at me, god-damnit."

Thumbs grub into my eyes and open them in a violent tug. That fat face staring at me.

"I'm going to tell you something, traitor," Gerry says and pauses to catch his breath.

"Anything but one of your Latin maxims," I reply and even manage a little smirk.

He grins, but only for a second and then a hard punch in the mouth jerks my head backwards forty-five degrees, thumping it into the back of the wooden wall.

Blackness.

Awareness.

The pain dissipating so that it becomes localized and specific, rather than one huge seething mess.

An hour or more since he was here.

My lungs seething.

But he's left the light on.

The kid in the corner, hooded, gagged. A dirt floor. Meat hooks in the ceiling for smoking venison and pig. A Coke bottle in the corner. A retro, old-fashioned bottle made of glass. Big one. Liter bottle with a broken neck.

Little pockets of pain.

Check it.

The burning gunshot wound. And the lads worked me over pretty good. The pain is bad in the testicles, where I must have been kicked hard. A stabbing soreness that jags and dissolves into the more general numbness around my lower torso.

The ribs. Head. My drowning lungs.

Thirst.

Above all, thirst.

The door opens.

A brief glimpse of light and the woods and the house. It's dusk. The deadline will be up in the morning. Peter and I have one more night. A shadow in the doorway. He comes in.

The bottle, focus on the bottle.

Because it's him.

It's Touched.

His big, menacing silhouette dominating the frame, overwhelming my field of vision.

The door closes.

He sits on the seat and lights a cigarette.

"Hi," he says quietly.

The good ones know you don't have to raise your voice to get things done. To make your presence felt. Let the weak yell and shout and waste time and emotion. The strong can devastate with a whisper.

"I'm going to have to kill ya to learn ya, is that right, Michael?" he says in an Irish purr.

Two can play at that game.

With him I will not speak at all.

That's the rule that will control him and beat him.

"I said I'm going to have to learn you to talk, am I right?"

I gave him a smile.

"Oh-ho, you're playing a game with me. A game with me? Dear oh dear. Big mistake, my friend," he says, a twinkle in those cold eyes.

My grin widens.

"Fuck me, Michael, you are fucking brave. Have to wipe that smile off your face. . . . Now, we'll try again. What's your full name?"

But I shake my head.

He waits.

The silence annoys him. Gets his goat. Makes him think that I'm smarter than he is.

He rubs his chin.

There are to be no imprecisions of belief permitted here and Touched must say something to cover the hesitancy and convince himself.

"No, Michael, you can't speak, because I have to teach you a whole new language," he says at last.

He gets up, and I look at the cigarette, flinch.

He spits. Shakes his head.

"So you think I'm here to burn ye with me fags, do you? Well, don't have any worries on that score. I just want to talk. See, we want this over with just as much as you. You're boring me. We just want to know what you've told your bosses in London and Washington. What you've told them about us."

I wink at him.

Touched leans on the back of the chair.

"You've seen what I'm capable of, haven't you?"

I nod my head.

His voice is soft again, almost loving.

"You know that that was just the beginning. Right? She was the appetizer. You will be my project, my life's work. That I assure you. They'll talk about you for years to come. You'll be the horror story they tell in Langley to the rookies. 'The worst I ever heard was about this body we found in Maine.' And I'll make sure they find you and they'll know it's you. You won't even look human when I'm done, but I'll carve a note in your skin explaining who you are and what you did."

My smile fades, but somehow I force it back onto my lips.

"How's your arms, Michael? Are they comfortable? Are your lungs starting to hurt? Well, maybe everything else hurts so much you haven't noticed. But you will. Eventually we'll tie you higher on the crossbeams, so your feet are off the floor. Later on tonight. When I've gouged out your eyes and castrated you. Not now. Later. You see, Michael, I'm patient. I've got all the time in the world. Think about it. You just think about that."

He pats me on the cheek, yawns, and walks over to Peter.

"And how are you, young fella my lad? How are you doing? Are you glad to have company? Let me take that out of your mouth. . . . There. That's better. The girls are bringing you supper. But no talking now. Understand? If you say one word to them I'll cut out your English tongue. Nod your head if you get me."

Peter nods.

"Good. You take care now, you too, Michael. I'll be seeing you."

Touched opens the smokehouse door. Pauses. The sun has set, but I notice that up at the house there's a person walking this way. Two people. Is she one of them? A hundred thousand synapses have been destroyed by blows to the head. And it's dark. Seeing is difficult. But yeah, that's her. Holding something, touching her fingers to her lips. Something glinting. A crucifix around her neck. Fine time to find religion.

She's nervous. Her chest breathing hard, almost hyperventilating in that big brown sweater.

Touched closes the door. But I've already seen them. Seen her. Walking over with food for Peter.

And I want to tell her. And I'll tell her.

Kit. The world is going to end tonight. No matter what happens.

Don't look for it in the skies.

And that cross won't protect you.

It's lying on the floor.

If I can get it.

I will get it.

Kit, honey, you *should* read *The Brendan Voyage* as a manual on perseverance in the face of the apocalypse. Aye. The world will end tonight, for one of us at least. Turn the handle. Turn the—

The door opens for the third time and the third character in the story enters. There are snowflakes on her sweater and hair. September snow. What a delightful rarity. Be another lovely Frost poem, but for the torture and the hostages in the bloody woodshed.

Sonia behind Kit, carrying a tray. They leave the door open and the cold air is a welcome balm. They come in and Kit goes to pull the light on but sees it's already lit and hesitates. Neither of them gazes at my side of the smokehouse.

"Hello, girls, remember me?" I say, lisping from a cracked jaw.

She doesn't want to, but then her head turns. She looks and it all collapses. Her face, the white of her hand, and it appears for a moment as if she might swoon. She steadies herself. I know your mantra. This is his just desserts. He betrayed all of us.

Sonia pours water from a bottle into Peter's mouth and feeds him from the plate.

"Sonia, I'm so thirsty, please," I say.

Her hand shakes but she ignores me, stealing only a quick glance back. Sonia is not the one to work on. She's been sucked into all of this and has accepted the journey down to hell. No doubt Gerry has comforted her with a line from the bloody *Aeneid*. I catch her in another wee look and she stares through me, blinking stupidly.

And no, I'm wrong. She's not going along with it, she's just overmedicated. Painkillers, booze. Numb.

In any case, she ain't the one.

Kit comes over.

"Hello, Kit."

"Hello," she says in two-point lowercase. Mouse speak. Barely a whisper.

"You did what you had to do, Kit. I don't blame you," I tell her.

"I did what I had to, yes," she says, as lifelike as Deep Blue.

She rubs at her eyes, trying to erase the sight of so much blood. She pulls down the sleeve of the massive sweater. It's too big for her, it's one of her dad's, and she looks lost in it. Like an orphan child.

She steps back.

"You weren't expecting snow, were you?" I ask.

She shakes her head.

"Sean, I, I . . ." she tries to explain.

"I know. Don't worry about it, Kit. You made your decision, and by this time tomorrow both Peter and I will be dead, murdered, and it'll all be over. You can think about it then."

On the other side of the room, Peter chokes on his food, but he's careful not to respond.

"I have to go," she says and walks to the door.

Hesitates.

And stands there in silhouette, the door creaking as she pushes it with feigned indifference and then the hint of a skitter smile, trying to be brave and hard, like Ming the Merciless. Snow falling on one arm outside and not on the one inside, teasing me with the scent of the external world.

This is much more effective and such sweet torture.

You, in indecision. Torn between the cause and the family and me. Standing there, emphasizing the alignments of power in the room and the fact that you have the control and are exercising it to close out the cool air and the snowflakes and the pale and sulfurous external light.

Sonia finishes feeding Peter.

She joins Kit at the door.

"We should go," Sonia says.

And if I could speak and think, what would I say to her? How would I convince her?

Oh, Kit, I lied, but your dad's the bigger liar. Your whole fucking culture is built on warped, pisshead sentimentalism. There were no old glories, just ugly massacres and men murdered on their doorsteps, or kids blown up in fish-and-chip shops, or taxi drivers gunned down behind a warehouse in the stinking docks.

You're going to kill me, and then what are you going to do? Wipe out every Protestant in Ireland until it's ethnically pure? Then the Jews, Chinese, blacks. It's so silly. It's so twentieth century. We're a couple of years from a new millennium. Don't you see that, Kit? I'm the future. You're the past.

Someone clears his throat and a man appears behind her in the doorjamb. It's too late to say anything now.

"What's keeping you two? You didn't give bloody Benedict any, did you?" he asks.

"No," Sonia says meekly.

It's Jackie, and such is the change in the dynamic of the group that he, who is half Sonia's age, has her cowed, scared.

"Out of there, the pair of you," he orders, and they go scurrying away up to the cabin. Jackie makes sure they're long gone, shakes the snow off his jacket, and walks in carrying something. A tree branch or a billy club or a—

He runs at me and thumps it down on the top of my head.

"That's your supper, mate," he says and, chuckling to himself, pulls the rope to the bulb, extinguishes the only light, and slams the door.

❁   ❁   ❁

I fought the blackout. If I passed out now I could die during the night, so I had to stay awake, conscious, sentient.

The pain was my great ally. They'd done me a favor, breaking my ribs and kicking my head in and punching me.

I heard the footsteps march away from the smokehouse and back to the main cabin. Where was it? That bottle, that fucking Coke bottle. The light was failing and there wasn't going to be much time left to look.

I blinked the blood out of my eyes and strained on the ropes.

There was going to be no Houdini on those cords. They'd tied me with a hangman's knot so that as I pulled it got tighter. The only way I was getting out of these bonds was if I could somehow cut them.

I stretched my body as far as it would go. Pointed the toes of my right foot. I leaned and strained with every muscle left.

The Coke bottle was a few inches away. Wouldn't matter if it was a few miles. I tried to reach it but it was impossible.

Come on, you son of a bitch.

I pulled and twisted. My lungs feeling as if I'd inhaled hot pitch.

I stopped the stretch and took a breath.

Lay back on the wall, tried to rest my ass on a raised knot of wood. Anything would be better than no support at all.

I sucked in the air.

A voice. English.

"Hello?" Peter said.

Sonia had forgotten to replace his gag.

"Hello," I replied once I had recovered.

"I've been listening to you all afternoon," he said in an Essex-boy London accent.

"Yeah?"

"I think they're gone for the day now," he said hopefully.

"Aye."

"I want to tell you something."

"What is it?"

"I'm afraid," he said simply.

"Don't be. We're going to be ok," I told him.

"They're going to kill us, aren't they? You're an FBI agent and I'm a British general's son. They're going to kill both of us."

"They're not going to kill us."

"They fucking are, oh my God, I don't want to die. I don't want to die," he said and cried quietly for a minute or two. I let him get it out and then I told him.

"Peter, if you're going to talk to me you gotta keep your voice down. They'll be back tonight to check on us periodically. So keep it down, pal."

"I don't want to die," he said, quieter now, but still sobbing.

"Listen to me, sonny. Every single word I say costs me a tremendous effort so I'm not going to repeat anything. We're going to be all right. I need you to keep it together. If I can find a way out of here, you're coming too. Whatever happens, I'm going to need you to be on the ball. If you're girning like a wean and paralyzed by fear and I have to worry about you as well as them, we're both as dead as a ham sandwich. Understood?"

He thought for a few seconds. Took a deep breath.

"I understand."

"Ok, good. That's what I like to hear. It's going to be ok, but you're going to have to work with me."

He shuffled a little against the pole. The way they'd tied him, he could stand or sit. Now he was sitting. The blindfold was a bandage they had wrapped round his head and covered in duct tape.

"What do you need me to do?" he asked, a wail creeping back into his voice again.

"I need you to calm down and trust me. I need you to compose yourself. It's going to be ok, but, Jesus, you've got to trust me. Ok?"

"Ok," he said softly.

"What are you tied to that thing by?"

"A chain."

"Can you get out of it?"

"I don't think so," he said.

"Ok, well, I want you to try. It looks like you're chained to a big wooden beam, so if nothing else the chain should be able to saw through the wood. Find a rough spot on the metal and start sawing. I'll tell you if anyone comes in."

"Ok," Peter said.

And I'll do my work.

I leaned as far to the right as possible, but even my out-stretched little toe could still not touch the goddamn bottle.

"What's your name?" Peter asked.

"Michael Forsythe," I told him. "No more talking. We've work to do."

I tried again. If it was another six inches to the right, I'd have no chance. But as it was, it was just close enough to exercise my frustrations. They'd done the same to that Greek guy, years ago. Tantalus. Poor fuck.

"They're going to kill us, Michael, aren't they? Tell me the truth," Peter said.

"The truth is, Peter, we have a pretty fair chance of getting out of this. I left a note for the peelers on your boat, telling them where we were taking you. I didn't know the exact location but, believe me, they're coming. They'll be here. Maybe not soon enough for me, but the deadline on you doesn't expire until tomorrow, so if you keep calm and your fingers crossed, you might make it out of here."

"Are you saying that to make me feel better?"

"No, I'm not. Now shut up for a minute."

He was quiet and I was quiet and he began sawing into the wooden beam with a smooth iron chain. He could do it if he had a couple of years, but it was better to keep him busy.

I spent the next hour trying in vain to touch the bottle with my foot.

But it was not possible. I'd need an atypical Maine earthquake or the assistance of a friendly Disney animal if I was ever going to reach it.

Nah, the only way would be to ask Kit if she could fill it with water for me if she came in next time without Sonia. She just might to do it out of compassion. Sonia wouldn't let her do it. But Kit might.

There was a noise outside.

A chain saw being jacked into life.

The door opened.

Touched was standing outside the smokehouse, obviously drunk, holding the saw, the chain whirring, smoke pouring out of the exhaust, a stink of sawdust and petrol.

I wasn't afraid.

If this was it, well, I'd given it a damn good shot.

He was grinning, stumbling, whirling the saw about his head.

"Here we go, Mikey boy," he said, laughing.

There was someone with him. Two people. Jackie and Gerry. They pulled the light, closed the door, and then there was an argument.

"What do you think you're playing at? Need to go lie down in the snow for ten minutes, this is fucking serious," Gerry was saying.

Touched said something incoherent.

The chain saw got turned off.

"Fucking show you both a thing or two," Touched said.

Wiser heads had prevailed.

"My way," Gerry said.

Touched muttered something.

Gerry opened the door.

Touched behind him, Jackie too. They'd all been drinking.

"Go ahead," Gerry said. Touched and Jackie clenched their fists, rushed me.

And it all began again.

* * *

Tenses change. The room implodes. Touched kicks me in the stomach and punches my limp head. My skull bangs against the log wall.

Punches and kicks. A yell and a swinging away of noise and light. Blood streaming onto my chin, a terrible noise that turns out to be me screaming.

Touched, Jackie standing back, breathing hard from the effort.

"Well, that's a sweet hello," I manage.

Jackie laughs.

"His name is Michael Forsythe, he told me, that's his name," Peter says.

Touched stops, turns to Peter.

"What did you say?" Touched asks.

"He told me his name. Michael Forsythe. See, I'm helping you. I'm on your side."

"What else did he tell you?" Touched asks.

Whatever you do, don't tell him about the boat, Peter, or he'll kill us both right now and flee the goddamn house.

"He, he just told me his name. Michael Forsythe. That's all," Peter mutters.

Touched looks at me.

"Michael Forsythe? Where have I heard that name before? Let me think," he wonders aloud.

"I'll spare you the trouble. I was the man that killed Darkey White, ratted out his gang, and went into the Witness Protection Program," I say.

Gerry nods his head.

"Yeah. That's right. I remember you, I read about you. Even in Boston that was a story. You killed some of his men, too. Isn't there a price on your head?" he says.

"Aye, there is, bound to be close to a million bucks," I mutter.

"Million bucks, dead or alive, actually," Touched says. "Nice wee bonus for us, Gerry, nice wee bonus."

I shake my head.

"I don't understand. Who is he?" Jackie asks.

"He was working for the feds, Jackie. Weren't you, Michael? You've been federaled up the ass for at least, at least five years now, I suppose. But why us, pal? You'd think you'd want to keep a low profile after Darkey White."

"I couldn't resist your charming personality, Touched," I tell him.

"Yeah, I heard you were a fucking cocky son of a bitch. Did you think you could take us down, like you took down Darkey? You were impressive then, but look at you now. Look at the state of you. This time you're a bit out of your league. Don't you think?" Touched says.

"Nobody said he'd only one fucking foot, though. That's a distinguishing feature they forgot about. And his hair doesn't look the same," Gerry says.

I say nothing.

"I can't believe this is what the feds make you do to pay the bills," Gerry adds, drinking from a flask and slurring his words.

Fear and a thought. Have they all got drunk enough so they can get the moral courage to butcher me?

"Have to talk about this one, won't we, Ger," Touched says.

Gerry looks pained and confused, but finally he nods.

"One more for good measure," Touched adds.

He kicks me in the stomach with his booted foot, a real good kick, nothing held back. I cough and spit blood and phlegm, wheezing and riding with the ripple of the blow. The pain almost knocking me out again.

"Come on," Gerry says, "we'll discuss this over a wee dram."

"Nah, one more, Gerry, I'll learn him for Darkey White, too," Touched says and takes his little green toolbox from his back pocket. He removes a thin knife.

"Now you listen to me, you wee bastard. You're going to tell us everything from the beginning or you're gonna wish your ma had a miscarriage instead of you, I swear, boy," he says.

With that he stabs me. The knife, small and cool, cutting into my flesh like a scalpel into tenderloin. The blade carving into my skin and the pain unbearable. Touched slicing up my skin, steady and relaxed, as if he'd done this hundreds of times before. Gliding it effortlessly under the soft membrane of my chest and digging through the tissue and blood vessels and hair with a harsh and unnecessary deepness. Touched coughs like an old man, leans forward with a bony hand and those yellow nails, and rips away a bloody square of skin and holds it up to me.

Someone's screaming.

It's me, the weak noise bounding back at me from the log wall. Screaming. Gasping at the air to breathe it in. I bite my tongue to stop it. I take a breath.

We face each other.

In the lines of dark with nothing between us.

Nothing.

It's not loss or rage or resentment or revenge. Nothing. Only the muddy light and an odd calm. One breath upon another.

Touched tosses away the patch of skin, irritated. He can read a situation like a master and he sees that he still has not yet mentally beaten me. He picks up the old wooden chair and smacks it into my legs, breaking it into pieces. I buck from the pain and fight another blackout.

"We have to go now, but we'll be back," he says.

He throws the remains of the chair onto the floor.

It clinks into the Coke bottle, knocking it against my foot.

"We'll be back and we'll bring Sonia and Kit, too, and we'll all take our turns on you, and you'll talk. You'll tell me everything. It won't be like that bitch, your boss, in Newburyport. Won't be in a rush. I can take it nice and fucking slow with you, pal. Jack, Gerry, let's go."

He spits at me, misses, turns, exits, and slams the smokehouse door behind him.

He will be back. I shiver uncontrollably, horribly scared, for a minute or two. And then I breathe and count to ten, twenty, a hundred.

And remember that this is the night and I should not be afraid because fear is the enemy.

Pain is the friend.

Fear is the enemy.

And down there on the floor is the Coke bottle that no one notices.

12: THE DEAD YARD

They return my armor from the sea. They improvise a weapon. They give it to me. Go and pay them back in kind, they say. The water burns, the air curdles, Kit comes to me in the moonlit hut.

Geologists say that Ireland was once joined to the coast of North America.

"Is that so, Kit?"

Greenland was tucked into Labrador, Nova Scotia and Newfoundland were squished together, and Ireland was soldered in there too. Galway hinged to the coast of Maine. There are rock formations that begin in the west of Ireland and end three thousand miles away in Maine and Massachusetts. So really I'm dying in a part of my homeland, separated by plate tectonics and several million years.

Is that comforting?

Is it fuck.

Kit. I smell sweet pea and look.

But she's not there.

She's not coming.

Shit.

I could never really have been asleep. More a hallucination. A waking dream.

And the dreams are done.

It's business now.

Self-rescue, as the instructors used to say in the army survival course.

Imagine, if you can, the situation.

An epic journey of about one yard.

First step.

You're holding the neck of a Coke bottle between your big toe and your next toe on your right foot. Your arms are spread-eagled, tied to crossbeams. The bottle has a ragged neck and if you can get it to your hands, you'll be able to use the broken glass to saw through the rope. But how do you get it from foot to hand?

You're going to have to swing your right leg up to shoulder height, hook it on top of your left arm, and then grab the bottle with your left hand. You're probably going to get only one shot at this. Because the bottle could slip or fall out of your grip with the violent motion you'll have to use to swing it. If it falls and rolls away, you'll never get it back or another chance at this, and basically you're done for.

Kit's not coming.

But Touched is.

This is not the time for mister fuckup.

You rehearse it in your mind a couple of times.

It's going to be tough.

And remember, also, they've taken away the prosthesis on your left foot, so for that second or two that your right leg is hooked over your left arm—if you can get it up there in the first place—you'll be dangling off the floor, the ropes digging into you, pulling apart your wrists and popping your shoulder blades.

It's going to take some time to saw through the ropes and they're probably going to kill you first thing in the morning. You can't be sure about the time right now but it's certainly after midnight.

At the most you've got about five hours.

One shot to get the bottle up to your left hand and then about five hours to cut the ropes.

And, to state the bloody obvious, the scales aren't even.

On the minus side, there's your ricochet wounds, you've a

one-inch square carved out of your chest, you've a couple of broken ribs, you've had the shit kicked out of you, and you haven't had any fluids or food in twenty-four hours.

On the plus side, if you don't do it, you're going to die.

Simple as that.

You'll die and you'll rob the Fates.

Oh yes, Michael. If you die now you'll never see what Bridget Callaghan's got in store for you—what she's been hiding away all these years.

Other things.

You'll never see the consequences of asking for that pardon from the Mexican government.

You'll never go to Los Angeles or Peru and you won't go back to Belfast on a wet June day seven years from now.

You won't do any of that fun stuff, Michael, if you can't get the bottle up there.

One chance.

You'll need to be a goddamn gymnast. One of those guys with the giant arms and the talc on their hands and their coach praying in Romanian as they swing their legs up above that bloody horse.

One chance.

Give you a minute to compose yourself.

Cut to the establishing shot. Midnight in the primeval forest. In Maine. A sepia film in a remote country of the dead. The uneasiness is everywhere. You can feel it. The hunters, the hunted.

But if you can get that bottle up there.

Well, I wouldn't like to be in that big cabin when I get free.

A deep meditation.

A silent countdown.

Here goes.

A final look out the tiny window to check for a light on at the cabin. I listen for anyone coming down the path. Nah. Just me and the woods and the boy, and the snow falling, steaming in the log fire. It's after midnight and they're done for the night. Those brave inheritors of Cuchulainn. With their tattoos of a maniacal fighting man tied to a stone. You should be

concerned about another man, tied to the beams of a smokehouse wall.

Enough procrastination.

Slowly and deliberately, I jam the broken bottle into my
big toe to give me a better grip. I hold it as tight as I can.

The night holds its breath.

If I don't do it now, I'll never do it.

Ten, nine, eight.

"Here goes."

I swing my leg up, feel the bottle slip, but grasp it tight as a
motherfucking vise, jamming the glass deeper into my skin.

I arch my side and my broken ribs, and in some kind of
miracle hook my right leg over my left arm.

With the fingers of my left hand I take the bottle from
between the toes.

I make sure I've got it.

Have I got it?

A desperate tenth of a second.

This is my poleaxe, my claymore, my fucking deliverer.

Have I got it?

Aye.

I hold it tight in my palm and fingers, I unhook my leg,
drop it back to the ground, take a huge gasp of air, spit, and
begin rubbing the ragged bottle neck over the ropes.

❀ ❀ ❀

The morning—dour and constant in a speckled half-light. A
snowy mist and an eerie quiet, as if the plague had come or
we were waiting for old eponymous in the moorland of the
Baskervilles.

The boy raised his head as the door opened.

A key jangled in her hand.

She was holding a tray with a plate of toast and a cup of coffee. I could smell the melting butter and the stench of Sanka.

She looked at me.

"You're free," she said, surprised.

I know.

"How? When?"

Only just now.

Her mouth opened.

This was the moment.

Slow-down time.

I swung the Coke bottle and smashed it against the side of Sonia's face. It caught her on the cheek and made a clubbing noise on contact with the heavy bones in her skull. I'd swung powerfully from the shoulder, and the crushing force of the blow hammered through the bronze dust of hair on her jaw and twisted her jawbone with a dry snap that shoved it almost forty-five degrees from the horizontal.

Before she could react, I hit her again from the other side. This second blow an uppercut. It knocked out teeth and splintered pieces of bone and cartilage through the roof of her mouth. Fragments slicing through the front of her gums and spurting thick blood down onto her chin. She swayed and staggered to the side. The tray dropped in a clatter on the floor.

"Ssssss," she groaned.

The two hits were enough to send her into a mild standing concussion, but I needed her to stay down. I held on tight to the wall and kicked her in the stomach with the heel of my right foot. I knocked the wind out of her and she fell backwards, bumping her head into the edge of a pine log and slumping to the floor.

For a second I thought she was unconscious and I hunted for a gag but then she began struggling up on one arm. Conscious, but still too stunned to react. She put her hand to her mouth and looked at the red blood on her fingertips.

Kneeling there before her executioner like Mary Queen of fucking Scots.

Our eyes met.

I lifted the bottle above my head.

She breathed in air to scream.

I knew I had to kill her in the next second.

I jumped up and, in midair, two-handed, thumped her hard on the top of her skull—so hard that the violence of the

contact shook her brain and the impact pressure wave retarded
back, surfing off the blow itself, and crashed into the bonded
silicon of the bottle, shattering it into a hundred micro pieces,
like a goddamn fragmentation grenade going off. Fucking
Christ. Glass everywhere. Tiny razors cast into life in the dead
black air, spraying in all directions. Some caught me and even
Peter at the far side of the hut. Like darts into a clayboard.
Sonia's scalp a minefield of little particles of glass. Glass in her
lips and eyes and bottle fragments stuck in her forehead.

"Huuuhhhh," she said and clattered to the smokehouse
floor. The holes immediately giving way to the steady progres-
sion of blood, oozing inevitably out from the myriad of
wounds. In a second, Sonia's head looked as if it had been
dipped in red paint.

I listened to the outside.

Nothing.

I turned her over.

It looked bad, but I knew it was still all superficial, not life
threatening, not immediately, anyway. She began shaking, flitting in and out of awareness, as if she was having an epileptic
seizure. Most of the glass still embedded in her face, some
falling out. She hadn't yelled, but that wouldn't last forever.

I was unsure of what to do. Tie her up? Gag her somehow?
Maybe use the rope they'd tied me with. A piece of glass
could cut off a long strip; I could bind her arms behind her
back and—

I'd hesitated too long.

She partially regained consciousness, began whimpering
loudly, and with trembling hands tried to pick the bottle fragments out of her face.

This was a goddamn nightmare and I had to finish it. I
grabbed the sheared-off bottle neck and slammed it across the
line of least resistance in her throat, nodding grimly as it
ripped through the epidermis and into the carotid artery. But
it just wasn't sharp enough. I pushed and pulled and the blood
vessel remained intact.

"Jesus."

I tossed the bottle neck and quickly found another fragment that looked sharper. I grabbed her hair, held her, and slashed the edge across her throat, lightning fast, before she seized that final chance to cry out. This time I cut the artery and the blood poured out in a long oxygenated red spout. I stood back, away from the curve and flow.

I looked outside the hut, checked on her, and in thirty seconds she was dead.

Thank God.

Ok. I had to move fast now if we were going to live.

I stepped over Sonia, limped to the other side of the smokehouse, and took the blindfold from Peter's eyes.

"Who, what?" he said.

I rummaged among the set of keys Sonia had brought, found one that looked like a padlock key, lifted the chain that tied him to the wall, put the key in the lock. It turned. I unlocked him.

No hugs, or thanks, or elation, because he was staring at the offal that had once been Sonia's neck and now resembled the stringy remains from an abattoir. A carpet of blood around her, seeping into all the corners of the smokehouse and out the door.

"You did that? What did you do? What did you? Oh my God, you—" he began to say, his voice rising with shock and a screechy panic.

I cut him off, putting my finger on his lips and forcing his mouth closed.

"You better chill the fuck out, sonny boy. If it looks like you're going to get us both killed, I'll top you before you do. So keep your voice down. Get me?" I said severely.

He nodded.

"Good."

He didn't seem capable of helping, so I took the padlock and chain and unwrapped it from the wooden support beam and released him. He rubbed his wrists, groaned, looked at me and again at Sonia.

"Did you have to kill her?" he asked.

"I had to stop her giving the alarm, it was the only way," I told him.

"Could we have tied her up or—"

"Enough," I said and gave him a shut-the-fuck-up stare.

I scanned the hut and spotted my boxer shorts and trousers, which had been thrown in a corner. I grabbed them, pulled them on, and searched for my artificial foot, but it wasn't there. In a burst of petty malice they'd probably tossed it or burned it on the log fire.

I thought for a sec. It was going to complicate things. The best I could manage was either an undignified hop or a shambling limp.

Test both ways of locomotion. I limped from one side of the smokehouse to the other. Hopped back. I moved slightly faster with the limp.

"What do we do—" Peter began, but I stopped. Someone outside.

"Sonia, did you drop something?" a voice yelled from the house. Jackie. I ran to the door, opened it a crack. He was standing at the cabin in pajama bottoms, slippers, and a leather jacket. He was holding a gun.

I looked at Peter.

"When it goes down, it's going to go down fast. You wait here and keep a lookout; when you think you have a chance, run for the woods. Don't come back. Just keep going. We're about ten miles from a town called Belfast. It's on the coast, so I think it's east of here. Do you know where east is?"

"Where the sun comes up."

"That's right."

"Keep going and call the police. You remember my name?"

"Michael Forsythe."

"Right, get them to call the FBI and tell them to get here as fast as fucking possible. This is Gerry McCaghan's cabin. Say that back."

"Gerry McCaghan. What are you going to do?"

"I'm going to have to stay here and fight them off. They've taken my prosthetic foot, so I'm not running anywhere. I've got to keep them at bay somehow," I said.

"I'll help you, I'll stay here and help you, two of us against the rest of them is going to be better odds. I was in the army cadets. I'm not completely usele—"

I put my hand on his shoulder.

"Thanks, but no thanks. I'm from the fucking midnight school and I'll do better if I don't have to worry about you. And I need you to get the peelers out here to save my bloody skin. Literally," I said, looking at the hole Touched had gouged last night.

"What do you want me to do?"

"You're going to have to take off. Fast. If they kill me, remember they'll be like mad dogs to track you down."

"Maybe we could talk to them, maybe we—"

I stood firmly on one foot to get balanced and then slapped his face.

"Listen to me, Gandhi, we're going to kill them or they're going to kill us. That's the way it's going to be. Your job is to live. To get out of here and live. Ok?"

He nodded.

I walked to the door crack.

Jackie had started coming down the path, muttering to himself, trying to keep the wet snow off his slippers. Not as cautious as he should be. Not by a long way.

"Ok, Jackie's coming. Don't say or do anything."

I found my shredded T-shirt, pulled it on, grabbed a piece of toast from the floor, wiped the blood off it, ate it, and sipped what was left of the coffee in the spilled cup.

"Sonia, are you ok?" Jackie asked when he was a few feet from the smokehouse. When there was no answer he hesitated, lifted up his gun.

"Sonia?"

Come on, Jackie, come on in.

He looked back at the house and at his gun to make sure it was loaded.

"Sonia, are you ok?" he asked.

Come on, Jack.

"Sonia?" he asked for a final time, his face nervous, his eyebrows scrunched up.

When again there was no reply, he stopped and backed away. I knew he wasn't going to enter now. He was going to go and get Touched. He was suspicious, afraid. Maybe the famous Michael Forsythe had pulled something. Maybe Sonia had had a heart attack. Maybe the police had shown up. Whatever it was, it was out of his league and was a job for Touched.

He turned his back and began walking to the cabin.

My best chance.

I picked up a large piece of glass. I opened the door and ran on bloody stump and bloody foot, through the wet snow, and leapt on his back.

My left hand struck out in the silence and curled around Jackie's mouth. My right stabbed the glass into his gun-holding arm.

I pulled hard with my left hand, turning his head sharply to one side, trying to break his neck. A schism of emotions as his face met mine. A terrified look. He was unable to speak. Snow blur and he hit the ground with a thud.

I couldn't break his neck now but at least he'd dropped the pistol.

We rolled in the snow, his eyes wide, his limbs fluid, and the piece of glass now moving towards his throat with such speed that he probably wondered if there wasn't some sorcery in it. And Jackie in such a state of petrification he didn't even have the wit to bite the hand covering his mouth. The piece of glass jerking fast and with it a swishing noise. It moved almost by itself like a cobra as it cut and recut his throat.

"Jesu—" he tried to say but the smoking pain and the satanic look on the man killing him froze the word. A deep puncture below his Adam's apple. A slash at his jugular vein.

And finally, attempting at last to save his life, he punched me with a left jab.

I was so beyond the pain that it didn't even register that he was hitting me until he did it again.

I remembered the gun, saw that it was only a few feet from us, and cracked my elbow into his bleeding throat, knocking the wind out of him. He made a grab at me but I head-butted his face so violently that it must have driven the cartilage in his nose a half inch into his brain.

In a last desperate play he thrashed out, knocking away the

piece of glass and almost shoving me off him.

But it only upset me for a moment.

I reached for the gun, got it, held the revolver by the stock, and with the butt hit him on the side of the head, three quick times.

"Bluhhh," he said and slipped into unconsciousness.

I couldn't shoot him, but I had to kill him right this second. I couldn't be exposed like this for much longer in plain view of the house.

I turned him over, slid beside him, rolled him, and wrapped my arm around his throat. With his neck in the crook of my elbow and my left hand pulling hard on my right wrist, I squeezed the remaining fight out of him. He woke for a moment before the end, thrashing, gasping. I drove my knee into his back and finally something suddenly snapped. His body went limp. But to be sure he hadn't just passed out I picked up the glass again and cut deep into his throat, the rough blade breaking the skin apart and scooping out flesh like a bad piece of fruit.

When I was finished, it was much worse than Sonia.

The personal must have slipped in because Jackie's neck had been severed in a huge gash that left him partially decapitated, his head hanging to his body only by the tissue around the spine.

Not so good.

A waste of effort.

I wasn't going on a rampage like a PCP freak. I had to do the minimum effort to stay alive.

I lifted Jackie's gun, spun the chamber, and checked the mechanism. A .22 Smith & Wesson revolver, a lovely little gun, just like the piece I'd had once in New York City.

Sweet.

I stood and limped back to the smokehouse. Peter was standing there, aghast.

"Now's your chance, fucking run for it and raise the alarm," I said.

"Are you hurt?"

"Are you still here? Get moving. Follow the old railway

line. It's bound to go somewhere."

"I don't—"

I slapped him on the side of the head.

"Go, you fucker," I ordered.

He ran out of the smokehouse in the direction of the woods, kicking up snow, shambling, limping, but moving. I watched him disappear between the trees. I sat down and took a breather, found the other bit of toast, ate it. I reached outside, grabbed a handful of snow, and swallowed it. It was cold in my mouth. Welcome.

Now what?

There was only one course of action. They had shotguns and were professionals. Touched, at least, was strong and fit and probably a competent tracker. I couldn't delay. A frontal assault on the house while I still had surprise.

Kill Touched, get his gun, and maneuver Gerry and Kit into a position where they had to surrender.

Simple.

I grabbed another handful of snow, bit into it.

I crawled to Jackie's body and looked at his watch. Seven a.m. They were all early risers in this family, but yesterday— Christ, was it really only yesterday?—Gerry had slept late. And Touched was bound to be knackered after two days of torture. And they'd been wasted in the wee hours.

I reconsidered my options. If only Jackie and Sonia had been awake and the rest were sleeping, that might have changed things. Maybe I could make a run for it into the woods, after all. Or, better yet, maybe I could even steal one of the cars.

Yeah.

It wouldn't take more than a couple of minutes to check it out.

I grabbed a pile of snow and threw it on Jackie's body, shoveling it on top of him as best I could. If someone did have a quick peek out one of the bedroom windows, I wanted them to think all was normal. I stepped back. It wouldn't do for a close inspection but it might fool them from a distance.

I limped to the snow-covered Mercedes-Benz, tried the

door handle. Unlocked. I opened it and got inside. I looked for keys. I checked the glove compartment and the sunshade and the drinks holder.

Nothing.

But wait a minute. Holy shit. It was Sonia's car, maybe the key was on that big bloody key chain she'd been carrying back at the smokehouse. It probably bloody was.

I got out of the car and closed the door.

"Where is everybody?" Touched suddenly shouted from inside the cabin. "I need me coffee."

His voice somewhere on the ground floor.

Goddamn it.

By the time I ran to the smokehouse, got the keys, and limped back to the Mercedes, he'd be standing at the cabin door with his pistol ready to shoot me down. It would be a fair fight, but only until Gerry heard a couple of shots and appeared at one of those upper windows with his shotgun. And with me pinned in the broad, from up there he couldn't miss.

No, forget the car.

It was either make a break for the woods right now, or the full-frontal attack while at least two of them were still sleeping.

"What's it going to be, Michael?" I whispered to myself. But I already knew the answer and I didn't need any more convincing to go after Touched.

Once before, long ago, I'd assaulted a big house filled with enemies and killed the occupants. Snowing then, too, come to think of it. Me, murder, and snow—fucking made for one another.

I held the gun tight and limped to the front door of the cabin.

A cigarette smell was coming from inside, limp and sweet from fresh-rolled tobacco. I listened for the sounds of conversation. But Touched was giving no one instructions. His coffee remark had been rhetorical.

Still, he was bound to be bloody suspicious.

I turned the handle and inched open the door. Touched

was sitting at the kitchen table with his feet up on another chair. He was in his usual brown slacks and a mustard working jumper. His graying hair was crushed under a woolen hat and he had a tattered dressing gown draped over his shoulders.

I opened the door a little farther and pointed the gun through the gap.

He didn't stir when I came in and he felt the outdoor breeze.

I sighted the .22.

He turned the page of a magazine called *Wooden Boat* and took a long draw on his cigarette.

"Pair of ya will catch your death out there," he said without looking up.

I checked to look for the .38 but it wasn't next to him. On the kitchen table: a newspaper, magazines, a coffeepot, but no gun. It might be in his pocket, but it might not. If I had to guess I'd say he was being careless, had left it in his room, and was in fact unarmed. Just the way I liked them.

I stepped completely into the cabin and closed the door behind me.

He turned another page of *Wooden Boat*. I looked for Kit or Gerry or anyone else waiting on the stairs with artillery, but there was no one, this was no trap.

I limped closer, trailing blood and snow.

"I really need some coffee . . ." he began and then he looked up.

In a single breath his face changed from amazement to fright to a gruesome composedness in the face of death.

He put down his magazine.

Took another puff of the cigarette.

"How the fuck did you get out?" he asked.

"Magic."

"What?"

"Magic. Now, Touched, me old china plate. Put your hands on your head and bloody keep them there," I said.

Touched left his fag in the ashtray and did as he was bid, resting his hands on his wool beanie hat.

I surveyed the kitchen and the stairs.

"Where's Gerry and Kit?" I asked.

"Sleeping," he said with a little disgusted shake of the head. Here they were letting him down again. Everybody always letting him down. Typical. And of course it was always someone else's fault. Never his.

His eyes narrowed.

He exhaled the cigarette smoke, a bubble of nervous spittle forming on his dry lips.

"So, Michael Forsythe, killer of Darkey White, informant, spy for the Federal Bureau of Investigation, what are you gonna do now? Arrest me?"

"I don't think so."

He looked puzzled and then smiled with recognition. That big friendly grin, that mix of hatred and bravado.

"Ah, I understand," he said. "It's personal. The woman in Newburyport. Right?"

"That's right," I said.

"Well, you certainly had me fooled. I'll admit that I was suspicious about you and her, but when you helped us put her in the ground and you didn't make a big song and dance about it, fuck, I didn't think she meant anything to you," he muttered a little louder.

"Keep your voice down, Touched," I said. "And keep those hands on your head."

Touched smiled again, a labored wrinkling of the face that made him lose his youthful arrogance.

And as he meekly put his hands back up I saw him afresh. The mystique had gone. The aperture of time worked its way with his features and suddenly he was just a middle-aged white guy, getter older, getting stupider, getting fatter, perplexed by the vagaries of life and the representative of the younger generation who had bested him and was, unexpectedly, about to murder him.

"And another thing. Neither of you bloody talked. I don't know what they teach you nowadays, but that was impressive. Or it could be that I'm getting soft," he said.

He reached to get his cigarette.

"Keep your hands where they are, Touched."

"Sorry, Michael, I forgot," he said and put his hands back on his hat, drumming them, pretending to be relaxed.

I limped closer until I was close enough.

It wasn't my style to gloat over him; to exult, to lecture him with famous last words. There wasn't time for that anyway. I just needed information and then I'd bloody get rid of him.

"Do you have a gun on ya?" I asked.

"No. No, I don't. If you believe me," he said.

"Stand up, shake out your pockets on the dressing gown."

He turned out the pockets.

"It's in the bog," he offered.

"Sit down again."

He sat and put his hands on his head unbidden.

"Ok. Where's the big shotguns?" I asked. "Where do you keep that big shotgun Gerry had yesterday?"

"Why should I tell you?"

"Tell me or I'll fucking kill you, Touched."

"It's in my room upstairs. I cleaned it," he said.

"Loaded?"

"Aye, think so."

"You know so. Is it loaded or not?"

"It's not loaded," he said.

"Where's the shells?"

"They're on the dresser in my room."

"Which one's your room?"

"First left at the top of the stairs. Two down from yours. What the fuck you want the shotgun for?"

I was going to kill Touched but I wanted the other two alive. The .22 wasn't going to impress Gerry. And I wanted them unarmed and intimidated by overwhelming force. If I killed Touched down here, the noise would bring out Gerry, he'd get that shotgun from Touched's room, and he'd blow my brains out. But if I took a little more effort, marched Touched upstairs, got the shotgun, killed him, and waited outside Gerry's room with those big double barrels pointed at him, he'd have no choice whatsoever. He'd have to surrender. It would be suicide to come at me then. Pointless suicide. He gives up. March him and Kit downstairs, find the phone. . . .

Nice and neat.

"Take that cord off your robe."

He unthreaded the dressing-gown tie and held it out to me.

"Turn around, put your hands behind your back," I ordered.

"I thought you were going to kill me," he said smugly.

"Plenty of time for that later, now spin around."

He smiled, spat.

"Hurry up."

He turned and put his hands behind him.

"Ok, Touched, one fidget, one move, and I blow your bloody brains out," I said.

I made a slipknot with one end of the bathrobe cord and placed it over his wrist and pulled it tight. Waited for him to try something since this was the best chance he was going to get. But he stood there and didn't move. I made another slipknot and put his other wrist into it. I tightened both loops and turned him to face me.

"This is how it's going to be. We're going to go upstairs and get the shotgun; if you behave yourself you just might live through this," I lied.

"Changed your mind, huh? That's what you get from hanging about with feds, it fucking weakens ya," he said with contempt.

"Whatever. If you try to shout a warning, I'll kill you. Understand?"

"Aye," he said and then a look went across his face that I couldn't interpret but it seemed to be concern.

"Tell me one thing, Michael, is the lad tied up out there too?" he asked. Of course, it wouldn't be fear for himself, he was worried about his protégé.

"What lad?"

"Jackie. Did you tie him up too?" Touched asked.

"I killed him."

He swallowed. Paled.

"And Sonia?" Touched asked, a trace of the composure disappearing from his dark eyes.

"Aye. Had to do it. Hated to do it. No choice."

"Ye wee fucker, peeler agent bastard," Touched said, anger making him slur his words.

"Keep your voice down. I won't tell you again."

Touched shook his head. His face tightened, his temple throbbed and then relaxed. He was no poker player. He was putting together a little plan.

It might have concerned me once. But I was transformed. I could see through him. He was obvious now. Old and obvious and tied. Let him plan.

I had the gun, I was ready.

"Ok, we'll go up the stairs and we'll get your gun and maybe you'll live to do jail time," I said.

I motioned for him to lead me up the stairs.

Yeah. Coming together. Up to his room, get that shotgun, kill that son of a bitch, arrest those other two, take them to the smokehouse, chain them up, then back to the cabin, untie Touched's wrists so I could claim it was self-defense and not an execution.

Touched began walking up the stairs. His dressing gown wafting backwards, his legs unsteady. He turned his head to look at me.

"I'm not sure I want to go to prison, Michael," he said.

"Don't see that you have much say in the matter."

He took another step.

"You know a comedy always ends in a marriage, a tragedy in a death," he said, sly and sleekit.

"Which one's this?" I asked cautiously.

"Oh, you know," he said, suddenly throwing himself backwards off the stair and crashing into me with his full body weight. We tumbled down the stairs, Touched landing on top of me, knocking the wind out of me and sending the gun awkwardly under a chair.

He head-butted me on the top of my skull.

"Fucking show ya," he muttered.

He struggled desperately to get out of the restraints, but I'd bound that bastard tight and good. I pushed him off me and he rolled to the side. He hooked the robe cord over his ass and down his legs, getting it over first his left leg and then the right. Fast for an old geezer. He tried to undo the knot but it was too tight. His hands still tied, but tied in front of him, which was more dangerous. He lunged at me, but I'd had a second to anticipate the attack and finally managed to get the gun round to face him.

Touched hadn't survived a couple of assassination attempts for nothing.

Before I could pull the trigger he kicked my hand and sent the gun clattering across the wooden floor.

He tried to kick me again but I caught the foot and violently twisted his leg and ankle.

He squirmed out of his slipper, turned, and spitting like a demon, jumped on top of me.

I punched him, breaking his nose with a right hook that sprayed blood into his eyes. Partially blinded, he swung wildly with his fist, missed my head completely but, luckily for him, managed to bring the side of his hand down onto my cracked ribs.

A tidal wave of pain rocked through me, paralyzing me.

"Fuuuuu . . ."

Touched took the opportunity to kneel on my arms, pinning me.

He pushed the robe cord down onto my throat and began to squeeze with all the controlled rage and seething elation of a professional killer. His eyes were wide apart, gray, emotionless.

This was what Samantha saw when he killed her.

"Have you now, Forsythe," he whispered, intimately, like a lover. He pushed down with all his weight, the blackout beginning with a ringing in my head and my eyes rolling back in their sockets.

If he'd had garroting wire or rope instead of a robe tie, Touched would be telling this story, not me. But as it was, the cord was too thick and too padded to strangle me. He needed more leverage, he needed to wrap the cord completely round my neck and pull with two hands.

He kept pushing down on my throat but he saw that I

wasn't dead yet.

"Kill ya," he muttered to himself, his breath a few inches from me.

He lifted my head up, slipped the cord behind my neck, and gave me one chance to suck air into my lungs.

I breathed deep and, in a desperate effort, I heaved myself forward and bit into his cheek, tearing out a chunk of flesh as large as a big bite out of an apple.

He screamed and I kicked him off me with my bloody stump.

He landed on his back and I scrambled to my feet.

"Gerry, Gerry, wake up, Kit, Gerry, wake up," he yelled at the top of his voice and crawled towards me, blood pouring out of his face.

I dived for the gun, got it, cocked it, and shot him square in the belly.

He slumped forward onto his knees.

"Gerry," he said again, desperately.

I could hear movement upstairs.

I'd have to bloody sprint if I wanted that big gun now.

Touched was reeling from the slug in his gut and it was a good hit but with a .22 you can never be sure, so I limped across the room, smacked him in the face with the pistol, kicked his legs, muscled him to the ground, shoved his cheek to the kitchen floor, turned his head.

"I'm still going to get you," he said weakly.

"You better move fast," I said and shot him above the ear— bits of skull, blood, and brains spraying over my weapon hand.

"What's going on down there?" Gerry yelled.

I turned Touched to face me and gave him one in the fore-head, too, the bullet drilling a neat hole above his right eye. I felt his neck pulse. *Nada.* I stood. I needed that shotgun.

I put the .22 in my trouser pocket and went up the stairs on all fours.

"Daddy?" Kit screamed from one of the rooms.

I got to the top and shoved open the first door on the left. It was Touched's room all right, there was his leather jacket, his sunglasses, a copy of *Hustler*. But he'd been lying about the shotgun.

Fuck.

"Get behind me, Kit," Gerry said. He was outside in the corridor. I took a look. And, shit, there he was, naked under a long black kimono, holding that big powerful 12-gauge. Kit behind him with a revolver. He saw me. I ducked inside as one of the barrels erupted, destroying the doorjamb.

"Give me a shell," Gerry called to Kit.

I closed the door.

Hot in here from the central heating. I wiped the sweat from my brow, opened the window, wondered if I could get out.

A second later, Gerry blasted the door apart.

Jesus.

I pointed my .22 at the wrecked doorway.

Talk to him.

"Gerry, listen to me, Touched is dead, Sonia's dead, Jackie's dead. I freed the kid, I dialed 911, and the police are on the way. The game is up. You have to surrender," I yelled.

"Fuck you, Forsythe. We'll fucking kill you. Come out of there and face me like a fucking man," Gerry yelled.

There was no way I was going out onto the landing, not with two of them armed to the teeth.

"Gerry, think of Kit. You don't have a chance in hell of getting out of this. I left a message on the boat, telling them it was you that kidnapped Peter. If you kill me it doesn't matter, you'll never go back to your life now. And Peter is running into Belfast and the cops are on the way. It's bloody over, Gerry. They might do you for being an accessory to murder, but Kit only has to go to jail for kidnap. Think about it, Gerry. If you give up now, come quietly, I'll make sure she's out in less than five. Better than a life term or the federal death penalty. It's a promise."

"What's your promise worth, Forsythe?" he snarled.

"I swear it, Gerry," I insisted.

Gerry muttered something under his breath but Kit was adamant.

"No, Dad, we can get away. We'll take the car and we'll

drive to Canada and they'll never get us," she said.

Good old Kit. Never say die.

It strengthened her da's resolve.

"Aye, you fucker, Forsythe. Sonia never hurt anyone in her goddamn life. She wanted us to let you go. Why'd you have to top her, you son of a bitch?" he said.

Before I could answer he lurched into the bedroom doorway with the shotgun.

Holy Christ. I shot at him, missed, Gerry flinched, slipped, and fired both barrels, tearing up the floor, missing me by half a room, but I couldn't help but catch a couple of pellets in the leg. I lost my balance, fell heavily backwards into the open window, smashed through the screen, and tumbled ten feet to the wet snow outside.

I landed with a soft clump, just missing the woodpile by half a yard.

Gerry appeared in the window.

"Reload me," Gerry screamed.

Kit handed him two more shells; he broke open the gun and slotted them into the smoking chamber.

I tried to get to my one good foot, but I was dazed from the fall. The house swimming before me, Gerry's kimono-clad form reloading his gun, Kit beside him wearing Hello Kitty pajamas.

If I didn't move I was a name in the newspaper. I pocketed the revolver, turned over, and crawled on all fours again, loping like a goddamn hyena for the bloody trees. The shotgun went off behind me. Gerry missing by a mile. He needed to calm down, shoot less, aim more.

And then I heard Kit's gun.

Blam, blam, blam.

A 9mm.

Jesus, Mary, and Joseph, she was firing at me too. Holes appearing in the snow, wide to the left and then after a big overcorrection wide to the right.

I made it to the edge of the forest, scrambled behind a tree, leaned against the trunk.

I tried to get my breath back. I felt in my pocket. The .22

was gone. Goddamnit. I looked behind me in the snow but I couldn't see it. It might be anywhere.

"Fuck."

Up at the house Gerry and Kit had gone from the window now. They were coming downstairs to get me and Gerry might not be the most mobile of psychotic killers but now he had all the cards: guns, a willing accomplice, and a good night's sleep.

Have to head.

I scrambled deeper into the trees.

Shades of déjà vu. But this was not like yesterday when I could run. There was no possibility of hiding from them because the snow had made tracking my blood trail a piece of cake.

"This way, Kit, you stay behind me now," Gerry yelled.

I looked back. He was huffing and puffing out of the house and into the first line of trees. That big elephant gun leading the way. Kit a step behind him with her niner. Gerry slipped on the snow, fired the gun by accident. Kit panicked and shot her gun too.

Jesus, neither of them was getting onto the Olympic biathlon team anytime soon.

"Do you see any sign of him?" Gerry asked, reloading.

I didn't catch her reply but if they had any sense at all they'd soon pick up the markers I'd left.

I hurried on, pushing my way through hanging trees and moss, limping over pine needles, pinecones, branches, rocks.

Foot and stump ignoring the pain, working together in a Quasimodo gait.

I crossed over the forest trail that led to the pond, and then up a slippery tree-lined embankment.

Another breather. Another look back.

Aye, they weren't pissing about. They were looking at the ground, seeing the big blundering path I'd taken and coming straight for me. Kit standing right next to her father, not heeding his instruction to stay a pace or two behind. It gave me an idea. One of the oldest mantraps in the book.

Not original, but who needs original when you don't have a bloody gun? I looked for a low-hanging tree branch.

A young bendy one, but a tree trunk thick enough for me to hide behind.

I selected a good, thick, pliable branch on a balsam fir tree and then limped about ten feet past it so that the trail looked like I had gone farther into the forest. Then I doubled back on myself, got behind the trunk, pulled back the long springy branch until it was at the snapping point.

They were coming and I waited, straining with all my might to hold the goddamn branch. This tree I did know the name of. The balm of Gilead. Balm of fucking Forsythe if this worked.

"Farther down there," Gerry said. "There he goes, come on, Kit, gently does it."

They came closer, but I couldn't look. Have to judge by sound alone. Have to judge it just right.

I waited until I could hear his labored breath and when I felt they were practically on top of me, I let go of the goddamn tree.

Feewooo, whack.

It smacked into them with a satisfying crash.

"Fuck," Gerry screamed as I ducked round the tree.

The branch had cracked Gerry in the skull, splaying him backwards. Kit had rolled with the blow and was getting up again but Gerry was down; he'd dropped the shotgun and his little leather pouch of shotgun shells. I jumped him, punching him hard on the nose and the throat and in his cheek and his right eye.

Then I rolled off him fast, grabbed Kit by the hair, and smacked her with a two-handed uppercut that sent her sprawling into a tree five feet away.

Gerry was fumbling for something in his pocket.

I bent down and grabbed the shotgun.

Gerry had taken out a revolver, he was trying to point at me, but he was probably seeing double from the punches I'd just given him. He pulled the trigger and the shot was so clumsy it nearly hit Kit.

"Drop the gun, Gerry," I demanded, pointing the shotgun at him.

He pulled the trigger again, this time missing by only a few feet.

I unloaded both barrels into him at close range. They took his head off, blowing his skull to pieces and scattering blood, brains, skin, and eyes over the lower limbs of the tree. The headless torso bucked wildly for a moment and fell forward.

Kit screamed and shot at me with the 9mm.

I hit the ground, grabbed the bag of shotgun shells, broke open the shotgun, removed the spent casings, reloaded, and jumped behind the nearest tree. 9mm rounds slammed into the space where I'd just been. She was a better shot than her old man. She must have lied to Touched about going to the range. Either that or she was a quick study. The latter. Kit was good at everything.

I heard her click out an old clip and slam home a new one.

She began shooting again.

I was in a bad position here, protected by the thin trunk of a pine tree and a couple of spindly branches.

At this range a lucky shot could sail right through the trunk and take me out.

Just up ahead, though, there was a little rise and a huge fallen tree that looked like excellent cover. A big tree that had toppled horizontally into the wood in the last year or so. An old log, easily about five feet in diameter. No 9mm was sailing through that motherfucker.

Fuck it, I said to myself and rolled forward, got up, limped for it through the snow, hobbled, limped, and I was goddamn there before Kit saw that I'd made a move and managed to get a shot off.

I dived behind the thick trunk.

Heard a couple of shots thud into the wood.

I got to my feet. Looked.

And yeah, there she was. I could see her easily, reloading. I rested my elbows on the trunk, pointed the shotgun, and took aim at her. An excellent position for me, a terrible one for her. I was protected right up to the shoulders by the fallen tree. She was exposed and to kill me she'd have to aim uphill into the light snow and then get me with a head shot.

She finished reloading and saw that I was standing up.

I waved to her.

She stepped out from cover and carefully held the 9mm, aimed, shot. A bullet clunked into the trunk in front of me.

"Kit, put the gun down. I don't want to have to kill you, but I will. If you shoot, I'll have to shoot, and this thing is going to blow you apart," I said.

"You killed my dad," she said, her voice quivering.

"Kit, I'm sorry. I had to. It was him or me. He understood that, Kit. He was a soldier, like me. He knew that. Him or me. But you don't have to die. Put the gun down on the ground."

She hesitated. Closed her eyes. Wiped the tears, snowflakes from her face.

"You killed him," she screamed and she began walking towards me, to narrow the distance and get a better shot.

"Kit, stop walking and put the gun down. Do it now," I commanded.

"You killed my dad," she said and stared at me with those cobalt eyes, that tubercular face, those serious lips.

"Kit, I'm not kidding, this isn't a finesse weapon, this thing will fucking kill you. Put your gun down now, and put your hands up."

"You killed my father, he was all I had in the world," she said, sobbing hysterically.

"Kit, listen to me. He wouldn't have wanted this. You've done your best, you've fought the good fight, now put down the bloody gun," I yelled.

But she wasn't listening.

She kept the 9mm pointed at my head and walked steadily up the rise.

Sober.

Determined.

She stepped over Gerry's outstretched arm and squinted into the snow.

Her feet were bare.

Her Hello Kitty pajamas soaked through.

The sky was clearing but there were still snowflakes on her arms and a light breeze blowing the loose strands of hair out of her face.

"Don't do it, Kit. If you shoot at me, I'll have to kill you. I won't have any choice. Please. Put the gun down on the ground and put your hands up," I begged her.

She shook her head. She was only ten feet away now. The pistol wobbled in her right fist.

"Drop the gun, Kit. Please."

Carefully, she placed her left hand underneath the right to steady herself. She closed one eye. Took aim.

"I'm sorry," she said and pulled the trigger.

The bullet missed by mere centimeters. I was desperate now.

"Kit, please, I'm begging you. You've got everything to live for, your real mother and father live in New York, Lilly and Hector Orlandez are their names, they—"

I gasped as the second bullet scorched up my left arm. It staggered me for a millisecond. It was only a superficial hit but it made me instantly react and squeeze the trigger on the shotgun.

The right barrel erupted in a spout of fire.

She fired one more time as the full force of the shotgun slammed into her, throwing her off her feet, eviscerating her, gouging a dozen holes the size of quarters in her chest and abdomen and throat.

She tumbled backwards down the slope.

"Kit," I screamed and dropped the gun. I scrambled on top of the horizontal tree, fell over it, crashed to the forest floor, and crawled to her.

Kit was lying in the snow. Her chest was open, exposing a destroyed mass of gore that had once been her internal organs.

Blood pouring everywhere.

There was no question.

The wound was fatal. The damage to her heart alone would be enough to erase her name forever from the big black book.

"Oh God, Kit."

I cradled her face.

She was so beautiful.

Kit, it didn't have to be this way.

My mouth opened to speak, to say anything, to comfort her, but there were no words. Her eyes blinked. A tear fell.

She whispered something.

I leaned in. I couldn't hear. I shook my head.

I didn't understand.

"What?"

With a superhuman effort she finally spoke:

"I love you, too, Sean," she said, and happy that she had communicated this thought, closed her eyes and breathed her last.

        ✿   ✿   ✿

The sun rises to banish specters. They'll watch me no more, these dead men. I'm glad. I was getting nervous under their reproach. And I'm becoming cold. The icy air penetrating through my soaked clothes. Gathering me away and into it. An ache to add to all the other aches, another rebuke for all I've wrought.

The sun rises over the wooded hills and clears those heralds tutting over the killing ground. Two women as well as the three men. One of them unarmed. But there was no other way that I could see. And that stupid kid, didn't he at least get out of here?

Anyway, they're all dead. The last of the Sons of Cuchulainn. Samantha was wrong. She overestimated them. They weren't the boys who make no noise. They weren't that smart. Do they even know the story of their name? The child Setanta was renamed Cuchulainn because he killed a dog. Blood transformed him.

Transformed all of us.

And I have lost a lot of it.

Red under my back and legs.

Red, all of today and yesterday.

I'm exhausted.

Lying prone on the ground, like a child making a snow angel. My hand cradling her white neck, massaging the capillaries to keep the rigor at bay for a few minutes yet. A vermilion hand. A flower of grief.

I'm too weak to get up. I can't move. So here I'll stay. Half-naked between the trees. The story of the precipitation running through the vultured rag of human paint that is smeared in great swirls across my body. In my hair and in my eyes that are almond now and black.

Stay here.

Under the ordered sky.

The growing day extinguishing the lamps of heaven and the yellow of unprayed-for souls. A big tiredness in every constriction of my rib cage. A lightness in my head that can only be oxygen deprivation. Death wants me, too.

About us, insects scenting putrefying flesh and descending onto the snow-draped soil where two bodies lie.

Five this morning. Five in the space of an hour.

One the day before yesterday.

I blink away the snowflakes.

I try to get up.

But it's too hard. And anyway it's better here on the ground, the earth licking my wounds in the protection of the trees. Better than up there in the afterlife of the accursed, caught between a massacre and the stretched attitudes of the hills.

If I get up, I know how it will be.

I know what will happen. A hushed absence and around me the sentient creatures will move aside in recognition. They know there will be more slaughters down the road. For I am the one, the master of the art. *I* am the favored son of Death. Touched was a mere pretender. They'll run and the skeleton will smile beneath his hood.

No.

I'll resist it. I'll stay here. With her.

An ocean wind. A faltering front. The snow is ending. Back in its box until December. The weather will return to something more autumnal, but the world will not be as it was before. I've changed it. Everything remade with a bitter quality. I see it manifest in the ghost of pine trees, in the clouds, the black bark, the dead girl next to me in the snow.

I shake my head.

I'll resist it . . .

A jet.

The moon.

Aye.

Do that, Michael.

Don't get up. Don't let them see you. They can leave you for a while yet. They can let you be. Those tongues of midnight. Whispering incantations. Casting glyphs. Biding their time. They'll weather well their wait, blessed as they are with the virtues of patience and fortitude and the knowledge of their propagation with the blood from the never-ending works of man.

You'll live to see another day. They'll let you have some years of peace.

You'll live because *she* is out there and *she* wants you. And her power is growing and will grow until she cleanses the deck of all the captains.

And you'll live because *he* is out there too. And no one knows. And *he* is coming. And the rage in you is as nothing to the bursting dam that is *him*. And you're the one that set *him* free.

It's a dangerous world, Michael. Stay in the woods. Hide. From the paramedics, the feds, the killers, hide from them all. Don't get up.

Don't get up if you know what's good for you.

Snow blinks into my eyelids.

I watch the sky.

Not a jet.

A helicopter.

Rotor blades.

Engines.

Sirens.

Cars.

A squeal of brakes.

A slamming door.

Voices.

Footsteps.

I get up.

Other Serpent's Tail titles of interest

Deadwater

Sean Burke

Deadwater begins with the murder of a prostitute in Cardiff's Tiger Bay. The novel's protagonist, the alcoholic pharmacist Jack Farissey, wakes up next morning in blood-stained clothes on a plastic sheet and no memory of what happened the night before. Lucky for Jack that the police soon finger local gangster Carl Baja for the murder.

What follows is a bleak journey through the dying Cardiff docklands as Farissey looks into his own heart of darkness and that of his childhood friend, the musician Jess Simmonds. Both Jack and Jess love the same woman, who is bent on proving Baja's innocence. Baja's release from prison will be the beginning of the end for all three of them.

'A strong, disturbing novel. As crime writers we forever want to achieve what seem (but are not) contradictory things: to document in as much detail as possible this most particular world about us, this life of the streets, and at the same time to represent the whole of an urban environment. Sean Burke's Cardiff ranks with Jonathan Lethem's Brooklyn, John Harvey's Nottingham or George Pelecanos' Washington — which is to say, among the best' James Sallis

'Downbeat but beautiful' *Guardian*

'A haunting, impressive novel, hardly suitable for the faint-hearted' *Western Mail*

'A notable entry in the genre of modern British noir, with characters hardened and almost dehumanised by the unforgiving city, but drawn with enough depth to suggest that redemption is still an option' *Leeds Guide*

'Disturbingly beautiful' *City Life (Manchester)*

'Now Cardiff has its chronicler. Now that powerful and political, blood-soaked and beautiful city has the ferociously talented observer it deserves and needs. Sean shares with James Lee Burke not just a surname but a lyrical despair, a committed wrestling with God, an unflinching endoscopic eye into the black chambers of our hearts and an ability to completely convince. He is a necessary alternative historian, a dark and barometric moralist. Deadwater will haunt me for years' Niall Griffiths

David Peace's Red Riding Quartet

Nineteen Seventy Four

'David Peace's stunning debut has done for the county what Raymond Chandler and James Ellroy did for Los Angeles…This is a brilliant first novel, written with tremendous pace and passion' *Yorkshire Post*

'His Red Riding quartet … set a new high-water mark for British crime writing. Their pace, tension, plotting, sheer in-your-face brutality and evocation of how corruption twists lives served notice that an utterly distinctive and prodigiously talented new writer had arrived.' *Writing Magazine*

Nineteen Seventy Seven

'Quite simply, this is the future of British crime fiction… the finest work of literature I've read this year - and its ending is as extraordinary and original as what precedes it' *Time Out*

'With a human landscape that is violent and unrelentingly bleak, Peace's fiction is two or three shades the other side of noir' *New Statesman*

Nineteen Eighty

'Peace has found his own voice – full of dazzling, intense poetry and visceral violence' *Uncut*

'A bleak portrait of those times, written in a stylised prose that takes a few pages to attune to but which admirably suits the subject matter. It's black and moving' *Observer*

'His best yet, a top-drawer thriller which grabs the reader by the scruff of the neck and doesn't let go until the last page...unmatched...his writing these days stands in comparison with American masters like Raymond Chandler, James Ellroy and Walter Mosley... Another winner from David Peace, whose name on the cover is these days a guarantee of existence, a must-read thriller of originality and style that confirms him to be one of the best crime writers anywhere' *Yorkshire Post*

Nineteen Eighty Three

'This is fiction that comes with a sense of moral gravity, clearly opposed to diluting the horrific effects of crime for the sake of bland entertainment. There is no light relief and, for most of the characters, no hope. Peace's series offers a fierce indictment of the era' *Independent*

'Peace is a manic James Joyce of the crime novel... jump cutting like a celluloid magus through space and time, reciting incantations and prayers, invoking the horror of grim lives, grim crimes, grim times' *Sleazenation*

'A gripping read, written in short breathless sentences - at times a sort of hardcore poetry... Not for the faint-hearted, this is as hard as a Leeds pavement on a Saturday night' *Birmingham Post*

Antwerp

Nicholas Royle

What connects the brutal murders of prostitutes in the seedy Antwerp underworld?

Cult film director Johnny Vos is making a low-budget biopic about the Belgian surrealist artist Paul Delvaux. He hires women from Antwerp's red-light district and from an internet voyeur house as extras to recreate the poses of Delvaux's famous sleepwalking nudes.

When two prostitutes end up murdered, English film critic Frank Warner, in town to interview Vos, turns investigative journalist and becomes personally involved when his own girlfriend goes missing.

'A chilling and exhilarating read' *Observer*

'Nobody writes novels quite like Nicholas Royle. His novels have this extraordinary texture: full of bizarre cultural reference points, but always shaped into something coherent and accessible by his natural gift for storytelling – a gift that few of his contemporaries can rival. His books are a tonic for our jaded palates' Jonathan Coe

'Uncanny, stylish and elusive: a fictional answer to the strangest art-house *noir*' *Independent*

Fiction
Non-fiction
Literary
Crime

Popular culture
Biography
Illustrated
Music

dare to read at serpentstail.com

Visit serpentstail.com today to browse and buy our books, and for exclusive previews, promotions, interviews with authors and forthcoming events.

| NEWS | cut to the literary chase with all the latest news about our books and authors |

| EVENTS | advance information on forthcoming events, author readings, exhibitions and book festivals |

| EXTRACTS | read first chapters, short stories, bite-sized extracts |

| EXCLUSIVES | pre-publication offers, signed copies, discounted books, competitions |

| BROWSE AND BUY | browse our full catalogue, fill up a basket and proceed to our **fully secure** checkout - our website is your oyster |

FREE POSTAGE & PACKING ON ALL ORDERS ANYWHERE!

---

sign up today and receive our new free full colour catalogue